P9-CLB-427

The Saving Graces

The Saving Graces

A NOVEL

Patricia Gaffney

HarperCollins*Publishers*

THE SAVING GRACES.

HarperCollins books may be purchased for educational, business, or sales promotional use. For information please write: Special Markets Department, HarperCollins Publishers, Inc., 10 East 53rd Street, New York, NY 10022.

FIRST EDITION

Designed by Nancy B. Field

Library of Congress Cataloging-in-Publication Data

Gaffney, Patricia.
The saving graces / Patricia Gaffney. — 1st ed.
p. cm.
ISBN 0-06-019192-9
I. Title
PS3557.A295S29 1999
812'.54—dc21 98-40003

99 00 01 02 03 ❖/HC 10 9 8 7 6 5 4 3 2 1

For Jan, Annie, and Marti.
Also for Carolyn, Jeanne, Jamie, Jodie, and Kathleen.
And Molly.
Most of all, in memory of Midge.

1

Emma

If half of all marriages end in divorce, how long does the average marriage last? This isn't a math problem; I'd really like to know. I bet it's less than nine and a half years. That's how long the Saving Graces have been going strong, and we're not even getting restless. We still talk, still notice things about each other, weight loss, haircuts, new boots. As far as I know, nobody's looking around for a younger, firmer member.

Truthfully, I never thought we'd last this long. I only joined because Rudy made me. The other three, Lee, Isabel, and—Joan? Joanne? She didn't last; moved to Detroit with her urologist boyfriend, and we didn't keep up—the other three didn't strike me at that first meeting as bosom buddy material, frankly. I thought Lee was bossy and Isabel was old—thirty-nine. Well, I'll be forty next year, enough said there, and Lee *is* bossy, but she can't help it because she's always right. She really is, and it's a tribute to her exceptional nature that we don't all loathe her for it.

The first meeting went badly. We had it at Isabel's house—this was back when she was still married to Gary. God, these people are straight, I remember thinking. Straight and *rich*, that's what really got me—but I'd just moved into a dank little basement apartment in Georgetown for eleven hundred a month because of the address, so I was a little touchy about money. Lee looked as if she'd just come from spa day at Neiman's. Plus she was single, still in graduate school, and teaching special ed. part-time—you know how much money there is in *that*—and yet she lived around the block from Isabel in snooty Chevy Chase, in a house she wasn't renting but *owned*. Naturally I had it in for these people.

All the way home I explained to Rudy, with much wit and sarcasm and disdain, what was wrong with everybody, and why I couldn't possibly join a women's group whose members owned electric hedge trimmers, wore Ellen Tracy, remembered Eisenhower, dated urologists. "But they're *nice*," Rudy insisted. Which, of course, missed the point. Lots of people are nice, but you don't want to have dinner with them every other Thursday and exchange secrets.

The other thing was jealousy. I was small enough to mind that Rudy had a good friend other than me. One night a week she and Lee volunteered to teach reading to inner-city illiterates, and had gotten to know each other during the training. I never worried, then or now, that they would become *best* friends; I mean, if ever there were two people with nothing in common, it's Lee and Rudy. But I was my old insecure self (then and now), and too neurotic to recognize the potential beauty of the Saving Graces even when it was staring me in the face.

We weren't the Saving Graces yet, of course. Even now, we don't go around calling ourselves that in public. It's corny; it sounds like a TV sitcom. Doesn't it? "The Saving Graces," starring Valerie Bertinelli, Susan Dey, and Cybill Shepherd. Notice these are all attractive, smart, funny women who happen to be a little long in the tooth. Anyway, the genesis of our name is a private matter. Not for any particular reason—it's kind of funny, and it reflects well on us all. But we just don't talk about it. It's personal.

We were driving back from dinner at a restaurant in Great Falls (we eat out when the person whose turn it is doesn't feel like cooking), taking the long way because Rudy missed the Beltway turnoff. We'd been a group for about a year by then; we'd just lost Joan/Joanne but hadn't yet acquired Marsha, transient member number two, so it was just the four of us. I was sitting in the back seat. Rudy turned around to catch my impersonation of the waitress, who we all thought looked and sounded just like Emma Thompson. Isabel yelled, "Look out!" and a split second later we hit the dog.

I can still see the expression on that yellow mutt face in the instant before the fender caught her on the shoulder and flipped her over the hood of Rudy's Saab—quizzical, curious, just mildly concerned. As if she were thinking, "Well, *hm*, isn't this interesting."

Everybody screamed. I kept saying, "It's dead, it's dead, it's got to be dead," while Rudy jerked the car off the pavement. To tell the truth, if I'd been driving by myself, I might've kept going: I was *sure* it was dead, and I didn't want to see. When I was twelve I ran over a frog with my bike, and I'm still not over it. But Rudy killed the engine and everybody piled out, so I had to get out with them.

It wasn't dead. But we didn't know that until Lee suddenly metamorphosed, right there on MacArthur Boulevard, into Cherry Ames, Highway Nurse. Have you ever seen a human being give CPR to a dog? It's funny, but only in retrospect. While it's happening it's sort of thrilling and revolting, like something that's still illegal in most of New England. Rudy whipped off her black cashmere cloak, which I have always coveted, and wrapped it around the dog because Lee said it was going into shock. "A vet, we need a vet," Isabel fretted, but there wasn't a house in sight, no store, no nothing except a darkened church on the other side of the road. Isabel jumped up and waved her arms at a car coming on our side. When it pulled over, she ran up and had a conversation with the driver. I stood there and wrung my hands.

Between them, Rudy and Lee got the dog in the back seat of the Saab. Blood spotted its muzzle, I noticed in my peripheral vision, the only vision I was capable of looking at it in. "Curtis will have a fit," I remember muttering, watching a dark stain seep into the 900 Turbo's honey-colored leather. But Rudy, the one who would pay for it if Curtis had a fit, never batted an eye.

"Okay, there's a vet in Glen Echo," Isabel reported, sliding into the front seat next to Rudy so she could give directions. I had to get in back with Lee and the dog. I'm not good with the bleeding and possibly dying: they make me sick. Literally; once I saw a man, a neighbor of mine, pull an electric lawnmower over his own foot, and I doubled up and vomited on the sidewalk. This is true. So I stared out the window, concentrating on the way the car headlights illuminated the sign in front of the church across the way, OUR LADY OF GRACE—and if you're wondering what the punch line of this story is and if I'll ever get to it, that's pretty much it.

Rudy drove like a stock car racer to the vet's in Glen Echo. He wasn't there—it was eleven o'clock at night—but he came when the sleepy-faced night guy called him. Grace, the dog, had a collapsed lung, a broken leg, and a dislocated shoulder, but she lived, and the bill was only eleven hundred and forty dollars. Nobody claimed her—*quelle surprise!*—but after she got out of the hospital Lee and Isabel had a fight over which one would get to keep her. Ernie, Isabel's old beagle, had just died, so she won, or lost, depending on your point of view, and has Grace to this day. She's old and grizzled, like us, and her highway-running days are over, but she is the *sweetest* dog, and I'm not even that much of a dog person. I've always thought she could hold it against us for hitting her, but instead she adores us for saving her. When we celebrate our group anniversaries, we say it's Grace's birthday, too, and regale her with lots of toys and edible gifts.

So that's it, the story of how we got our name. You've noticed I'm the only one who didn't actually do anything, who performed no semiheroic act whatsoever. The group, like Grace in its benevolence and generosity, chose to overlook this. Nobody's ever pointed it out even for a joke (something I myself couldn't have resisted, at least *once* in nine and a half years). No, I've always been unquestioningly accepted as a Saving Grace, and that alone, even if there were no other instances of support and love, kindness, fidelity, sympathy, comfort, and solidarity, would have guaranteed my loyalty for life.

But there are. A thousand. And since I didn't join an order of nuns, I should mention there have also been instances of jealousy, pettiness, pigheadedness, and let us not forget the occasional nervous breakdown. But they're nothing, and now I find it scary to think that prejudice against the upper middle class almost persuaded me to beg off with a polite excuse after that first meeting at Isabel's.

Good old Rudy, she kept me on the straight and narrow. Which is funny when you think about it. Because of us all, Rudy's by far the one who comes closest to being genuinely certifiable. Lee's the normal one. We even call her that—she takes it as a compliment. Which sort of says it all about Lee.

2

Lee

The women's group held its first meeting on June 14, 1988, at Isabel's house on Meadow Street. She made Thai chicken in peanut sauce with cellophane noodles. There were five of us that first time—Isabel, Rudy, Emma, Joanne Karlewski, and me. At my suggestion, we made the rule about pot luck contributions that night, after four of us showed up with salads. We said that, unless you were making the main dish because the meeting was at your house, the assignments would be: Rudy, hors d'oeuvres; Emma, salad; Joanne, bread; Isabel, fruit; me, dessert. Except for Rudy's, the assignments have stayed the same ever since. (We had to switch her from hors d'oeuvres to desserts because she's never on time.)

Meetings were on the first and third Wednesdays of the month until September of '91, when I went back to school and had a conflict with an evening class. So we switched to Thursdays, and we've pretty much stuck with them ever since. We begin at seven-thirty and break up around ten or ten-fifteen. For the first few years, we would have a semiformal discussion of a topic we'd picked the week before—mothers and daughters, ambition, trust, sex, that sort of thing—beginning immediately after dinner and lasting for an hour or so. However, this practice has fallen by the way, and I for one miss it. From time to time I'll suggest to the group that we reinstate it, but I never get any support. "We've already talked about everything under the sun," Emma argues, "there's nothing left." There's some truth to that, I'll admit, but I think the true problem is laziness. It's so much easier to gossip than it is to organize one's thoughts around a genuine, objective *topic* and stick to it. I like gossip as much as the next person, but I'm quite sure we had better discussions when we were organized.

It was when Susan Geiser was a member (February of '94 to April of '95) that we instituted the fifteen-minute rule, and that one is still in effect, although we don't need it now that Susan is gone. The Saving Graces had been without a fifth member for quite a while when Isabel met Susan and proposed her for membership. She had some lovely qualities, Susan did, and she could be quite interesting and funny. But she had one flaw: she never shut up. I didn't mind it that much, but it drove Emma and Rudy wild. So one night Isabel suggested the fifteen-minute rule—in some wonderfully tactful way, as only Isabel could—and from that time on we've each taken fifteen minutes at dinner to tell how we are, what we've been doing or thinking lately. We're not rigid about it, nobody looks at her watch or anything; it's simply a guideline. I'm usually finished in five minutes, whereas Rudy needs at least twenty, so it works out very well.

Emma and Rudy always say I'm the one who thought up the idea for the group and did the original planning and organizing, but in truth it was Isabel at least as much as me. We'd been friends for about a year and a half, Isabel and I, ever since that Halloween night when Terry, her son, threw up on my new shoes. It was my first Halloween in the Chevy Chase house, and I was having the nicest time giving out popcorn and candy apples I'd made myself to all the little trick-or-treaters. Dozens and dozens of them—I'd moved from a high-rise in College Park, and I couldn't get over how many children lived in my new neighborhood. And they were so dear, so sweet in their little costumes, the tiny princesses and witches and Power Rangers. I'll admit I was having what Emma calls a "kid Jones." By eight-thirty the doorbell had almost stopped ringing, though, and by nine o'clock, Halloween seemed to be over.

I was turning out the porch light, getting ready to go up and take my shower, when something fell against the door. A heavy thud—I thought someone had thrown something, perhaps one of the pumpkins I'd carved and set out on the steps. I looked through the peephole and saw a boy. Two boys. One I recognized, so I opened the door.

"Trick or treat."

That cracked them up; both boys, neither of whom was wearing a costume, bumped against each other and bent over double, convulsed with laughter. Drunken laughter.

"Are you clowns?" I asked.

"No, we're thugs," said the one whose name, I later learned, was Kevin. That sent them into more gales. They were holding pillowcases weighted down with candy, evidence of a long, successful night of trick-or-treating. Which meant no one had taken them in hand. And people wonder why today's youth is in trouble.

These two had finally come to the wrong house. "I know you," I said, pointing my finger in Terry's face. "You live on Meadow Street, the white house on the corner. Does your mother know what you and your friend are up to tonight?"

"Sure," he said. But he stopped laughing. The chilly, drizzly night had spiked his blond hair and reddened his cheeks. Terry was fifteen then, but he looked much younger in his slouchy, cocky, too-big clothes, like a little boy playing dress-up.

I whipped around on Kevin. "Where do you live?"

"Leland Street," he muttered, backing away toward the steps. I have this effect on children: when I'm stern with them, they sober up. (In this case, literally.) But it's not from fear, I assure you; it's a way I have of making them see reality the way I see it: sensibly.

"Which side of Connecticut?"

"This side," said Kevin.

"Good." I didn't want him crossing that busy street drunk. "You go home, right now. And whatever you're drinking, I'll take it." I held out my hand.

Kevin looked like a baby, too, but not a very nice one. He had a buzz cut and a fake tattoo of a skull on his cheek; going for the Nazi look, I supposed. "Fuck you," he said, "and anyway, Terry's got it," while he tottered down the steps and wove a crooked route to the sidewalk. I turned my back on him. "See ya, T! See ya when the bitch is gone!"

"Nice talk."

Terry backed up and hit the screen door with a thump. He was trying to smile carelessly, but it wasn't working. "Kev's an asshole," he slurred. "S'cuse me." The pillowcase slipped out of his slack fingers and thunked on the porch floor.

I picked it up. An almost-empty pint bottle of vodka sagged at the bottom under the candy. I moved a pumpkin and set the bottle on top of the newel post.

"Can you make it home by yourself?"

"Sure." But he didn't move, and all that kept him from sliding to the floor were his locked knees.

I sighed. "All right, let's go."

I took his arm to get him moving. We were about the same height then—now he's over six feet, and burly—but I was stronger, and it was no effort to take half his weight as we staggered and tacked down the empty sidewalk to the corner. He protested at first but said less and less the closer we got to his house. The porch light was out; otherwise I might have noticed Terry getting paler, greener, and the dots of perspiration popping out on his whiskerless upper lip. He hung back at the front door—reluctant to face the music, I thought.

I knocked, and almost immediately Isabel pulled open the door, smiling, holding out a bowl of bite-size Snickers. I recognized her and couldn't help smiling back. She was that pleasant-faced older woman who walked her beagle in the same vacant lot—"the dog park," we call it in our neighborhood—where I walked Lettice, my Brittany spaniel.

"Terry?" She saw her son behind me and frowned in puzzlement.

"Mom?" Well, no, what he actually said was, "Mo—?" If he'd gotten his mouth closed in time, my shoes could have been saved. But up came a disgusting stream of half-digested M&M's, Mounds, Milky Ways, and vodka, and most of it landed on my one-day-old, dove-gray suede Ferragamos.

Isabel rushed outside. Right behind her came Gary. I can't remember what I thought of him that first time. Not much—husband, older, short and stocky, nondescript. He ended up taking care of Terry, and Isabel ended up taking care of me.

I've sat in her kitchen a thousand times since that night. Isabel isn't like any friend I've ever made, and, at first, even though I was drawn to her and liked her a lot, I couldn't imagine us ever being close. She was older, for one thing—only eight years, but it seemed like much more. It's because she's from another generation, Isabel says, but I think it's something else as well. Some people are born knowing things the rest of us spend our lives trying to learn. Then, too, she *looked* so much older, with her streaky gray hair in a bun, of all things, and no fashion sense whatsoever. (I've helped her a lot with her sense of style over the years.) But she was still beautiful. To me, that night, she looked like an aging Madonna—I don't mean the singer. This was in 1987, so her real troubles hadn't even begun, but already there was sadness in Isabel's face, and serenity, and that lit-from-within quality that's so extraordinary to me.

And I . . . well, my life was busy and full with part-time teaching and a full course load, as well as a thesis to write for my M.Ed., but I was still a bit lonely. And maybe . . . in the market for a mother. Not that I haven't got a mother. As my husband says, *Oy*, have I got a mother. What I mean is—I might have been in the market for a little mothering.

Emma says I don't understand irony, but I believe this is the definition of it: except for Isabel, none of the Saving Graces has ever had children, and the only one who wants any is me. And I can't. Plus—this is ironic, too—I think Isabel and I were born to be mothers, and yet we both had rather cold parents. I'm dying to be a mother, to be mothered. And she mothers everybody, but who mothered her? No one.

On second thought, perhaps this isn't ironic. Perhaps it's just pathetic.

She made me take off my pantyhose and put on a pair of clean socks—Terry's—and she gave me a mug of hot mulled cider to sip while she cleaned my shoes in her powder room sink. When she came back, we had the nicest, most comfortable conversation. She asked me all about myself. In particular, I remember telling her about some of the scrapes my two brothers used to get into as teenagers, and how they've both turned into pillars of the community, as the saying goes. I said that so she wouldn't worry too much about Terry being on the road to ruin. I didn't stay long, but as I was leaving, it occurred to me that she'd found out a lot more about me than I had about her.

Terry came over the next day with a very nice apology, and also an invitation to dinner. So that's how it started. Isabel and I became friends. When we weren't visiting in each other's house, we were walking Lettice and Ernie in the dog park, or playing tennis together, or going for drives in the country. I cried with her when Terry decided to go to college at McGill in Montreal. She listened to every detail of my husband's long, shy courtship. After she walked out on Gary, she and Grace lived in my spare room for three weeks, and when she got cancer I felt as if it had happened to me. I can't imagine not knowing Isabel, can barely remember what my life was like before I met her.

A year or so after Terry's Halloween escapade, we were sitting on the linoleum floor, drying our dogs after their last bath of the summer, when Isabel said, "Leah Pavlik, you spend too much time with me in this kitchen. You ought to go out and play with friends your own age." I said, "*You* ought to go out and play with friends my own age." We laughed, and then—I'm not sure who said what, but before we knew it we were talking about starting a women's group.

All my life I've had a lot of girlfriends, and I admit I enjoy organizing them. I founded a girls-only club that met in my basement during sixth and seventh grades, and in high school I was cocaptain of the pompom squad, then president of my sorority in college. But since moving to Washington, I guess because I was so busy, except for Isabel I hadn't made that many women friends. I *loved* the idea of starting a group. It wouldn't be a book club, and not a political group, not a feminist organization. Just women we liked and respected and thought we could learn something from, meeting every so often to talk about issues of interest to us. Quite a modest agenda. Little did we know we were planting the first seeds of a beautiful garden.

Isabel said that, not me, years later. She said we were growing wholesome vegetables for sustenance and gorgeous flowers for joy. I asked her which one I was, certain she'd say a wholesome vegetable, but she said I was both. "We're all both, you dolt," were her exact words.

First impressions. After we'd been a group for about a year, we had a meeting at which the topic (at my suggestion) was what we had all thought of each other—those of us who didn't know each other already—at the first Graces' meeting. I started us off, saying I'd thought Emma looked like someone in the arts, or the fringes of the arts, possibly a rock star. (More of a *fading* rock star, I really meant, because of the sort of blasé, world-weary air Emma likes to project. In reality she's not jaded in the least, and I don't understand why it's so important to her to look "cool" all the time.) Well, she was *thrilled* to hear that she looked like a rock star. She wanted to know which one, and I came up with Bonnie Raitt—thinking they both have pretty, sharp-featured faces and (it must be said) the same slightly snotty expression at times. Also the same hair—long, reddish blond, and, to put it charitably, *self-styled.* (I am dying to introduce Emma to Harold, my hairdresser, but she says she can't be bothered.)

Rudy and Emma both said they had loved Isabel on sight, thought she was wonderful, although maybe a little old-fashioned, just a tad conservative. "Matronly, but in a *good* way," Emma said, and Rudy said, "No, *motherly.*" I do remember that during that first meeting Isabel wore a red denim apron over her sweater and slacks—kept it on the whole evening, just forgot to take it off. That's how lacking in vanity she is. But conservative? No, no, no, no, no. Here is obvious proof that first impressions can be wildly inaccurate.

Isabel said she thought Rudy was one of the most beautiful women she'd ever seen in real life, and of course Emma and I agreed. The rest of us are fairly attractive women in a normal, average way, I would say. But Rudy's special. Everybody notices her; we can't go anywhere together and not attract attention. She has skin like an angel, a cover model's body, shiny, perfect, blue-black hair that does anything she wants it to. If she had only a gorgeous face, you could hate her, but behind the classic features there's such a sweetness, so much innocence and vulnerability, she brings out everybody's protective instincts. Everyone wants to save Rudy—men especially, she says. But so far, I'm sorry to say, I don't think anyone has.

As for me, Emma claimed she'd thought *I* looked like a rock star, too. Who? I asked eagerly. (Once an old beau told me I reminded him of Marie Osmond—"the perkiness," he'd said.) But Emma said, "Sinéad O'Connor." *What?* "Oh, not the baldness, although your hair was pretty short, Lee. More that, you know, humorless, self-righteous schtick you do." Oh, thank you very much! I was offended, but Emma added, "No, Sinéad O'Connor's *gorgeous*, haven't you ever noticed her eyes?" No. "She's a beautiful woman, Lee, I meant that as a *compliment.*" Oh, really. I doubt that, but in any case, I look *nothing* like Sinéad O'Connor. I look like my mother: small, wiry, dark, and intense. And I am never self-righteous, although it's true that I'm frequently right.

So, again, so much for first impressions.

When I married Henry, it crossed my mind that I might not need the group as much anymore, or that my enthusiasm would slack off, I might not have the same time and energy for it. None of that happened. There was a period of seven or eight months when I was so fixated on sleeping with Henry, very little else registered on my consciousness, but that was an across-the-board phenomenon and didn't reflect on the Saving Graces specifically.

Emma and Rudy got a great deal of amusement out of that time in my life, I must say. I don't know what they thought I was like before I met Henry—a prude, I suppose. Which I am not, and never have been. I don't happen to swear, and I do like to keep certain thoughts to myself, not share them with the world at large. Or if I do share them, apparently I put them in terms that sound old-fashioned, even quaint to certain people. So when I met Henry and suddenly the only thing on my notoriously rational and unimaginative mind was sex, they thought this was hilarious.

I could have put a lid on their fun by simply keeping quiet, but for some reason, I guess the hormone circus going on inside, I couldn't stop talking about it. Could not keep my mouth closed. Nothing like this had ever happened to me before, and I was thirty-seven years old. One Thursday night, I made the mistake of telling the group how Henry looked in his blue cotton uniform, with his name in gold over the front pocket, and PATTERSON & SON HEATING, PLUMBING & AC on the back. And he wore a tool belt. A *tool belt*. Who knew? Rudy and Emma said they knew about tool belts—I'm talking about the ultimate in male allure, that irresistible combination of sexuality and visible evidence of problem-solving capability—and even Isabel allowed that the concept wasn't new to her. I wonder where I've been.

Then I made an even bigger mistake. I told them about the first time he came to my house (which at that point was only to fix a stopped-up toilet; I hadn't hired him yet to replace the old pipes and put in new heating ducts), and he showed me a diagram in a plumbing book so that I could see exactly what was wrong and how he was going to fix it. "It's pawd o' the suhvice," he told me in his low, thrilling, solicitous southern accent. "An infawmed customah is a satisfahed one." He had his sleeves rolled up, and the sun through the bathroom window illuminated every golden hair on his—well, I believe in this case the word really is *sinewy*—forearms. You would have to see the diagram he showed me to understand what I mean, but believe me when I say that the drawing of the "closet auger" angling its long, tubular way into the narrow, back-slanted overflow passage of the toilet looked exactly, *exactly* like a man's penis in a woman's vagina.

You can imagine the "plumbing" jokes I've had to put up with for the last four years.

Here is some more irony. In addition to the clean, liberating lust I've felt for Henry since almost the moment we met, I also knew he would make the world's most wonderful father. My genes called to his genes, I used to say, in a joking way. Together we were going to make beautiful Jewish/Protestant, intellectual/blue-collar babies (the intellectual component coming from my parents, not me; my father teaches quantum physics at Brandeis and my mother is a stockbroker). But things are not looking hopeful in the baby-making department nowadays. Something seems to be wrong with my plumber's plumbing. Or maybe it's me, they're not quite sure.

I try not to think about the worst that could happen to us: childlessness. Such a forlorn word. And alien. I've never associated it with myself before. I feel mocked now by all the years I religiously took the pill or used foam, an IUD, a diaphragm, scrupulously making sure I kept myself barren.

I've managed to hide the worst of my fears from the group better than I hid my oh-so-funny libido, but I probably won't be able to for much longer. And why would I want to? To preserve their image of me as the sober, sensible, coolheaded one, I suppose.

But Isabel knows already. As usual. Once she told me she couldn't have gotten through her divorce and then the cancer and chemo and all that without me—which is very kind, very typical of her, but not true. But it will be in my case. If the worst happens—if Henry and I can't conceive a child—I'm quite sure that, without Isabel, I won't be able to bear it.

3

Rudy

I don't know why my friends bother with me, I'm so high-maintenance. I would run if I saw me coming. But they're always so patient and supportive. They put their arms around me and say, "Oh, Rudy, you are doing so *well*." That's code; it means, since nobody's put me in a straitjacket yet, I must be all right. I agree, but I always feel like knocking on wood after they say that.

What I don't tell anybody, not even Emma, who thinks she knows everything about me, is how large a part norpramin and amitriptyline have been playing in my mental health. And before them, protriptyline and alprazolam. And meprobamate. I could go on.

Nobody knows this about me except Curtis, my husband, and Eric, my therapist. I'm frank about the rest, my family's total dysfunction, the decades I've spent in counseling, my fights with depression and melancholia and mania. Everybody in the world is on Prozac or Zoloft, so there's no shock value there anymore, no shame, as Emma says, in better living through chemistry.

But I keep it to myself. The thing is, I need my friends to believe that what I do, how I behave, is *real*. Because it is real—but if they knew about my secret army of psychopharmaceuticals, anything I did right would be "because of the drugs," and anything wrong—same thing. Nothing about me would be authentic. In their minds, there would be no real Rudy.

Wait till I tell them what I did today. I already know what their reactions are going to be: Emma will laugh, Isabel will sympathize and console, and Lee will disapprove (gently). And all of them will be wondering in private, *Well, what were they thinking of when they hired her in the first place?* But it's not their judgments I'm worried about. It's Curtis's.

What happened was, I got fired from the Call for Help Hotline. I'm ashamed to say I only lasted a week. Mrs. Phillips, my supervisor, said I got too personal with one of the callers, in direct violation of training guidelines. I know I handled it wrong, I *know* there have to be rules, but the truth is, if this girl—Stephanie—if she called again, I know I would do the same thing.

They tell us to be cautious at first, and already I had taken some prank calls from teenagers. But Stephanie's young, thin, strung-out voice gave her away so quickly, I was sure after only a few seconds that this was no game.

"Call for Help Hotline, this is Rudy speaking. Hello? This is Rudy, is somebody there?"

"Hi, yeah. I'm, um, calling for a friend."

"Hi. Okay. What's your friend's name?"

Long pause. "Stephanie."

"Stephanie. Does Stephanie have a problem?"

"Yeah, you could say that. She's got a lotta problems."

"A lot of problems. Okay, which one is the worst? The one that's making her the most unhappy."

"Oh, God, I don't know. She cries a lot. You know. Over, you know, a lot of stuff. Like, her family. Her friends."

"What's wrong with her family?"

Snort. "What isn't?"

I waited.

"Her mother, okay, she's a real mess."

"In what way?"

Silence.

"In what way is she a real mess?"

No answer.

"I bet she drinks too much."

"*What?*"

"Does Stephanie's mother drink too much?"

"Jeez. Yeah. She does. So—did you just, like, *guess* that?"

"Well, my mother drinks too much. So, yeah, I guess I just guessed it." Why did I say that? Why?

"Really? So she's a drunk? My mother's a total drunk, it's so awful, I don't see how I can . . . Oh, man. Oh, shit."

"No, wait, that's okay. Hey, Stephanie? Listen, it's okay, really. About ninety percent of the people I talk to start out telling me they're calling for a friend. But, you know, I think it's good—you probably *would* call for a friend, because you're a nice person." (This is not exactly how I usually talk; I mean, it's not quite my *voice*. But whoever I'm talking to on the Hotline, I find myself—found myself—falling into their idiom. Mrs. Phillips, before she fired me, said it was one of my most effective counseling strategies.)

"Right," Stephanie said skeptically.

"No, you are, I can tell."

"How old are you?"

"Me? Forty-one."

Scoffing sounds. "Yeah, so like, what do you know about teenage angst?"

"Teenage angst." I laughed, and Stephanie started to laugh with me—I thought she was laughing, but then I realized she was crying.

"Oh, man . . ." I heard her fingers slide on the receiver—she was going to hang up.

I said very quickly, "Yeah, my mother was a drunk, she tried to kill herself when I was twelve. When I was eleven, my father *did* kill himself."

Long, long silence. I had plenty of time to ponder what made me blurt that out. I knew it was against the rules, but at the time, I couldn't think of any other way to keep her on the line.

Anyway, it worked. She started talking. "My mother . . . almost every day when I come home from school she's, like, plastered. Or else she's sick. And I have to take care of her. I can't bring anybody over, so I don't have any friends. Well, one, I have one friend, Jill. But she doesn't . . . you know, I can't tell her what's going on, so . . . "

"I know what that's like. I didn't have any friends, either, the whole time I was growing up. But that was a mistake. I made that mistake."

"How do you mean?"

"Well, I mean, I did it all to myself, because I couldn't stop feeling ashamed. Like *I* was the one with the problem. But, Stephanie, listen to me, you didn't do anything, you really didn't. You're innocent. You're a baby. You don't deserve what's happening to you."

She burst into tears then. I did, too. Neither of us could speak for quite some time. I'm not sure, but I think this was when Mrs. Phillips started listening in.

"And, you know, this isn't even the main thing," Stephanie went on when she could talk. "Except it is, it's like *over* everything, you know?"

"I know."

"But right now it's something else, something even . . . "

"What? What, Steph?"

"God." She started to cry again. I just waited. I was crying, too, but silently now. I thought of Eric, my therapist, and how he *never* cries, no matter how badly I go to pieces in his office. And yet I never think he's cold or indifferent—oh, no, just the opposite. But he doesn't cry. Which is good, thank God, because *somebody's* got to stay composed.

So I tried to pull myself together for Stephanie. "What happened?" I finally asked her. "I know it's something bad."

"It's bad. Something I did."

"With a boy?"

Stunned silence. Then, "Well, *shit*."

I had to laugh again. "It's okay, really, just another wild guess. What did you do? You can tell me if you want to."

"Are you married? What was your name, again?"

"Rudy. Am I married? Yes."

"For how long?"

"Four and a half years, almost five."

"So you were, like, thirty-seven?"

"Yes. Old," I said, before she could. I could tell that's what she was thinking.

"So did you ever, like . . . do anything with a guy that . . . "

"That I felt ashamed of afterward?"

"Yeah."

We're not supposed to tell parallel stories. We're trained to listen and ask questions, and refer callers to the appropriate social service agencies. So all I said—and I don't really think this was so bad—was, "Steph, I've done things with men that I haven't even told my therapist about."

She gave a nervous, relieved laugh. "So you mean, like, you go to a shrink?"

"I'll give you his name. Eric Greenburg, he's in Maryland—"

"Hey, wait—"

"No, write it down. Just in case." I gave her the phone number, too. I think she wrote it down. Needless to say, this is something else we're not allowed to do.

"Okay," Stephanie said, clearing her throat, "this guy, he's in my math class. His name is George but everybody calls him Spider, Spider Man, I don't know why. I don't even like him that much, I mean, he's not my boyfriend or anything, but he was in the mall with these other guys last night, and I was with Jill, and we started talking and everything, and pretty soon Spider said why don't we come out to his car because he's got some stuff, you know, and we can smoke it. So Jill goes, no way, we're leaving, and—okay, this was really, really stupid, I know, but I told her to go on, because I was staying."

"Uh-huh."

"So she left, and I went out in the parking lot with Spider and these two other guys and got high."

"Uh-huh."

"I've smoked before, it wasn't the first time or anything. I think it was my mood or something. And, you know . . . "

"Not wanting to go home."

"Yeah."

"Wanting to shake things up a little. Bust out."

"Yeah. Oh God, Rudy."

"I know. So . . . "

"So . . . you know what I did after that."

"I guess so. How was it?"

She giggled—but then she started to cry again. My telephone is on a table with two fiberglass panels on either side that are about chin height. If I don't want anyone to see me, I have to hunch over, practically put my face on the table. I covered the back of my head with my hand and listened to Stephanie cry and cry. "It's okay. It's okay. You're all right," I told her over and over. "You're still yourself. You're still you."

"It was awful, Rudy, it was so awful. Oh, God, and I don't even like him! And he'll tell everybody, all his friends, and then . . . "

"Who cares? You're not like that and *you* know it. Screw them."

"Jill's not even talking to me!"

"Well, she's angry, but—"

"No, she *hates* me, my best friend *hates* me."

"No, she doesn't."

"Yes, she *does*."

"She's confused and she's mad at you, but she doesn't hate you, Steph. Is she really your best friend? For how long?"

"Since sixth grade. *Four years*." She said that like I would say *forty years*. "Oh, what am I going to do?"

"Well, I guess you have to talk to her."

"She won't talk to me! And anyway, I can't tell her all this stuff."

"Well, you can. You told me. It'll just be really hard."

"I can't. She's so straight. And she's good, she's always been good.

Sometimes I think if I had a sister, it wouldn't be so awful. Or even a brother, if I just had someone—"

"Well, not necessarily."

"No, I mean, if I had a sister or something, then at least there would be somebody to share it with, all this *crap*."

"Well, you'd think so."

"No, I think it would be a lot easier. A lot. You know, being lonely and everything . . . "

I did it again. I said, "Well, I'll tell you, I've got siblings, and they just made everything worse. When I was your age."

"I don't get that."

"You know how your mother's drinking makes you feel like a failure?"

"Yeah?"

"Well—think if you had a brother and sister, and you felt as if you were failing them, too. Instead of one person to worry about, you had three. I'm just saying, it doesn't necessarily make anything better."

"I still wish I had someone."

Why couldn't I just leave it at that? "Listen, Stephanie—Claire, my sister, ran away when I was sixteen and she was eighteen and joined a religious cult. She still belongs to it."

"Huh."

"Yeah. This is a cult that believes we should revere *cats* because they're the direct descendants of Yahweh. *Cats*."

"Who? Yahweh?"

"God—Yahweh means God."

Stephanie burst out laughing.

"I'm not kidding. And this is just *one* thing they believe. And my brother, Allen, well, he's just lost, he's gone. *This is my family*, Steph. My father committed suicide and my mother was a lush, my sister joined a cult, my brother's a lost soul—and here I am at this crisis center, acting like a sane person! So—no, listen"—she was still snickering—"I think the first thing you should do is call Dr. Greenburg, and the second thing is, call Jill. Because you really need her right now."

"Yeah, but I don't know . . . "

A little red light on the telephone starts blinking when the supervisor wants to break in. We're supposed to put the caller on hold, hit the button, and see what she wants. My red light had been blinking for about two minutes.

"I'm just saying, I think you should probably go for it with Jill. That's what I'd do if I were you. Do you really love her?"

"Yeah. I guess." She started to cry again. Really cry—she was sobbing. What a nerve I'd touched that time.

"Hey, Stephanie, it's all right. Oh, baby, it's okay, it's okay. Shhh, you're all right." The red light kept flashing, flashing.

"Rudy?"

"What, baby."

"Are you really okay now?"

"I am, I really am."

We're allowed to lie. And if we're not, we should be.

"Well, but . . . what about your mother?" Stephanie asked in a small voice.

"She's around. We both survived. She lives in Rhode Island with my stepfather, and we talk on the phone sometimes." No point in mentioning I haven't seen her in almost five years, not since my wedding. "She says she's sorry. Well, she said that once."

"She did?"

"Yeah. That meant a lot to me."

"God, Rudy." She heaved a sigh. "It sounds like your family's more fucked up than mine is. Oh—I'm sorry—can I say that?"

Oh, sweet Stephanie. "My family. Steph, if I started to tell you about my family, you'd be late for school tomorrow." Tickled laughter. I liked her so much. I had an idea. "Hey, do you live in the District?"

"Yeah, Tenley Circle. I go to Wilson."

"You know, if you wanted to, I could meet you sometime and we could talk some more. Would you like to? It's just an idea—"

"I'd like it. Like some Saturday or something?"

"That would be great. My husband usually works on Saturdays, so we could have lunch—"

"Oh Jeez, I forgot you were married."

"Yeah, I'm married."

"So—is that cool?"

"Being married? Very cool. You know. Usually."

"Yeah, usually." Her voice dropped one whole, cynical octave. It broke my heart.

"So," I said, "how about Saturday? Do you want to meet?"

"Oh, that would—"

Click.

"Hello? Steph? Stephanie? Hello?"

I stared at the dead receiver in my hand. On my console, six or seven green lights flickered, indicating callers talking to volunteers. Had they transferred Stephanie to somebody else? I pushed a button at random.

". . . coming out at this particular time, it's *inconvenient*, and that queen *knew*—"

Click.

"*Mrs. Lloyd.*"

I jolted up straight. Mrs. Phillips never called me "Mrs. Lloyd"—I called her Mrs. Phillips and she called me Rudy. She's a large, beautiful, statuesque black woman, and she scares the hell out of me. She was standing over me, looming, really, her intimidating bosom heaving. I couldn't do anything but stare up at her. I felt like a guilty child.

"Mrs. Lloyd, hang up that phone, get your things, and get the hell out of this office."

"Wait, I know I was—"

"Out." She pivoted sideways and pointed through the window to the street. She had painted, one-inch fingernails and a lot of rings, a lot of clattering bracelets. She reminded me of a goddess, an Amazon.

"Please, Mrs. Phillips, if I could just talk to that girl for two more minutes, I think she—"

"Lady," she said, incredulous, "you are *fired*. What were you thinking of?" She wasn't indignant, she was furious. Until now I'd never even heard her raise her voice.

"Mrs. Phillips, I was wrong, I know that, and I'll never—"

"We serve clients, Mrs. Lloyd. What do you think we're here for, to give *you* therapy?"

"No, I—"

"You're lucky if I don't decide to have charges brought against you."

"Charges!"

It was every nightmare come true. *Access your anger*, Eric tells me—but if I had any now, it was buried too deeply, under too much guilt and remorse and misery and mortification. This was—this was one of the most classic failures of my life.

Poor Stephanie, I agonized all the way home. What would happen to her now? What if she went back to Spider Man? If I could find her somehow—she lived in Tenley Circle, she went to Wilson High, she was fifteen years old . . .

What made me think *I* could help her? All I'd done was tell her about myself, *my* alcoholic mother, *my* screwed-up family. Mrs. Phillips was right about everything. I deserved this disgrace, and much more.

Well, I would get more. The worst punishment hadn't started yet, but it was about to. As soon as I tried to explain all this to Curtis.

4

Isabel

I've been reading a book by a woman who believes that, in her most recent past life, she was a Nazi sympathizer. She collaborated with the SS, she says, spied on her neighbors, and made herself rich (or rather *him*self rich; she's positive she was a man in this life) by shameless war profiteering. She bases this conviction not only on past-life regression therapy, but also on the circumstances of her current life. Poor woman, she's a quadriplegic; she lost the use of all but her facial muscles in a horrific automobile accident when she was sixteen. She says the suffering she endures now is in payment for the sins she committed in Germany in the 1940s.

Karma. What goes around comes around.

I have never been hypnotized or regressed, and if I've lived past lives, I've lost track of them. But I would not rule out the possibility. Skepticism is a luxury I don't indulge anymore—I leave that to the young and immortal. But if it's true that the yin and yang are always counterbalancing each other, I'd like to think they're doing it within me *now*, in *this* life. I even know where I'd place the fulcrum for the most perfect equilibrium: at the center of my forty-sixth year. Before and after that dubious milestone, the halves of my life fall away like wings, like a heart broken in two. I am reborn. Here in the third year of my new life, I try to balance the old one with hope and love, sympathy, warmth and superfluous kindnesses, gratuitous outbursts of delight. There is so much to counterweigh (although nothing so heinous as the erstwhile Nazi's sins); I only hope I have time. It would help if I could live to ninety-two. Forty-six and forty-six.

* * *

Among good friends, ten years isn't much of an age difference, and yet sometimes I feel as if the Saving Graces and I come from different centuries. I'm not quite fifty; technically I'm a boomer. My father was a missionary, though, and I spent half my childhood in Cameroon and Gabon, the other half in Iowa. Then, too, my husband's job kept us stationed in Turkey for the first six years of our marriage; our son was born there, in fact. These are the most obvious explanations for my lifelong uneasiness with the popular culture, but I think something else is also at work. Something in me. Terminal unhipness, Emma would call it. That's as good an explanation as any.

We're all productive, tolerably sane, functioning adults, we Graces, with no more emotional baggage—well, except for Rudy—than you would expect in a random sample of aging yuppie women. And yet our childhoods were disasters. Some more than others, of course. Rudy could write a book; Emma probably *will* write a book. Lee's family and mine have in common an outward appearance of normalcy, a very different reality inside. Occasionally we four play the intriguing "What keeps us together?" game, and the fact that we all survived our childhoods is mentioned early and often.

I wonder if I could have survived my cancer without their loving-kindness. Survived—yes, probably. But only that: barest survival. Nothing, no other experience has ever leveled me to such an extent. I believed I would never recover, that I was forever changed. And I was, but not in the way I expected. I'd read all the pamphlets and books on the disease, as many as I could find. The first-person stories of women who claimed that cancer changed their lives, turned them into different people, *was a blessing in disguise*—oh God, these stories infuriated me. I felt cheated and betrayed, lied to, and deeply, personally offended. And now—now I'm one of those women. It's been two years since I lost my breast, and I hear myself uttering the very same sentiment that used to make me grind my teeth: "Not that

I'd wish it on anyone, but it was *good* that this happened to me. It's turned my life around."

Well, it needed turning around. It had taken a little detour, my life, occasioned by, among other things, the discovery of my husband's chronic unfaithfulness. I don't know why, but I've been thinking about Gary quite a lot these days. I've been wondering if I was right to turn his last act of betrayal into the catalyst for our breakup. If we were still married and it happened today, would I forgive him? I believe I would. I hope so. Because I'm not the same person; I don't have that anger inside me anymore. Thank God. Oh, but what would Lee say if I told her this? Or Emma, or Rudy? It doesn't bear thinking about! The only bright spot in the long horror of my divorce was their friendship, the way they rallied around, united in loathing Gary. In the space of one women's group meeting, they went from being rather fond of him to wishing him dead, and at the time I found that enormously comforting.

To this day, I haven't told the Graces the whole story of his infidelities. Too embarrassed, I guess; it's shameful, Gary's behavior, and some of the shame has stuck to me, as if part of the blame were mine. Perhaps it is—I'm sure it is. But I'll never forget and I'll always be grateful for their savage, righteous fury when I told them how I discovered his *first* peccadillo. It happened on the night of our nineteenth wedding anniversary—which, in retrospect, seems fitting; as long as I've known Gary, he's always had terrible timing.

He took me to a new Turkish restaurant in Bethesda—a little gift of nostalgia for the good old days, when we were first married and lived in Ankara. I was surprised and touched. We drank raki and ate skewered lamb with eggplant, and went home and made love on the couch. Most unlike us, but Terry was in Richmond on a glee club overnight, and for once the house was ours. I fell asleep afterward, and woke up in the dark. Carrying my clothes, I wandered upstairs, feeling cozy and smug because my marriage was nineteen years old and I still had sex on the sofa. Gary's voice, low and confidential, came to me from the half-closed bedroom door, and I paused on the landing, nothing but curious. Who could he be talking to on the telephone at midnight? In that voice?

Betty Cunnilefski—a name that didn't amuse me in the slightest until much, much later. She worked as an administrative assistant in his office. I'd met her once, recalled her vaguely: small, wispy, beige, the sort of woman you see dining alone in restaurants, who's careful to keep the cover of the book she's reading facedown on the table.

Gary confessed everything that night in a rush. He wouldn't see her again, he swore, and he'd have her transferred to another office. Even in the midst of my hurt and anger, I felt a small pang for Betty—who, true to his word, Gary moved to a different department within the week. And presumably never saw again. I believed him at the time, he wept so convincingly, begged my forgiveness so sincerely. He seemed almost as shocked as I was, and unable to explain why he'd done it. Which was just as well, because if he'd claimed he was lonely, misunderstood, sexually deprived, drunk, seduced, in midlife crisis—*any* excuse would have ignited the silent, seething volcano of anger in me. I was barely aware of it, frankly thought myself incapable of it. And Gary would have been flabbergasted if he'd guessed at a fraction of it.

It took three years for the volcano to erupt. Betty may or may not have been his first mistress, but she wasn't his last. How did he get these women? That's all I want to know, now that the fury has burned itself out. Gary is short, jowly, on the stocky side; he has a full beard, and still plenty of salt-and-pepper hair. He's bull-chested, thick-necked, and short-legged. In bed he's ramlike, a batterer. Fine if you like that sort of thing, but over the years I grew to hate it. Behind a friendly smile, he's really quite cool and measuring, predatory. He flirts energetically and ineptly; it's impossible—was impossible—to imagine him scoring with any woman. But he does. What is it about him?

For one thing, he's an earthy, passionate man—that's why I fell in love with him. And for another, he chooses needy, lonely, awkward girls, the pathetic sure things of this world—girls exactly like I used to be. I can't say if it's deliberate on his part, and therefore cruel and calculating, or only blind, unerring instinct. I've never been able to decide. I want to give him the benefit of the doubt. I want to forgive.

This is not altruism, not saintliness. There's no room inside for bitterness anymore—it's that simple. At the risk of sounding fatuous, I'll make an observation that life is full of Bettys. I don't know whom I have to thank for this new, sanguine attitude, and it's amusing to think it may be, in part, my minister father's Lutheran God. But only in part. I'm equally drawn nowadays to what Emma calls woo-woo, meaning crystals and rocks, the Tarot, reincarnation, past lives, astrology, numerology, meditation, hypnotherapy—anything and everything under the rubric of New Age (anything spiritual other than orthodox Protestantism, according to Emma). I believe in them all. My friend's scorn knows no bounds, and yet she teases me so gently, so affectionately. It's a lovely form of play between us. Emma and I are closer than we've ever been.

I could tell her how purely delighted I am to see God in so many new places. The dual burdens of conventionality and rationality fell away when I realized I might die, *I really might die*. Now I'm free. Free and forty-nine, and so grateful to be starting life over again. Yin and yang. I've gone back to school, I've moved from Chevy Chase to Burleith to Adams-Morgan—a progression that speaks volumes all by itself. I color my hair. I might take a lover. Waking up in the morning isn't a tedious and dutiful act, it's the start of a possible adventure. I've recreated myself. No, that's not it. I have *been* recreated, by a new definition of mortality forced on me by circumstances. And it was worth it: all I had to give in return was a breast.

The deal of a lifetime.

5

Emma

Bad news doesn't hurt as much if you hear it in good company. It's like—if somebody pushes you out a fifth-floor window and you bounce off an awning, a car roof, and a pile of plastic garbage bags before you smash onto the pavement, you've got a pretty good chance of surviving.

This analogy is too unwieldy to go on with, plus I can't decide whom to equate with the plastic garbage bags. So I'll just say, the night I found out Mick Draco was married, I thought of my three best friends as fall-breakers extraordinaire.

We were having dinner on a Thursday, our regular meeting night, at La Cuillerée in Adams-Morgan instead of at Isabel's apartment because her stove was broken. "My short story got another rejection," I had just announced to Rudy, Lee, and Isabel, and I was in the process of laughing off their concern and sympathy, even though it felt like balm, so they wouldn't know how wrecked I was—when all of a sudden Lee looked past my shoulder and said, "Mick Draco."

I froze, disoriented—five minutes ago I'd been fantasizing about him. *Lee read my mind*, I marveled, and then, following her gaze, I glanced around and saw him. An X-rated dream come true.

She said his name again and waved, but since Lee's the kind of person who would rather eat a cockroach than raise her voice in a public place, he didn't hear her. But—*Lee knew him?* Flustered, I stood up and shouted, "Hey, Mick!" and he whipped around, grinned, and walked over to our table.

I had been thinking about him for the last four days, ever since our brief, pre-interview meeting in the seedy coffee shop across from his grungy art studio on Eighth Street. He'd told me he lived in nearby Columbia Heights, but still, suddenly seeing him in this middling-trendy French bistro on Columbia Road threw me off.

He still looked good, though. Still straight and lean and not too tall, my favorite body type. And he still had dark, silver-streaked hair, a big, intelligent head, and light brown eyes that warmed when he saw me. "It's that guy I told you about," I had time to whisper to Rudy, before he loomed over us with his hands in his pea jacket pockets, smiling and glad, a little nervous, a little self-conscious. And then I thought, *Shit—he'll take one look at Rudy and forget my name.* That's what men do—I've gotten used to it, I'm philosophical about it. Tonight, though, I wanted to stuff a bag over her head.

Lee said, "Mick, hello, it's nice to see you. I've been meaning to call Sally. Do you and Emma know each other? I had no idea."

Sally, who's Sally, I thought while Lee introduced him to Rudy and Isabel. But then I knew. The little wife. Oh, *perfect,* the story of my life. And it wasn't even going to make for a good joke, no funny routine about the date from hell or the newest hilarious bedroom blunder by one of my famously inept sex partners. No, this just hurt. I was blindsided, totally unprepared for how bad it felt. Do you think this was peculiar of me? Immature or unstable? I mean, to react this strongly to the married status of a man I barely knew? Well, so do I. I can't explain it. It's never happened before.

"Mick's son Jay goes to the Center," Lee was saying, sparkling her black eyes at him, obviously pleased to see him. "That's how I met Sally."

Another jolt: a wife *and* a kid. In Lee's day care center, no less. I put on a big smile and told everybody how *I* knew Mick. "We just met a few days ago. Mick's going to be the star of an article I'm writing about midlife career changes." Rudy and Isabel made interested noises. He didn't pick up on it, so I said, "He used to be a patent attorney, and now he's an artist."

He moved his hands around in his pockets and muttered, "Struggling, would-be artist," with a crooked smile.

Shy—he was shy. Oh, God. That's my other weakness. I have two: men who are shy, and men who are smarter than I am. He hadn't been shy before, though, not when it was just him and me in the coffee shop. And now he wasn't blinded by Rudy, either; in fact, he kept glancing at me while he and Lee made small talk. Isabel sat quietly and watched, not saying anything. Absorbing it all.

Technically we were having a meeting, so nobody asked him to sit down with us. I was glad—why torture myself until I had to? When the conversation got sparse, he told Rudy and Isabel it was nice meeting them, told Lee he'd tell Sally to call her. *Sally*. I've never known one, but I had no trouble picturing her. *Sally* would be a natural blonde with a wholesome, perky outlook. She'd wear an apron when she baked special, complicated but healthful cookies for her men. That's what she'd call them—"my men."

Mick backed up a step, looking directly at me for the first time. "So, Monday," he said.

"Right. Monday."

"Would you like to get some lunch first?"

"No, can't, let's start in the studio like we said." My voice sounded snippy—how stupid. He hadn't done anything wrong. He didn't wear a wedding band, but he hadn't lied, hadn't even done that shuffle-dance men do to *imply* that they're single without saying it. If this was anybody's fault, it was mine, for making an assumption based on nothing but wishful thinking. Rookie mistake. I could've sworn foolishness like that had been bled out of me years ago.

We all said good-bye, and Mick went off to join a stoop-shouldered man with a white ponytail at a window table. I watched them out of the corner of my eye while Lee chattered about *Sally*, how nice she was, how they were thinking of taking ballet lessons together. The moment came and went when I could have blurted out that my heart was broken—in a humorous way, of course. I still have a few secrets I keep from the group, but this kind of thing, man trouble, isn't usually one of them. Why didn't I speak up? Lee knowing the wife made it sticky, that was one thing. The other was Isabel. Her divorce isn't that old, and adultery is still a touchy subject with her.

Not that I was contemplating adultery. God, no, I hate cheating, cheaters, infidelity, the whole sleazy package. But still. Something about Isabel, quietly sitting there with her gentle face and her Buddha smile, something in her that's fine, not judgmental, kept me from making any cynical, self-effacing quips about the crush I had on married Mick Draco.

We'd saved Rudy for last, as usual, because her fifteen-minute allotment has a way of stretching to thirty, forty, forty-five. Nobody minds; it's just better to plan ahead. She told a long, funny story about losing her job at the Help Hotline.

"Well, I knew *you'd* laugh," she said to me. "But I'm telling you, it wasn't that funny."

"You really gave her Greenburg's phone number? Oh, Rudy."

"Why not? He's a family therapist, he counsels adolescents. And if ever a girl needed—"

"Because it's a violation of the rules," Lee said in that tolerant, teacher-to-student voice she uses a lot on Rudy. She doesn't use it on me, because if she does I use it right back. Only I exaggerate, make it sound even more irritating, which is saying something.

"I know," Rudy said, "but—"

"Places like that aren't allowed to recommend individuals, Rudy. Didn't they explain that? Wasn't there any training before they let you start answering phones?"

"Yes, there was training. They told us all about not recommending individual doctors or clinics or hospitals, not even programs. I know it was wrong, but I couldn't help it. If you'd heard her"—deliberately, she turned from Lee and me to Isabel—"you'd have done the same thing."

Isabel smiled. "I hope I would have."

"But you can't *do* that," Lee insisted, "because then the hot line becomes nothing more than an advertising service. Just think of the potential for abuse."

Isabel sat back, fluffing her soft cap of ash-blonde curls—a dye job, she looks *fabulous* these days, not a minute over forty-five. "Rudy," she said mildly, "how many charitable organizations do you volunteer for?"

"Right now?" She counted. "Four."

"Really. What are they?"

"Literacy, Sunday Soup Kitchen, humane society, and story hour."

"Story hour—"

"At Children's Hospital."

"Ah."

Moment of silence while we took that in. There's an old black lady who plays slide guitar on the corner of Fifteenth and G. Sometimes I drop a dollar in her cigar box as I'm rushing past. Except for some Christmas checks, assuming I'm flush, that's the extent of my charity work.

Isabel didn't press the point. She didn't have to. Lee stopped lecturing and I stopped laughing. Rudy, sweet, oblivious Rudy, asked the waiter for more water. She didn't even know Isabel had made a point.

Rudy caught me beaming at her. "What?" she said, smiling back.

"Nothing."

I really love Rudy's squinty-eyed smile. Twelve years ago, on the student side of the reference desk at the Duke University library, she must not have smiled much, because otherwise I'd have noticed. We were only nodding acquaintances then, harried grad students who knew but never really registered on each other. Nowadays we love to marvel about luck, timing, providence—*fate*, if we're drinking—and what a tragedy it would've been if we hadn't moved to D.C. the same year, and then, clearly a miracle, joined the same book club.

"What did you first see in me?" We never get tired of asking each other that question, although we word it more artfully, less baldly. "You laughed at all my jokes," I always say; "nobody else in that group had any sense of humor whatsoever. Plus you've got a terrific laugh."

True, but an even truer reason is because Rudy always said out loud the things I was only thinking. She had *words* for everything, and they fit with my inner life, meshed with my deepest feelings, as if she were me. It was as if I'd met my double. I'm her best friend, but she attracts other people for the same reason. I don't know if it's all the years in therapy, but Rudy has a way of saying the unsayable and making it sound normal and human. Forgivable.

When I ask what she saw in me, she says, "You were so funny." That's nice; I like making people laugh, and I don't need a therapist to tell me why. "And you were honest. And sort of snotty, but in a good way, not really mean. A smart-ass with a heart of gold."

It's the nicest thing anybody's ever said to me.

Over dessert, my mind wandered. Also my eyes. Mick Draco had incredible shoulders. Draco—it's Greek, isn't it? But the bump in his nose looked Roman. I put on my glasses. He had a mole at the flared end of his right eyebrow. And the neatest, tidiest hairline, something so clean about it, even though his straight, streaky hair was too long. (For fashion; not too long for him.) He laughed at something his friend said. I couldn't hear the laugh over the restaurant din, but it made me smile in sympathy.

Lee smiled back at me.

I took off my glasses and pulled myself together. Mick Draco's a dead end. And I'm a bust at the man-woman thing. Half a lifetime of trying and failing to connect with the opposite sex for longer than a year or two can't be discounted or called "finding myself" anymore. I'm never going to find myself, because I'm a loser.

"What would I do without you guys?" I interrupted Rudy to ask, out of the blue, in the middle of the crème brûlée. Everybody smiled at me fondly; Isabel glanced at my wineglass—just checking, a tolerant, motherly gesture. "No, I mean it. If my luck was as rotten with women as it is with men, I'd have to shoot myself."

Rudy gave me a little pat on the shoulder and went back to a story she was telling about her shrink. But, you know, it's true. I might die an old maid, but I'll always have my pals. God knows there are worse things than living alone. Most men are only speed bumps anyway, aggravating distractions scattered along life's otherwise pretty nice highway. You might run into a good one every long once in a while, but even then he's usually got something wrong with him. Good women, on the other hand, are everywhere. You can pick and choose, find the best ones, start a club, and have friends for life.

Walking out of La Cuillerée, Lee turned at the door and waved good-bye to Mick Draco, but I didn't. I sailed on out, didn't even glance his way. I was over him. Thanks to my friends, I had it all in perspective. Saved by the Graces once more.

Then, too, I'd be seeing him again on Monday.

6

Rudy

I had an awful dream last night. I was rushing, late for something, the dream was half over before I realized what—my session with Eric. I was driving Curtis's car instead of mine, and there was no place to park, so I drove right over the curb and parked on the sidewalk in front of Eric's office. *Uh-oh,* I thought, *he won't like that.* Now I'm not sure who I meant, Eric or Curtis. Eric, I think. Anyway, I was wild to see him. I had something important to tell him, something about my father. (What?) I ran into the building, up the stairs, through the waiting room and into his office, I didn't even knock—and—there he was, having sex on the floor with somebody.

I couldn't see the woman's face. They still had their clothes on—funny that the dream censored that—but they were definitely making love. Eric looked up at me and smiled, just the way he always does, and then I saw the woman's red hair and her pale, laughing face. Emma.

Should I tell Eric about this dream? Should I tell Emma? She'll laugh, I can hear her. It wasn't funny when it was happening, though. Not in the least.

I started to cry. My heart was broken. I went behind the door, hiding so they couldn't see me. But they did, and then I felt humiliated. Then—then it changed, and it was Eric and *me* making love, on his velour-upholstered sofa. With our clothes *off.* Emma appeared, hands on her hips. She said, "Well, *this* is just great, wait till Curtis hears about *this,*" and as soon as she said *Curtis*, I woke up and started shaking.

I could see the outline of his shoulder under the quilt, his back turned to me. I stared and stared, watching him breathe in and out, so frightened that somehow he knew what I'd dreamed and he was only pretending to be asleep. *It didn't mean anything,* I wanted to tell him. *Don't be sad, it didn't mean anything, I love only you.*

But, of course, the longer I stared, the more I woke up, and after a little while I slipped my arm around his waist and pressed up against him. And then I was safe.

But—should I tell Eric about this dream? At least he would know what it means. I could never tell Curtis, oh God, never. The sex wasn't even any good. If that makes a difference. In fact, it was better watching it than doing it. It meant something else besides sex, I'm sure, control or domination, maybe even love. Why is it that sex in dreams never seems to really mean sex? Like the death card in the Tarot never means death. Or so they always tell you. But was my dream a dream about what I want or what I fear? Or both?

I don't know, I don't know. But then, I never know anything. Once Eric said, "Rudy, what is the worst that could happen if you had a strong opinion about something and you were wrong?" But I don't think that's it, quite. I don't fear being wrong, I'm wrong all the time, ask Curtis. It's that—if you pick one thing to believe, you eliminate all the others. So it's not fair. Why choose, then? It's better, it's *gentler* not to. And also, it's important to leave yourself room to escape, always make sure there's a way out. Always have a hiding place.

No, I've decided. I'm not telling anyone about this dream.

Eric is fascinated by the Saving Graces. Whenever he gets glassy-eyed because I'm droning on about something that bores him, I can always wake him up by mentioning them. I think there's something sexual going on. He would probably deny it, but if you ask me, my therapist not only likes hearing about the Saving

Graces, he wouldn't mind sleeping with them, too. All of us, all at the same time.

Not that he would, of course, even if he could. Nobody's straighter than Eric. But deep, deep down in that noble unconscious, I'm pretty sure old Eric would like to shag us all.

"What do the Graces look like?" he asked me once. "What does Emma look like?"

"Oh, she's beautiful. I think—she doesn't, she thinks she's fat. She has reddish hair and white, white Irish skin that freckles in the summer and turns pink when she blushes—she can't hide anything. She tries to look cool all the time and she's got this careless air that fools people, but she's really—well, I was going to say as neurotic as I am, but let's not get carried away."

"Ha. And Isabel?"

"She's older, of course, but really pretty. To me. When I first met her she had gray hair, but now it's blonde. She has blue eyes. She's tall, but not as tall as me. She keeps in shape by walking a lot. In fact, she looks better now than before she got cancer." I couldn't really think of anything else to tell him. Isabel is a quiet person, and her looks are quiet, too. You have to be especially observant or else know her for a long time to really see how lovely she is.

"Lee's cute—which she hates, but it's true. She's tiny, she looks like an elf. Kids love her, and I always think it's partly because she's about their size. Dark hair, and for as long as I've known her she's worn it really, really short. She says it's more practical. Which is Lee to a *T*."

"So you're all good-looking," Eric said, rubbing his chin, with that certain light in his eye, innocent but interested, that always makes me laugh. He's so transparent sometimes.

"Why, thank you," I said, acknowledging the compliment to me. "I've never thought about it much, but I guess we are."

Yesterday he asked me, out of the blue, "How does Curtis feel about your women's group these days?"

"Curtis? Oh," I said, "he's ambivalent." A good catchall word that Eric, of all people, appreciates.

"But he was against it at first, wasn't he?"

"Oh . . ." Had I admitted that to him? It seemed disloyal now. "Maybe a little, but only in the beginning. And he never came out and said so, not in words. It's just that he's so busy."

"So . . . ?"

"So, he likes me to be there when he gets home."

Curtis is a legislative aide to Congressman Wingert; his days start at six and go until eight, nine, sometimes ten at night. He says, "I spend all day talking to assholes, Rudy, and when I come home I'd like you to be there." (I don't think this is unreasonable.) "I need to spend time with you," he says, "just the two of us. I *need* it, I don't just want it. You keep me in sync."

Imagine me maintaining anybody's equilibrium.

Eric said, "So . . . he didn't want you to join the group because it would—what? Take you out of the house too much?"

"No, that's not it. Nothing so—I don't know, what would you call it?"

He shrugged, but I knew what he was thinking: passive-aggressive.

Once I made the mistake of telling Eric about how Curtis enjoys warning me that biology is destiny. The biological imperative. Curtis says the strain of psychosis in my family runs so strong, it's probably congenital. Naturally Eric took offense at that. That's the last thing a psychiatrist wants to hear. (It's the last thing I want to hear, too, but I can't escape it. If Curtis isn't reminding me, I'm reminding myself.) The "heredity connection" goes against everything Eric believes in. He even questioned Curtis's motive in suggesting it.

But in the dark times, it makes perfect sense to me, and then Curtis is my comforter and my solace. He folds me in his arms and swears he'll protect me, and as long as he holds me like that I know I'm safe. I'm safe.

Eric says I take care of Curtis too much, but he doesn't understand. If anything, it's the other way around.

"And how do the other three Saving Graces feel about Curtis?" Eric asked after a couple of silent minutes.

"Oh, they don't talk about him much. That's not really what the group is, Eric. I mean, it's not like we sit around talking about men all the time."

He made a patient face. Eric usually knows, although not always, when I'm hedging.

"Okay, we do talk about Curtis some. Obviously. Away from the group, I probably talk most to Isabel about him."

"Really? Not Emma?"

"No, not Emma. No. Actually . . ." This memory is so painful, I try never to think about it. "Emma and I . . . the worst fight we ever had was over Curtis. Years ago. So now we just leave him out. Pretty much. Pleasantries—how's Curtis, fine, tell him I said hi—that's about it."

"You never told me this. A fight with Emma? When did it happen?"

I didn't want to tell him now. "A long time ago. I still think most of it was her fault."

"Why?"

"Because she waited until the eve of my wedding, I mean literally, the night before, to tell me what she really thinks of Curtis. I've forgiven her—well, there's nothing to forgive. But it's hard to forget."

"Well, tell me."

"It's really old news, Eric."

"I know, but I'm interested."

"Why?"

"Because. Come on, tell me."

I sighed, and told him.

It was four years ago, five in December. Curtis and I had been living together for years, forever, but on the night before the wedding he moved out, just for fun, and Emma came over to stay with me. She was maid of honor, and she was taking the job seriously, being very solicitous and practical and take-charge. Which was good, because I needed taking care of. My mother and stepfather had flown down from Rhode Island that day, my brother from L.A. that night, and my sister had a one-day pass from the cult and was due in the next morning. It was going to be the first time we'd all been together, all of us in one place, in about twenty-five years. Since my father's funeral.

So there was that, plus Curtis's parents who had come up from Georgia two days earlier and were staying at the Willard. I can never decide whose family makes me crazier, his or mine. He calls his people "Old South aristocrats," although how you can be aristocratic and stone broke at the same time, I'm not sure. The Lloyds have a kind of slow, brittle southern charm that freezes my New England blood. They smile and smile, but in their hearts I don't think there's anything but contempt. And none of them talk, they all *drawl.* They remind me of fat brown lizards sunning themselves on hot rocks, too lazy to move a muscle. They drink all the time, and publicly, not in secret like my family—gin martinis, three fingers of bourbon, scotch from tarnished sterling flasks, beakers of warm, smoky brandy. They've refined drinking to a delicate, sensual, obscene art. When we go for visits, I watch them like a voyeur; I feel like I'm viewing erotica from behind a hedge of magnolia or honeysuckle, and everything is sweet and cloying, and I can almost hear that character from Tennessee Williams yelling, "Men*da*city!"

Well, I'm exaggerating, but not much. Curtis claims I hyperbolize his family's eccentricities in order to minimize mine. That's true.

The night before the wedding, Emma came home with me after the rehearsal dinner. The plan was for her to spend the night, then get up early and help me dress for the wedding. We were both starving, even though we'd supposedly just eaten, so we made Spanish omelettes and opened a bottle of wine. This was after about two dozen champagne toasts at the rehearsal dinner, but by then I wasn't counting. I know I drink too much, but on this particular night that was only part of the problem.

We couldn't make ourselves go to bed. Midnight came, but we kept drinking and talking, singing along to the stereo. Exchanging final confidences as single women, I guess. But we were careful not to say that. In fact, we were pretending just the opposite—that nothing would change, my marrying Curtis was only a technicality. I remember Emma was sprawled on the floor in the living room—this was in my old D Street house on Capitol Hill, a dark, skinny row house with six rooms on three floors—and I was on the couch, in my oldest, raggediest nightgown, because I'd packed the good ones for the honeymoon.

"Of course I knew she didn't like Curtis," I told Eric. "I'd known that since I introduced them to each other ten years ago, not long after Curtis and I moved to Washington. But until that night she'd never said so. Well, not in words."

"Nice timing," Eric said sympathetically.

"Yeah."

It started out harmlessly. We were talking about Curtis's new job on the Hill, how much money he would make, how soon we could move to a bigger house. Emma said, "Yeah, that's great, but what I still don't get is the marriage part. I mean, why exactly do you have to *tie the knot*?" I was surprised by how riled she sounded, but I just said something about ritual and ceremony and public commitment—that standard answer.

It was June; hot; Emma had on a sleeveless football jersey and her underpants. She stuck her knees inside the jersey and wrapped her arms around her calves, shook her wild red hair out of her eyes. "Yes, but why not just keep living with him? Why bring the *law* into it?" And she made some joke about Mickey Rooney or Liz

Taylor, how much trouble they'd have saved themselves by just shacking up. We laughed, but it wasn't real. I saw anger when she flicked her eyes away from me.

That scared me, of course, but I said, "This might come as a surprise to you, but Curtis makes me happy. The problem is, Em, you've never known me without him. You don't know what I'm like when he's not around." I gave another false laugh. "I mean, if you think *this* is bad—"

"That's not true. Why are you saying that? I see you with him and I see you without him. When he's around, you don't even talk, Rudy. Or—you look at him, you check with him to make sure what you said was okay. That makes me *sick*."

The revulsion in her voice shocked both of us. I said, "That's a lie," without smiling, and we recoiled again. I got up and turned off the stereo.

Not once in all the years we'd been friends had we used that tone with each other. Or said words that blunt. *Lie*—that's such an ugly word; you only say it to a close friend if you're kidding.

Eric said, "You were frightened."

"I was. Scared to death. We'd had our differences, things that irritated us about each other, but we'd always smoothed them over with humor. Emma's good at getting a serious point across by making a joke—that's her style, and it works for her. She doesn't think anybody knows it, but she'll do almost anything to avoid a confrontation. Because she's afraid of anger. Especially mine, I think." I laughed. "If you can believe that."

"You were *both* scared."

"Yes. Scared and mad and drunk."

That night she tried to pacify me by saying, "Is it because you want children? You and Curtis? I could understand getting married for kids."

"No," I said, "of course not. I want kids, but that's not why I'm marrying him. Emma, why are you being so . . ." Awful pause while we both looked at everything except each other. "I love Curtis. Why is that so hard to understand? Curtis is *good* for me."

"No, he's not." She stood up, glass of warm Chardonnay in one hand, lit cigarette in the other, big maroon "28" on her chest—some Redskin's number. Emma doesn't drink that much, and she only smokes when she's with me, so this was really an incongruous pose. And. . . cute. There's no other word for it. I was dying for her to say something funny now, to erase this conversation, get us back where we'd always been. But she said, "I don't know how, but he's made you *think* he's good for you. Can't you see that's just his trick?"

"His trick? Oh, for—"

"Oh, Rudy, you are so much stronger than he lets you believe! Would you have dropped out of school if it weren't for Curtis? No, and you'd have a real job by now, you'd have a profession."

"Oh, now you don't like my job, either. Well, great, this is just wonderful." Oh, that really hurt. I was selling designer jewelry in a Georgetown boutique, and okay, it wasn't my life's work, but it was all right and I was pretty good at it. But it certainly wasn't Curtis's fault. We moved to D.C. after he graduated from law school, and—well, I just never went back to finish my art history master's. I said, "How in the world is Curtis responsible for what my job is? What do you think he did, *force* me to quit school?"

"Yeah, that's exactly what I think. Only he did it so you didn't even know he was doing it."

"Oh, that's funny. You are so full of it, it's—"

"Rudy, he's manipulative and controlling—those words were *invented* for Curtis Lloyd, and I don't know why you can't see it! He makes you think *you're* crazy, and meanwhile he's this creepy southern sociopath, like Bruce Dern when he used to play those psychotic bayou maniacs—"

I threw a CD at her. It hit her on the side of the throat and made a little cut—tiny, but it bled. She went paper white. We gaped at each other, completely horrified, and both wanting the other to apologize first. If we hadn't been drinking since five o'clock in the afternoon, I know we'd have found a way out, some face-saving retreat. Oh, but we were drunk. And we were both just so tired of lying about Curtis.

Eric was staring at me as if I had two heads. "You did that? You really threw a CD?"

"You can't picture it, can you?" I didn't blame him; I'm notoriously nonviolent.

"What happened? How did it end?"

"I told her if she felt that way about Curtis, maybe she ought not to come to my wedding."

Eric has enormous brown eyes, like a figure in a Velázquez painting. When he opens them wide behind his steel-rimmed glasses, I know I've said something amazing.

"And she said, 'All right, if that's what you want,' and I said, 'I think it's what you want.' She said, 'Well, what do *you* want?' and we went around like that for a while. That's another thing Emma's good at—hiding behind questions, throwing up diversions. People who don't know her think she's really frank and open, but she's not. She's one of the most reserved people I know."

"Did she go to the wedding?"

"Oh, sure. But we didn't resolve anything."

"Did she spend the night?"

"Yes, because we just let it go. We chickened out. I started taking plates and glasses out to the kitchen, and when I came back she was standing over her suitcase, pulling on her jeans. I was shaking inside, walking stiff, like a puppet. I said, 'So you're going home?' She said, 'Yeah.' She didn't look at me, but I could tell by her voice she was crying. And that did it, that just killed me. Because she never cries. So we both started crying, and I told her I wanted her to come to my wedding, and she said she wanted to come, and that was sort of the end of it. But we didn't make up, not really, and neither of us ever apologized. We just went to bed. Or passed out, in my case. I took some pills and went to sleep, just—got *out* of there.

"The wedding—God, the wedding was horrible. I woke up with a headache that lasted for three days. I could see the little scratch on her neck above the collar of her maid-of-honor suit, and every time I saw it I'd sink down into this black hole of depression. Lee and Isabel were the bridesmaids, and it only took them about thirty seconds to realize something was wrong between us. Emma and I stayed mad at each other for three months."

"But you reconciled."

"Yes. Finally. I wish I'd known you then," I said, and Eric smiled.

"How did it come about? The reconciliation."

"Oh, well . . . I can't tell you that. It's Emma's story, not mine. Another calamity involving a man, but that's all I can say. But it was her man that time, not mine."

Eric couldn't stop shaking his head. "How did you feel when she told you Curtis was manipulative and—what was it? Manipulative and—"

"She called him a sociopath, Eric, that's what she called him, and how do you think I felt? It was like a stab in my heart. These are the two people in the world I love most, and I can't stand it that they hate each other. But he *doesn't* hate her, and that makes it even worse. He never says *anything* bad about her, he never has."

"Do you think so? Rudy, do you really think Curtis likes Emma?"

I said, "The only good thing about my wedding was, we finally got to meet Lee's boyfriend. Although he wasn't her boyfriend yet, it was their first date. 'Henry the plumber' we'd been calling him. We were dying to meet him, because you know Lee, the original Jewish American princess, and she was absolutely in *lust* with this man who was installing heating ducts and copper wiring in her basement. But we all ended up falling in love with him, and so did she, and nine months later she married him."

And that was the end of our fifty minutes.

7

Emma

What do you do when you look at a piece of modern art and it looks like nothing at all, your mind goes blank, and you can't even think of a joke or something smart-mouthed to say about it if you happen to be viewing it with a pal, and all you can think is, Either I'm crazy or you are, Mr. Big Shot Artist, and since you've got this exhibit in a real building and all these people are standing around contemplating your stuff and saying intelligent things about it, it must be me? Well, what do you do?

What I do is get out as fast as I can without saying much of anything, and I also try to drink as much of the cheap white wine as I can if it's an opening, so at least the night isn't a total loss, and plus I find I have a lot more to say about the artist's oeuvre if I am, how shall I say, slightly oiled.

But these solutions don't apply if you're in his studio with the artiste himself, and it's just you, him, and his work. And say his work mystifies you; it might be priceless, it might be dreck, you don't have a clue. And say you're supposed to be doing a serious, paid, legitimate piece on the artist for the major newspaper that employs you, and, oh yeah, you also have this painful, yearning, lustful attraction to the artist's body, not to mention a helpless and wholly out of character passion for his heart, both of which are married? Then what?

You're fucked.

"So, Mick. Tell me the story of how you went from patent law to fine art. Constitution Avenue to Seventh Street." It's never too early to start thinking in headlines, I always say. "Bourgeois to Bauhaus. Buttoned-down to PoMo."

"Well—"

"And while you're at it, what exactly is postmodernism?"

When I'm nervous, I become insufferable. I can see it happening, but I can't stop it, can't shut up, and the more important the occasion is to me, the more obnoxious I get. Today, boy, I was really outdoing myself.

We were standing in the middle of Mick Draco's chilly, cluttered studio, which was smaller than I'd expected, considering he shares it with two other people. Richard, the photographer from the paper, had just left after taking about two hundred pictures, from every angle you can imagine and some you'd never dream of, of Mick smearing yellow paint on a canvas with a trowel. I got a good, long look at him then, because I didn't have to talk, I could just stare. I lied, I have three weaknesses. I don't like to admit to the third one. It's physical beauty. I know, I'm shallow, and I hate it. Sometimes I go out with unattractive men on purpose so no one can accuse me of superficiality. But in truth, all other things being equal, I'd rather they were good-looking.

Watching him, I decided Mick's beauty came from the way he moved as much as from his great-looking body, and his facial expressions—humor and self-consciousness, patience, rapt concentration, finally impatience—as much as the handsome face itself. He was wearing black slacks, a tweed jacket, a blue work shirt, and a red tie, and I had on jeans and a T-shirt, and I was thinking it was funny, maybe kind of sweet, that he'd dressed up and I'd dressed down. As if we'd been thinking about each other when we put our clothes on this morning.

To his credit, he didn't even try to answer any of my facetious questions. He said, "Would you like to sit down?" He took an oily rag from his work table and swished it around a coating of plaster dust on the only chair in the room.

I gave the dirty chair a look and said, "Uh, no thanks," sort of deadpan.

He has a beautiful smile, truly self-deprecating. He lowers his eyelashes, which are longer than mine, and curves his lips up at the sharp corners, and you imagine he's thinking, *That's a good joke on me.* He sort of mumbled, "Yeah, I guess this isn't the best place to talk. Want to go across the street?"

Yes! Yes! Let's go there again, Murray's, that dump with the rotten food and congealed air, where everybody looks like a corpse and the coffee tastes like antifreeze! Let's sit across from each other in a cracked booth by the smudged window in the livid light, like we did last week, and talk and talk and talk!

"Yeah, okay," I mumbled back. "If you want to."

On the way, huddled in our coats against the November drizzle, he answered the main question, or I guess he thought he did. I was struck again by the idea that he was shy, or at least deeply reserved, because of the way he turned away from me, peering down shiny, wet G Street while he explained what had to be one of the most significant events of his life. I could barely hear him. And he'd picked the least focused, most distracted moment to deal with the subject—us in the middle of traffic—as if he wanted to slip his answer in without anyone noticing. "I got into art when it felt like I could get into it," he said—or I thought he said; he was muttering again. "You were joking about postmodernism—"

"No, I wasn't."

"—but you know it redeemed representation in some ways, made the figure respectable again, I guess you could say. Brought back the concept of meaning in painting. Which wasn't allowed so much during modernism."

He took my arm in the intersection, and we scuttled across. I said, brilliantly, "Come again?"

He cleared his throat. "Abstraction never appealed to me, I

couldn't feel it or understand it. I looked at it and knew I couldn't do it, and I was proud or stupid enough to think that meant I couldn't be an artist. Yeah, stupid. Stupid enough. Years." He muttered something I couldn't hear. I started to say, "What?" but he was holding the door open, so I passed him and went inside.

Murray's has a counter on the right with cracked red leatherette stools, and on the left a row of cracked red leatherette booths. Last week we sat at the counter, but today we took a booth. The decor . . . think of a bus station coffee shop in Trenton. The walls are lined with blurry, sepia-colored mirrors, and you start when you first catch sight of yourself, because in the sick fluorescent glare you don't look nearly as bad as the person you're talking to does; the grease on the mirrors acts like a gauze filter, and you actually look pretty good. The temperature hovers around eighty degrees, which is why artists in the lofts and studios in this neighborhood come here, Mick says: to get warm. "Coffee?" he asked. I nodded, and he went up to the counter to get it. You wait on yourself at Murray's.

"So," I said when he returned, my pencil poised, notebook open. Ready for business. "You're saying you became a painter because the postmodern atmosphere in the art world finally freed you to feel like one."

"No, that sounds ridiculous. Don't write that."

I'd thought it sounded pretty good. "Well, what? This is a piece about people who give up straight jobs that aren't satisfying them for a dream they think will." I'd explained that before, but I was thinking we both needed to hear it again. "What I'm looking for is policy wonks who decide to be forest rangers. Dentists who want to write mystery novels. Washington's perfect for this, people love to read about some guy at the Bureau of Standards who threw it all away to become a horse jockey or a mime, a dog trainer, a Deadhead—"

"I know, I understand what you're after."

"Okay. Well, let's try it this way. What was wrong with patent law? Why did you leave that profession?"

He smiled at me, light eyes twinkling. "I'm impressed."

"How come?"

"You asked me that with a straight face."

I laughed. I felt light and airy inside, buoyant for some reason. Well, he looked so appreciative. As if he was noticing things about me and he liked them. But he wasn't coming on to me, he just liked me. We sat for a minute, not talking, just stirring our coffees and pulling one-ply napkins out of the metal dispenser.

"Well, anyway." My notebook recalled me to my purpose. "Back to postmodernism. Now, you—"

"No, Emma, forget that. I'll tell you the truth." But he looked pained.

I said, "Fine," uncertainly. "But it's not a police interrogation or anything. Don't tell me anything that's going to hurt anybody." The hard-hitting investigative journalist at work. Earlier, he'd asked me not to tape our conversation, and usually I push that a little, try to assure the interviewee that it won't hurt a bit, it's for my convenience but also for his protection, blah blah. But when Mick asked, I gave in without a fight.

He rested his forearms on the table and hunched his shoulders, circling the thick, stained coffee cup with his hands. Nice hands, by the way, bony and smart, long-fingered. "It's . . . well, it's not exactly a secret." He looked up, looked me in the eye.

I stared back without blinking, trying to project professionalism and integrity. But I felt like a doe caught in a flashlight beam. It was so obvious he was sizing me up, trying to decide if he could trust me. I kept quiet—what could I say?—but the phrase that kept coming to my mind was *Oh, Mick, if you only knew*.

He sat back, twisting sideways so he could slouch against the wall, one foot drawn up on the cracked seat. He loosened his tie. "Draco is a Greek name," he said conversationally. I scribbled down "Greek," although I didn't know what to think yet, wasn't sure what he'd decided. "My father is Philip Draco. Do you know the name?" I shook my head. "Percy, Wells, Draco, & Dunn. Pretty well-known law firm, offices in most of the big cities. My name isn't Draco, though."

I looked up. "It's not?"

"I mean it's not my real name, my birth name. I was adopted. Never knew my real parents."

"Oh."

"I was an only child, and I grew up knowing what I was supposed to be—a lawyer like my dad. Who is a good man," he added, "really a great man in some ways. He's brilliant at his work, probably one of the top fifty lawyers in the country."

"Did you grow up in Washington?"

"Chicago."

"How old were you when you found out you were adopted?"

"I always knew."

"Even when you were little?"

"I never remember not knowing it." He hesitated, started to fiddle with the paper place mat, a child's map of D.C.'s major tourist attractions. "Believe me, no one wanted to make me feel as if I were on trial. My parents were terrific. Anything like that, I did it to myself. Because . . ." He held his empty cup up and scrutinized the manufacturer's name on the bottom.

I know better than to prompt someone I'm interviewing. But I said, "Because you didn't want them to be sorry. For choosing you."

"That's it." The surprise and the gratitude in his face were too good—they made me dizzy. I grabbed his coffee cup and mine, got up, and went to the counter for refills. Now all I could think was, *We have to stop having these moments.*

But when I came back and sat down, and stirred and sipped and acted normal, I noticed he was looking at me in a new way. You know how you can tell when you've done or said something, inadvertently or not, that makes the other person go to the next level, so to speak, some alternate way of seeing you? And sometimes that's good, and sometimes you wish you'd been more circumspect? I couldn't decide which it was in this case, but one thing was clear: Mick didn't just interest me anymore. I interested him.

I picked up my pencil. He resumed.

"About four years ago, after giving it a lot of thought, I made up my mind to try to find out who my birth mother was. By then I'd been practicing law for seven years. Not very happily. Miserably," he said with a laugh, glancing up. "I was married, my son was almost two. Sally—that's my wife—she'd quit her job after Jay was born so she could be a full-time mother."

"What was her job?" I sounded businesslike, as if the story would crumble without that vital tidbit.

"She was a paralegal. That's how we met."

Paralegal, I wrote. "And did you find your mother?"

"Eventually. I should tell you something about myself first. I've always painted or sketched or sculpted or built constructions, collages—I've always made things. Even as a kid."

"You've always been an artist."

"Well, but I didn't call it that. It would never have occurred to me. We didn't have any artists in my family, not even remotely. A second cousin who dabbles in photography—that's it. Except for him, nothing."

It hit me. "*Your mother.* You found her—and? Who was she? What was she?"

He smiled; he liked my excitement. "Yeah, I found her. When she gave me up, she was a second-year student at the Art Institute in Chicago."

"My God. Mick, oh, wow, that's amazing."

"I thought you'd like that. It makes a good story for you, doesn't it?"

"Are you kidding?" My CPA-turned-bluegrass fiddler, my UPS man-turned-pentecostal preacher—they were in danger of looking anemic in comparison. "This is terrific, this could be the *whole* story. So do you see her now? What does she do, is she still—"

"I've never met her."

"Oh. No?"

"I wrote her a letter, and I know she got it, but she didn't write back. So I had to let it go. I never tried to see her."

He has a way of compressing his lips in a tight half-smile when he says things that pain him. It discourages sympathy. I took the hint and didn't offer any. But I hurt for him.

"The point is," he said after a moment, "finding that out about my mother was like"—he touched his fingertips to his temple, then flung his hand out—"an explosion. When the smoke cleared, everything fell into place—I knew what I was supposed to do. For the first time, I really understood myself."

"Wow." I felt a definite spark of envy. "Like figuring out you're gay and coming out of the closet or something."

"Exactly. Not that it happened overnight. Don't misunderstand—it took about a year for the smoke to clear."

"Well, that was the lawyer part, I guess. You know, being cautious."

"Partly."

He didn't elaborate on that, and I started thinking how I might phrase a question about his wife, how all this had sat with her. But then—I didn't. In the same situation, I'd have asked it of somebody else. But my motives were impure. I couldn't quite bring myself to ask it of Mick.

Instead I asked him about the early days, and if it had been scary resigning from his job. He said it was terrifying; his paycheck went from—he caught himself. "It dropped about ninety-eight percent," he said, watching me write that down. "I've been a full-time painter for three years now, and I've sold two paintings, both to friends. I may *never* make any money." But I don't think he believed that, because he said it without any anxiety, and he didn't strike me as the kind of man who could indulge himself without guilt indefinitely.

A kindred spirit.

He'd opened the door, though, and I had a responsibility to walk through it. "Your wife—um—"

"Sally."

"Sally." I wrote it down. "So she's okay with all this, she's—"

"She's been great. She's been great." He nodded and nodded, and I scribbled, *S. been great.* I looked at him expectantly. It's amazing how much you can get out of someone by saying nothing, just waiting. Mick rubbed his cheek in a raspy circle—he needed a shave—and finally said, "Jay's in day care—well, you know that, you know Lee Patterson—because Sally's had to go back to work. She's an administrative assistant at the Labor Department."

"Uh-huh."

"She had to do it. Otherwise we'd've starved. And we've moved to Columbia Heights."

"From?"

"Q Street, Dupont Circle. Near the Park."

"Uh-huh."

"We're fixing up an old row house."

"Been there."

"Really?"

"Well, no, I mean, I just bought one. An old town house. Somebody else fixed it up."

"Uh-huh." He smiled, but I think he was mimicking me. "Well, that's a little different."

"I guess." The change of address suggested he'd come down in the world, and his manner said he minded. What wasn't clear was if he minded for himself or for Sally, and I couldn't think of a way to ask. Not that it was any of my business.

I glanced over my notes. "So tell me, what would you call the kind of art you're doing now?"

He put his chin on his knee, frowning. "What would you call it?" I gave a nervous laugh, but he wasn't being hostile or aggressive. He sounded curious.

"Listen, Mick, I have to tell you, I don't know the first thing about art. Honestly, I'm a complete dunce, so if you want this article to sound good and be true, you should talk to me straight. In fact, you should talk down to me. Pretend I'm your kid." He laughed. God, I liked making him laugh. I liked it too much. "Failing that, just talk very, very slowly."

So he did. At length. The gist of it was that he hadn't found his own style yet, or even his true subject, but he was working in a formalist, figural mode because he needed the practice and because abstraction was a dead end for him. He thought postmodernism wasn't a real epoch, just the last gasp of modernism before the next phase started. He wouldn't presume to say what that would be like, but when I pressed, he said he thought it might involve a revival of formal excellence, which contemporary art was incapable of and had therefore cynically dismissed.

I asked him who he admired, and he said Rembrandt, Fantin-Latour, Arshile Gorky, Alice Neel, Eric Fischl. Who did he hate? He said he would tell me, but only off the record, and then he rattled off about five names, all men, none I'd ever heard of. He saw himself moving more and more toward portraiture, he said; in fact, lately he'd noticed a recurring character in his paintings and sketches, a young man, maybe an adolescent, whom he was calling "Joe" and who he thought was probably himself. Color was his strength, drawing his weakness; he took two different drawing classes, four nights a week, and he was beginning to see a little progress. He wished he had the time and money to go for a master of fine arts somewhere, because he was at a point where his lack of formal training was becoming more and more of a handicap.

I got most of it down, but the longer he talked, the more distracted I got. He was so beautifully intense. Art was his passion, obviously, it bordered on his obsession, and I am such a sucker for men who really love their work. I find their single-mindedness incredibly sexy and desirable. And the best part is, they don't depend on *me* to make sense out of their lives.

I ran out of questions. I glanced at my watch.

"Let's eat something, I'm starting to shake." Mick held out his hand; sure enough, his fingers were trembling. "I never drink coffee like this," he admitted and got up to go to the men's room.

We ordered cheeseburgers, french fries, and milkshakes, the kind of food we both swore we never ate, but I noticed we polished it all off without any trouble. While we ate, he asked *me* questions. At first I didn't even notice; it seemed like the usual give-and-take, just normal conversation. But when he said, "Is newspaper work what you've always wanted to do? Or—if you suddenly found out you had a different birth mother, who would you like her to be?"—I realized he was turning the tables and interviewing me.

Okay, I was flattered. In my experience, the majority of people don't care that much about other people's inner lives. They're nice, they're polite, they ask how you're doing—and as soon as you start telling them they click off. Their eyes glaze, they go into wait mode, and what they're waiting for is you to run down or take a breath, so they can jump in and tell you how much more interesting their lives are than yours. This isn't cynicism. I'm telling you, it happens all the time.

The exception, of course, is men who are trying to sleep with you. The better they are at it, the harder they listen; the more they want you, the more entranced they become by your every random utterance. What's funny is that this tried-and-true method really works, at least on me. As one who has, as they say, been around the block a few times, I ought to know better, but I don't. It gets me every time.

So it was with considerably mixed feelings that I stared back into Mick Draco's intelligent brown eyes, currently focused on me with much interest and expectancy, and contemplated his acute question. *Are you trying to seduce me?* I asked him via mental telepathy. *God, I hope so.*

No, I don't, I'd hate that.

"Mary McCarthy."

His eyebrows shot up. "The writer?"

"Yeah, or Iris Murdoch. Katherine Anne Porter. No, not really—I was trying to think of who'd be the right age to give birth to me about forty years ago. Thirty-nine." *Shit,* I told him my age. And he was younger! Only one year, but still.

"Oh, so you'd like to write fiction?"

Now that was the really disconcerting thing, not that I'd told him my age but that I'd told him my secret dream. Not that secret—the Graces know, although Rudy's the only one who knows how *much* I want it; and my mother knows; a couple of ex-boyfriends know, because I was stupid enough to blurt it out to them. But it's *supposed* to be a secret. Why? Because I hate to fail in public. And because the journalist-who-yearns-to-write-the-great-American-novel is such a foolish, humiliating cliché, I don't care to be associated with it.

But I was speaking to a man who had given up lawyering for painting. If anyone would understand the dream, it ought to be Mick. So I didn't back down or try to wriggle out with a joke, I looked straight at him and said, "Yes, I would. Someday. It's what I want to do most. But I'm, you know. Afraid."

"Yeah," he said, as if nothing could be more natural. "Because it's terrifying."

"It is, it's terrifying." Just thinking about it was scaring me.

"So what are you going to do?"

"Hm? Well, I've written some short stories that stink, nobody wants them." Defenses creeping back; arms halfway into full metal jacket. "And I'm playing around with something longer, but it's no good. Really. I'm not being modest."

"Has anybody read it?"

"Are you kidding?" I laughed, ha ha. "Luckily, I've got a very highly developed sense of shame, it keeps me out of all sorts of trouble."

Mick smiled and looked away.

I went cold, realizing he was a little embarrassed. For me. Because what I'd said was so transparent.

"I wonder," he said slowly, "which is more personal, a painting or a poem. I wonder which one is more revealing."

"That's easy. A poem."

"How come?"

"Because it's easier to hide behind a painting."

"Is it? Why?"

I grinned, trying to win him back with candor. "Because I don't understand paintings."

"I don't understand poems."

I laughed, but he didn't. "Okay," I said testily, "I get your point."

"What point?"

"You're braver than I am. You're a hero, I'm a chicken. Look, I'm not arguing with you, you're right. No contest."

"That's not what I meant. Wait a second, that's not what I'm saying, I'm—"

"Okay, my mistake. Forget it, it doesn't matter anyway. I don't even know what we're talking about."

His sigh sounded exasperated. "I'm quite sure I'm not braver than you are, Emma."

"Well, but you don't know me."

"True, but I can tell you're not a chicken."

"How?" Oh, how embarrassing, how childish, how immature, how pathetic, how needy. "Hm? How can you tell?"

He never got to answer. The ear-splitting siren of a police car, then an ambulance, then another police car made it impossible to talk. Mick smiled and shrugged, and turned around to watch them roar by in the bleary, grease-smeared window. “Oh, no. My God, it’s ten to three.”

I saw the clock over the front door. “So—?”

He started rooting around in his pockets, hunting for his wallet. He looked stunned. “I’ve got to pick up Jay. I’m sorry, I had no idea it was this late, I’ve got ten minutes to get to Judiciary Square. But I can make it. But how did this happen? So—did we finish?”

“Yeah, I guess.” I couldn’t think; my mind had blanked. “I’ll get this,” I said, shoving dollar bills back at him.

“No—”

“It’s on the paper. I’ve got an expense account.”

“Oh. Okay. Look, I’m sorry I have to go, but I have to.”

“Sure. Go. Take the subway, it’s only one stop.”

“No, I think I’ll just run.” He stood over me, frowning and smiling, smoothing his hair back, harried, uncertain. “Well, so. If you need to ask me any more questions, you know how to get in touch with me, I guess.”

“Right. And here’s my card, you can call me if, you know, you think of anything else.”

“It should be a great article.”

“Thanks for a terrific interview.”

“I really enjoyed it. Obviously.” He made a sheepish gesture back at the clock.

“Yeah, me, too.”

“Well. Good luck to you.”

“Thanks. I’ll be looking for your stuff in *Art World* from now on.”

“Ha.”

I finally had to stop smiling. Mick’s face changed from hectic courtesy to awareness. For the space of about three seconds, we were both naked. I started to say something, but then I couldn’t.

He couldn't either. It was over, it was ending. Hello, good-bye. If we shook hands—

But no—he just said my name and bowed his head, and I saw his lips press together in that grimacing smile he makes when things aren't good. And then he walked out of my life without touching me.

Which was just as well. Close call. I might not have let go.

I took the bus home. I've got a car, but I like to take the bus or the subway around the city, it gives me time to think. If I'm in a good mood, I like to look at my fellow passengers and speculate on their lives, measure them on the narrow, unforgiving scale of Emma's Criteria for Normalcy. If I'm in a bad mood, I like to sink deeper and deeper into it while I stare lifelessly out the window of the No. 42 or the Red Line Metro, converting every building, every pedestrian, every telephone pole into a metaphor for corruption, decay, and urban ennui. It cheers me up.

But today I was beyond bad moods or good moods. I was flummoxed. I couldn't understand myself. I'm my best friend, I trust me, I keep a constant conversation going with myself—audible, if I'm alone—and it's important to me that I know myself. Vital. Otherwise, *chaos*.

Why was I devastated? Oh, please. Even the word *devastated* offends me, it's so melodramatic. I drank coffee all afternoon with a man, and we talked. It was a good conversation, and there had been bursts of honesty that thrilled me, little explosions of candor that don't occur that often between me and other people, except for Rudy, and hardly ever between me and the men I've been seeing for, oh, the last five years or so. Especially sober.

Fine, but it still wasn't that extraordinary. If Mick had let me record the interview, I could play it back, and I bet I'd scratch my head and think, *What's the big deal?* On the surface, not that much happened. Why was I in such disarray? And pain. I felt like an accident had happened to me, but I was hurt in a place I couldn't put my finger on. All over.

Sense of proportion needed here. I saw something I wanted and I can't have it, that's all. They call it loss, and the standard reaction is grief. So I'm normal. And how long can it last? Not long—I'm Emma DeWitt, not Emma Bovary.

At four o'clock in the afternoon, my house was as dark as nighttime. I went around turning on lamps, turning up the heat, wondering if I should get a cat. Or a bird, one that would make a lot of noise when I came home. I made a cup of tea—more caffeine, that's the ticket—and leafed through my boring mail. Then I watched the rain glide down the kitchen window in long, slow, monotonous trails.

The phone rang, and my heart flipped right into my throat.

"Hello?"

"Sondra?"

"Who?"

"Oh. Sor—" Click.

Same to you.

Well, that was a revealing little incident. I felt weak in the knees. Elbows on the counter, I held my head in my hands and wallowed in misery for one full minute.

Mick wasn't going to call me. In my heart, I didn't even want him to. And I wasn't going to dream up some specious, last-minute interview question and call him. Both of us were better than that.

There's some comfort in finality, even if it's grim. I hate ambiguity, give me all or nothing. I can take nothing as long as it really is nothing, undiluted by hope or *yes, but maybe if.*

I would take a bath, I decided. I'm a shower person, but there's something healing about submersion in scalding water when you've got the blues. A bath, or a bowl of hot oatmeal with lots of butter—those are the two best depression remedies I know. Well, no, but they're the two wholesomest. And I'd take the phone in the tub with me and call Rudy. Curtis wouldn't be home yet, she'd be able to talk.

Upstairs in my study, the answering machine was blinking a message.

"Hi, Em, it's Lee, it's Monday, it's approximately. . . two-forty-seven in the afternoon. I'm calling to see if you can come to dinner on Friday."

Great! A diversion. And I hadn't seen Henry, who cracks me up, in ages.

"Are you still seeing that Brad, the engineering consultant guy?" Unfortunately, yes. "Well, anyway, bring him if you want to, or anybody else, whoever you'd like. Or come alone if you'd rather, it doesn't matter. Although the table won't be balanced." Gotcha. "So, I really hope you can make it and it's not too short notice." Lee has a wonderfully flattering misconception of my social life. "Very informal, just pot luck, come in anything." Meaning I'd show up in leggings and a sweater, and she'd wear a two-hundred-dollar hostess gown. Do they still call them that, "hostess gowns"?

"I think the only other couple I'm asking is the Dracos. I ran into Sally yesterday, and then I remembered you already know Mick, so I thought it might be fun if we all got together. You'll like Sally, Em, she's smart. And nice, I'm really having fun getting to know her."

Oh Jesus Christ God Almighty.

"Well, okay, call me when you get a chance, I'll be home all evening. Or tomorrow—leave a message if you're out all night gallivanting. Ha ha. B'bye."

As I say, I hate ambiguity. It makes dealing with simultaneous joy and wretchedness a special challenge. I headed back downstairs because it was time for the big guns. A bowl of oatmeal *in* a scalding hot bath.

8

Lee

I'd have enjoyed my dinner party more if Emma and Mick Draco, Sally's husband, had gotten along better. I think it's rude to bring your personal animosities to a social function; it discomfits everybody. Not that they had a fight—far from it; they didn't even speak. They barely *looked* at each other, and I for one think that's discourteous. To each other, certainly, but even more, to the hostess. Me. Clearly their interview last Monday didn't go well, but that's not *my* fault.

I smoothed things over as best I could, and a less perceptive observer probably wouldn't even have noticed anything amiss. Henry didn't, as he told me afterward when we discussed it. But that's a man for you. Women are the discerning ones when it comes to the dynamics of interpersonal relationships.

After dinner, I served dessert (apple mousse with drizzled calvados sauce) in the living room. "How long have you two been married?" Sally asked sociably, sipping coffee.

"Four years," I said. "And you and Mick?"

"Six. Six?" She looked at her husband, who nodded. "Gosh, it doesn't seem that long. How did you meet? I love to hear stories about how happy couples first got together, don't you?" She's such a friendly woman, and I appreciated her effort to keep the conversation fresh and interesting—like me, she must've noticed the strain between Mick and Emma.

I started to answer, but Henry spoke first. "Well, I was driving home from work one day, and I got a call on the car phone from my mom. She was stuck on a job in Alexandria and wanted me to take her last call."

"Oh, your mother's a—?"

"She's a plumber, like me. I'm the son in Patterson and Son."

"Oh, really? I didn't realize that."

"Yeah, so she asked me to take her last job for her, some lady in Maryland with a stopped-up toilet."

Sally laughed. "How romantic! I'm assuming this was Lee."

Henry nodded. "I drove over to Chevy Chase and knocked on the door—this door—and that was that. One look, and I was gone."

"Aww," Emma said. "What were you wearing, Lee?"

"Oh, golly, I don't remember."

"I do." Henry grinned, slanting me a lazy-eyed look that brought back some memories. "A little checked suit, with a vest and a black bowtie. Masculine, you know, which made me want to laugh, 'cause she sure wasn't masculine. And she had on real high heels, red ones, but still she only came up to my chin. She was cute as a basket o' kittens."

Now, I've never owned a pair of red high heels in my life. Burgundy, yes, and a pair of medium-heeled cranberry patent leather pumps, but no red. I don't mention that when Henry recounts this story, however; the memory is so clear to him, and evidently so satisfying, I would never want to correct it.

I, on the other hand, remember perfectly what *he* wore that first day: his blue uniform and his tool belt. With scuffed work boots. And he had that gorgeous southern accent, and even though his eyes said he wanted to eat me up, still he was *so* polite and painstakingly gentle and careful of me in every way, even then, when all we were talking about was toilets. I'm the one who was "gone."

"After I finished the repair, she gave me a cup of tea and a cookie—"

"A scone." I had to correct that.

"A scone, and we sat at the kitchen table and talked for an hour and a half."

"What about?" Sally looked fascinated.

Henry and I glanced at each other and shrugged. "I couldn't tell you," he said, "but by the time I left, she'd hired me to tear out all her old water pipes and put in new copper."

"And after that, all new heating ducts."

"And then whole-house air-conditioning."

"Then we had to get married," I joked, "because I was broke."

Sally got up to pour everybody more coffee. "What about you, Emma? How did you and Brad meet?" She smiled invitingly, trying to disarm Emma, who squirmed and scowled and pretended she wasn't uncomfortable.

"Oh, you know," she mumbled, "the usual. A bar."

"Uh-oh," Sally said humorously, "*this* sounds interesting."

"Not really."

Brad, beside Emma on the sofa, put his hand on her thigh. She looked very pretty tonight, I thought, with proper makeup on for a change and her hair in a French braid. She'd dressed up, too—I couldn't remember the last time I'd seen Emma in a skirt. She must like Brad; she doesn't usually go to so much trouble for her dates. Brad said, "Well, *I* thought it was pretty interesting. She played hard to get, I had to use all my masculine charm."

"You just had to keep buying drinks."

"She's kidding," I assured Sally—Emma's humor can be a little difficult until you know her. And even then.

"I was with a couple of guys from the office, and Emma was with a girlfriend—"

"Who?" I interrupted, curious. I'd never heard this story.

"You don't know her," Emma told me, "a woman from the paper. You know, it really isn't all that—"

"This was at Shannon's on L Street, a weeknight, a Wednesday night," Brad went on, "that time between happy hour and dinner, when you can't decide whether to go home or stay and make a night of it." He's an engineer, and always very precise. Except for being good-looking, he's not really Emma's type, I wouldn't have said. Too normal.

"My table was next to hers. I'd been staring at her all night, of course, and when she got up to go to the ladies' room, I stood up too. I said—well, you tell it."

"No, you," Emma said quickly. She looked completely blank.

"Okay—I said, 'Can I tell you a joke?' and she said, 'Why?' and I said, 'Because you've got a great laugh and I want to hear it again.'"

"Oh, that's a *wonderful* line," Sally said. "Isn't that a good line?" she asked her husband, and he said yes, great.

"So then it took another hour to talk her into having dinner with me—right, Em?—and by then we were both feeling no pain, so—"

"See?" Emma interrupted, crossing her leg to move his hand. "This isn't interesting at all."

"—so then it only took *two* more hours to talk her into letting me take her home. And then we—"

"Story over," Emma snapped. "We lived happily ever after."

"Okay, okay," Brad said, laughing, "fade to black. I'm getting that the rest of this is censored."

Sally laughed knowingly. "And how long have you been together?"

Emma shrugged.

Brad said, "Four, going on five months now. That's right, because it was the night after the Fourth of July, and the subway was still littered with trash. Remember, Em?"

"Right," she said, shaking her head no.

I looked at Emma more closely, to see if she was really blushing. *Yes*—she ducked her head, but I saw her cheeks flush. Well, how interesting. She doesn't make it a habit, as far as I know, to pick up men in bars and take them home with her—but at the same time, she's not the kind of woman who would care that much if anybody *thought* she did; she'd say, "Screw you," and go on about her business. But here she was, turning red from embarrassment because apparently she and Brad had slept with each other on their first date. Very interesting. It had to be because of Sally, who's so fresh and wholesome. Emma must be worried about offending her.

"Well," Sally said, sliding her arm through Mick's, "*we* met when he rescued me. My shining knight. He foiled a mugger who was trying to rip my handbag off my shoulder in McPherson Square."

"Wow, *that's* exciting," I said. Mick leaned over to pet Lettice, who was dozing with her chin on his shoe; I couldn't see his face. He and Sally make a very attractive couple, and such a sharp contrast to each other—he tall and dark and quiet, she fair, petite, and animated. They really look as if they were made for each other.

"Wait, it gets better," she said, sitting forward. "He wouldn't stay and let me thank him, he said he was late, had to run—he just made sure I was okay and then he left. Well, I was bereft! I thought he was *so* good-looking in his three-piece suit. He even wore suspenders! I'm *mad* for a man in suspenders."

I laughed. "I've never thought about it."

"Really? Emma, don't you love a man in suspenders?"

"Sometimes. I guess."

"And *vests*—I love it when they take off their suit coats, and all they have on is a vest and their crisp shirtsleeves. So sexy." Sally wriggled her eyebrows at Mick, who ran a finger over his lips, half smiling.

"I'll have to remember this," Brad said, nudging Emma. "Remind me to take my coat off more often." She sent him one of her famous quelling looks, but he just laughed.

"So then—this was on a Thursday—on *Fri*day, guess who I ran into at the office Christmas party. Yes!"

"No, really?" I marveled. "Mick?"

"It turned out we worked in the same building on Vermont Avenue. Can you believe it? For the same law firm."

"We'd never met before," Mick cleared his throat to say, "because she was new, plus I'd been out of the office a lot on travel."

"Still, quite a coincidence," Brad said.

"I thought it was a miracle," Sally said, leaning back against Mick's shoulder. "Definitely a sign that we were fated to be together. Kismet!"

"Very romantic," I said.

"Yeah, Romeo and Juliet." Emma stood up. We stared at her; she looked a little surprised to find herself on her feet. "I'm sorry, I have to go. I forgot, I have to work tomorrow."

"On Saturday?" Brad looked amazed.

"What can I say. It's a seven-day newspaper."

So then *everybody* decided they had to go, and the evening ended much too early. While I held her coat for her, Emma apologized under her breath. "I'm sorry, Lee, I've broken up your nice party."

"Well, I wish you'd told me."

"I know, I just forgot, I was having too good a time. Really sorry, and it was great, everything was perfect, as usual. You're the *best* hostess."

I whispered, my back to the others, who were busy putting their coats on and talking, "I'm sorry you didn't like him."

"Who?"

"Mick," I mouthed.

Emma kept blinking, jerking her head toward me in small spasms. "*What*?"

"Shh. I'll call you, we'll talk."

"Okay." And then she laughed. She threw her head back and crowed. Everybody stopped talking and looked at her.

"What's funny?" Henry wanted to know.

I said, "Nothing," and turned away to open the door. I thought, *Well, maybe I was mistaken*. But then Sally hugged me and everybody else, Brad shook hands with Henry and Mick, Henry hugged Emma, Mick hugged me—and Mick and Emma didn't even look at each other. I think they might've mumbled, "G'night," but that was it. So I knew. I rarely err when it comes to this sort of thing.

"Good dinner," Henry said later that night, peering at his teeth in the bathroom mirror.

"It was." I'd made *thaazi saag aur narial* (beef with curried spinach and coconut); the recipe said "serves ten," but six of us ate it all. That's my definition of a successful dinner. I said, "Sally's awfully nice, isn't she?" Henry grunted. "And you and Mick really hit it off." But that didn't surprise me; I've yet to meet anyone who doesn't like Henry.

"Yeah, I liked him. Interesting guy. Know what he said? Prob'ly won't come to anything, but he's gonna recommend me and Jenny to his studio landlord for plumbing work. And guess who his landlord is."

"Who?"

"Carney Brothers. If we could get any kind of a foothold downtown in one o' those big ol' buildings—something's always going wrong, they're a gold mine for repairs. Just a couple o' maintenance contracts, and we'd be set. Wouldn't that be something?"

"It would be."

"I'll call Jenny tomorrow—guess it's too late tonight. Prob'ly won't come to anything," he said again, "but it was nice of Mick to offer. Most people wouldn't think of it."

Henry calls his mother Jenny. I used to think it was strange—I can't imagine calling my mother "Irene." But he grew up in a women's commune in North Carolina back in the 1960s, so he had a lot of mothers. No fathers, but a lot of mothers. Rather than call them all "Mom," he called them by their names, including his own mother. I guess it makes sense.

"Yeah, it was a nice party, but something was in the air, I thought," Henry said, moving aside so I could take off my makeup in front of the sink. "I thought maybe Emma didn't like Sally, or maybe she and Brad were fighting. Can't figure out what she sees in that guy anyway."

"Brad? Oh, I think he's nice. No, Emma likes smart people, and Sally's so clever, that's not it. It's Mick she doesn't like."

"Mick! You think?"

"Well, did you ever hear them say two words to each other?"

Henry said, "Huh," thoughtfully.

"They looked at each other, but they never talked. That interview they did together for the paper didn't go well, obviously."

"Huh."

I finished brushing my teeth and yawned. "Tired?" Henry was watching me in the mirror. I was tired, but I shrugged and said, "Oh," in a noncommittal voice. In case he had anything in mind.

But then I spoiled the mood by saying, "You know those fruit-stuffed game hens I make? Do you think they'd be good enough to serve to my parents when they come in December?"

He'd been giving me a little back rub. He took his hands away and said, "Prob'ly not," and walked out. Throwing over his shoulder, "But then, what could be?"

I finished what I had to do and followed him, with Lettice shuffling down the hall in front of me. Henry was already in bed with his reading light out, eyes closed, hands folded over his stomach. *Oh, no, you don't,* I thought. I settled Lettice in her dog bed, then sat down on Henry's side of the mattress so he had to look at me. "Don't you want them to come? It's only for two nights."

"Sure I want 'em to come. They're your parents."

"Really?"

"Sure. But it's not two nights, honey, it's four."

"No, two."

"Two on the way down, two on the way back. Four."

"No, *one* on the way down, one back." My parents were planning to stay at our house on either side of their annual trip to Florida.

"Oh."

He looked so relieved, I laughed. I twisted the ends of his mustache between my fingers, trying to make them curl up. He smiled and closed his eyes again. My husband looks like an aging hippie. You might not think I'd like that look, but on him I do. He wears his hair in a neat, tidy ponytail during the day, but at night he lets it down and it falls across the pillow like a shiny, dark red flag, thick and gorgeous. I can't keep my hands out of it.

"Anyway, it won't be so bad," I told him. "They like you, they really do."

"Sure they do."

"They *do*."

"Lee, give up. You married a blue-collar gentile. A *redneck* blue-collar gentile. As far as your parents are concerned, you couldn't have done worse if you'd married an Arab."

"Oh, boy, *that* really shows what you know." I got up and went over to my own side, flouncing down in bed, yanking the sheet out from under his hip to cover myself. "You married a heterosexual, but your mother doesn't hate *me*."

Good one. Score a point for Lee.

Henry started laughing. I didn't see anything funny, so I just lay there. When he saw I wasn't amused, he turned away, clasping his hands across his forehead and staring up at the ceiling. Brooding.

I hate to say it, but my family intimidates Henry. They honestly like him, but he can't see it. He can't get over it that my father is a physicist, my mother's an economist, one brother is a psychologist, and the other is a cardiologist. And he's a fatherless plumber from the South, in business with his mother. It's true I have more money than Henry has, but it's not because I earned it. My field is early childhood development, a woman's profession, which means no status and no money. I happen to be well off because my mother tells me what stocks to buy, and she's rarely wrong. I'm sorry to say that this is another sore point with Henry. He doesn't blame me, he blames himself, and then he gets quiet and moody. Our troubles conceiving a child aren't helping anything either, believe me.

I touched his ankle with the side of my foot, then held still, pretending it was an accident. Every night he puts on clean shorts and a fresh T-shirt before bed. I love the fragrance of the fabric softener and that fresh, linty, dryer smell. It always puts me in the mood.

But sex between us has gotten so complicated. It's almost not even connected to love anymore, it's all about temperature charts and fertility windows. Getting up early to pee in a cup, and botching a test that only has three steps. Ask me anything about urinary LH—luteinizing hormone. I have three ovulation prediction kits in the bathroom. We thanked God when we found out Henry had a varicocele—a varicose vein in his scrotum; it raises testicular temperature, and it's the most common cause of male infertility. So he had microsurgery to repair it and we started over. Nothing. Now we're back to basal thermometers and fertility periods and little pink sticks that turn blue. You have to make love when they turn blue whether you want to or not.

I moved my foot a little, stroking, fluffing the hair on his calf. This was a good time for me, hormonally speaking. But he knew that—I'd told him so this morning. If I made a suggestion now, he'd think it was because of the timing. And the truth is, it would be. Partly.

Oh, God, what's going to happen? Sometimes Henry can't perform. Not often—only twice. It's because of the stress, obviously, we both know that. The second time, he said, "I've never been impotent in my life!" and I said, "Well, I'm impotent, too, it just doesn't show!" That helped us a little. It hasn't happened since then.

Oh, I want a child so badly. I'm stuck, my life is stalled, I can't get on with it until I solve this problem. I know it's not fair to anybody, especially Henry, but I don't know what to do. I don't know how to get out of this cycle of trying and failing, trying and failing.

I sighed and turned out the light. We always kiss, the last thing before going to sleep. Once in a while it leads to something, but usually it's just a sweet, good-night peck. We groped for each other in the dark, finally found each other's lips.

"Night."

"Night."

I started to roll back to my side, but Henry kept my hand and pulled me over, halfway onto his chest. He has a very deep chest. It's not comfortable to sleep on—I've tried, it's like a too-high pillow. I said, "Honey—"

But he reached down and grabbed me around the hips, hauling the rest of me on top of him. "Hey, I was thinking."

Well, this was better. I stretched out, getting comfortable. "Thinking what?"

He slipped his big hands inside my pajama bottoms. "Thinking you might like to ravish me."

I yawned. "I might, but I'm pretty tired."

He tried to see my face in the dark. I'm not what you would call a big kidder—he didn't know if I was teasing or not. "Really?"

"No, not really." I put my arms around his neck.

So we made love. And it was good, it's always good, but at the critical moment I didn't climax. I don't think Henry knew. I wanted to, but my mind was distracted. All I could think of was, *This time it's going to work. This time. This time for sure.*

9

Isabel

Kirby kissed me last night. I couldn't have been more surprised if he'd drawn a gun and shot me. I thought he was gay.

I've assumed it for months, and now I see the assumption was based on very little, hardly anything at all. I'd never known him to have a date, and he didn't talk about women he used to date—that was one thing. He's a part-time actor—that was another. (I'm deeply embarrassed. Honestly, I deplore stereotypes.) There's something rather monklike about him, a certain contemplative quality. He's a quiet, very kind, extraordinarily gentle man, who would rather listen to me than talk about himself.

On second thought, what else could I think?

We were walking home from a play at the Church Basement Theater on Seventeenth Street, an experimental production by a local playwright in which Kirby had played a mute turnpike tollbooth operator. I hadn't understood a word of it, and he was trying, with much diffidence and tact, to explain it to me. It had just begun to snow, the first fall of the season, and we'd stopped to watch the thick, wet flakes swirl in the halo of a streetlamp. We had never touched before, never so much as held hands. Still, it felt quite natural to turn my head and rest it, just lightly, on his shoulder and say, "Isn't it lovely?" We might have been actors in a movie—because he looked into my eyes and echoed, "Lovely." And he touched my face with his gloved fingertips.

He kissed my cheek. All I could do was stare at him, nonplussed and suddenly shy, fumbling in my mind for an explanation for this confusing turn of events. I thought, *But you're gay!* And then he kissed my mouth, and I knew he wasn't. It was like discovering that someone you thought you knew has been in drag all along. Exactly like that—like finding out your woman friend is really a man.

He drew back to smile at me, but I couldn't smile back, couldn't even speak. I was utterly dumbfounded. Gradually my silence began to embarrass him. "I'm sorry," he said. "Isabel, I'm very sorry."

"It's all right," I said automatically. Meaninglessly. We started to walk again. He went back to explaining the play, but of course now it was terribly awkward. And I couldn't do anything to smooth the situation over—I was too busy trying to rearrange everything I had ever thought about him.

We live in the same building, in the noisy heart of Adams-Morgan. His third-floor apartment is directly over mine. He's a quiet neighbor, and yet the walls and floors are so thin, I can still hear him with rather unsettling clarity; I can tell what room he's in, for example, and more often than not, what he's doing. I daresay he can hear me almost as well—the first time we spoke, he called on the telephone to ask if I would please turn my stereo *up* so that he could hear the "Appassionata" without straining. His deep, cultured voice intrigued me, even though I thought at first he was being sarcastic. Another false assumption.

When we met in person, his looks neither confirmed nor contradicted the mistaken impression which was to grow, slowly but surely, the longer I knew him, that he was a homosexual. He's tall, thin as a stalk, almost completely bald. His eyes would be piercing, because of the intense way he has of staring at people, if they weren't such a benign shade of soft brown. His nose is like a blade, sharp and pointed on the end, but his lips are soft. Surprisingly soft. As I have discovered. He looks malnourished, but he's really quite strong—I know this from all the furniture-moving and household repairs he's done for me over the course of our friendship. What drew us together, a passion for music, is still our strongest bond. We love to go to concerts together, and now we marvel that we never met before or at least noticed each other, for we invariably occupy the cheapest seats at the Kennedy Center, the DAR, the Lisner, the Baird Auditorium.

Last night, after our awkward walk home in the snow, Kirby came to my door, as he always does, to see me in and say good night. But of course it was different this time.

"Would you like to come in?" I asked.

"No, I'll go up. Thanks. It's late."

I almost let him go, but then I couldn't. Something needed to be said. To pretend nothing had happened would be insulting to him, cowardly of me. On the other hand, what if I were making too much of it? What if his kiss had been an impulse, a gesture of friendship, no more? No, it *was* more than that for him, I was sure of it.

"My life is changing, Kirby, *I'm* changing, so quickly these days, I can hardly keep up with myself. I'm completely self-absorbed just now. It's simply the wrong time for me to form a—a romantic attachment. I'm too selfish, too caught up in myself to do justice to anyone else. I love our friendship, I don't want it to change. I'm so fond of you. Please understand."

I said more, I can't remember what, and through it all he listened intently, his body inclined toward me, his head cocked in polite attention. He really is the most wonderful listener.

Finally I stopped. I felt sheepish and dissatisfied, and very much as if I were missing something.

He said in a low, controlled voice, "Isabel, the last thing I wanted to do was upset you. I didn't know it would take you so much by surprise. The truth is, I've wanted to kiss you for a long time."

I may have blushed. I said, "I had no idea."

He frowned, as if that amazed him. Whatever may happen between us, I can never, ever tell him what I thought. Already it's almost inconceivable to me that I believed, as recently as yesterday, that this man was gay.

He put one hand in his coat pocket and looked down at his feet. "You could think about it some more. Let the shock wear off. Then . . ." He made a casual, hopeful gesture, stealing a glance at me through his eyelashes.

"I can truthfully say that tonight I'll think of little else."

"Well, that'll make two of us."

A good exit line. He made a little bow, murmured good night, and walked away. Nice timing, too. Must be the theatrical background. He's the reverse of Gary in that way—Gary had awful timing. But then, he's the reverse of Gary in almost every way.

I kept my word and thought about him at length. It's possible the time has come for me to find someone. I divorced Gary four years ago, and there's been no one at all since Richard Smith. "The aptly named Dick," as Emma always calls him. I try never to think of him; he comes with too many bad memories. A year and a half after the divorce, three months after Richard and I began a relationship—he was an instructor in my graduate school program—I found the lump in my breast. Or rather, Richard found it, fooling around at the movies. "What's this?" he whispered, breaking in on a touching scene in *Sense and Sensibility*.

I knew exactly what it was. In fact, I knew everything in an instant, all that would happen, up to and including my death. Fortunately, I was half wrong. But half was enough for Dick. He stayed around for the surgery, but after that he "couldn't see us going anywhere." I wasn't angry—I left all that to Emma. What would I do without her? My surrogate man hater and grudge holder.

But Richard was over two years ago, and since then there's been no one. I haven't felt the lack; I'm delighted by the pleasures of my solitary life. I love my cramped apartment. I painted it peach, white, and sea green, and I ripped up the rusty carpets and left the scarred wood floors bare. There was too much furniture in my Chevy Chase house, Gary is welcome to all of it. I have my bookshelves, my rocking chair. An old sofa, an assortment of rickety floor lamps, and for my friends, oversize pillows to sit on when they come to see me. I have enough dishes and silver to serve dinner to eight people, the perfect number. I have raucous neighbors, quiet neighbors, eccentric neighbors. My landlady, Mrs. Skazafava, barely speaks English. Lee says I'm living like a hippie, and I suppose I am—I missed that era when I was young. Ramakrishna says our lives move through cycles in no prescribed order. I'm traversing a circle that my contemporaries experienced thirty years ago. No matter; it's only the journey that counts.

I was daydreaming at my desk in the afternoon, petting Grace and staring out the window instead of studying for my families-at-risk exam when, overhead, I heard the door to Kirby's apartment open and close. I hear it all the time and unconsciously, unwillingly, keep tabs on him that way. Soon I heard footsteps in the hall, a knock at my door.

Grace stopped barking the second I opened it and she saw Kirby. He had on his uniform: corduroy trousers and a baggy sweater. And something in his hand. "Look what I bought," he said, and held out a still-wrapped CD. It was Beethoven, the Triple Concerto. "Would you like to hear it?"

So I made a pot of tea, and we sat and listened to the concerto, and it was almost like old times. Except that it wasn't. When the music ended, I decided against small talk and asked him a straight question. No pun intended.

"Have you ever been married?"

"Yes."

"Really." I masked my surprise by fiddling with the tea strainer. "You've never mentioned it."

"I was married for nineteen years. I had a son and a daughter." He stirred sugar into his cup and sipped. "They were killed eleven years ago. All three, in an accident on the Beltway. Julie was twelve, Tyler was eight."

"I'm so sorry." Why do those words always sound feeble, heartbreakingly inadequate? You wish and you search for better ones, but there aren't any. But Kirby said, "Thank you," as if he meant it, and that sad little ritual was over.

"Eleven years," he said after a pause. "It's a long time to be alone. It suited me at first. Not anymore." And he looked at me with frank meaning over the rim of his cup.

I stood up and went to the stereo, took his CD out of the player, put it back in the box. Leaned over and ran a finger across the titles in my music holder, looking for something suitable to accompany what I was going to say to him next. I couldn't find anything.

"Kirby . . ." I leaned back against the windowsill. "You know about my breast cancer." He did—I'd told him months ago. It's not something I keep secret, but then again, I don't go around blurting it out to people, either. But I'd told Kirby. Just the bare fact of it, no details. "I thought that . . . maybe you thought I only had the tumor removed, a lumpectomy. Or that I had had reconstruction. But, no. I just have—nothing. Here." I gestured. "A prosthesis in my bra."

Except for medical professionals, no one has ever seen my naked; asymmetric chest. Of late I had been coming, quite easily, to terms with the idea that no one ever would. And so I had stopped imagining myself having this unbelievably awkward conversation with a prospective lover.

Kirby unwound his long legs and levered himself up from the floor, coming to stand in front of me. I folded my arms across my chest. His narrow face looked stern and ever so slightly impatient. "That doesn't matter to me in the slightest. I don't give a damn. I couldn't care less."

"Well," I said. I believed him.

"Isabel, I'm falling in love with you."

I moved away from him, shocked. That I *didn't* believe. I wasn't interested in falling in love with anyone. I've done that. Now I'm too old, too selfish, I want to concentrate on me, not someone who's *falling in love* with me.

"Oh, Kirby. I wish you hadn't said that."

He turned, and it was a huge relief to see that he didn't look miserable or angry or embarrassed. He looked thoughtful. He smiled. "Then I wish I hadn't said it, too." He took something from his pocket and came toward me, holding it out. A ring—I started back in horror. "I brought down some washers to try," he said mildly.

"You . . . What?"

"The faucet in the kitchen. It's still leaking, isn't it?"

I nodded stupidly.

"I'll see if I can fix it." He went out of the room, into the kitchen, and started puttering.

I sank down on the floor, right where I was. Grace hauled herself up from her place by the radiator, padded over, flopped down beside me. Grace loves Kirby, I mused, stroking her soft gray muzzle. Other than that, there wasn't a coherent thought in my head.

On Tuesday, I would be having my last six-month checkup. After that, assuming all was well, I'd only have to see my surgeon/oncologist once a year. Another breast cancer milestone. Petting Grace, staring into space, it came to me that I'd made a decision. If I was all right, no spread, no lumps or bumps, no fishy X rays—and I was sure there wouldn't be—then I would think, *think* about the possibility of a relationship with Kirby. Just consider it. No pressure, no timetables, no agendas. I'd just give it some thought.

Meanwhile, it was nice to sit here with Grace and listen to the rattles and thumps and clanks of a man doing a chore for me in my kitchen. Mysterious, masculine sounds. Comforting. They made me feel like a woman. Now, that's something I haven't felt in a long time.

10

Rudy

Curtis thinks I shouldn't get a real job because we don't need the money. He says my volunteer work (excluding the Call for Help Hotline) helps others and satisfies me, and any sort of paying, full-time career would make me crazy, I couldn't handle the stress.

I don't know. I'm not sure. I guess he's right.

But I look at Lee, a Ph.D., director of a federal child care center. She always knew what she wanted, and for her it's been a matter of taking step after logical step to get it. I can't even *imagine* being that responsible or that clear-sighted. And Isabel, going back to school at fifty, methodically working on a degree that will get her exactly where she wants to go. How do they *know* what they want? Even Emma knows, although she's careful not to let anybody in on her secret.

Like me, she's afraid. Her fear comes from pride, though, and not wanting to make a fool of herself. Mine comes from understanding my own incompetence.

I tried to explain that to her, driving home from the movies last night, but I couldn't. Curtis is the only one who really understands. Emma and I almost had a fight. I stopped the car in front of her house, wishing we'd gone for drinks instead of ice cream after the movie, because then I'd have been able to argue better.

She glared at me with one hand on the door handle, the other crushing out her cigarette in the ashtray. She wears a black wool beret when the weather's bad; she pulls it low over her forehead, almost past her eyebrows, and her crazy red hair shoots out like fire all around. "Rudy, you're an *artist.* You are incredibly talented, you could be anything you want, but it's like you're frozen or something. You're stuck, and for the life of me I can't figure out what's holding you back."

Cowardice. Inadequacy. Inertia. I felt defensive, but I didn't want to fight, and throwing Emma's own fears back in her face would've hurt her feelings.

"I *am* doing things. I might enter some prints in a photo contest at the Corcoran. Oh, and they want me to teach a pottery class at the Free School next year."

"A pottery class? But you don't even throw pots anymore."

Another sore subject. Emma blamed Curtis when I sold my potting wheel. I kept it in the basement, and it's true his exercise equipment started crowding everything else out, but that's not really why I gave up potting. It took up a lot of time, and Curtis said, and I eventually agreed, that if I wasn't going to do it full-time, actually make a career for myself in ceramics, why do it at all?

"I don't do it actively," I told Emma, "but I could still teach it to beginners. So anyway—I am working on some things, I just don't always tell you."

"Yeah, okay. I know you are." She was backtracking; she knew she'd hurt my feelings by being so blunt. "I'm sorry if I came on like your mother. Well, not *your* mother. Some normal mother."

"Yeah, not my mother." I laughed, to make her laugh, and then we were okay again. But when she asked me to come in, I said I'd better not. In spite of that last-second mollifying, Emma was in a feisty mood, and I was afraid she'd start in again if I stayed.

"Night," she said, and gave me a light slap on the shoulder—she's not much of a hugger. I waited while she ran up to her front porch in the rain. Once inside, she flicked the porch light on and off—our signal that we're safe, no rapists hiding in the shrubbery—and I tooted the horn and pulled away.

The rain turned to sleet as I drove home along Rock Creek, and then I was glad instead of sorry we hadn't ended the evening with a few drinks. And when I got home and saw all the downstairs lights on in my house, I was more than glad.

Thank God I'm sober, I prayed as I circled the block, looking for an empty space. Curtis was back from Atlanta a day early, and I should've been there. He hates to come home to an empty house.

I thought of Eric's advice about pointless guilt—I'm supposed to ask myself exactly what I've done wrong, and the answer, he says, will almost always be nothing. Well, maybe, but I never *feel* innocent. There's always this sense, especially with Curtis, that I could do, should do, more, better, something else.

"Curtis?"

He'd left the lights on, but he wasn't downstairs. I went up, taking my coat off as I went. He wasn't in the bedroom, wasn't in the bathroom. "Curtis?"

I heard a noise from his darkened study. I went in, but he didn't turn around; he stayed slumped in his chair at his desk, staring at his black computer screen. "Curtis?"

He still had on his suit. I touched his shoulder. When he didn't move, I slid my hand to the back of his neck, feeling the tight tendons there bunch and flex. "What are you doing, baby? All by yourself in the dark."

His hair grows to a perfect little V at the back. He hates it; he instructs his expensive Capitol Hill hairstylist to blunt it every two weeks, but it never quite goes away. I used to like to play with it, but he doesn't let me anymore. It annoys him.

"Where've you been?" he asked in his slow, meticulous southern drawl.

"I thought you weren't coming home till tomorrow."

He waited for the real answer.

"I just went to the movies."

"Alone?"

"No, with Emma. She wanted to see this French film, a love story, I've already forgotten the name. She liked it, but I thought it was silly." That wasn't quite the truth. "It had subtitles you could barely see," I added. To make it clearer that I hadn't had a very good time.

I slipped my fingers under the collar of his jacket and started a soft, slow massage. I could smell his cologne, still fresh after his long day, and the musk-scented mousse he puts on his neat, glossy hair. His head bowed slowly, a little at a time, and I felt him begin to relax. "How was Atlanta?" I asked.

A mistake. I shouldn't have asked him that, not yet. All his muscles tensed. "A disaster."

Why did I feel responsible? Whatever happened in Atlanta, it didn't have anything to do with me, but still I heard his words as an accusation.

I waited, but when he didn't explain, I said, "What happened?"

"Morris."

"Oh, no." I made a scornful, sympathetic sound, squeezing his shoulders. Frank Morris is Curtis's enemy. He has much less seniority, but he wants Curtis's job, and he always tries to make him look bad in front of the congressman. "What did he do?"

No answer.

"Hm? What did Morris do?"

"What do you care?"

I could feel that heavy, smothering fog of guilt seep inside, bog me down. From where? Why? "You know I care." But what had I done? Something, I knew it was something. Curtis knew what it was, but I didn't dare ask him.

A long minute passed, and I realized he wasn't going to tell me. That was his worst punishment—not letting me in. But why couldn't he see that it punished him, too?

I put my arms around him, leaning over to rest my cheek against his ear. "Oh, baby," I whispered. If I could just warm him, soften him. "Curtis, it's—"

He stood up. My hands fell away as I stepped back. Without a glance, he passed beside me and walked out of the room.

We have a ritual. This was just part of it, this would pass. He wasn't really shutting me out. No one understands that Curtis needs me as much as I need him. More sometimes. But he's the strong one. I would be lost without him. Eric says no, but I would.

Later, I brought him a glass of cognac in bed. "I don't want this," he said, and he wouldn't take it.

I sipped it, watching him. I'd put on the nightgown he likes best, black and cut low, soft crushed velvet. "Tired?"

He shrugged. He almost smiled at me.

"You have such long days." I set the glass down. He let me take the *Forbes* out of his hand and put it on the night table. A lock of his hair fell across his forehead; he looked so boyish and young, and I thought of the early days, in Durham, when we first moved in together. The happiest, safest time of my life. He really loved me then.

"Morris is such an idiot," I said. "I've never been able to stand him." Curtis grunted. "And he's going bald awfully fast." He sniffed his breath out, a kind of a laugh, and reached for my hand. His smile meant the beginning of forgiveness.

"I'm getting out of there," he said, pulling on the black ribbon bow at the top of my nightgown. "I'm going with Teeter and Jack."

"You're what? You are?" He kept yanking at the ties; I had to cover his hands to make him stop. "You mean you're quitting?"

"I decided tonight."

"But—"

"Assholes, Rudy, I can't deal with it anymore. And I don't have to."

"No—no, you *should* leave, you haven't been happy in ages." What a surprise! I could hardly think. But he *hadn't* been happy in his work; there was too much back stabbing in Congressman Wingert's office, he said, too much hypocrisy. Teeter Reese and

Jack Birmingham were old friends from law school. They'd started a lobbying firm, and they were making tons of money, according to Curtis. Maybe that would be perfect. He couldn't bear authority. But if he could be a partner, his own boss instead of somebody's underling, he might thrive. And the springboard to political office—Curtis's true ambition—was almost as direct, I imagined. It was just a different route.

He was peeling my nightgown over my shoulders, starting to caress me. "Wingert can fuck himself," he said, his eyes shining, white teeth flashing. "He can fuck Morris, too. They can fuck each other." His vulgarity shocked me—he rarely swears. He pulled me down. I let him touch me too roughly, but he needed to, because of the strange mood he was in. But he finally stopped when he realized I wasn't with him, wasn't ready. He gentled his hands, grew tender.

Tenderness—it breaks me down, and he knows me so well. He knows I'll be anything he wants if he's tender with me. He stroked the tears off my face with his fingers, murmuring, "Good, Rudy, that's right," and spreading my legs with his knees. I wanted him to fill me, take up all the empty space inside with himself. Complete me. He never, never lets go of himself, never loses control, but he can make me so hot. I was panting for him, calling him baby, calling out, "God, God," wanting it so much. He buried his face in my hair. Then he stopped.

"Oh, Christ."

I went still, too, appalled by the disgust in his tone. "What's wrong?"

His lips curled, still wet from kissing me. "What's wrong? I'll tell you. You smell like a God damn ashtray." I reached for him. He shrugged off my hand and rolled away.

"I'm sorry." My skin prickled everywhere, I was freezing. "I'm sorry. I thought I had quit, but Emma and I, we just—she had some and I started again, I smoked in the car. I'm sorry—" I made myself stop. It wasn't the smoking, anyway.

"I *hate* when you do this," I whispered to his back. I touched his hip with one finger, but he jerked at the covers angrily, and I snatched my hand away. "Curtis, *please*."

He wouldn't answer, not if I went on my knees and begged him. It's easy for me to hate myself, harder to hate him. But sometimes he even manages that.

I got up and took two Phrenilin for my head, a couple of Nembutals for oblivion. Deep, black sleep is the only analgesic for this particular kind of pain. Too bad it's impossible to come by naturally. I need a guarantee.

The next morning, my mother called.

I hadn't spoken to her in about three months. I suppose that sounds like a long time, but it's not unusual for us. She sounded awful. I shut my eyes and thought, *Shit, shit, she's drinking again.*

"Rudelle? Oh, it's good to hear your voice. How are you, darling?"

"I'm fine, Mother. Is something wrong?"

"August is in the hospital."

"Oh, no. What's wrong with him? Mom?" A sharp noise hurt my ear—I had to pull the telephone away. "Are you there?"

"I dropped it." She started to cry.

I took the phone into the hall outside the bedroom. I lay down on the floor, curled onto my side on the crisp mauve carpet.

"Please don't cry, Mom, don't cry. What's wrong with August?" My stepfather turned eighty in September. He's sixteen years older than my mother.

"His heart. Late last night. I called Allen, but he won't come. Oh, Rudelle, if only you would."

"Mother—"

"I'm not drinking. I haven't been."

Maybe. Maybe not. "Did he have a heart attack?"

"An episode, they called it. I don't know what else they said, I can't listen."

"But—then he's going to be okay?"

"They're making him come home today."

"They're—" I opened my eyes. "Okay, then, he's all right. It was just a warning. It can't be serious, Mom, or they wouldn't let him leave." I lay still, thinking, *She called Allen first*, while she blew her nose. My brother is an alcoholic with two ex-wives, a drug habit, and no job, and my mother called him first for help. I could feel my muscles getting weak, lax, my face going slack. The start of my own "episode."

"Can you come? It's been so long, Rudelle."

"I don't think I can right now."

"You could come for Christmas. It's beautiful here. Remember? How beautiful at the holidays? You and Curtis. It's been so long."

"We can't. Curtis has to work." That probably wasn't a lie. "Mother, I'll have to call you back."

"Rudelle—"

"I've got another call. Have to go, I'll call you." I clicked off and cut the connection.

She used to be beautiful. I wonder if she still is. I haven't seen her in almost five years, not since my wedding. To my friends I call her Felicia, not "Mother" or "my mom," so that's what they call her to me. "How are Felicia and the playboy?" Emma will say. The eighty-year-old playboy. August is Swiss; Mother met him in Geneva the year before my father killed himself. They were lovers, of course. They must have been.

Every once in a while my mother decides she wants to see me. She'll call up and go on about how long it's been, how wonderful it would be, how much she misses me. I can't bring myself to follow through and arrange a visit. Eric thinks I should. He thinks I've got issues with my mother I need to resolve. But I don't do anything. Can't.

I got a mental picture of how I probably looked, curled up in a ball on the hall floor. Eric taught me to do that—see myself, visualize the way I look when I think I'm getting sick. It works sometimes. Shocks me into doing something.

I got up and started toward the bathroom. I made it through the doorway, but as soon as I flicked on the light, I couldn't go any farther. I froze with my foot in midair, inches from the white tile floor. *Stop it,* I thought in a panic, but I couldn't go in. I could make my hand work—I turned out the bathroom light. And then I could go backward, back out into the hall. I kept going and went into the bedroom and sat on the edge of the bed.

I still had the phone in my hand. I hit memory and the number two. The receptionist in Wingert's office said Curtis was in a meeting. Was there a message? "No, thanks." I couldn't recognize my voice. I disconnected quickly and dialed again.

Emma's voice on her answering machine steadied me. I could see her so clearly, trying not to laugh, eyes dancing while she made her witty, tongue-in-cheek recording. When I spoke into the machine, I almost sounded normal.

"Hi, it's me. I was hoping you'd be home. Guess you're at work. It's nothing . . . nothing important." I had to whisper, "Bye," because all of a sudden I was crying.

Rudy, Rudy. Rudelle. How I hate that name. It's German for "famous one." I was born in Germany. My parents liked Europe better than America. I called myself Rudi when I was a child. I was Rudi O'Neill until my mother married August. I had to take his name, Lacretelle. Rudelle Lacretelle. In college I took my mother's name, Surratt, and changed Rudi to Rudy. Rudy Surratt. I liked it. I felt comfortable. But when I married Curtis, he asked me to take his name, so now I'm Rudy Lloyd. Emma loves to say my name. She calls me "Roodie," high and soft like a song, for no reason at all—if we're driving somewhere, for instance. She just starts singing my name.

I got off the bed and dialed again, memory-one. Eric's machine answered, but he picked up in the middle of the message and said hello.

"Can you see me today?"

"Rudy? Has something happened?"

"No, not really. Eric, can I see you? Something—yes—happened, but I don't know what."

"Is four o'clock okay?"

"Thank you. Thanks. Thanks."

"The first two years after my father died were the worst. We were living in Austria for some reason, a ski resort in the mountains. Have I told you this? My brother was living with us because he'd flunked out of his prep school in Rhode Island. Claire and I went to a convent school in the village. August stayed with us most of the time, but he hadn't married my mother yet. We lived in a hotel. I've told you this, haven't I?"

"It doesn't matter."

"You know this part. My mother. That day I found her."

"Tell me again."

"I am, I have—I want to. It was the summer when I was twelve and Claire was fourteen. Allen, my brother, he'd go away every day, we didn't know where. Walking, he said. My mother couldn't make him stay home. But she couldn't do anything. Well, no—she could drink and sleep, and when she took the right pills she could be loving and so very, very sweet. I loved her so much, Eric. I have never felt so much pain. For anyone. Not since that summer. I think . . . I've been sort of numb since then."

I stopped talking and closed my eyes. Eric stayed still and quiet, waiting for me. Behind my eyelids, the scene came on like an old movie, black and white except for the blood.

"My sister and I found her together. Dead, we thought. Naked on the white tiles, the bathtub full of bloody water. *Get help, get a doctor*—I kept screaming at Claire. But I should've known from her face, half smiling, blank, as if she were falling asleep. She just walked out. Some people found her and brought her back the next day. Riding her bike, they said."

"Rudy," Eric said.

"I'm all right. I didn't tell you this before, did I? That I stayed with my mother, just me, for hours? She was almost as white as the tiles. And cold, she felt like rubber. I thought if I let her go, she'd die. A bruise on her face from where she fell, but—the blood, like red coins on the floor—the blood—it was menstrual blood. Because she'd used pills, not a razor. Pills and vodka. Didn't she know? Oh, how could she not know who would find her! Her little girls, her babies. Oh, Mother. I held her and held her, thinking we'd changed places, mother and child, my child was dying and I couldn't stop it, could not keep her."

I was choking, blood pounding in my head—Eric's hands took my hands and squeezed tight, tight, and I stopped sobbing. "I'm all right. I am. I'm fine."

When I was calm, I told him about my mother's phone call this morning. "So—that's why all this came back. It's funny. Years pass and you think it's gone, but it isn't. Does it ever go away?"

"I don't think so."

"No. I knew it," I said.

"It doesn't have to be so painful, though."

"What makes it stop hurting? Not time. It's been thirty years. Thirty years. Eric?"

"Yes?"

I smiled at him so he would think I was teasing. "Am I ever going to get well?"

I didn't expect him to answer, that's the kind of question he usually ignores. But I had frightened him today. His face, when he'd held my hands, hadn't been calm, for once. "I think you are," he said, nodding solemnly. "I wouldn't see you if I didn't believe that."

"You wouldn't see me?" I rubbed my chilled arms.

"I wouldn't keep seeing you. If I didn't think you'll get better."

But I'm worse now than when we started. Couples therapy,

that's what he wants to try next. I've told him that's impossible, but it makes no impression on him, he doesn't understand. Curtis won't come here. If I were dying and it would save my life, Curtis wouldn't come here.

"I'd better go," I said, although we still had ten minutes. "Curtis thought he might come home early tonight, and he likes me to be there."

Eric said nothing. He pressed his lips together and let me go.

11

Emma

"This isn't worth it for women."

I actually said that, out loud and with force. Sure, I had cause: deveining shrimp brings out the worst in anybody, and twenty-five minutes of it hunched over the sink with nothing but *All Things Considered* for company could drive Patricia Ireland, or whoever it is these days, around the p.c. bend. Nevertheless. I'm supposed to be a feminist. It's part of my identity, my persona, it goes with Irish, agnostic, lapsed Democrat. Old maid. I'm supposed to be *above* thinking that excessive shrimp-cleaning, apple-peeling, and snow pea string-pulling are only worth it if men are coming for dinner.

Ach, but I do love my gerruls. I was thinking in a Scottish brogue, because I'd just heard this guy interviewed on NPR, Lonnie McSomething. He wrote a profane Glaswegian coming-of-age novel, big deal, and now they're treating him like the Second Coming. No jealousy here, though, no siree. I flicked off the radio with the side of my wrist and started on another pile of shrimp.

Anyway, I go to at least as much trouble when it's my turn for the women's group as I do for dinner parties with couples. And a hell of a lot more trouble than I go to for individual guys, who are lucky to get a cup of coffee in the morning before I push them out the door. Politely—I'm always polite. And I enjoy cooking for my gerruls. Three of us are in an unspoken competition for second best chef (Isabel has a lock on first), and tonight's curried shrimp with snow peas and apples is a tough contender. Plus I have made a cake. Not from scratch—what am I, June Cleaver?—but I did add red food coloring to the white frosting and write in big letters, over an extremely artistic rendering of an hourglass, "Two Years & Counting—You Go Girl!" That's how long it's been, two years this month, since Isabel found the lump in her breast. They say you can't really start to relax until five years have passed, but this is still an anniversary, and by God, we're celebrating.

Seven-fifteen. Rudy was late. I told her to come at seven so we could talk. Should've known; should've said six-thirty.

I finished the shrimp and squeezed dishwashing soap on my palms, wondering how many other people can't clean the smell of fish from their hands anymore without thinking of Susan Sarandon. Hey—would that make a good piece for something? American film iconography, how it intrudes on our everyday lives. Some pseudosmart mag might go for it if I threw in enough sarcasm. My specialty. But I'd rather write it straight. Sweet. There have to be a hundred examples—indelible psychic connections between, say, whistling and Lauren Bacall. Tricycles and extraterrestrials. Question: Why do you feel sexy when you see an Amish guy in a field? Answer: Harrison Ford, *Witness*. Okay, trite example, but still, there have to be hundreds.

"Stinks," I decided. Too obvious, nothing behind it; once you said it, you'd said it. Which is the trouble with about 90 percent of my story ideas. Still, I scribbled "Sarandon/lemons/cult. assn." on the scratch pad stuck to the refrigerator. Because you never know.

The doorbell rang. I flicked on the porch light to see Rudy through the beveled sidelight, looking tall and glamorous in her long black cloak—the same cloak she wrapped Grace in eight years ago on MacArthur Boulevard. The cloak I still want. Her face looked morose, distracted, before she saw me through the glass; then it brightened in a wide, sparkling, squinty-eyed smile. I pulled open the door, and Rudy swept in on a blast of cold air, cashmere, perfume, and—gasoline?

"I ran out of gas. Can you believe it? In the middle of Sixteenth

Street, and nobody stopped, nobody helped me, I had to schlepp all the way to Euclid and back for one lousy gallon."

"Wow, that's terrible." But what an excellent excuse, and so unexpected. Rudy's chronically late and never thinks a thing of it, never even apologizes. I was thrown off my stride. "I never get that," I said peevishly, "how anybody can run out of gas. Don't you look at the gauge when you start your car?"

She just laughed. "Hey, you look great! You got your hair cut."

I'm not too good at hugging, or so the group is always telling me. I braced for Rudy's strong, one-armed embrace, wondering what we were crushing between us in the grocery bag she had in her other arm. "Yeah," I said, "I had to do something with it. It's not too short, is it? I told him medium. Look at my new coat rack—a Christmas present from me. So, come on in the kitchen, let's get a drink."

I found glasses, opened wine, poured peanuts in a bowl, while Rudy prowled around, looking for new things since she'd been here last. "Oh, you hung it," she exclaimed, pointing to the "kitchen collage" she had made me for Christmas. "That's a good place for it, over the door."

"I absolutely love it." It's truly a masterpiece: an assemblage of 1950s-style aluminum kitchen implements that somehow suggest a face. It's got two measuring spoons for eyes, a cheese grater for the nose and eyebrows, a bent orange jar cap for lips—oh hell, I can't describe it, you'd have to see it to appreciate it. But trust me, you can't look at this piece without laughing. Rudy could make a living doing this stuff.

"I can't get over how much I love home ownership," I told her, handing over a glass of merlot, her favorite. "It fills me with a lot of revolting middle-class satisfaction."

I've lived in classier places—Georgetown, Foggy Bottom, Woodley Park—but I didn't *own* those apartments, so they didn't count. My eighty-year-old Mt. Pleasant town house doesn't look like much, especially from the outside, and the neighborhood is what they call transitional, meaning you're smart not to go out at night without your own personal pit bull. But it's all mine.

"To the Sloans," I said.

"The Sloans."

We drank to the previous owners, who rehabbed my house within an inch of its life, then did a white flight when the wife got pregnant and decided they'd rather bring Junior up in the suburbs. "Their paranoia is my gain. I'm even starting to like the bars on the windows."

"Why not?" Rudy said. "White wrought iron is beautiful. It's just a matter of separating form from function."

"And not getting hysterical."

"Hey. You choose to live in our lovely and historic nation's capital— "

"You takes your chances."

We toasted again.

"So," I said, settling down on the bench at the kitchen table, making room for Rudy. "How did it go with Greenburg?" Sometimes you can tell if she's been talking to her shrink because her eyes look puffy and bloodshot. Not tonight, though. "Wasn't this a Greenburg day?"

"Yes." She shook two Winstons out of a pack and offered me one. "It was good. We talked about my father. Which is always pretty intense. Eric says it's all right to think he might not have killed himself."

"Might not have killed himself? Wait—he did, didn't he? That's what you've always said. You mean he didn't?"

"Well, I'm just saying, it's possible he might not have. No one knows. It's a myth in my family that he did it on purpose, but it could just as easily have been that he got drunk and fell out of the boat."

It wasn't only a family myth, it was a women's group myth, too. I heard the story years ago, and now I have an image of it in my mind that's as vivid as a home movie. It happened on Lake Como about thirty years ago, when Rudy was eleven. I can see the blue sky and the white sailboat, the soft yellow Italian light. It's dusk. Rudy's dad, Allen Aubrey O'Neill, has on baggy white trousers and a white sweater. He's barefooted; he smokes Camels; he looks like Joseph Cotton. He tosses back the last of the vodka in his leather-covered hip flask. He reaches for the stanchion, hauls himself up. Seagulls dip and soar, and he listens to their hungry, heartless cries for a second, takes a last sniff of the sweet, sunny breeze. Then he steps out, into the air and the smooth, cool blue of the lake.

That's the end of the movie—no unseemly splashing or gasping, and I never follow him down or try to imagine his panic or his sick second thoughts. Rudy's handsome, aristocratic father has simply taken himself off.

"Well, I guess," I said slowly. "He drank a lot, didn't he?"

"Oh, God."

"Yeah. So . . ." I started to nod. "Why not? You're right, he could just as easily have fallen overboard. In which case, my God, everything changes. Oh, Rudy—" I leaned forward, beginning to get an idea of what that would mean to her. "So he didn't commit suicide. Maybe. This is great, because if he was just a drunk, not—"

"He was still manic-depressive. It doesn't mean he wasn't crazy, Emma."

"No, I know, but still—"

"It's just something to think about, that's all."

"Yeah."

"It's not that big a deal."

"Right." I backed off with a joke. "I bet Greenburg gets more APA journal articles out of your family than he does from the whole rest of his shrink practice."

She smiled, craned her long neck to blow smoke at the ceiling. "Well," she said, and then she laughed self-consciously. "I thought I was ready to hope for this, but it looks like I'm not. Not out loud, anyway. Not in public."

"Well, I'm not public."

Rudy has fine gray eyes, as they used to say in books about English governesses. I watched them soften and mellow, turn tender. "No, you're not." She set her glass down. "Okay. I hope he got shit-faced and fell in the damn lake and drowned, because then I'll only have to worry about my genetic predisposition to alcohol, depression, drug addiction, and paranoid schizophrenia. But not suicide."

Neither of us mentioned her mother, and we laughed the loud, too-long, healing laugh that's part of our therapeutic repertoire and as vital to us, to our relationship, as kind words or sympathy—no, more so. And after that there was nothing left to say, at least not now, on the subject of Rudy's father's death. We'd covered it all.

We poured more wine, lit up again. I was thinking I ought to get up and start chopping onions or something; Lee and Isabel and the new woman, Sharon, would be here any minute. But this was too nice. Sitting in the kitchen with Rudy, smoking and drinking and talking about life—like the beer commercial said, it doesn't get any better than this.

"Well, I had a rotten day," I said cheerfully, and told her about the piece for the *Washingtonian* I was bogged down in, couldn't seem to finish even though it was due Monday. Rudy sympathized and told me about a landscaping course she really wanted to take. It started in the spring, and it was a two-year program, you got a certificate in residential landscape design, and then you could probably apprentice with a landscaping company or a master gardener and be on your way. She was excited about it, but she backed off at the end, saying it was just a thought, she probably wouldn't do it, it cost a lot, it would take too long.

"Oh, but it sounds terrific, like something you'd really love. And you'd be great at it. Landscaping? You love to garden and you love to design. Oh, Rudy, it's perfect for you."

"I don't know, I don't know. Anyway, I don't think I have time.

This would be full-time, very intensive, so I don't know, I just don't think . . ." She crossed her ankles and slid down on her backbone, sleek as a seal. What Rudy *could've* been is a model. "I probably won't do it. We haven't even talked about it."

"We" meaning Curtis. I've gotten used to biting my tongue in situations like this, it's not even that hard anymore. "How is Curtis?" I said in my best neutral voice. But I was kissing our pleasant conversation good-bye.

"He's fine." She kept her eyes on the glowing tip of her cigarette. "Said to give you his love."

Sure he did. Curtis is brimming over with love for me. "Give him mine," I lied back, and got up to chop the onions.

A long time ago I learned that, on the subject of her husband, the price of Rudy's friendship is smiles, lies, and teeth-gritting silence. I hate this deal, I despise the hypocrisy and the unfairness, but I stick to it like a sacred vow. What choice do I have? It's Rudy. But there's nobody else in the world I'd do it for.

I heard her stand up. "So, Em. Tell me. What's new on the Mick Draco front these days?"

I couldn't believe it—my heart actually missed a beat. Good thing my paring knife is dull or I might've sliced off a digit. I had to duck my head so Rudy wouldn't see me flushing. *Christ, it's worse than I thought.* The other thing I hadn't realized was how badly I wanted to talk about him.

But I was cool. "Oh, not that much. We had coffee again on Friday. Thursday or Friday. Friday. In that dive across from his studio again. We just, you know, talked."

"Talked."

"Yeah, about stuff. His kid, my work. His painting."

"His wife."

"Ha. No."

It's been three months since I met him. Three months. Of torture. I'm used to men torturing me, but not like this. We'll call each other up and say something like, "Guess what, I happen to be in your neighborhood right now, want to have coffee?" if it's me calling him, or "I just learned how to do lithographs, want to see them?" if it's him calling me. Since neither of us likes coffee that much and I don't even know for sure what a lithograph is, it's safe to say these are subterfuges. Innocent ones, though. Excruciatingly innocent. I'm dying here.

Rudy leaned in, elbows on the counter, her Acqua di Gió adding class to the odor of the onions. "Well? What's going on? Come on, give me the lowdown."

"*Nothing*. Nothing's changed, we just, you know, we see each other every once in a while and we talk. We're friends. That's it." I put down the knife and met her eyes. "Oh, Rudy. I'm going insane."

She smiled, and her eyes crinkled with sympathy. "Poor Emma."

"I can't stand it. We've never even touched hands. But I'm falling, I'm really—and it's the same for him, I think, although he would never say. And nothing can change, nothing can ever happen."

"Look at you," Rudy said wonderingly. When she put her arm around my waist, I had the stupidest urge to burst into tears. So I shuffled away, muttering, "Oh, I'm okay," laughing to cover it. I was torn between wanting to blurt out everything—even though there honestly is nothing to tell—and wanting to keep it all to myself. But what I wanted most was to get over him and tell Rudy about it in retrospect—"You wouldn't believe how gone I was on that Mick guy—remember him?"

"If it's making you this miserable," she said, "maybe you ought to stop seeing him."

"I'm not miserable. Not all the time." Misery alternates with euphoria. "But I know I have to stop seeing him. And then Lee has a party and invites Mick and the lovely Sally—she's done it twice now—"

"You have to tell Lee who he is."

"I can't, it's too late, I waited too long. So even if I *try* not to see him, I do see him, and I'm just—I'm losing my mind! And he's—"

The doorbell rang.

"Shit," we said in unison.

"But it's okay, I'm fine, I really am. I'll tell you the rest later. Listen," I blurted, backing toward the hall, "don't say anything, his name or anything, you know—" Rudy's expression, *Don't insult me*, made me laugh nervously and blush again. "I know—I'm just crazy. Oh, God, Rudy!"

Chaos rules for the first twenty minutes or so of every women's group meeting while everybody hugs and kisses, pours wine, tries to find a cutting board, a knife, jockeys for a place at the sink, catches up on everybody else's news—all at the same time, and all, except for Lee's, in kitchens the size of really big bathrooms.

"Are you through with that colander?"

"Em, your hair looks darling."

"This cheese is good—is it Saga?"

"Can I take a shower? I just came from ballet class."

"Isabel, make your rice in the microwave, okay? I need this whole stove. And nobody talk to me while I'm doing this shrimp, I need five minutes of peace and quiet."

"Oh, heck, I'm not taking a shower."

"She is so bossy when she cooks."

I love this. Making a nice meal for my best friends, listening to them joke and laugh and tell how they've been, throwing in a zinger of my own now and then—this is the *best* time. Wine, cheese, gossip, and pals. If you could get sex in there somehow, you'd have it all.

The telephone rang. "Can somebody get that?" I was at the Dijon-and-cream-sauce stage, very tricky. Lee picked up the phone and said, "DeWitt residence. Oh, hi, Sharon. No, this is Lee. Oh, no, really? Oh, I'm sorry."

"I *knew* it," Rudy said in a stage whisper.

"I didn't like her that much anyway," I said. Lee made a face at me and took the phone into the dining room. "I didn't. She plucks her eyebrows and then pencils them back on. What is that?"

"This is a record, though. Usually they last longer than two meetings."

Lee came back in, grim-faced. "Another one bites the dust." She slumped down on a stool. "Is it something we're doing?" She looked so dejected, Rudy and I burst out laughing. "No, I mean it." She turned to Isabel. "This is the third in—what?"

"About two years."

"Well, I knew she wouldn't last."

"Me, too," Rudy agreed with me.

"Did she say why she was quitting?" Isabel asked.

"She doesn't have time."

"Right."

"Oh, right," said Rudy. "What else did she say?"

"Nothing. Well, she did say she thought we'd discuss issues more. Topics."

"Topics? Please." I snorted. "Women in the workplace. Post-feminism in a preliberation era. Authenticating your life. Juggling work and family in a—"

"Didn't you tell her," Isabel interrupted mildly, "that we quit having topics quite a few years ago?"

"Yes, but—"

"Topics," Rudy said, "are what people talk about when they don't know each other well."

"Topics," I said, "are what men talk about."

Lee shook her head at us, disappointed.

"I think it must be hard for someone new to break into this group," Isabel said. Sharon was another one of Lee's finds—Isabel didn't want her to feel bad. "We're established now, a unit. Any newcomer's bound to feel like an outsider, no matter how welcoming we try to be."

"Well, I don't see why." Of course Isabel was right, but I wanted to keep it going. "Aren't we a fun buncha gals?" I turned to Rudy. "Remember the bald one? Sort of a middle-age punk deal going on. What was her name—"

"Moira, and she was nice," Rudy said defensively—she'd proposed her.

"I didn't say she wasn't nice, I said she was bald. Bald as an egg, bald as a cue ball. Bald—"

"How long have we been a group?" Isabel said to divert me.

Somebody asks that question every fourth or fifth meeting. Lee always knows the answer, and everybody always acts surprised and disbelieving. "It'll be ten years in June," Lee said.

"Ten *years*."

"My God."

"Who'd've thought."

Rudy lifted her glass high. "To us."

"To us." Everybody clinked, and we drank. I was thinking two things: *God, we're so lucky*, and *I want this to last forever.*

"So tomorrow," Lee wound up, "Henry has his third and last sperm test. They've been inconsistent up to now, so we're hoping this one finally tells us something."

"His sperm have been inconsistent? I hate when that happens."

"The test results. After the first one, they said his count was low, and after the second they said it was normal. The morphology was okay in the second, but abnormal in the first. And in both tests the motility was Grade II, which means slow and meandering."

"What's morphology?" Rudy asked.

"The shape. If the sperm is too tapered, it could be missing the acrosome, which is the packet of enzymes at the tip that helps it bore through the egg's coating."

"Hey, I'm eating here." I just wanted to lighten the mood. Lee's battles with infertility have been going on for about two years now, half the length of her marriage, and it's really starting to get to her. I'm so used to her being the cheerful, normal, competent one in the group, it's hard to watch her playing in a game she keeps losing. You know how some people are so chronically, outrageously successful, you can't help feeling a little satisfaction when they finally fail at something? Well, I do. But not with Lee. She has a terrific job, plenty of money, a hunk of a husband who adores her. I've known her for almost ten years, and in my opinion she deserves everything she's got. I never want to see her disillusioned or disappointed, never. It *hurts* me. A couple of meetings ago, during her fifteen minutes, she got tears in her eyes talking about how much she wanted a baby. That's all—but I couldn't stand it, I had to get up and go in the kitchen. I couldn't look at her.

"Well, at least after tomorrow you'll know more," Isabel said. "The uncertainty has to be the worst part."

"The worst," Lee agreed. She stuck her fingers in her short brown hair and ruffled it, a body-language change of subject. Lee is five-foot-two, small-boned and delicate-looking, but she's anything but fragile. She plays golf and tennis, swims, dances—upper-class sports—and she's good at all of them. One night I had too many gin and tonics and challenged her to an arm-wrestling contest. She twisted me right under the table.

"Well, I'm done," she said briskly. "Rudy, you go next."

"That's it? Work's fine, your parents drove you crazy over Hanukkah, and Henry's got a sperm test tomorrow?"

"That's it." Lee grinned. "That leaves you twenty minutes, which I'm sure you can use."

Rudy laughed, but it's true.

"Well, okay, I'll go. One thing that's going on with me . . ." She leaned toward Lee and touched her hand. "Curtis and I, we've been thinking a lot about it lately, and . . . "

"What?"

"Well, we've decided it's probably time for *us* to try for a baby."

She kept her eyes on Lee and didn't look at me after she delivered this news. I joined in the surprised exclamations and good wishes, but inside I went numb. As long as they were childless, the inevitable collapse of Rudy and Curtis's marriage could only hurt two people, and I only cared about one of them. *Oh, no, not a baby*. Deeper and deeper. Across the table, Isabel sent me a quick, veiled glance. She was thinking the same thing. Her opinion of Curtis Lloyd is a kinder, gentler version of mine, but when I pin her down we agree on the basics: he's an asshole.

"I thought a lot about whether I should tell you this right now," Rudy was saying to Lee, "but it seemed worse to keep it from you. Like I couldn't trust you to be able to handle it or something—"

"Oh, no, I'm glad you told me. Oh, Rudy, I'm really, *really* happy for you."

"And then I thought, well, what if I do get pregnant? Will I have to hide that from her, too?"

They started laughing, making jokes about giving the baby to a family of gypsies to raise in secret. Lee might or might not be pretending, I couldn't tell. If anyone in her situation would be glad for Rudy, it would be Lee. But Jeez, what timing. Lee's only human. If Rudy gets pregnant, how can it be anything for her but a stake through the heart?

I got up to get more bread, and when I came back Rudy was talking about the landscaping course again. I kept my mouth shut and let Lee and Isabel urge her to do it, enroll in the program. But I bet she doesn't. Last year she was excited about a job that would have involved consulting on corporate art purchases for one of the big associations in town, the home builders or the franchise owners, I can't remember. It would've been a miracle if she'd gotten it, since she threw away her master's in art history with nothing left to do but the thesis. But it was good to see her interested in anything, so we all encouraged her to go for it. In the end she never applied, though, never even sent in a résumé. Oh, Rudy, why not? we asked her. Well, it would've involved a lot of travel. So? Curtis didn't go for that.

I cannot stand that slippery, psychotic little prick.

When it was my turn, I told a pretty funny story about the blind date I had on New Year's Eve—which, believe me, wasn't funny at all while it was happening. Lee laughed so hard, she had to get out a Kleenex and wipe her eyes. "Oh, Emma, that is priceless," she wheezed, "where do you *find* these guys?"

"I'm a rotten date magnet, they stick to me like lead filings. You girls have no idea how lucky you are. Well, that's it, I'm done—Isabel, you go. Nothing else is new with me. I've got this *Washingtonian* deadline on Monday, that's it. Now, Isabel."

Lee said, "Wait a second, not so fast. What about your married guy? Anything happening there?"

A couple of weeks ago, in a really stupid moment, I made the mistake of mentioning Mick to Lee and Isabel. But I didn't say his name or give any details that would've identified him. I just said I was occasionally seeing a man who happened to be married and we didn't do anything but I was incredibly attracted to him and it was driving me out of my mind. Which trivializes what I feel, but I figure the group knows me well enough to decipher my self-protection codes. Anyway, it just spilled out—I couldn't control it. And it didn't even give me any satisfaction, since I couldn't go into any gory specifics. Lee's taking dance lessons with Sally now, and Henry's becoming pals with Mick, and it's all just a big, ugly mess. So I told them he was "somebody from work," which you must admit is technically true.

"Nope," I said, "nothing new on the married guy scene."

"You've stopped seeing him?"

"Oh, I still run into him every once in a while. We just talk."

"So—does that mean you're still interested in him?"

"Oh, you know. It's hopeless, so—" I grinned, shrugged, got really interested in spacing my silverware just so.

Lee got the hint. "Okay, I just wondered, because you haven't mentioned him lately. But you're okay, Em, right?"

"Sure, I'm fine, and the reason I don't talk about him is because there's nothing to talk about."

"Okay."

"Okay," I said, laughing. Rudy sent me a very dry look, which I ignored. "Now, Isabel. Tell us how school's going."

"School is wonderful—I got an A minus on my families-at-risk final." Cheering and table thumping. Isabel's getting a master's in social work at American U. "Other than that . . ." We waited, but she just shook her head and smiled. She was unusually quiet tonight, I realized. I looked at her more closely. Isabel grows younger and prettier to me all the time. Most of her long gray hair fell out while she was having chemotherapy, and when it grew back it came in curly and soft, like a young girl's hair. It suits her, doesn't look incongruous or too youthful, because her calm face is almost unlined. She doesn't look placid, though; that's not what I mean. Serene. Beneficent. She has a quality of repose I associate more with medieval saints than social work grad students. She's not like anyone else. Isabel is unique.

"Nothing at *all* is going on?" Lee pressed.

"Not really. Nothing much."

"What about your neighbor? And didn't you have a doctor's appointment—"

"Well, I *was* thinking about Gary today," she said quickly. Everybody groaned. "Or more precisely, I was thinking about infidelity and forgiveness. Sexual infidelity, how it's different between men and women. For us, it's all but unforgivable. For them, it's nothing."

"Not all men," Lee corrected.

"No." The softness in her voice when she said that one word, the way she touched Lee's arm just for a second—there's so much love between those two, I felt a stab of jealousy. "Definitely not all men." She put her chin on her folded hands. "I'll tell you a story during my fifteen minutes," she said. "Gary's been on my mind lately. I'll tell you about his last girlfriend."

"You mean Betty Cunnilefski?" We snickered—as we always do when Betty's name comes up.

"No, Betty was his first girlfriend. Or at least the first one I knew about. There were others."

"Others? *Plural*, Isabel?" I glanced at Rudy, who looked as surprised as I felt. Lee said nothing—she must already know about this.

Rudy blurted out what I was thinking: "Why didn't you ever tell us?"

"It was—I just—" Isabel gave a helpless shrug. "Because—I didn't want to. Until now."

"Were you embarrassed?" Rudy theorized gently.

"No. Well, yes. Yes, partly. It is hard to admit you've loved a man who was unfaithful for most of the twenty-two years you lived with him."

"Oh, but—"

"But mostly—I think I had to be able to forgive him myself before I could tell you."

"*Forgive* him? Forgive that bastard? Isabel, it was bad enough when it was only the cunnilingus bitch. Now—how the hell many women are we talking about?" I was swearing at Gary, but the truth is I was angry with Isabel, too, for keeping this little detail about her life a secret from us. She knew it, too; she held her hand out toward me along the tablecloth.

"Emma, it was too ugly. If I'd told you, there would only have been more anger, more bitterness."

"You're damn right."

"But don't you see, it wouldn't have helped. It would only have added to the negativity."

"Oh, okay. I get it. Balance, you wanted cosmic balance. Well, say no more."

She made a patient face. "Don't be mad. There's a time for everything, and the time for telling you this about Gary and me wasn't right. Until now."

"It's all right." I smiled—no hard feelings—and didn't mention that the time for telling *Lee* this had been right quite awhile ago, apparently. But that would have been admitting to childish jealousy, a card in my hand of character flaws I like to keep close to the vest.

Rudy broke an uncomfortable pause to ask, "So who was this last floozy, Isabel?"

"Her name was Norma, and she wasn't much of a floozy. She was an accountant, another one of Gary's office conquests. After Betty, I always knew when he was seeing someone, but this—"

I couldn't keep quiet. "Jesus, Isabel, how many were there?" *Gary Kurtz?* I still couldn't picture it. He's this stocky, middle-aged guy with a beard, sort of a Santa Claus type of fellow but without the heartiness. A government drone, probably a GS–14 or so, does something in the Commerce Department that's so dull I can't remember what it is. Back when I used to speak to him, he talked a lot about his grass.

"I don't know how many," Isabel answered, raising an eyebrow at me in a rare show of testiness. "I just know the last one wouldn't go away. So I went to see her."

We gasped.

"Really?"

"You went to *see* her?"

"I looked her up in the phone book, and there she was—Norma Stottlemyer, in an apartment on Colesville Road."

"How did you know her name?"

"Gary told me. He never denied anything, I'll give him that. He never lied to me."

"I just think that makes it worse," Lee said fiercely.

"I picked a Saturday morning when he was home, and told him I was going to the Safeway. I drove over to Silver Spring, one of those brick garden apartments set close to the road on Colesville. Children outside, plastic toys everywhere—I was terrified she was married and I'd end up wrecking *her* home. But I had a story in case a man answered, or a child—I was collecting for leukemia."

"Good one."

"Except you didn't have any I.D.," Lee noted, always practical.

"Anyway, she came to the door herself, wearing a pink corduroy bathrobe. Even before I went in, I knew she lived alone. Just something about her."

"How old?" I asked.

"Late twenties."

"Rat bastard. What did she look like?"

"It was still early, I'd caught her off guard, she hadn't fixed up yet."

Rudy and I shook our heads at each other: *Are you hearing this?* Trust Isabel to make excuses for the slut who was banging her husband. "So she was ugly," I said.

"No, not ugly, just not attractive. Not sexy, not even interesting-looking. Quite ordinary. When I said, 'I'm Isabel Kurtz,' she looked blank. Then I said, 'Gary's wife,' and I thought she was going to faint."

"She didn't *know*?"

"Yes, she knew he was married, but she was shocked, not thinking fast. She backed up, sort of waved me in, and that's when I knew we weren't going to be having any dramatic scene. There was just no fight in her."

"Wimp. Dirtbag wuss."

"Her apartment was all Pier I and Door Store—you'd have written something scathing and funny about it, Emma." I decided to take that as a compliment. "She took me into the kitchen, not the living room. I could hear music from the apartment next door, just the bass thumping. There was half a bowl of soup on the counter, I remember—she'd been eating soup for breakfast. Bean with bacon." She smiled with one side of her mouth, dry and wistful and bitter at the same time.

"She had one of those cheap, six-jar spice racks over the stove. Glass jars with name tags. She bought spices and poured them into the little jars and wrote CINNAMON and BLACK PEPPER and GARLIC POWDER on the labels. Only six." She looked around at us in pity and amazement, but I don't know what she found more pathetic, the fact that Norma labeled her spices or that she only used six. "And—she had kitten magnets on the refrigerator. One played a tune. She backed up against it and it fell on the floor and started to play 'You Are My Sunshine.'"

"Isabel," I said, "you're killing me."

"So what *happened*?" Rudy said.

"I could see she wasn't going to start us off, so I said, 'I just wanted to see what kind of person you are.' I meant it literally; that's exactly why I'd come, to *see* her, try to understand what Gary found so attractive. But she took it as a condemnation and started to cry."

"Oh, Jesus."

"What did you do?"

"I cried with her. I did. We turned our backs on each other and buried our faces—well, I had my handkerchief and she used a paper towel."

Rudy was trying not to laugh. "God, I can see it."

"After that, I just lost interest. She was such a pitiful enemy, I couldn't even hate her. But for the first time, I felt contempt for Gary. Just utter contempt."

"Gary's a pig," I said.

"Norma stopped crying and said she was sorry, so sorry, and she would stop seeing him. I asked her if she was in love with him, and she said yes." She smiled faintly. "But, you know, I don't think she was. And I think she realized it at that moment. I said it didn't matter to me if she kept seeing him or not, because I was leaving him. And I said I thought she could do better."

I clapped my hands. "*Good* one."

"After that, I went home and told Gary it was over. My only mistake—"

"Was leaving him instead of throwing him out," Lee finished for her, and we all nodded grimly. That satisfying gesture had cost Isabel the house in the divorce settlement. Gary the pig is still living there in suburban splendor, still mowing his fucking lawn, while Isabel makes do in a cramped, one-bedroom apartment on a tough street in Adams-Morgan. She got breast cancer less than two years after she left him, and Gary demonstrated what a class act he is by trying to get her cut out of his government health insurance policy. She finally won, but it wasn't a battle she needed to be fighting at that particular time in her life. I think I hate him for that more than anything, even the womanizing.

"Well, I'm not sure why I told that story," Isabel marveled, shaking her head. "I honestly haven't thought about Norma in ages."

"It's a sad story," Rudy said.

"You said you'd been thinking about infidelity," Lee reminded her.

"Yes. But not for any particular reason."

Was it my guilty imagination that Isabel flicked a look at me then? A quick, appraising glance to see if I'd gotten a message? Because infidelity has been on my mind lately, too. I don't know if I could commit adultery. If she was trying to tell me something, she'd done a clever job. It's useful to keep in mind that if I began an affair with Mick Draco, there would be nothing more than her Door Store furniture to distinguish me from the Norma Stottlemyers of the world.

Isabel put her forearms on the table, leaning in. "No, I do know why I told you." She spoke in a low, earnest tone; we bent toward her, catching her intensity. "I wanted you to know that I've forgiven him. No, wait"—I must've made somc scornful noise—"listen to me, it's important. Nobody knows why a man does what he does—"

"Isabel, there are *standards,* there's—" She made a violent slicing motion with the side of her hand. I closed my mouth.

"No one knows why someone acts in a certain way, not all the reasons, not the compulsions or inducements that led up to it, what weapons a person has inside himself to fight temptation. We can't know that. Listen, all I want to tell you is—life is so short. It's so short, and I can't waste any more of mine on resentment. Forgiveness isn't weak, it doesn't mean you have no moral center. Buddha said wanting revenge is like spitting in the wind—you only hurt yourself." She spread her hands—honest to God, she looked like an angel in the vanilla-scented glow of the candles. "I believe it's true that we're all one, all . . . one." Her smile was wry and self-conscious, perfectly aware of how daffy this sounded to someone like—say—me. "And separations are an illusion. When I forgive Gary, I forgive myself."

Talk about a conversation stopper.

"Yeah, except you didn't do anything," I threw in, mostly to break the silence. Isabel's sad smile said I'd missed the point, but she loved me anyway. I got up to make coffee.

I dimmed the lights to bring in dessert—Isabel's homemade, candelit cake. It was a big hit. We sang "For she's the jolly good fellow," and she blew out her candles.

"Oh, why didn't I bring my movie camera?" Lee wailed. "I'm so proud of you," she told Isabel, kissing her on both cheeks.

"Me, too," Rudy said, leaning over to hug her. "I love it that you're doing things for *yourself* for a change. And from now on it's just going to get better."

"Right," I said. "The second half of your life is going to be great."

"To the second half of Isabel's life," Lee proposed, and we toasted with our coffee cups and waterglasses and wine dregs.

I didn't think she was going to be able to say anything. I've never seen Isabel so overcome; it almost made *me* cry. Her soft blue eyes were shimmering, but finally she managed to say, "To all of us."

"To all of us," I seconded, and added my all-time favorite toast: "May we live forever."

Rudy stayed after Lee and Isabel left. I put on my coat and we went outside on the porch to smoke cigarettes and look at the moon. My neighborhood is about one-third black, one-third white, one-third other, mostly Hispanic, and I like it that way. It's real. Sometimes it's a little too real, like when you wake up to sirens and cop radios at four in the morning, or read about a mugging in the next block, or stumble into a drug deal in front of the Latino grocery store. Still, I like the mix of colors and classes, most of us law-abiding, all of us just trying to get along, as Rodney said. Tonight it was peaceful, the quiet sweetened by the soft yellow light in the windows of my neighbors, nobody out except the dog walkers.

"Isabel was awfully quiet, wasn't she? Except for the Norma story," Rudy said, and I said I'd noticed that, too. "Emma, do you think Lee really doesn't mind about Curtis and me? Trying for a baby?"

I answered carefully. "I think it's bound to be hard on her. Whether she knows it yet or not. I think she and Henry are in for a pretty rough time." Rudy sighed. I watched my breath condense in the cold, silvery air. "So. A baby. I thought Curtis wasn't interested in having children."

She got that pleasant, determined look we both wear when we talk about him. "He wasn't at first, but he's come around. The new job I was telling you about is almost a cinch now, and when that happens our income will more than double. And that's only to start."

"The lobbying job? So he'll be a lobbyist?" Perfect.

"Yes, so money won't be an issue anymore."

"Money was what was holding him back?" And here I thought it was total self-involvement.

"Mostly. Oh, Emma, I'm so excited. I didn't want to show it because of Lee. But, God, can you imagine me a mother?"

I sidestepped that by asking, "What does Greenburg think about it?"

She took a nervous drag and flicked ashes over the porch rail. "He won't say, he just keeps asking what I think. So . . ." She laughed giddily. "He's probably against it."

"Well, you can't live your life according to what your shrink thinks." Although sometimes it wouldn't be a bad idea. I'm always trying to find out, in clever, oblique ways, what Greenburg thinks about Curtis. Rudy never tells me, which either means she's too smart for me or Greenburg's too smart for her. I'm not even sure I'd *want* Greenburg to disillusion her about Curtis. Sometimes I think he must be in the same conspiracy I'm in, which involves saying nothing bad about Curtis in order to keep Rudy from getting hurt.

"That's right, and you also can't put off having a child until you're in perfect mental health. God, I'll be *dead* by then."

"Well, I hope it's a girl and it looks like you, not Curtis," I said, pretending that was a joke.

She hugged herself, laughing. Her eyes were shiny with wistfulness and hope, and it finally hit me how much she wanted a child. "Oh, think of it, Em. I could be somebody's mother in nine months." She turned her face up to the moon, and when she shivered, it wasn't from the cold.

"I hope so," I said truthfully. "I really hope so, and I think it's great. I hope it happens soon."

"Thank you. Really. That means a lot. Well, hey, it's late, I'd better get going."

She gave me a strong hug, which I returned weakly. She'd forgotten to ask me about Mick. And I'm so screwed up on this subject, I couldn't bring him up first. "Do you really have to go? It's only eleven." Hint, hint. *Stay longer and ask me about the man I'm obsessed with.*

"No, I should go, Curtis doesn't like me driving at night." She started down the steps.

"Want me to call him?" Yuck. "Tell him you're on your way?"

"That's okay, I've got my phone." She patted her purse. "Thanks for dinner, everything was great. Hey, do you want to go to the movies on Monday?"

I brightened. "Sure. I'll call you Sunday night."

"Sunday's good." She blew me a kiss. "Night, Em."

She'd parked half a block up the street. *Rats*, I thought, watching her negotiate the grass strip between sidewalk and curb with the dog shit–avoiding grace of a D.C. veteran. Thoughtlessness, self-absorption, preoccupation, negligence—you expect these from the average run of your acquaintances, but not from your best friend. From her you want perfection. You want her to read your mind.

Parking is a bitch on my street. The car behind Rudy's khaki-colored Wrangler had boxed her in. She inched back and forth, back and forth, about ten times before she finally jerked free of the space. As she started to pull away, a speeding car roared past, practically sideswiping the Jeep, and slid to a long, screeching stop fifty feet down from the front of my walkway. My heart stopped but started again and began to race when I saw what kind of car it was—Volvo station wagon—and who was getting out of it. Lee.

Rudy and I converged on her. "What happened, where's Isabel? What's wrong?"

She grabbed us both and held on. She was crying and couldn't talk, I had to shake her. "I took her home—she told me. I'm not supposed to tell—"

"*What*?"

"The cancer."

"Oh, my God."

She kept swallowing. I had her hand, I felt it shaking. "A recurrence. The doctor's almost sure. She has to have a bone scan." Lee broke down, and Rudy hugged her. I hung my arms around both of them; we stood there in the middle of the street, holding on for our lives.

A car came and honked at us. I gave it the finger. "Let's go." I started for Lee's car, which was still idling. "Rudy, you drive."

"Where? You mean to Isabel's?"

"Well, where the hell else?"

"But I wasn't supposed to tell you," Lee cried, "you're not supposed to know!"

I just stared at her.

"Right," she said, coming out of her trance. "Let's go."

12

Isabel

A lot of my youth is a blur, great chunks of it simply missing, as if I periodically contracted amnesia along with the usual measles and chicken pox of childhood. And yet my recollection of the night I gave up on my parents is as clear and vivid as a piece of clip art. I was eight. I know because I tagged it in my consciousness as if with a book mark, quite aware that something significant had happened. *I'm eight*, I thought, *and this is true. This is something I know about Mother and Daddy*.

It was in Marshalltown, Iowa, early on a winter evening. I remember the lamps burning in the living room, the smell of hot dust from a hissing radiator. The sound of a page turning, and then the dry, unnecessary cough, *uh ehh*, of my mother. Creeping down the staircase, I paused to look at my parents, peering at them over the banister rail. Our small house had no office; my father wrote sermons in the living room seated in his morris chair, using the broad arms for a desk, notebook on one side, Bible on the other. He sat with his foot propped up on the needlepoint stool, his elbow on his knee, forehead on the heel of his hand. Slowly, steadily, and without pausing, he composed the dry, ineffably dull discourse he would deliver in a passionless monologue next Sunday at the Concordia Evangelical Lutheran Church.

Across the blue oval of the braided rug, in the cheap, sixty-watt, old-gold beam of the tole lamp, my mother bowed over a fall of heavy cloth on her lap—curtains, perhaps, or some dark, dreary garment of my father's. Her forehead furrowed slightly at the first prick of each stitch, cleared with every long, smooth pull of the thread. There was no music playing, no television, no radio. Definitely no conversation. My parents faced each other in perfect half-profile, still and silent as coins.

In that moment I understood—without knowing the word, of course—the meaning of stasis. And the futility of hoping that anything could change, not here, not in this room. Silence reigned; silence saturated. There couldn't possibly be any communication between them, or among us. My father spoke more in church on Sunday than at home the rest of the week. And here is the insight that ultimately saved me: *Something is wrong. Other people aren't like this.*

Arrested, I came down the rest of the way and drifted over to my mother, stood beside her chair. She made some gesture, a nod or a shrug of her shoulder, but she didn't look up or speak to me. She wore a tan woolen jumper with a mustard-colored blouse, white kneesocks, and loafers. She was fifty-three years old. I leaned against her tough, stringy shoulder, watching the changes in her face, thinking how gray her dry, wavy hair was. When I pressed my arm against her arm, she looked at me, startled. "What's wrong?" And she covered my forehead with her cool, spidery hand. To see if I was sick.

I considered my answer. "I don't feel good," I could have said. Had said in the past. I was a clever child, not above malingering for attention. Not above hypochondria, either.

But this night was different; this was the night I grew up. I said, "Nothing," and sidled away. My father never looked up or stopped writing. And I gave up on them. In that moment, I ran out of hope.

How lugubrious that sounds. Poor little me. In fact, it wasn't that dire. And much better to give up cleanly then and there, I think, than to yearn and long and nurse false hopes for a closeness that can never come. My parents weren't monsters. I never hated them. Years later, when my father was dying, I kept watch with my mother and sister as he lay in his steel hospital bed, stone-faced and speechless as ever. "I love you, Daddy," I told him once—only once. He was still conscious then. He turned his pale blue eyes on me and blinked. His tongue came out to wet his lips, and I thought he was going to speak. He didn't. But he nodded a little. And I thought—maybe he thinks it's understood. All these years, maybe for him it's been a given, not worth saying out loud. Maybe.

My sister is just like them. I barely know her. Eighteen years older, she's more like an aunt than a sister, some relative I rarely see. I write her spare, jovial thank-you notes when she remembers my birthday with a card. Lately I've been hearing from her more often, though. "Shall we put Mother in an assisted living facility?" she wonders. Oh, I should think so. Mother is ninety-four and losing her mind. Odd: she never gave much of herself to me, my mother, only the bare essentials, no frivolous extras like hugs, silliness, laughter, conversation. And yet now that she's all but gone, I miss her very much. My father, too. It's odd.

Why didn't I grow up remote and cold, or frightened and clinging, pursuing one wrong man after another in search of the elusive embrace of acceptance? Maybe it's only in self-help books or on television talk shows that such a fate lies in store for every lonely child. Real life is much more complicated. Or much simpler. One thing I know: love or the search for it is stronger than neglect, or indifference, or rejection. I looked for it in other places, not in my parents' house, and I found it. Occasionally.

The Graces didn't come to see me after all, that night Lee raced back to Emma's and told her and Rudy what I had just asked her not to tell them. They drove to my street and parked in front of my building for ten minutes, debating what to do. They decided to reconnoiter—drive through the alley to the back, see if my lights were on. If they were, they would park, knock at my door, and demand entrance.

The lights weren't on.

They debated again, and eventually drove back to Emma's. Where they sat in Lee's car for an hour and fifteen minutes, talking about me. This was the best of all possible resolutions, since talking about me that night would have been infinitely more satisfying for everybody than talking to me. "Nobody wanted to get out of the car," Lee reported afterward. "We didn't want to *land*. We didn't want to go in, sit down, drink coffee, look at each other in the light. So we just sat and talked and stared straight out the windshield. Like we were at the drive-in."

Emma's feelings were hurt because I'd told Lee but not her. (She didn't confide that in me, of course; Rudy did. Emma still imagines that if she hides her vulnerabilities, no one will notice she has any.) But there was no help for it, nothing I could have done except what I did. The news was too fresh—I was too raw. I shouldn't have gone to Emma's house at all that night, but at the last minute I couldn't stay away. I knew it would be warm there, and I was freezing cold.

"A metastasis, I'm almost certain," Dr. Glass said. "I'm very sorry." It was hard to listen after that. I heard "stage four," though. And I heard "bone," and thought of the mild ache in my hip I'd thought was a muscle strain. After that, my mind went blank. The oddest thing. I turned icy cold all over, a gelid, numbing horror. I remember leaving Dr. Glass's office, but not getting on the elevator or going out of the building. I remember men digging up the sidewalk on P Street with jackhammers. The noise was so deafening, it jarred me awake and I realized it was raining. The bus stop was blocks away. I thought, Should I take a taxi? But it would only take me home, and what was the point of that? What was the point of anything? I stood on the curb and watched pedestrians come and go in the crosswalk, listened to the Walk/Don't Walk light click on and click off, on and off. A woman bumped me. "Oh, sorry," she said with a quick smile, and I stared at her in dull surprise. *Do you think it matters?* I asked her retreating back. Whether you hit me, or say excuse me, or wear a warm wool coat, or buy an expensive briefcase or read the newspaper—or make an appointment at the optometrist's for new glasses, or have a dinner party, or get enough sleep, or dream about your vacation, or meet a man, or take your vitamins, or buy flowers from the vendor on the corner? Do you think any of that matters? *Nothing* matters. I know it—why don't you?

I had fallen into the rut in my mind from the last time someone told me I had cancer. A habit. Chill rain soaking the shoulders of my trench coat woke me up, like the jackhammers. Mundane reality forced movement on me. I could go home, get warm, get on with it. As long as you're not dead, you're alive. I lifted my hand. Immediately a braking cab splashed water on my shoes. I told the driver my address and he took me home.

Since then, I've survived by getting from one moment to the next moment. I feed the dog, take in the mail, wipe crumbs off the counter. Contrary to how it felt, my life didn't stop in Dr. Glass's office; it keeps moving on, the future as big a mystery as ever. Well, no, that's not quite true. As a matter of fact, the only good thing I've come up with about my situation is: at least the suspense is over. It's looking as if Isabel Thorlefsen Kurtz will die of breast cancer, not in an automobile accident, not peacefully in her sleep of old age, not of AIDS or a heart attack, not in a drive-by shooting. No more wondering; finally knowing. It's something.

I want to be wide awake to the truth, not pretend and not hide, quaking, behind irony or passivity. Acceptance is dead last, though—forgive the pun—on the famous list of five stages. First comes denial, but I seem to have bypassed that one. Because of immediate past experience, I suppose; having had cancer before has inured me, to some small extent. What is the difference between hope and false hope? Who's to say what is "the best way" to die? How am I, how is anyone expected to know that? Oh, I see it's just beginning—I'll be on intimate terms with these and all the other unanswerable questions soon enough.

But I have things to do, decisions to make. I have to keep my head clear, not cloud it with thoughts of loss and dread. Plenty of time for that, too. I'm not ready for the sympathy of people who love me (this is what Emma couldn't understand, and I'll make her understand, but not yet, I can't do it yet), I have to hang on a little longer to my impersonality, my anonymity. That's why I haven't called anyone. I have to put my house in order. It's crucial to keep working, planning, going on with my life just as before, as if it still had meaning. And—I must confess to a little loop in my brain that keeps insisting I still might get out of this. A low, adamant voice saying, *You're only fifty, you won't die. It can't be finished.*

The last two years have been the best ever, and I wouldn't have had them if I hadn't gotten sick in the first place. So, inevitably, I must ask, was it worth it? Is this a fair trade? On the outside, it looked as if the best was just about to happen to me—satisfying work, finally some security and stability, maybe even a man to love. But on the inside, I already had everything. Life is for living, not relishing in retrospect. I've been given two splendid years of rich, tantalizing uncertainty and unexpected contentment. Was it enough?

I'm afraid of the question. I said I wouldn't do this. But everything is conspiring against me, all the things I love. I made a pot of Indian tea and drank it with saffron honey, and I savored the musky, smoky taste as never before. If I had scotch, I would pour a little glass and let it prickle on my tongue, let the hot, masculine fire burn all the way down. An inch of snow fell last night. I opened the window and scooped up a handful, let it melt on my palm. I stuck out my tongue and tasted it, and it was dirty and metallic and delicious. I can't get enough of anything. Music—but I put on the Beethoven piano sonata that always makes me cry, and when the adagio came, I broke down.

Grace suspects something. She watches me. I look up and catch her brown eyes on me, steadfast and worried. Sweet old girl. She's ten, we think, and might outlive me. I never expected that.

Little things. The thought of losing them makes them unbearably dear. It's easy to forget at a time like this that life also features cruelty, indifference, brutality, perversion, bigotry, starvation, greed, venality, madness, corruption. I only think of the sweetness. Simple things. The quarter moon, the taste of an orange. The smell of the pages of a new book. If I pause to listen, I can hear Kirby moving around in his bedroom, right over my bedroom. Would he have been my lover? I listen to the voices of my friends who call and leave me messages—"Isabel, oh God, I don't know what to say," "Isabel, please call me, I love you"—and I know I can't stay away from them much longer. I have to tell my son, my mother, my sister. Oh, the world is hurtling toward me, all the pieces of my heart flying at me at once, I'll be leveled by love if I don't take care.

A bone scan on Tuesday—pro forma; Glass already knows—then his office again on Wednesday. He says he'll tell me everything. I'll take a notebook and write it all down. I have to be smart, stay focused. I'll go with a list of questions. Maybe . . . no.

Yes. I'll ask Lee to go with me.

13

Lee

At first I thought I was the only one who couldn't stand Dr. Glass, but it turned out we all hated him. Except for Emma, though, we managed to be polite.

"I don't understand what you're talking about," she said, leaning forward with her head jutting, as if a leash around her neck was holding her down. "You're the only doctor in the room, notice, so would you mind speaking English?"

I'd never heard her sound so shrill. It would have embarrassed me—in the majority of situations, I think we accomplish very little by being confrontational—but I was angry, too, and in her way Emma was speaking for all of us.

A lot of framed certificates hung on the wall behind Dr. Glass's desk. He had a tasteful office, a large staff, several prestigious hospital associations. What he lacked was a bedside manner, or even one that hinted he cared at all about the people who came to him to hear the worst news. Maybe he did care, but you couldn't tell it from his dead eyes or his thin smile, and not from his virtually inaudible speaking voice. He moved his lips like a ventriloquist—hardly at all. We had to bend over to hear him, me with my notebook pressed to my chest—I was the official note-taker—and strain to catch his low, rapid-fire mumble.

"I'm saying there is no surgical cure for a cancer that's already spread beyond the site of origin. Still, the patient who presents with stage four metastatic breast disease has a number of treatment options, although some or none may be indicated in the individual case. In this case, we have—"

"In *Isabel's* case. She's the 'patient presenting,' and her name is Isabel."

"Emma." Isabel was chalk white but calm, calmer than we were. Even when Glass had enumerated the metastases—"mets" he called them—in her spine and pelvis, both femurs, and her rib cage, she'd sat with her hands folded in her lap and stared straight back at him, not flinching. I could hardly take notes, my fingers were shaking so. It wasn't only the doctor's delivery that made it hard to write down what he said. My mind kept switching on and off, the strangest sensation, as if my fear was shorting out the circuitry in my brain.

At least I wasn't crying. Rudy was crying. To hide it from Isabel, she got up and walked to the window, pretending to look down at the traffic on Reservoir Road. But I saw her sneak her handkerchief out of her pocket and hold it over her mouth and nose. I wanted to shout at her, *Don't you dare break down!* That's all we would need. Emma's rudeness made a distraction, at least—we could focus on it instead of the horrible, devastating things, one after another, Dr. Glass would not stop muttering.

"In *Isabel's* case," he said, narrowing his eyes behind his Ralph Lauren bifocals, "where we have carcinomatosis in a distant site, a patient presently in menopause, with a positive estrogen but negative progesterone receptor status, as well as a prior history of cytotoxin—chemotherapy—I'm saying the treatment modalities available to us have narrowed and are somewhat limited."

"What about a bone marrow transplant?" Emma kept squeezing the arms of her chair with both hands, as if she'd fly out of it if she let go. "That could cure her, couldn't it?"

He bounced his fingertips together and retracted his lips in a slow, annoying rhythm, like a guppy. "There are a number of factors to consider before I would endorse ABMT/BCT. Autologous bone marrow or blood cell transplantation," he said when Emma uncrossed her legs and stomped one boot heel on his carpeted floor. "A number of factors." He turned cold eyes on Isabel. "I wouldn't rule out antiestrogen therapy to begin with, although the fact that you've already tried tamoxifen, with obviously unsuccessful results, makes me less than hopeful on that score. Down the road, there's chemo. At this time there's no way to tell whether you'd respond better to HDC or SDC—"

"High-dose or standard-dose chemotherapy," I interrupted. "I read about it on the Internet."

He actually smiled. "Very good." But the surprise in his voice was insulting, and I sympathized with Emma when she sucked her tongue, *tst*. "Eventually—it's too soon to say yet—you may decide to undergo what we call induction chemotherapy, a prelude for patients considering HDC with ABMT/BCT. It's not a therapy in itself, but it's helpful sometimes in determining whether a cancer will respond to the drugs we use in high-dose chemo. On the other hand, responding to or 'passing' induction therapy doesn't mean HDC with ABMT/BCT will be any more effective than SDC, it simply means the cancer is sensitive to chemotherapy. Also, it doesn't mean you'll live longer or have an equivalent or better quality of life with HDC than SDC."

"So really, it doesn't mean anything."

"It means exactly what I said it means."

We stared back and forth between Glass and Emma, whose eyes were locked. He seemed nettled, but she looked like a witch, a Fury; I could swear her hair was standing on end. Even Rudy turned around, caught by the hostility in the room, thick as a mist.

In the middle of the tense silence, Isabel stood up.

"I'll call you. About hormone therapy, and to set up the test. Tests. What you said, the induction . . ." She waved her hand gently—the real name wasn't important, she meant. All of us, even Glass, especially Emma, looked rueful and embarrassed. Because, for a few minutes, it had been easier to behave as if the problem here were a personality conflict instead of someone's life. Isabel's life.

We rode down in the elevator in a strange, self-conscious silence until Rudy asked where we should go for lunch. Sergei's in Georgetown, we decided, because we could walk there. We couldn't seem to look in one another's faces, and yet we stayed bunched together in the elevator, arms and shoulders touching, like marchers in a demonstration. Isabel had asked *me* to go with her to see Dr. Glass, not Rudy or Emma. Somehow they'd found out, though, and insisted on going with us. That had made me mad; how pushy, I thought, how insensitive. Now . . . oh, God. Now I didn't want to think what I'd have done without them.

We asked for a booth in a corner of the restaurant, and I went to call the office, tell my assistant I'd be a lot later than I'd thought. When I came back, Rudy was ordering drinks.

"Double scotch, rocks," she said—like a man, like my father. Isabel and I asked for iced tea. "Hey, you guys—" Rudy started to protest, but Emma said, "I'll drink with you, Rude. Beer, please, whatever's on tap."

When the drinks came, nobody toasted. That's something we always do, at least for the first one. But this time we just sipped, still not really looking at one another. Everything I thought to say sounded either too light or too dark, so I just sat there. Finally Emma said, "Is it me, or was that guy a flaming asshole?" and we all started talking at once.

Glass had been awful, but I wouldn't have said so in case Isabel still liked him—he'd been her oncologist for the last two years, after all. But she told us, "I went to him because I'd heard he was good, and after that there wasn't any reason to switch—I thought I was cured. But I've always thought he was arrogant."

"*Arrogant*. He's a cartoon," Emma said. "I hated him as soon as I looked at him. Did you see the way he held the door for us? Sarcastic bastard."

He hadn't wanted all of us in his office. "Just one," he'd said with a fake smile. "Don't you think?" Implying it was silly of us, but cute, a girl thing, to want to stay together. But, no, we didn't think. Part of me could even see his point, and yet I'm the one who said, with particular force and composure, "We think it's important that we all hear what you have to say, Doctor. We're acting as Isabel's surrogate family." He chuckled and spread his hands, trying to suggest that that was absurd. We just looked back at him, not budging, and finally there wasn't anything else he could do. Emma was right: he had held the door sarcastically.

We ordered lunch. *We're eating,* I thought. Just like always, just as if something horrible hadn't happened. Isabel got the seafood salad. We could talk about some things but not others. For example, nobody could say, "How do you feel right now? What was it like when he said those things about the cancer in your body? Are you afraid?" All we could do, it seemed, was be together, ourselves, the same as always.

Emma asked the first really personal question. "Have you told Terry or your mother yet?"

"Not yet. I was waiting until I knew for sure." Isabel laid her fork down and sat back. She'd eaten almost nothing. "My mother won't understand—I probably won't tell her at all. There's no point." Her mother just went in a nursing home; she has Alzheimer's disease. "I'll have to tell my sister, though. And Terry. Oh, God," she whispered, and shut her eyes tight.

Rudy's face turned red; she put her hand over her mouth. Emma looked away.

I said, "I'll call Terry. If you want me to."

Isabel reached out and rubbed my arm up and down, hard, smiling with her jaws clenched. "Thanks. I'll call him tonight. It's better." She squeezed my elbow. "Thanks," she mouthed. That was as close as she came to crying all day.

"I can start a Web search," I said, trying to sound brisk. "I've done it before at work. It's amazing how much information is out there, and it's easy to access."

"As a matter of fact, Kirby's already doing that."

"Kirby? Your neighbor?"

Isabel nodded.

"Wait a second. Kirby *knows*?" I couldn't believe it. *Kirby* knew, and Isabel hadn't even told Terry yet?

A little color came into her cheeks. She turned her teaspoon over and over on the tablecloth. "I didn't tell you this yet. I didn't have a chance."

"Tell us what?"

"Kirby . . ." She looked up and laughed. "Kirby's in love with me. He says."

"*What*?"

"But he's gay!"

"You *said* he was gay."

"Yes, well. Apparently I was mistaken."

"Wow." Emma sat back and started to laugh.

"So," Rudy said, grinning, pleased. "Do you like him?"

Isabel shrugged. "Oh," she said, and nothing else.

"Well, are you, you know . . . "

"Lovers? No."

Emma stopped laughing to ask, "Are you going to be?"

Isabel's face had been lively for a minute, but now the animation faded. "I might have. I hadn't decided. Then . . ." She shook her head. "He's a friend, a good friend."

A good friend. It was the first I'd heard. And she'd told him about her illness even before she told her own son. But she'd told me first, and that was . . .

Maybe she hadn't. Maybe she'd told Kirby first. Even before me.

I hate jealousy. At least it's its own punishment; it makes me feel like hell.

After a while, we started talking about other things, normal things. I wondered if anyone else was as surprised by that as I was. *This is how it's going to be*, I realized. Whatever happened, Isabel was going to try to make it as easy for us as she could.

Over our coffee, she asked about Henry. "What happened with the sperm test, Lee? Did you get the results yet?"

"Yes," I said, "the nurse called yesterday. They've figured it out."

"They have?"

"What's the story?"

I had been feeling guilty for being happy, for having twinges of gladness in the midst of my closest friend's crisis. But now the Graces' expectant faces and excitement, *Isabel's* excitement, erased all that. "You won't believe it. Henry has *too many* sperm."

Their mouths dropped, then they whooped with laughter—I knew they would.

"He's so relieved. Normal is between twenty million and two hundred million per millimeter, and Henry's got over a billion."

"Get *out*."

"A billion?"

"It's a rare condition."

"Oh, what a manly man," Emma said breathily. "Tell him I'm awed."

"So what happens now?"

"Well, we probably can't get pregnant in the normal way. It's a motility problem—he's got so many sperm, they clump together and can't move. So we'll have to do AI. Artificial insemination."

"With donor sperm?"

"No, they can use Henry's."

"Oh, Lee, that's wonderful!"

"I am so happy for you."

"The nurse said I could be pregnant in six months."

Isabel leaned over and kissed me. This was the news that had kept me going. How could I lose hope for her when this blessing was happening to me?

"This is so great. But you know," Emma said, "fifty years ago you'd've been out of luck. Thank God for the miracle of modern medicine." I saw her start to reach for her glass, then stop.

A sheepish silence fell. Emma had been going to toast the miracle of modern medicine. Then she'd remembered: the one most in need of a miracle here was Isabel.

"All right," I said, pushing my plate away, "what's the plan? How are we going to work this? I'll get on the 'Net again. Kirby, too—that's great, two heads are better than one." I really meant it. "It sounds like you probably need to decide about hormone therapy first, so that's where I'll start. We still have plenty of time to figure out the HDC and SDC or the BMT, if you decide to go that route. My father knows one of the head oncologists at Sloan-Kettering, they used to be golfing buddies, so I can call him and try to get some referrals, preferably local. You'll need at least two second opinions, don't you think? A different one from Glass's, whatever his turns out to be, and a tiebreaker, that would be ideal, but we'll see how it goes. How is your health insurance? Have you checked to see what it considers standard practice versus experimental?" Emma started to laugh. "What?" Isabel joined her—even Rudy looked amused. "What's so funny?"

"Nothing." Isabel put her arm around me.

"Am I being bossy?"

"No."

"No, you're being great," Emma said.

"You are," Rudy said.

"Well, *somebody's* got to get this thing organized. And I'm assuming time is of the essence, right? Am I right?"

They stopped smiling.

"You're right," Isabel said quietly, when no one else answered.

14

Rudy

"She has to be all right, Emma. She looks great, God, she looks beautiful."

"I know. She's never looked better."

"How could this have happened? How can she be so sick?"

"I don't know." Emma shook her head, miserable. It was just us now; Isabel and Lee had left Sergei's together at about three, but Emma and I never even got up. It was understood that we were staying. Like old times.

The waitress came over. "Can I get you ladies some more coffee?"

"No, but I'll have another scotch," I said. "Just a single this time."

Emma lifted her eyebrows at me. "Well, shoot. Guess that means I'll have to have another beer."

So we started drinking. Sometimes alcohol really works for me, really is the answer. Not always. But sometimes, something about the way it goes down, easy and clear and—*bright* or something—well, I can't explain it. But every once in a while, I just know it's going to be perfect.

This time, it gave me the courage to say, "I'm so frightened. It's all I can feel. Oh, Emma, what if she dies?" I could only whisper it. "What if Isabel dies?"

She slid out of her side of the booth and sat down on mine, making me shove over. "I'm scared, too. It's all I can think about."

"I just can't believe it. Still. Last week she was fine, and this week she might be dying. How can that be?"

"She's not dying. People beat it, people have remissions for years, decades. People are *cured*, you read about it all the time."

"That's true."

Emma drew vertical lines through the condensation on her beer glass. "My father died of cancer."

"You were little, though, weren't you? You didn't see it."

"I was eight, and they were already divorced. I don't know anything about it, just that he died of cancer. Of the liver."

"I hate cancer."

"Because it's slow, so you know. God, I'd rather be hit by a bus. Anything."

I stopped tearing my napkin into shreds to stare at my hands. What if I were dying? My skin . . . the shapes of my fingers, the gray-blue veins in my wrists. How could I lose myself? To be something, and then to be nothing. To cease. "She won't die," I said. "She's too young." But I meant, *I'm too young*.

Emma said, "Can I have a cigarette?"

"I quit."

"Oh. Okay, that's cool, we'll both—"

"Let's buy some."

"Okay." She got up and bought us a pack of Winstons.

"Can you believe I've got a date tonight?" she said, blowing a smoke ring at the ceiling. She was back on her side of the booth, and she was changing the subject, changing the mood. For me. She takes care of me.

"Who with?"

"Brad. Same guy."

"I thought you broke up."

"We did, then we sort of reunited. Out of inertia. But tonight I'm telling him it's really over."

"What's wrong with him?"

"Nothing."

We smiled, recognizing that we've had this conversation, about different men, a thousand times. "What's wrong with him?" "Nothing." Emma could write a book and call it that.

She squinted, using her thumbnail to peel the label off the Sam Adams bottle. She was wearing her hair up, to show off the enamel earrings I made her for her birthday. Emma thinks her skin is too pale, she thinks her hips are too big, she thinks her hair is too red or too brassy or something—I've never gotten that one. None of this is true. It used to worry me, how out of touch she is with her own looks, but now I just accept it. It's Emma. Anyway, I have a theory that feelings of inadequacy make people kinder and more tolerant of one another. They help keep us civil.

"Are you in love?"

"Am I in *love*?" She smirked, pretending she thought I was still talking about Brad. She rolled bits of label into balls and dropped them in the ashtray. Finally she quit playing and said, "How could I be? I hardly ever see him."

"Why do you see him at all?"

"Well, for one thing, he's helping me with an article I might do about the D.C. art world."

"*Another* article?"

"This is different, freelance. It wasn't even my idea," she said defensively. "The editor at *Capital* liked the piece I did for the paper and suggested I do something like it for them. The state of art in Washington."

"Do you know anything about the state of art in Washington?"

"No." She laughed. "So Mick said he'd help me."

"But doesn't it hurt, Em? Wouldn't it be better if—"

"We're *friends*, Rudy."

"I know, but—*secret* friends."

I wished I hadn't said that. It made her blanch. She lit a cigarette without looking at me and stopped talking.

I thought of the night we finally patched up our quarrel over Curtis. She called me at two in the morning, and I came. I found her sitting on the sofa in the living room of her old Foggy Bottom apartment, crying bitter tears and cursing Peter Dickenson, whom she had just thrown out. She'd gone with him longer, been more serious about him than any man since I've known her. They were even talking about marriage.

She'd really scared me that night, but in some ways this was worse. It wasn't that violent grief, that brokenhearted anger that I'll never forget—this was quiet and invisible. It was stealing parts of her, eating her up.

We ordered more drinks. Emma cheered up, and that cheered me up. I love the slow, warming sensation of my body going numb when I drink. It starts in strange places, my cheeks, my triceps, my thighs, and eventually it seeps into everything. It's no wonder people sleep with anybody when they're drunk. I feel such loving calm, such understanding, as if I'm everybody and everybody is me. I can control it now, but when I was younger I would screw anybody. I mean anybody. After a few drinks.

Just then, sure enough, a couple of guys came over from the bar and hit on us. One was cute. Sergei's is good for lunch, but later in the day it turns into a singles bar. Emma scowled at the two guys, who looked like lawyers, both younger than us. She reached for my hand across the table. "Hey, do you mind? We're trying to break up here. Jeez, the insensitivity of some peno-Americans."

They said, "Heh, heh," and went back to the bar.

We ordered another round. Emma said, "How did it get to be happy hour?"

"Oh, no. Oh, *no*."

"What?"

"Curtis is coming home. I'm supposed to pick him up! Oh, my *God*."

"What time? Take it easy, he can get home by himself. He does it every—"

"The airport. I'm supposed to pick him up at the *airport*."

"Oh, the airport. That's different." She giggled. "What time?"

"Five-fifty."

"Uh-oh. You're in trouble, Rude. It's six o'clock."

I pressed my hands to my eyes, making everything black. Emma's laughter was catching, but mine sounded hysterical.

"What airline?" she asked.

"Delta."

"Okay, sit tight, I'll call National and leave a message. They'll page him—he'll like that. 'Mr. Curtis Lloyd, Mr. Curtis Lloyd, please come to the white courtesy phone.'"

"What will you say?"

"That you're sloshed and can't drive, what else?" I must have looked terrified, because she squeezed my wrist. "*Kidding*. What do you want me to say?"

"Say . . . I'm with Isabel."

"That's good. It's no big deal, he can take the subway to Eastern Market and walk home, can't he?"

"No, he'll take a cab."

"Of course he will," she said in her bland, ironic, Curtis voice. "Don't worry, Rudy, I'll fix it."

But when she came back, she looked worried and amused and sheepish. "You're screwed."

"Why?"

She sat down on my side again. "I had to leave a message."

"So?"

"They've got a new deal, voice mail. So he'll know it was me who called. I mean, he's going to hear *me*, not some page lady, with a message from you. He'll know I called and not you. I should've hung up."

"What did you say?"

"I said we were all here at Sergei's, comforting Isabel. You wanted to go pick him up, but she was in a bad way and we wouldn't let you leave."

"Oh, Em." One lie was bad enough, but that was about three.

"I know, but I got into it and couldn't stop."

I laughed shakily. I knew I was in trouble, though, even if Curtis believed Emma's lie.

The waitress came over and asked if we wanted another round. We looked at each other. All of a sudden I felt wonderful. "What the hell?" we said together. It really was like old times, when we first moved to D.C., and we'd hang out in bars or restaurants and talk for hours, six hours, eight, start at lunch and talk right through dinner. Before I got married.

"Hey, Rude. You're not really afraid of him, are you?" She must've been drunk. She would never have asked me that question sober.

I must've been drunk, too—I didn't mind it. I didn't lie, either. "Sometimes I am, but it's not his fault."

"Why isn't it?"

"Because I'm afraid of everything."

"How come?"

I shrugged.

She said, "Has he ever hit you?"

"*No*. Jesus, Emma!"

"Okay, I just wondered. I'm sorry. No offense."

"Well, now you know."

"Okay."

"Okay."

He had, though, once. Just one time, and it was so long ago, I never thought of it anymore.

"So what are you afraid of?" Emma asked me again.

"Everything."

"What? Gimme a list."

"Let's see. That he'll stop loving me. That we'll never have a child. That if we do have a child I'll ruin its life." I held my face in my hands and stared into my drink. "That one of these days I'll go crazy, kill myself or something. That Isabel will die. That I'll never make anything of my life. That I'll end up like my mother. That my brother's going to kill himself with drugs."

"Shit, Rudy." Emma put her arm around me. "That's enough for now."

I stopped trying to think of things I was afraid of. "Those are just off the top of my head," I said, and we started laughing. I laughed until my drink tasted salty from the tears trickling down my face. "People are watching us," I noticed, blowing my nose on a napkin.

"Now they really think we're lesbians."

We lounged in our booth, smiling around vacantly. We stared at people. We ate some of the free hors d'oeuvres.

"We should go, probably," Emma said.

"Yeah. Don't forget, you've got a date."

"I *did* forget. Shit. I'd better call and tell him the deal's off." She got up, only a little wobbly.

"You're canceling?"

"God, yes. Shape I'm in, I'd either start a fight or propose to him. And either way, I'd jump him first." She went off to the telephone.

I waited, not thinking of anything much. Feeling pretty good. One of the lawyers came back.

"Hey, did your friend run off and leave you?"

"No," I said, "she had to make a phone call."

"Oh, yeah? What's your name?"

"Rudy."

"Hi, Rudy. I'm Simon."

Simon had a sweet smile and a five o'clock shadow. A yellow tie. Definitely a lawyer.

"You're not really gay, are you?"

He looked friendly, and he didn't sound coy or hostile. So I said, "No, we're not. I'm married, though."

"Ah. What a shame." He sat down on Emma's side and folded his hands in his lap. I liked his unaggressive body language. But then he looked away and nodded, lifting his eyebrows. A signal. His friend got up from the bar, scooping up drinks and cigarettes and change, and started to come over. *Emma's going to kill me,* I thought while Simon said, "So, do you two work around here?"

Three things happened at once. Simon's friend sat down next to me, Emma came back, holding two new drinks and frowning, and I saw Curtis at the same time he saw me.

He must've come straight from the airport—he had his Hartman carry-on over his shoulder. He moved toward me slowly, his eyes huge and dark, gleaming with hurt and calculation. I tried to stand up, but the man, Simon's friend, was big and heavy and he didn't know what was going on, he wouldn't move.

"Curtis," Emma said jovially, putting the drinks down, facing him. Making a shield between him and me. "What a nice surprise! So you got my message, great, great. Have a seat? Too bad you missed Isabel, just missed her. These guys . . ." She bit her lips. Her voice dropped to normal; she quit trying. "Who the hell are you guys?"

"Curtis, please don't—" What? His tight, violent smile was paralyzing me.

"Ready to go home?" Polite. Reasonable. Behind the pain in his face, some kind of resigned excitement showed. *I've got you now,* he was thinking.

Simon's friend finally slid out. I got to my feet in slow motion, fumbling for coat, gloves, purse.

"Don't let her drive," Emma warned.

Curtis whirled around. "Don't tell me what to do with my wife." The naked hate between them shocked but didn't surprise me. *Do you really believe Curtis likes Emma?* Eric asked me that once.

Emma reached past Curtis and touched me. "Are you okay?"

"Yes, sure." I tried to laugh, tried to lessen the awfulness. She looked wound up but indecisive. Sparks were all but shooting off her.

"Hey, why don't we all sit down and cool off," she said unexpectedly, and I realized she was afraid—for me. Curtis stood unmoving, silent. I wanted to tell Emma there was nothing to fear from him, I only feared *for* him.

"We're going. 'Bye." I hugged her. "Call me. Don't *you* drive, hear?"

She nodded. Curtis didn't even look at her when he turned me, just a light hand on my back, and made me walk out ahead of him.

Out on the street, I froze for a minute, my mind a blank. I couldn't remember where I'd parked the car. I started toward Wisconsin, then remembered—the lot on K Street. "Oh, no, this way," I said casually, and Curtis turned around with me without a word. But he knew. I was loaded, and he knew it.

He drove.

"I'm sorry, I'm *so sorry* about the airport," I told him, huddling on the cold car seat, shivering because the Jeep's heater hadn't kicked in yet.

Instead of answering, he turned on the radio.

His handsome face looked sharp and clean against the lights flashing past his window. He'll never look old. He'll die with that boyish mouth, that child's hairline. I tried not loving him—just for a second; an experiment. To my horror, it worked. I jerked my head away and stared past the streetlamps at the icy, empty Mall. The heat came on. Even though I turned the fan up high, I never stopped shivering.

At home, I sat on the bed and watched him unpack. Socks and shorts in the hamper, shirts in the pile to the cleaners, shoes on wooden trees, suit on a padded hanger. He has an electric tie rack. I bought it for him for a joke, but he loves it.

I tried again.

"Listen, I'm sorry. Those men in the bar—you *know* that was nothing."

No answer.

"And I *was* with Isabel before, but she left. Before you came." Four hours before. I caught sight of myself in the mirror over the bureau. Red-rimmed eyes, mascara in blotches like paw prints. A mess. I looked drunk, which I was. The hangover was just starting.

"How did it go in Atlanta?" I asked.

"Badly." He turned away and went into the bathroom. He didn't close the door.

"Oh, no!" I called. "What happened?"

"I was going to tell you about it tonight. I thought we'd go out and talk."

Guilt feels like being smothered under a pile of rocks and mortar and pieces of glass. Buried alive. "We can still go. I'll get dressed, it's only eight o'clock."

"I couldn't eat now." He came out of the bathroom in his pajamas and bathrobe—navy blue with white piping and bright tartan plaid. He looked like a Brooks Brothers model, blond and ruddy-cheeked, healthy and urbane. I was surprised and grateful when he sat beside me on the bed.

"I'm sorry." Sometimes if I say it often enough, he relents. "It was my fault. I had too much to drink and forgot the time. Emma just made that up, that we were still with Isabel. She left much earlier. Oh, Curtis—poor Isabel, it was horrible in the doctor's office, sitting there and listening to him—"

"So Emma lied," he interrupted.

"What? Oh, but that wasn't—she didn't—"

"Rudy. I know how much you like her, but I don't think Emma's the good friend you think she is."

"Oh, no—"

"Listen," he said gently. He touched me, and I leaned into him, limp with relief. He forgave me. The world had stopped when he came into Sergei's and saw me, and now it was starting again.

I turned my head to kiss his clean-smelling neck, sliding my arms around his waist, but he held himself stiffly. I drew back.

"I don't want you to see quite so much of her."

I stared stupidly. "You mean Emma?"

"Look what it's doing to you." He touched my smudged cheek with distaste. Even I could smell the cigarette smoke in my hair, my clothes. "I know you've known her for a long time. I don't expect you to drop her."

"Drop her?"

"But I think it would be better if you didn't see her outside the group." He looked into my eyes, cupping my face in his palms. "For your own good, Rudy. In a way, I'm surprised Greenburg hasn't suggested it already."

My mind was spinning. I took hold of his hands. "Eric likes Emma, he'd never tell me that."

He sighed and pulled away.

I tried to keep his hands. "Don't be angry. Don't—"

He got up and went to the door. Turned. "So you won't do what I'm asking. For your sake."

"Stop seeing Emma? She's my best friend!"

"So you won't?"

"Curtis, don't do this. *Please* don't." I could feel the door shutting, me freezing. He would go away, take his love, take everything. "Please," I begged. "Curtis, please."

"Yes or no."

For my sake, he said, but it was cruel. "No, I can't. I'm sorry, please—Emma is my closest friend. Curtis!"

He'd turned and gone out.

I heard his leather slippers on the stairs. He would go down to the kitchen and make a toasted cheese sandwich in the broiler, with low-fat margarine on one side and nothing on the other. He'd eat it at the kitchen table with a glass of 2 percent milk while he skimmed the latest *Time*, *U.S. News*, and *Money*.

I went in the bathroom and took three sleeping pills. I was afraid to take more after the scotch. Three should do it, though. In bed, I pulled the covers over my head. Blackness, please. I needed a meditation to keep everything out, and I chose, *It's starting*. A time of penitence was coming, and only Curtis could say how long it would last. He held the key.

I slipped into a dream about God. He was sitting in a gilded chair, surrounded by vague-faced, worshipful angels. He looked at his watch, a Rolex like Curtis's. "She's late," he said with terrible sadness. "I'm very sorry, but she's late." He wept just, righteous tears. He reached up over his head and pulled the chain to a big Tiffany lamp, and the world went black.

15

Emma

In March I crossed three onerous tasks off my master To Do list. In increasing order of difficulty, I: broke up with Brad once and for all, drove down to Virginia to see my mother, and turned in my resignation at the paper. Actually the last two tied for degree of difficulty.

Just kidding. My mother's not so bad. After she stopped carping about what an idiot I was to quit my job, she was almost nice to me. I think I've figured out the secret to civility between us: only see each other twice a year.

The scariest part of the visit was realizing how much I'm starting to look like her. Or she's starting to look like me—there's a thought. My mother—Kathleen—looks like me if I stayed up for a week, drinking, smoking, shooting smack, and whoring. And worrying. That's what being sixty-five does to you, I guess, because the only pastime on this list my mother actually indulges in (as far as I know) is the last. But at that, she is truly world-class.

Oh, I'm too hard on her, I know. Force of habit. But I'm getting too old to react to her clumsy manipulations and machinations like the sulky, insufferable teenager I used to be. Anyway, I've won. I won a long time ago. I got out of Danville, Virginia; I didn't get married; I didn't go to state college and become a teacher "for something to fall back on," i.e., in case, like hers, my husband left me. Oh, and I developed this charming wiseass persona on purpose to annoy her.

Quitting my job turned out to be harder than I thought it would be. Because of the money. I'd gotten used to having some. I had started to buy things I saw in shop windows—walk by, stop, look, go in, and *buy*. "I'll have that." "I'll take it." This is what it means to be a grown-up, I'd think, flashing my gold Visa, my platinum MasterCard. I sent my mother a VCR for Christmas. I was planning for a new car in the spring, something sporty, maybe a Miata. The tips I left waitresses had gotten positively philanthropical.

But there was one thing I was even sicker of than poverty, and that was my excuse for not writing a novel, my so-called heart's desire: "I don't have time." Never mind that it was true; working for the paper, freelancing on the side, and writing short stories nobody bought had left me pretty much written out by the end of the day. Something had to go. So I've dumped the nine-to-five, kept the freelancing to pay the mortgage, and hung up the short stories. Now we'll see what I'm made of.

I say that with such gusto, such verve. As if I haven't been procrastinating since birth to avoid this very thing. Could it be? Could I be growing up?

No. Unfortunately. The reason is more craven and doesn't do me nearly as much credit. It's Isabel. Over the years she's taught me many lessons, but this is one I really didn't want to learn, not from her, not like this. It's the one about how short life is, and how foolish we would be to waste it.

I try to understand why this happened to her, why not to Rudy or Lee, or me. Why Isabel? She's the best of us. She has the biggest heart. She believes in everything—I don't believe in anything. It's *chance* that this happened to her, isn't it? She says no, there's no such thing as chance, it happened for a reason. What reason? "Maybe I can stand it and you can't," she said to me. But that's nonsense, isn't it?

She ditched that jerk Glass and got a new oncologist. Searle, this one's name is; he started her on antiestrogen therapy, some drug called Megace that made her gain weight and have hot flashes, but otherwise didn't do anything. Now she's trying two new drugs, Arimidex and something else, I can't remember the name, and we've all got our fingers crossed. Get this: at first Isabel wanted to skip the whole medical model and go for self-healing. *Self*-healing. That's your wheatgrass and coffee enemas, Indian sweat tents and acupuncture and hypnosis. Guided imagery. Bio-fucking-feedback.

But I didn't open my mouth. I bit my tongue and did not say one word. Rudy and Lee finally talked her out of it, and apparently Kirby—gay-guy-turned-hetero-heartthrob—did, too. (I'm sorry; that's snide. I apologize, Kirby. Whom I still haven't met. Isabel says there's nothing between them now except friendship. Maybe, but for some reason I don't like him. So what if the reason is jealousy and possessiveness?)

I can't stand it that this is happening to her. When I call, I never know the right thing to say. I feel awkward and stupid, because this thing between us that neither one of us really wants to talk about anyway has gotten so huge, we can't see around it. So I put off calling her, and then whole days go by when I don't even think about her. That's the worst: that I could forget all about my kindest, truest friend, whose life has turned into an absolute nightmare.

No, that's wrong. *My* life would be a nightmare if I were in Isabel's shoes. Who really knows, but it *seems* as if she's getting through it with the same grace that's seen her through the other rotten deals life's handed her. And speaking of Gary—he hasn't called her, hasn't so much as sent a get-well card. Terry wanted to come, fly down from Montreal for a long weekend, but she told him not to. What a nice kid. I've always liked him. Always wished he were about fifteen years older.

Oh, me, me, me. Nothing like a loved one's crisis to really bring home your own self-absorption. Isabel's illness is all relative: relative to me. How will *my* life change if she gets worse instead of better? How will *I* live without her if she dies? Oh, guilt, guilt, guilt. I thought Jews were the ones plagued for life with guilt, not us ex-Catholic agnostics. Lee's Jewish, and she's the most guilt-free, nonneurotic woman I've ever met. Irritating, but nonneurotic. Isabel's situation is just making Lee more efficient and organized. Bossier.

She's not pregnant yet, by the way, but her spirits are good. Lately, instead of calling, she's been sending me E-mails. I guess it's more efficient.

> To: Emma [DeWitt@Dotcom.com]
> From: L.P. Patterson [LeePatt@Dotcom.com]
> Subject: Healing Circle
>
> Emma:
> Just a reminder about Wednesday night, 9:00 to 9:30, EST. I've mentioned it twice to Rudy, but if you speak to her between now and then, would you remind her again? You know how she is. >g<
> Cheers,
> Lee

On Wednesday we're having our second "healing circle" for Isabel. At a prearranged time, everybody—not just the four Graces but her other friends and family across the country, plus any acquaintances so inclined—stops doing whatever they're doing and meditates on Isabel and her recovery. Some people pray, some imagine bad things happening to her cancer cells, some people "send white light," whatever that means. Rudy stares at a candle flame in a dark room and chants things—she told me this. "What things?" I asked, fascinated. "Just things. It's sort of private." Well, hmpf. I was just looking for some guidance. Because I am such a flop at this. It's never mattered much before, the fact that I'm no good at anything New Age, in fact I'm the poster child for Old Age. But now, when I try to pray or chant or send white light and I end up daydreaming about Mick or hot fudge cake or my car inspection, I worry that I'm personally letting Isabel down.

To: Emma [DeWitt@Dotcom.com]
From: L.P. Patterson [LeePatt@Dotcom.com]
Subject: Anniversary

Emma:
It's all set—we can have the Cape Hatteras cottage the second weekend in June. I wanted the third because, as you know, that's the true 10th anniversary of the S.G.'s, but it was already booked. Henry's planning to drive down Sunday late after everyone else leaves, and we'll stay three more days. Might invite another couple. Care to join us? With or without beau—up to you.
Looking forward to Friday night,
Lee

To: Emma [DeWitt@Dotcom.com]
From: L.P. Patterson [LeePatt@Dotcom.com]
Subject: Friday night

Emma:
You're coming to my cocktail party, aren't you? (I ask because you never RSVP'd.) Assuming you are, I have a tiny emergency. Henry and I have an A.I. appointment tomorrow at 3:30. (Our 4th, and this one is it, I'm positive!) So we'll be rushing and may or may not get home in time to pick up the salmon mousse at Fresh Fields. It's on your way—could you do it? Many thanks. It's paid for; all you have to do is pick it up. Meanwhile, guess who's coming to the party and BRINGING A FRIEND?
Hurriedly,
Lee

Ha! Must be Jenny, Lee's mother-in-law. And "BRINGING A FRIEND." This should be good. I love to watch Lee's liberal superego fight it out with her conservative id.

And here I thought the only one suffering anxious moments at

Lee's party was going to be me, trying to act natural around Mick and Sally, the Dracos, *en famille*. My, what a fun night this is going to be.

I won't deny that I was watching the door, and yet somehow I missed Mick's entrance. By the time I saw him, he was leaning in the archway to the sunroom, holding a drink. The setting sun poured in through the jalousie windows like fire, backlighting the food-laden buffet table. Backlighting Mick's tall, straight silhouette. Our eyes met. As they say. I started to smile, but bodies came between us, a knot of chatting people shifting to make room for Lee and her tray of crab puffs. When the way cleared, he was bending down, saying something in his wife's ear.

Sally's shy at parties. She needs a drink or two before she ventures away from his side and talks to people on her own.

How do I know that? He told me. I forget in what context. An innocent one, though. All our conversations are innocent, and greasy, sleazy Murray's is still our trysting place. He doesn't help me with my coat, doesn't take my arm when we cross the street. Except for when our knees accidentally bump under the table, we never touch. But I am having the hottest, riskiest, most intense love affair of my life. I think it's the same for him.

Lee glided up. "Thanks for bringing the mousse, Em. It wasn't any trouble, was it?" She looked hostessy in a floor-length skirt and a silk tank; Emanuel Ungaro, she'd told me in an E-mail.

"Oh, no," I said, "it was right on my way. Hey, you look great. So does your house."

"You, too! That's quite a suit."

I guess she meant it, sarcastic understatement being more my style than Lee's. But now that I was here, I was feeling a little unsure of my choice: no blouse under a low-cut cocktail jacket with a matching midthigh skirt. It showed a lot more skin than I'm used to revealing. "Well, it's a cocktail party," I said defensively. "Where else can a girl show off her assets?"

"The beach?" Lee laughed, pleased with her little joke. "Oh, Emma, something I've been meaning to mention—we can't talk about it now, but I just want you to be thinking about it."

"What?"

She glanced over her shoulder and lowered her voice. "How do you feel about asking Sally to join the group? The women's group. The Graces," she specified when all I could do was stare. "Does it sound like a good idea to you?"

I was speechless.

"You've met her a couple of times now. Do you like her? I think she's really nice. And smart, and interesting. And different enough from the rest of us to bring something new to the group." Diversity was important to Lee. Once she vetoed a woman I knew at the paper because we had the same job. "Then we'd have *two* journalists," she'd argued. "It's redundant. Don't we want variety?"

Sally would add variety, I could see that. A young mother, a Southerner, a primary breadwinner: all unique traits. The trouble with Sally, I've thought more than once, is that there's nothing wrong with her.

I fell back on a craven but obvious excuse. "Well, but don't you think it's not the best time to be thinking of a new member? Because of Isabel? Where is she, by the way?"

"She said she might be late. No, I don't think it's—"

"Hey, gorgeous, you look good enough to eat." Henry smothered me in a huge bear hug. Frowning at the interruption, Lee absently took his arm and leaned against him. Mutt and Jeff. He could put her in his pocket. They're so cute together, so . . . unliberated or something. If he *did* put her in his pocket, neither of them would think a thing of it.

"I don't necessarily see that, not at all," Lee said to me. "As soon as they hit on the right drug with Isabel, the worst will be behind her. Then I should think it would be good for her *and* the group to have someone new to get to know. And she's met Sally," she added, dropping her voice again. "I asked her, and she said she likes her."

"You asked her? You asked Isabel about—"

"Not about joining, just if she liked her. And she said yes."

"Oh." But Isabel likes everybody, she's like God that way. "Oh, Lee, I don't know. I don't have anything against Sally, it's just that—I'm still not sure it's a good time for us to be taking on somebody new."

"Well, I don't agree, but if that's your opinion. I'll ask Rudy what she thinks, of course."

You do that. "Sure," I nodded vigorously. Rudy wouldn't let me down. "And Isabel, of course."

"Naturally."

She went off to do hostess duties. Henry hung around, shooting the breeze with me, telling a couple of his cornball dirty jokes. Then he said, "Y'know, Em, I hope I'm wrong, but . . ." He fluffed the carpet with the toe of his shoe.

"What?"

"I'm not sure Lee's being that realistic about Isabel. Her condition. I don't say anything, because I don't want to discourage her. And miracles do happen." He bent his head, rubbing the back of his neck. "What do you think?"

"I think we're all trying hard to handle it in our own ways. Lee's an optimist, she's coping with it optimistically." A more polite way of saying she's in denial. "Rudy's scared to death, but hiding it."

"What about you?"

I looked at him frankly. "I'm a pessimist."

"Yeah." His rugged face softened with sympathy. "I'm just scared Lee might get blindsided. You know, if something bad happens. She's not gonna be prepared."

"I know." Neither am I. If something bad happens. "Well," I said, "good thing she's got you to take care of her." I sidled closer. "So, Mister Horn o' Plenty. Mister hunka burning love. How's it going in the fertility department these days?"

Henry is such a guy, he loves this routine I've been doing since Lee told us about his sperm count. I think he's relieved to be able to talk about the problem, and before, we couldn't. Isn't that ridiculous? It was a taboo subject when it might've been a *low* sperm count, but now it's okay.

After a few more nitwit sperm jokes, he sobered and said, "The timing's perfect for us, considering what all else is goin' on. Lee's counting on it to work this time. Even if it doesn't, we've got two more shots. Being pregnant, you know, it would get her through. If . . ."

"It'll work," I said, not wanting to hear about *if*. "Because you are awesome, Patterson. You are so damn potent, you'll probably have triplets. All sons."

He threw back his head and laughed. And blushed. Oh, I do love Henry. He's like a big, sleepy bear, calm and sturdy, dependable as dawn. He's good to Lee, and he tones down her anal retentiveness like . . . I don't know what. A good sedative. Lee's live-in Seconal prescription.

The party got a little louder, a little sloppier. Not much; Lee's parties never get out of hand. She'd stocked it with all her preschool and early-childhood-development cronies: smart, interesting, good-hearted women whose husbands make more money than they do. I schmoozed with the ones I'd met before, introduced myself to a couple of new ones. Lee's parties are notoriously low on single men, I'm not sure why. My only theory is it's because her friends are so wholesome, they never get divorced.

Tonight I wasn't trolling for single men, of course. Even though I never looked for him, I always knew where Mick was. Radar. We circulated, but always kept the width of a room between us, a clutch of moving bodies. Me, deliberately; him—I couldn't say. But what a painful, addictive game I was playing. It's true that I hurt all over because of the hopelessness of this infatuation, but at the same time I'd never felt so alive.

As usual, Rudy and Curtis arrived late. He may be a schmuck—

no, he's definitely a schmuck—but there's no denying that Curtis Lloyd is a good-looking man. In that Earnest Young Nazi mold, but still. And Rudy, well, besides being beautiful, she's got this effortless model-chic that makes normal people feel gawky and flat-footed and too made-up when they're around her. People like me. I waved to her, hoping she'd extricate herself from Curtis and come over alone. No way. I should've known; he hardly ever lets her out of his sight at parties. Either he doesn't trust her or he's afraid to be by himself. Probably both.

Rudy and I kissed cheeks, while Curtis and I managed to hug without actually touching. "Where's Isabel?" Rudy asked after some small talk.

"Not here yet. Lee said she said she might be late."

"I can't wait to meet this Kirby."

"Me, too."

I can't talk to Rudy when Curtis is around. It's like trying to talk on the phone through glass while the prison guard watches. The only thing worse is talking to Curtis when Rudy's not around.

That's why I could've killed her when she said, "Oh, there's Allison Wilkes, I haven't seen her in ages. I'll be right back," and walked away.

With anyone else I didn't particularly care for, I might've said, "Alone at last," at a time like this, on the theory that getting the worst out of the way early, even if you do it sarcastically, helps dissipate the tension. But I keep my true feelings for Curtis to myself—that time at Sergei's was an exception. Rudy says she's not afraid of him, but I am. Slightly. Because he's creepy. So I'm civil and one-dimensional and deliberately dull with him, practically zombielike in my self-restraint. Pretty admirable, when what I'd really enjoy is punching him out. Anything for Rudy.

Empty-handed—Curtis doesn't drink in public; might lose control—he bounced on his toes a little, surveying the crowd. Checking to see if anybody here could do him any good, I was sure. He's a born politician, except for one thing. He doesn't like people.

"Well, Emma," he roused himself to say. "Rudy tells me you've quit your job."

I said that was true.

"And you're all set to write a book. A novel." He laughed his hard, sharp, machine gun laugh, *Ha ha ha ha.*

"Is that funny? You find that amusing?" I kept smiling, smiling, the hostility only coming out of my eyes. He didn't bother to answer. My anger was out of all proportion, but he's like a marksman, an archer with perfect aim. With one shot, he'd hit me in my tender spot.

"How's *your* new job?" I countered. "Lobbying. That seems so right for you, Curtis. Really a"—I pretended to hunt for the word—"a *noble* profession."

He only smirked. My arrow hadn't even nicked the target. I thought the little game was over, but he said, "So, what is your book about?"

Ah, the question a writer hates most. How do you suppose he knew that? "It's still in the incubation stage," I said, still smiling. Talk about understatement. "I'd really rather not discuss it." Across the room, I could see Mick talking to Henry. Laughing with him, kind of bobbing and weaving the way men do. Their new friendship surprises me a little. They're so different from each other.

"They say you should always write about what you know best," Curtis was telling me.

"Yeah, well. Up to a point."

"So your story would probably be . . ." He frowned and pursed his lips, thinking. "Promiscuous spinster's dark dreams of adultery . . . something like that?" I turned to stare at him. He raised his blond brows innocently, half smiling. His eyes flicked up and down over my body, slowing down contemptuously at the areas of exposed skin.

Guilt and fury are a lethal combination. My neck and throat

flushed with heat. I loathed him, I despised that knowing look on his smug face. I knew if I opened my mouth, I would curse him.

"Well. Think I'll go find my wife. You take care, Em." He sauntered away, hands in his pockets.

On the way to the bathroom, I nodded, smiled, spoke casually to people. But once inside I locked the door and gripped the sides of the sink, staring at myself in the mirror. Curtis saw this stricken face? No wonder he'd looked so satisfied. "Don't fall for it," I warned, fumbling in my bag for mascara and lipstick. This was what he'd wanted: me to feel hurt and betrayed by Rudy.

But how could she tell him my secret? Not that I'd ever told her not to. I didn't think I had to! I thought she treated my confidences the same way I treated hers, sacredly, respectfully. "Promiscuous spinster"—oh, please. To hell with that, that only proves he's as sick as I've always said he was. But, oh, Rudy, how could you tell him about Mick?

Somebody knocked.

Shit. "Just a sec!" Give me a minute, for Pete's sake. I looked as if I'd been crying.

"Sorry, no hurry!"

I recognized the bright, convivial voice of Sally Draco.

Perfect.

I smiled. Grinned. Threw back my head and mimed delighted laughter. My party face. Smoothing down my skirt, I made a decision to confront Rudy later, not tonight, not here, while we were both drinking. We did that once. Never again.

Sally was leaning in the hallway, gazing out across the crowded living room, and she turned when she heard the door open. "Oh, hi! It's you."

The second drink must've kicked in; she really looked glad to see me. In fact, if I hadn't folded my arms, I think she'd have embraced me. Which would've been excessive, considering I'd only met her twice in my life, both times at Lee's dinner parties.

"How've you been, Emma? I keep meaning to call you, but you know how it is—"

"Oh, yeah," I said weakly, "working *and* having a child, that must really keep you busy. Well, so how's the job going?" I asked when it looked like she wanted a real chat, not a hit-and-run.

She rolled her eyes. "Let's just say, it's not my life's work."

"No?" What was she, a paralegal? I can never remember people's jobs. No, she was a paralegal when Mick met her; now she was something in the Labor Department.

"But I guess only one person to a family gets to do his life's work." She laughed with rueful good nature, but I know passive aggression when I hear it. "Oh, that is a *gorgeous* suit, where did you get it?"

So we did girl talk while I checked her out and returned the obligatory compliment on her little white cocktail dress. She was an attractive woman, no question, with straight, sleek yellow hair, cut short and styled in a way women admire more than men. Her wide-spaced eyes and strong cheekbones made her face exotic. The mouth was enormous, but not happy. No, it was worried. But sensual—her whole face was sensual. It eclipsed her body, which seemed oddly asexual in comparison; you hardly noticed it.

"Mick tells me you're almost finished your article. I'm glad he could help you with it."

"Oh, yes, he's been great. I couldn't have done it without him."

"When does it come out?"

"It's hard to say. Maybe June. Whenever they decide to print it."

"I can't wait to read it," she said, eyes big and sincere.

God knows I've tried to be objective. I've asked myself, would I like Sally Draco if Mick didn't exist? If I met her at a party and we just started talking, would I want to be her friend? And the honest answer is no, but not for any good reason; I mean, she's not Satan or anything. She exudes a lot of warmth you're not sure is real, and the longer you talk to her, the less authentic that initial burst of self-confidence seems. She watches carefully, hopefully, waiting for something. Behind the big eyes, I see big need.

Our conversation, such as it was, petered out. She went in the bathroom and I drifted away, thinking about her. Why did she marry Mick? They're total opposites: he's real, she's not. (Not that I'm biased.) He rarely talks about her, and then only in the most politically correct generalities. Which is no more than I would expect of him. It's frustrating, but I like his discretion, his courtliness. But he's no Mr. Rochester; I think he'd have told Jane about the madwoman in the attic on the first date.

I saw Lee in the middle of the living room, holding a plate of miniature lamb kebobs and looking pained. I followed her gaze—she was glaring through the doorway into the kitchen.

Aha. Jenny was here, with A FRIEND. You could tell they were friends because they were holding hands.

"My, what a striking couple." I couldn't resist.

Lee closed her eyes for a second. "Come with me, okay?"

"Sure." I even went first. I like Jenny.

Henry was talking to her and her *friend* while he took little quiches out of the oven and put them on a plate. "Oh, Lee!" Jenny exclaimed when she saw us. "Lee and her friend. Oh, look, Phyllis, it's Lee, my lovely daughter-in-law"—and she scooped Lee up in a terrific embrace, lifting her completely off the floor. I got a similar treatment, although I could see my name escaped her. She can't quite keep the Graces straight, but she loves us, one and all.

"Emma," I said helpfully, offering my hand to small, handsome, fiftyish Phyllis. Jenny was doing a little cradle-robbing. Phyllis sparkled her eyes at me and said how do you do.

The tip-off that Jenny was smitten was that she was wearing a dress—a first in my experience. A nice dress, and technically it fit her, but the sight was so incongruous, she made me think of a guy in drag. Jenny is five-eleven—six feet in her work boots, she loves to say—and what they call big-boned. She dyes her hair dark brown and wears it up in an old-fashioned pompadour. Except for the southern accent, she reminds me of Julia Child.

"Lee, this is Phyllis Orr, my very good friend." Except she said, "Mah verra good *free*-in," in her slow Carolina drawl, like a female Jesse Helms. Henry only has a shadow of it.

"Well, how do you do? It's lovely to meet you, just lovely," Lee burbled, overcompensating. "Welcome to our home. Yes, indeed, any friend of Jenny's . . ." She tapered off, hearing herself. Henry and I gave each other tickled looks. "And how did you two meet? I mean if that's not too—you don't have to—I was just wond—"

"Phyllis manages my apartment building," Jenny said, in a tone of wonder at the unexpectedness of life's gifts. "Somebody tried to break into my place—I told you, Henry, remember?—but all they did was crack the dead bolt. She fixed it." She gave Phyllis a playful but proud jab on the shoulder.

"Well, isn't that something. How about that, and you've been friends ever since," Lee marveled. "I think that's wonderful, I really do."

Phyllis, a slight, wiry, darkly attractive woman who looked as if she'd know her way around a dead bolt, looked at Lee curiously.

"Look who's talking about *friends*," Jenny boomed. "Tell Phyllis about your group, Lee honey, go on. Lee started a club just for women, *years* ago, Phil, and they're still going strong. Emma here is one of her members." *One o' huh membahs*. "How many years have y'all been together now?"

Lee said, "It'll be ten years in June."

"Oh, is that right," Phyllis said.

"We're going to Cape Hatteras to celebrate," I threw in. Lee's family has a cottage they rent out for all but two weeks in June and September. The Saving Graces have celebrated four of their nine anniversaries there so far, so it's a sporadic tradition.

"Well, I'll swan, isn't that marvelous." *Idn that mahvelous*.

Jenny rested an affectionate elbow on top of Henry's shoulder.

Patterson & Son looked great together, both of them so uncharacteristically dressed up this evening. Lee glanced around, rubbing her hands together and smiling anxiously. A couple of her education friends had come in for ice or something, and now they were gathering around, listening in.

"When I was your age—Henry, when was that?" Jenny demanded.

He thought. "Late 70s."

"That's right—twenty years ago when I was your age, I had just about had it up to here with living with women in a group. Did you know I used to live in a commune?" she said to me. "Out in the country near Asheville, *beautiful* place. That's where Henry grew up. I used to worry about him not having a daddy—his was killed in Vietnam, you know—but look how he's turned out." She got his neck in an armlock and squeezed.

"Huh!" I said—as if I hadn't heard these reminiscences from Lee, Henry, and Jenny herself several times already.

"Quiche?" Lee held the plate under her mother-in-law's nose hopefully.

"Women united! There's nothing we can't do when we work together. Right, Emma? Lee honey? Oh, what a bunch we were, though, back then. Free love, and no men allowed. Does y'all's group have a name? We called ourselves the Viragos."

"But you know," Lee pointed out amid the laughter, "we're—ha ha!—not that kind of a group." She lifted her hand to Henry, the one here with the penis, as if to say, Look: living proof I'm heterosexual.

"And radical? Oh, my goodness, we'd demonstrate at the drop of a hat, as long as it was for something militant. I remember one time, we went to an antiwar rally in Raleigh, and named ourselves 'Lesbians for Mao' on the spot. My girlfriend and I took off our shirts and nursed our babies on the Capitol steps. Henry, you've seen that picture."

"Yep. I was eight years old."

"You were *not*," Lee said, aghast.

"Oh, but it didn't last. Couldn't, I guess, and plus we were all so young. We left, one by one, and I hear there's not even a farm there anymore. Out in that pretty place. You remember Sue Ellen Rich?" Jenny asked Henry. "I got a note from her last Christmas—we still keep up—and she says there's a Saturn dealership there now. Mm mmm." She shook her head mournfully; Phyllis patted her arm and said, "Aww."

"We're not very political," Lee said brightly. "We just have dinner."

"But you're still *together*, that's what I envy. Ten years, and you're still a group. Y'all still love each other."

"Oh, we do," I agreed, sliding my arm around Lee's waist. "We still love each other *so much*." At the last second Lee figured out what I was going to do—kiss her on the mouth—and jerked her head away in a panic. All I got was cheek.

"Well, I'd better pass these," she muttered, sidling out of my affectionate grasp. "Before they get cold. Excuse me?" Always polite. But the look she threw me on her way out glittered with homicidal longing.

"I'm so sorry we're late. Kirby dropped me off in front," Isabel said breathlessly. "He's parking the car." Lee started to take her jacket, but she said, "I think I'll keep it." She spied me. "Hi, you," she said, and I gave her a soft, one-armed hug. She felt good, exactly like she always did—not breakable or anything.

Rudy came striding over, beaming with gladness, and wrapped her up in a long, strong Rudy-hug. "I was worried, I thought you'd never get here."

"No, I'm fine, just couldn't get organized."

"How *are* you?" Lee demanded, taking both of Isabel's hands and staring intently into her eyes.

"You *look* wonderful," Rudy said.

That was partly true, partly false. Isabel had on a great dress, the kind that reminds us why basic black is a classic, and she was wearing her hair in a new style that really flattered her. But her complexion was off, too yellow or something, and her eyes looked too big. She claimed she hadn't gained or lost a single pound on the new drugs, but then, why was she slightly puffy-looking around the jaw and throat? Not much; anyone who didn't know her probably wouldn't even notice. But I could hardly see anything else. I monitor her these days like a mother with a sick child. We all do. She hates it.

"How do you *feel*?" Lee persisted, still doing the eye contact thing.

"Fine, great, couldn't be better. Your house looks so pretty." Isabel glanced around, withdrawing her hands. "That's a new mirror, isn't it? I'd give anything to have your taste, Lee. How do you do it?"

O-kay. Even Lee got that message: *We're not talking about my health*. So we four stood in the middle of the living room in a tight, protective circle, laughing and chattering about nothing, Isabel's pretty earrings, my great new shoes, Lee's plans for Passover, was that Obsession Rudy was wearing?—until even I was seduced into forgetting that something dark and menacing had settled over our precious solidarity and changed us forever.

Kirby arrived. Isabel introduced him to Rudy and me—Lee had already met him—with none of the watchful, oh-I-hope-you-like-him anxiety I'd have felt in her situation. And he was kind of an anxiety-inducing guy. He towered over us, although he couldn't have weighed more than 150, 155, soaking wet. Virtually bald; sharp, bony features; stoop-shouldered. Gawky. There was nothing birdlike about him, though; he looked stringy and tough, athletic in spite of the gauntness. His eyes dominated his priest's face, soft brown and sad.

I just said, "Hi, how are you," and kept quiet. We formed a little knot in the sunroom, we four and Kirby, and had a light, semistiff, getting-to-know-you chat. He didn't say much either, although he wasn't aloof or creepily silent. He had to know we were checking him out. Funnily enough, Lee claimed she liked him, and she's more possessive of Isabel than any of us. But she's also famous for her poor judgment of character (witness Sally, not that I'm prejudiced), so her endorsement meant nothing to me. Frankly, I was disposed not to like him, but I was trying to be objective for Isabel's sake.

It wasn't anything he said, and if I hadn't been watching like a cat at a mousehole, I wouldn't even have known it was anything he did. Not that he hovered—it was more like he *guarded* Isabel. A body language thing. And something else—Lee had taken all the chairs out of the room for more space; Kirby vaporized for a few seconds, then reassembled, as it were, holding a kitchen stool, which he placed behind Isabel all but invisibly—the whole transaction had the unobtrusive feel of good magic. In the same way, he brought her a glass of club soda with a lemon slice. Then he made her a plate from the buffet table, and frowned sadly, playfully, until she began to nibble from it. He was like a guardian angel. Inconspicuously benevolent.

It would've been easy to write him off as weird because of his looks, or ghoulish because of the way he'd attached himself to a woman who was, at the least, seriously ill. And I could see why Isabel had thought at first that he was gay; not because he was effeminate, but because he was different, he fit no type. Under the strangeness, though, I came to a realization that he was gentle. I decided to trust him. After half an hour, I felt delighted for Isabel. A man less like Gary Kurtz she couldn't have found without advertising.

He suggested we go sit in the living room, and by now I knew it was because he thought she'd be more comfortable there. As we dispersed, Isabel hung back in the doorway and buttonholed me.

"Well?"

"Well, what?" She made an impatient face, and I laughed. "I like him, I like him."

"Do you? Really, Em?"

I can't tell you how it made me feel, knowing Isabel cared what

I thought of her boyfriend. It was like—the pope clearing his blind date with me first. I was really moved. Isabel is *my* mentor, although neither of us would ever say that out loud, and certainly we'd never use that word. She approves of *me*, not the other way around.

"Of course I like him, who wouldn't? But"—I couldn't resist asking—"what happened to 'just friends'?"

"But we are friends. That's exactly what we are."

"Oh? Have you told him that?"

She smiled slightly, eyes downcast.

"He's in love with you, Is."

"If he ever was, that's over now."

"Why?"

She didn't answer.

"How come? You mean because you got sick again? Well, if he's that— "

"Emma, it's complicated now, that's all. You must admit it's complicated."

"Everything's complicated, Isabel. You're telling me Kirby only likes you when you're glowing with health?"

"No, that's not what I'm saying." She looked shocked. "You really don't understand."

I had a brainstorm. "You're doing it," I realized.

"I'm doing what?"

"*You're* the one who's pulling back—because you're sick. It's not Kirby at all." What a relief, especially since I'd just decided I trusted him.

Isabel stared at me with abstracted eyes, thinking it over. She shook her head, going back to, "No, it's more complicated than that. Really."

"Well, if you say so. But you want to keep a clear head, Is." Amazing how cocky I can get about other people's business after a little encouragement. "It's true I've only met him once, but Kirby doesn't strike me as a guy who can't stand complications. He doesn't look like a deserter, in other words."

Isabel started to say something, but Lee interrupted. "Movies!" she chirped, and she waved the dreaded video camera. "Everybody in the living room, Henry wants to take us all on the couch."

I laughed.

Lee frowned. "What?"

"Nothing." I've never known anybody as oblivious to double entendre.

Henry was such a mensch to put up with this. Candid shutterbuggery was one of Lee's most annoying amusements. It was bad enough when she did it, but when she dragged him into it, too, he proved he's a saint.

We four squeezed onto the damn sofa. I had Isabel on one side, Rudy on the other. Rudy wasn't drunk, but she was feeling no pain. She mugged for the camera, made faces, pretended to stick her tongue in my ear. I didn't want to laugh—I was mad at her—but she made me. I saw Curtis milling among the party guests who were watching us. He didn't laugh with the others; he didn't even smile. That helped me make up my mind.

I'd been stupid and naive to think Rudy would keep my secrets from Curtis. Grow up, Emma. Husbands and wives tell each other things. Marriage supersedes friendship, even marriage to a prick. I wasn't angry with her anymore, I wouldn't make an issue of it, wouldn't even bring up the subject. That's what he wanted me to do. Screw him. I wasn't driving a wedge between Rudy and me to spite myself.

I caught his eye. While he watched, I put my arm around Rudy and gave her a smacking kiss on the temple. Take that, jerkoff.

It wasn't a total victory, though. Because of Curtis, I'd have to watch what I told Rudy about Mick from now on. Thinking of that made me angry all over again.

* * *

"Hi."

"Hello."

All night I'd felt like a bird circling a thicket of prickly bushes, unable to light because of the thorns. Lee's back patio was a wide, soft meadow I'd spied at last with my bird's eye, and Mick was there waiting for me.

Well. I don't know if he was waiting for me. He was just there, smoking a cigarette beside the tastefully faded, Boston ivy–covered stockade fence that separated the Pattersons' house from its neighbor. He wasn't even alone; at the bottom of the yard other guests, three or four men and one woman, laughed and drank and smoked cigars around a rusting swing set as old as the house. It was warm and cloudy, the moon only a smudge in the gray, starless sky. Unlike mine, unlike Mick's, Lee's neighborhood was quiet on Saturday nights.

"Doesn't feel much like home, does it?" I said, and he smiled, moving back a step, inviting me to stand next to him on the last bit of concrete before the grass started. I smiled, too, but I looked down at my feet so he wouldn't see. Euphoria was making my chest tickle. It was alarming, this tension between us. It meant everything was true, everything I had hoped and dreaded.

"I'm surprised that you smoke."

He looked at the burning tip of his cigarette with interest. "Somebody gave it to me. I don't. Once in a blue moon."

"I do, but only with Rudy."

"Want one? I could get you one."

"No." I laughed—euphoria again.

Bugs smacked into the light over the patio. A couple of yards down, somebody's dog barked out of boredom. A plane droned overhead, invisible. Gradually, even though we didn't talk, we began to relax. We were spinning a web around us, making a cocoon. We did this at Murray's, too, so we knew how. But still, I was amazed. How easy.

"My article's almost finished," I said. "Nothing but the final run-through left, and some fact-checking."

He nodded. He didn't say, "Good," I noticed. Finishing the article for *Capital* on the D.C. art world meant I wouldn't have any more excuses to call him at his studio or meet him for coffee and ask questions. There would be no legitimate excuse to stay in touch now. Except friendship. Secret friendship, as Rudy had been good enough to point out. Which more or less negated the legitimacy.

"Thank you for your help," I said formally. "I couldn't have done it without you."

"I didn't do anything."

"That's not true. I wouldn't have known who to talk to and who to keep away from if you hadn't told me. I wouldn't even have known where to start." The *Cap* editor told me to slant the story from the viewpoint of an art know-nothing, a good thing for me, since that's the only way I could have written it.

"You're a reporter," Mick said, "you'd have figured it out."

"Why don't you just say, 'You're welcome'?"

He ducked his head, smiling. "You're welcome."

"Course, they may not like it. No guarantees. They might even turn it down."

"Well, then you can say it was all my fault."

"Oh, don't worry."

This was a little bit of disingenuity on my part. I loved the way the piece had turned out; if they rejected it, I'd be astonished. But I'm nothing if not self-deprecating. It's a form of bet hedging, keeping hope firmly in the middle range so disappointment can't hurt too much. At least not in public.

Through the closed patio doors, we watched the slow-mo shifting of the guests from bar to table, group to group. Their mouths moved, inaudible except for the occasional whoop of laughter. Mick's wife was deep in conversation with Curtis Lloyd, I saw, and my mind spun off in a symmetrical fantasy that they fell deeply in love, left their spouses, and ran off together to Ibiza.

"I spoke to your friend Isabel," Mick said.

"But you've met her before." Here, in fact, at Lee's last dinner party.

He nodded. "But we've never really talked. We did tonight, a little. I like her very much."

"You couldn't not."

He watched me. "It's hard," he said.

Once, at Murray's, I started to tell him how scared I was, and I ended up in tears. Which I *hate*, I would rather eat dirt than let anybody see me cry. So now he was being diplomatic, he thought, showing his sympathy but not saying anything to set me off.

He said, "Lee told Sally about the healing circle, and Sally told me."

"Did you do it?"

"I did," he nodded. "Didn't you?"

"Of course. Sort of. Where were you?" I tried to picture him and Sally hovering around a candle, chanting in harmony.

"On the subway, coming back from a drawing class. I didn't remember until about quarter to ten."

"What did you do?"

"Well, you know. I meditated. What did you do?"

It was so nice to be talking like this. With Rudy and Lee it had seemed too private, and of course with Isabel it was out of the question. "Well," I said, "I *tried* to meditate, but I'm not very good at it. How do you shut your mind off? Mine keeps jumping around."

"I don't know if I really meditated," he said—trying to make me feel better. "I just thought about her. I closed my eyes and . . . wished her well."

"That's what I did, too. I *wished her well*."

A woman I didn't know opened the patio door and peered out into the semidark. Somebody—Lee, undoubtedly—had turned off

Henry's Drifters tape and put on Stephane Grappelli; the jazzy, staccato sound shattered the quiet, like driving by a playground at recess. The woman smiled, decided against coming out, and pulled the door shut. Silence rolled back.

We were quiet, too. Except when I slipped my shoes off and Mick asked if I wanted to go inside and sit. "No," I said, "it's too nice. Unless you do."

"No." He looked at me then. Looked at my body. Something he usually takes pains to avoid, or so it seems to me.

How is it that some men can look at you and make you feel like the sexiest woman in the world, and other men can look at you and make you feel like mashing your spike heel through their instep? With Mick, I was suddenly aware of everything about myself. A fantasy kept intruding on my restless attempts to make small talk, a fantasy that I was holding him. Standing on tiptoes, my arms around his shoulders, leaning into him. It made my mouth dry up, it made me forget what I was saying. My clothes felt too small, or too intimate. Too revealing. I was showing a lot of skin, and I wanted him to have it. I wanted to give myself to him.

I put my drink down on the wrought-iron plant stand. This wasn't like flirting with some cute guy at a party. What I felt was a dangerous lust that could destroy lives. The disaster potential sobered me up like a plunge into cold water.

"What are you working on these days?" I asked, pleased with my assertive, no-nonsense tone.

"Something new. Some watercolor portraits. Come and see them," he invited. "Anytime. Come anytime, Emma."

And there we were, right back where we had been.

I hedged. "That would be nice. I'd like to. Someday."

He never asked me how my writing was going, because a long time ago I had asked him not to. "Nine times out of ten, that's the last thing I want to talk about," I'd told him. "What's to say, anyway? It's going fine, it's going lousy. Either way, it's a conversation stopper." But now I wanted to tell him something, and it was my own fault that I had to bring it up first.

"I'm having trouble with my writing," I said. Yes, that bit of candor amazed me, too. So unwonted. "The thing I'm working on isn't going well. I've been thinking, quitting the paper might have been a mistake."

"No. I don't think it was."

"Well . . . ," I said, so he'd keep going. So far he'd said exactly what I wanted to hear.

"In any case, it's much too soon to tell. How long has it been?"

"A month."

"Not long enough."

"How long will it be before I know it's a mistake?"

"Such an optimist," he said, smiling. "A year. Minimum. Two years would be better."

"How long did it take before you knew you hadn't made a mistake?"

"I still don't know it."

"I wouldn't have done it if you . . . You inspired me," I said with a lopsided smile. "I wouldn't have done it if I hadn't met you. So you get some of the blame when I pancake."

"You won't. You'll be good."

"How do you know?"

"Because. You have a strong voice. For one thing."

"You mean a loud voice."

"And a strong heart. You're alive."

I am with you, I thought.

"You have a—I don't know what to call it. An attitude, and it's going to appeal to people, smart people."

Good thing it was dark, because I actually blushed. "I would give anything if that were true," I admitted, a little breathless. "But I haven't even figured out what I should write *about* yet."

"That'll come. You want everything now."

"I do, I hate to wait. Am I going to make it? Is this going to work? Will I be a success? I want to know it all *now*."

"What if the answer was no, and you knew it? What would you change?"

I shook my head.

"For me," he said, "I knew painting was what I should do when I realized it was the *only* thing I wanted, even if I never succeeded. That was the test. It isn't a question of what other people think, it's—*my* process. Watching myself get better, understanding things that used to be complete mysteries to me. Moving. Changing."

I nodded a lot. Talk like this makes me feel exhilarated and worried and cheered up and inadequate. I take it in and think about it later.

It confirmed one thing, though, something I'd suspected for some time. Mick's more grown up than I am.

I said, "Well, anyway. I wanted to tell you, if I hadn't met you, I probably wouldn't have quit my job. That seemed like taking a big chance to me. What it must've been to you—I didn't appreciate it before. Now I do. I admire you."

He looked down; all I could see was the top of his head. He reached around to his back pocket, and for an awful second I thought he was getting his handkerchief, because he was crying. I felt stupid, but relieved, when he pulled out his wallet and said, "Want to see a picture of Jay?"

His son was beautiful, of course. What else? A towheaded blond with pink cheeks and a goofy, angel smile. "He looks like you," I said. "But I don't know why. None of his features . . ."

"No. People always say he looks like Sally."

"Yeah, but there's something, something . . ." Jay was building a snowman with Dad in the front yard. I recognized the narrow gray town house in the background because, God help me, I once drove past it. On purpose. I wanted to see where Mick lived, I just wanted to fill in that one harmless blank. In the picture, Jay had on so many clothes—blue quilted snowsuit, muffler, a cap with earflaps, soggy wool mittens, clumpy yellow boots—he looked incapable of movement, rooted to the spot with the three snow blobs stacked beside him. My mother's got a picture of me in the same getup, a classic kid pose; I'm holding my sled by a rope, and the little boy who lived two doors down is standing behind me, bigger, older, a tricky look in his eye. But I have no recollection of the event, the day. Will Jay look at this photo one day and not remember anything about it?

"Oh, Mick, he's lovely. Six?"

"Five and a half, he'll be six in December."

"Did you always want children?"

"Not really. Jay was . . . a surprise." I looked up. His face had grown still, inward. He was choosing his words with care. "I never thought anyone else's life could mean more to me than my life. I think Jay's happy. I think he is. His innocence is what scares me the most. I want to protect him, and I know I can't." His low voice dropped lower. "Emma, I couldn't do anything that would hurt Jay. No matter how much I wanted to. No matter . . ."

He let that hang. I handed him his photograph back, with nothing to say. Message received.

It was a relief, really. Like a child, I function better when somebody sets limits. Now that I know the rules, I'll follow them to the letter. *What were you thinking?* I was already asking myself.

The patio door slid open. There was a new innocence in the way we turned at the sound. Sally came toward us, with Lee behind her. Mick appeared to wait until his wife was beside him before he slipped the photo of his son back in his wallet. More blamelessness on display.

We chatted—we women. Mick didn't talk. I felt numb and light, barely there. Lee said Sally wanted to fix me up with a man in her office. Lawyer, late forties, divorced, works for the general counsel. "Now, don't say no without even thinking about it, Em, because he really sounds nice, he—"

"Okay."

Lee blinked. "Hm?"

"Thanks, Sally. Give him my number, tell him to call me."

She looked as surprised as Lee. My reputation preceded me. "I sure will," she said. She took Mick's upper arm in both hands and leaned on him, rested her head on his shoulder. A wifely message: *Let's go soon, honey, I'm tired.*

I made the mistake of looking at him. I wonder how much hurt I could have saved myself if he had turned away then, or if he'd disguised what he was feeling, or even if the light had been bad. But it was bright enough, and Mick's not half as good as I am at dissembling. I saw all his pain, and it was big and raw and humbling. All this time, I had been holding back from loving him. The illusion that I had a choice evaporated.

Two weighty lessons I could have done without: I can't have him, and we are in love with each other.

16

Isabel

Spring is my favorite season, May is my favorite month. I love May's innocence after treacherous April, its artless hope. Sweetness. I can't decide if it's good fortune or another of fate's low blows that the worst experience of my life is unfolding in gentle, good-hearted May.

Antiestrogen therapy didn't work for me. Given my history, Dr. Searle was not hopeful from the beginning, but we'd both wanted, for different reasons, to put off chemotherapy as long as possible. My reason was that I'd had it before and it frightened me. Not only had it failed to stave off a recurrence, it had made me sicker than I'd ever been in my life.

But I didn't know what sick was. Dr. Searle has devised a new cocktail since my last party with chemo. It's called CAF—Cytoxan, Adriamycin, and 5-fluorouracil—and if it doesn't kill me first, I could almost pity my poor cancer cells.

Kirby wanted to go with me for the first treatment, but I dissuaded him; I told him I'd been through it before, I knew what to expect. Anyway—I didn't tell him this—if there were going to be problems, they would begin later, seven to ten hours after the infusions.

My appointment was for one-thirty. At twelve-fifteen, Lee knocked at my door. "I'm taking the afternoon off and going with you," she announced. I knew before I tried that, unlike Kirby, Lee wouldn't be talked out of it, and I was right. But I must confess that under a veneer of exasperation, I felt a prodigious relief.

The doctor had already written my chemo orders, but there was still red tape to go through before the treatment could start: registering, meeting the chemo nurse, getting vitals and blood counts taken, waiting for the drugs to be processed at the pharmacy. I didn't sit down in the comfortable, too-familiar lounge chair in my own private little cubicle until after three. Lee sat on a hard stool beside me and chattered. Who knows what about—I was too wrought up to listen. I doubt that she knew herself because if anything, she was more nervous than I. But, relatively speaking, getting the chemo's nothing, I could have told her. It's *after* when the fun begins.

The staff had changed in two years; I didn't know Dorothy, the petite, pretty, dark-skinned nurse who bustled in, smiling and efficient, with her tray of drugs. "Brought your friend, have you? That's nice," she said in a pleasant English accent while she slapped at the inside of my elbow for a vein. The stick was smooth and quick—thank God, I thought, she's good at it. Some of them are awful.

"What's in that?" Lee asked, eyeing the bright red syringe Nurse Dorothy was attaching to my catheter.

"Adriamycin. That's the one that makes your hair fall out, love." She looked straight into my eyes, her face gentle as a mother's. Her sympathy was real, and it was almost too much. My emotions were ragged, and nothing on earth makes me feel sorrier for myself than chemotherapy. I believe if Lee hadn't been with me, I'd have wept. But I always feel obliged to cheer up anyone who's kind enough to try to cheer me up, and so I made a stupid joke, "Hair today, gone tomorrow," and closed my eyes, while Dorothy monitored the slow, steady pump of red drug in my vein.

Cytoxan came next, via a slow drip. I knew this one; I was prepared for its disconcerting and instantaneous side effect, a feeling as if you've just eaten Chinese mustard and your sinuses are prickly cold and wide open. Five-FU was last, and afterward the nurse removed the catheter and told me to stay where I was, she'd be back in a while to take my vitals and give last-minute instructions on side effects.

I lay with my eyes closed, morbidly alert to every sense, trying to gauge what I felt. Nothing much—too early. Lee had gone very quiet. I thought she would start talking again when I heard her draw her stool up close beside me. Instead, she slipped her hand, which was trembling slightly, into mine. "Let's do an imagery thing," she murmured. "Let's visualize the chemo killing the cancer cells. Want to?"

I don't know what form her visualization took, but mine made me smile. "What's funny?" she asked, but I only shook my head. I didn't think she'd find it as charming as I did—Lee as a gladiator in star-spangled tights and a leotard, smacking hoodlum cancer cells off a platform, one by one, with a giant styrofoam sword.

"Henry and I are fighting," she told me over an early dinner in a Spanish restaurant near my apartment. I was hungry, watching her push pieces of scallop and shrimp around on a plate of saffron rice. But I ordered a cup of lentil soup and a small salad, and worried that even that would prove too much.

"What are you fighting about?"

"Everything. Everything he says or does makes me furious. I just can't help it."

"It's the stress. You're both—"

"I know that. I yelled at him last night that he had to quit drinking, and we haven't talked to each other since."

"Quit drinking? But Henry doesn't drink much, does he?" *Henry?*

"He has a beer sometimes after work. Alcohol affects a man's sperm, Isabel, it's a known fact. I don't think I'm asking that much. *I'm* the one who's doing everything. All he has to do is—is—jerk off in a bottle every few weeks, while I have to—do everything else—" She dropped her fork on her plate and covered her face with her hands.

"Lee, oh, honey—" I was so surprised, all I could do was reach across and pat her arm.

"Sorry." She fumbled in her purse for a tissue. "It's been an awful day." She looked up, red-faced. "I got my period," she whispered, and dissolved into tears.

"Oh, no. Oh, I'm sorry."

"I don't know what's happening to me. I'm sorry to tell you all this now, of all times, but— "

"Doesn't matter."

"—but I can't help it, I'm not *myself* anymore, I can't control my emotions and I just want to cry and cry and *beat* on something. I'm so afraid, oh, Isabel, I'm so scared that we'll never get a baby, and if that happens— " She put her hand on her throat, glancing around in mortification, appalled at the thought that someone might have heard her.

"But there are more things to try, aren't there? If the insemination doesn't work— "

"There are a *million* more things to try. There's in vitro, there's GIFT, there's ZIFT, something called ICSI, there's gestational surrogacy—we're just at the beginning, and everything takes forever and costs a fortune. Henry keeps asking, 'What do *poor* people do?' and I know it's driving him crazy to spend all this money, but it's *my* money, but when I say that, it just makes him angry and hurts his feelings. Oh, God."

I'd never seen her like this. Emma and Rudy joke, fondly, about Lee's self-possession, her rationality, her tendency to see things in black and white and not delve for nuance—but the truth, of course, is that she can be as passionate as any of us. Her private sense of what feelings are fit for public disclosure is strict, though, strict and old-fashioned, and that's exactly what made tonight's outburst so shocking.

She recovered quickly, and then she couldn't stop apologizing. I wanted to pursue the subject, ask her to finish that sentence that had trailed off with "if that happens." But it was the wrong time and the wrong place.

When we finished eating, she insisted on going home with me. "You might feel sick, Isabel, and someone should be with you."

I protested, knowing it was pointless, but once again secretly relieved. I probably would be sick—in fact, I was planning on it—but I told her there was nothing she could do about it. "Anyway, what about Henry? You should go home, Lee, it's Friday night."

"So? He's fine on his own. I'll call and tell him I'll be late, don't worry about him."

Her way of punishing her husband because she was miserable. If only all married couples took their anger out on each other so harmlessly, I thought, remembering Gary and me.

At home, although it was only eight o'clock, I undressed and got in bed. I probably wouldn't sleep, but at least I could relax for a few hours before—or *if*; I was trying to be positive—I began to feel sick.

"How do you feel now?" Lee asked, leaning over me, smoothing the sheet over the top of the blanket. Tucking me in.

"Hard to describe. Warm, and my skin feels a little tight. I just feel odd. A sort of humming."

She sat on the edge of the bed. "No fever," she noted, resting her hand on my forehead. "Don't worry, Isabel, I'll stay with you. We'll get through this."

"Of course we will." I wanted to tell her what a wonderful mother she'd have been—would be—but I was afraid we'd both cry.

"Do you want some water?"

"Yes. Yes, I forgot, I'm supposed to drink lots of water."

"That makes sense. You don't want poison sitting in your bladder and kidneys any longer than necessary," she said practically, and got up. "Want the light out?"

"Yes, please."

"Okay. I'll bring you some water, and then you try to go to sleep."

"What will you do?"

"I'll sit and meditate for a while. Okay if I turn the TV on low?"

"Sure."

"Okay, then. Night, Isabel."

"Good night. Thanks for everything."

She blew me a kiss from the doorway.

A few minutes later, I heard her talking softly on the telephone. To Henry, I guessed. I hoped they made up. I meant to listen, monitor how the reconciliation went by the length of the conversation, but I must have drifted off. I jolted awake when the phone rang.

Lee answered it immediately, before I could get up. "She's fine," I heard her say in a voice, crisp and formal, borderline impolite, that made me certain the caller was Kirby. Seconds later, a wave of sickness rolled over me.

I staggered up. The bathroom was adjacent to the bedroom, across a short, narrow hall. A matter of ten or twelve steps, no more, but I didn't make it.

I vomited on the carpet in the hall and on the pink tile floor and on the round throw rug in front of the sink. An explosion. Everything I'd eaten, dinner, lunch, breakfast, a massive quantity of thick black bile—everything spewed out like a geyser, utterly uncontrollable. I huddled over the toilet, retching and coughing, while Lee put her arm around my waist and said, "There, now, that's much better."

"Hell," I said when I could. "Don't clean up—I will, just—"

"Hush, Isabel. Are you through?"

No. I threw up again, holding my stomach, gagging at the end until there was nothing left. But when I tried to rinse my mouth out at the sink, sickness hit again and I swerved back to the toilet.

Lee finally guided me back to bed, where I lay in a sweaty heap, listening to her scrub the carpet, mop the floor. The smell of Lysol jerked me up. She barely got out of the way before I was heaving again into her spanking clean toilet.

It wouldn't stop. "Where's it coming from? There can't be anything left!" And finally there wasn't anything, but that didn't stop the nausea. "I'm calling the doctor," Lee kept threatening, but I told her there was no point, I'd already taken the antinausea medication. "It's like this, this is how it is, they can't do anything." But this time was worse than before. It had to be the Adriamycin, the new drug in the cocktail. I crawled back to bed and tried to rest, but I couldn't lie still, couldn't find any position that was comfortable for more than a few seconds. The muscles of my stomach felt tender and achy, all my nerves were on fire. Lee wanted me to drink water, but I couldn't—just the thought of it made me gag.

Someone knocked at the door. I looked at the clock: twelve-twenty. Lee went to answer, and presently I heard Kirby's low, solemn voice raised in solicitous questions. I turned my face into the pillow, senselessly mortified. Of course he'd heard me; our bathrooms might as well be connected for all the soundproofing the ceiling provided. I wasn't sorry when Lee sent him away. "All right, I'll *call* you, but there's nothing you can do. But thanks." She closed the door firmly.

I wished we had never had that abortive, semiromantic interlude last December, I wished he had never kissed me, never said those words to me about love. Then the conspicuous absence of a follow-up would not have been so embarrassing to us both. Emma was partly right when she said I was the one who had pulled away from the relationship. But she was partly wrong. Kirby disappeared, didn't call, didn't visit, for six days after I told him about my new diagnosis. A long time for us; we were used to seeing each other daily. When he reappeared, he behaved as if nothing had happened, and since then he'd been helpfulness itself, a model of sympathy and selfless friendship. It was obvious that decency motivated him, not "love," and, of course, I didn't blame him. He'd lost his wife and children to senseless early deaths. He would have to be crazy, he would have to be pathologically self-destructive to choose to be intimate with a woman in my situation. No, no, no, I didn't blame him, but I hated it that here was one more loss to grieve.

When did I become the sort of person who puts *love* in quotation marks?

"Go home," I told Lee at one o'clock. "I think it's getting better." A lie; I was shuddering with sickness, red-skinned and hot, exhausted but unable to lie still.

"I've already called Henry and told him I'm staying. I just wish I could *do* something. Shall I rub your back?"

I shook my head. "Thanks. Don't want anything touching me."

"What about some nice music? To take your mind off it."

"I don't know. I don't think so."

"Well, we could try it. All right?"

I said yes, to humor her. "Terry sent me the Glenn Gould Brahms intermezzos. Put that on."

She did, and minutes later I was stumbling for the bathroom. "Turn it off, oh God, don't ruin it— " I was crying from weakness and frustration, and now fear that this wretched sickness might turn me against something so beautiful, something I loved so much. "Oh, take it off, Lee, stop it, stop— "

She looked scared when I came back into the bedroom and sat down gingerly beside her. "I think we should call the doctor," she said again. "This can't be natural."

"It's not, that's the point. It's poison." I hugged my legs to my aching stomach. "All that gets me through is thinking of it eating the cancer. Like acid."

"But this is too much. Let me call, Isabel, and just ask."

"No point, I'm telling you. This is what it does."

"Let me just *call*."

"Call, then." I was too weak to keep arguing.

She got up and called. I heard her murmuring into the phone, but I didn't listen, didn't care enough.

"I told the answering service it's an emergency," she announced with satisfaction from the doorway. "The doctor's going to call."

I grunted. At least one of us felt better.

A few minutes later the phone rang.

"He's calling in a prescription at the all-night on Columbia," she reported after another low-voiced conversation. "I'm going to pick it up. You'll be okay for about twenty minutes, right? I'll be—"

"You are not driving to the drugstore at one-thirty in the morning." The effort to talk brought on a fresh wave of queasiness.

"Don't be silly. I'll be—"

I sat up. "Don't, Lee, I mean it. I forbid it."

She didn't laugh. To her credit. She stared at me speculatively for a few seconds. "Okay. I'll call Kirby, then, and he can get it."

I said no and started to swear, but she only raised her eyebrows at me and waited until I had to lie down, moaning.

That's how it came about that I was lying under a blanket on my living room sofa at three o'clock in the morning, listening to Lee and Kirby make polite conversation, and beginning to feel just a little bit better. The interludes between episodes of vomiting had lengthened to about thirty minutes, and I no longer felt so feverish. But I still couldn't drink water, and my reaction to Kirby's innocent, never repeated suggestion that I try a few saltines was predictable. Lee made tea; they sipped it quietly, and took surreptitious bites of something, Oreos, I think, when they thought I wasn't looking. As far as feeling awful went, that night was the worst ever, and yet, unexpectedly, I didn't feel like slinking off somewhere to be alone in my sickness, and I had no interest in being noble and not inflicting myself on others. In fact, I craved company.

Kirby sat on the floor like a yogi, legs crossed, wrists rather elegantly draped over his knees. Beside him, in the easy chair, Lee yawned without covering her mouth, a grave lapse for her, and a sure sign of fatigue. "How long have you lived in D.C.? Kirby—is that your first name or your last?"

"Last. Since 1980. My wife and I moved here from Pittsburgh."

"Oh, Pittsburgh, I have friends there. Do you know the Newmans? Mark and Patti?"

Kirby said no.

"So you're *from* Pittsburgh?" Lee asked.

"No, originally from New York. Upstate. And you?"

"My family is from the Boston area."

"Ah."

Pause.

"How did you first meet Isabel?" Kirby asked sociably.

"We used to live two blocks from each other in Chevy Chase. This was back when she was married to Gary. I met her son, Terry, first. On a Halloween night."

I smiled faintly at the memory.

Kirby said, "The first time I saw Isabel, she was talking to the bag lady who used to camp out on the corner by our building. The woman was sitting on the sidewalk, all her possessions piled around her, and Isabel was squatting down beside her so they could be eye-to-eye. Isabel had on a dark green skirt and a light blue blouse and low-heeled shoes. The homeless woman did most of the talking. A couple of times they both laughed. Isabel didn't give her money, but when the visit was over, she squeezed her by her tennis shoe. Gently. I thought the gesture looked very . . . loving."

I turned my head to look at him.

"The second time I saw her," he continued in the same low, matter-of-fact voice, "she sat down beside me on the No. 42 bus. At first I didn't quite recognize her; I thought it might be the same woman who'd spoken so kindly to the homeless lady, but I wasn't positive. This time she wore slacks and a brown sweater. And boots. She was carrying an armload of books, textbooks, I thought, but I couldn't read the titles. Her fingers were ink-stained.

"On F Street, she took a tape player out of her purse and put on a set of headphones. I watched her out of the corner of my eye. Her face smoothed out and she smiled. Just slightly. Her hands in her lap went limp. The music was barely audible; try as I might, I couldn't make it out. I had already decided she was perfect, and yet I was filled with a terrible dread that she was smiling beatifically to Megadeath or the Beastie Boys. Imagine my relief when, at Dupont Circle, she opened the machine to turn the tape over, and I saw that it was a Mozart symphony. The G minor."

"Goodness," Lee said faintly.

"She got off the bus at my stop, and began to walk down Ontario Road toward Euclid. I followed. When she went up the steps to this building and then buzzed herself through the front door, I wondered briefly if I were hallucinating. A wish-fulfillment fantasy. She saw me—for the first time—from the elevator, and held the door for me. We rode up to her floor in silence. Everything I thought to say to her sounded . . . frivolous. Not important enough for the occasion. The door opened, and then I did say something—I don't remember what; I've blocked it—and she ended up telling me her name. I told her mine. The buzzer warned that I'd held the elevator door too long, and she stepped back and said, 'Well,' and waved good-bye."

He stopped talking. The story was over. He didn't look at me, but Lee did, with wide, fascinated eyes.

I sat up. Slowly, I thought. I didn't know what I would say, but something certainly seemed to be called for. But despite my intention, I had moved too quickly. The worst happened—sickness broke over me without warning, and I had time to mutter, "This isn't personal—truly—" before throwing off the blanket and making a mad and extremely undignified dash for the bathroom.

When I returned, Kirby and Lee were talking and laughing with much animation about something else, some completely neutral subject. The loaded moment had passed, and of course that was a relief—and yet, a tender, unused spot in me wanted it back, and didn't care how awkward that would be. I lay on my side and watched Kirby, examined his narrow face, the skin fine and pale over the sharp-boned surfaces, his brown eyes hooded and slightly sunken. I listened while he told a story about his daughter, Julie, whom he'd lost when she was twelve, and as he spoke I saw him patiently, thoroughly, and almost surely unconsciously turning Lee around, from a jealous, suspicious critic to a friend. My eyes blurred, blinked shut, and I finally dozed.

Dawn.

"Both of you, go home."

Kirby had fallen asleep on the floor, Lee in her chair. I huddled inside my blanket, shivering in spasms; I wasn't hot anymore, I was freezing.

"Could you drink some tea now?" Lee asked, staggering up, stretching.

I could. A miracle. We slurped tea and didn't talk. I don't know which of us looked grayer; me, probably, but I wasn't going to look in a mirror.

"What a night." I used both hands to scratch my head. "Scalp itches," I explained—then froze. They looked at me uncomprehendingly. I took my hands away. "Adriamycin," I said, trying to laugh. "Complete hair loss in all takers. No exceptions. I'll be bald in two weeks."

"Oh, Is." Lee came over and sat beside me, put her arm around me and kissed my head. I stiffened, sensing the start of a good cry. I might have enjoyed that if Kirby hadn't been there.

"Why don't you cut it yourself?" he said.

I looked at him. "Pardon?"

"*Yes.*" Lee sat up straight. "Cut it before it can start falling out."

"Cut it myself?" I touched my soft, curly hair with my fingertips. "What—now?"

"Show it who's boss," Lee said, ruthless excitement snapping in her eyes. "Screw it before it can screw you."

"I could shave it for you," Kirby said quietly, watching me. "With my electric razor. We could do it together now, the three of us."

I did cry then, but only a little. I cried for the losses in store for me, and for the love of my friends, and because sometimes kindness is as excruciating as cruelty. And—a little—for my hair.

17

Lee

The Saving Graces have celebrated more anniversaries (four) at Neap Tide, my family's cottage on the Outer Banks, than anyplace else, so deciding where to spend our tenth was simple. We left on Friday morning, later than planned because of some trouble Rudy had getting Curtis's car, and then it took forever to get there because Rudy and Emma had to stop every hour to go to the bathroom. They denied it, but I think it's entirely possible they had a flask and were passing it back and forth in the front seat.

"You two aren't drinking, are you?" I asked after the third pit stop. Emma turned around and looked at me as if she thought I'd lost my mind. So—I don't know. I do know they got louder as the day went on, laughing at nothing and singing along to the tapes she'd brought, old rock and roll songs I didn't care for when they were new, and then country songs that were even worse, sung by Tammy Wynette and Dolly Parton and God knows who else. I finally had to tell them Isabel was trying to sleep, which was the truth. She took a nap every afternoon now that she was on chemo, and even Rudy and Emma weren't immature enough to disrespect that.

Neap Tide is really Neap Tide II, Neap Tide I having suffered so much storm surge damage during Hurricane Emily that it had to be rebuilt. The new cottage is bigger and has a few more amenities, ceiling fans, another roof deck, brand-new appliances, but in the main it's still as homey and unsophisticated as the original. Nothing, in other words, like the half-million-dollar mansions they're building on the ocean side these days. Henry and I come down twice a year; my parents, maybe once every two years; my brothers, never: they prefer Cape Cod. The rest of the season, my family rents Neap Tide out to tourists.

We were exhausted by the time Rudy pulled the car between the stilts under the long, weathered front deck. Emma had to go look at the ocean immediately, while Rudy and I hauled our stuff (and hers) up the two flights of outside stairs and decided on rooms. I suggested Isabel and I each have a room to ourselves, and Rudy and Emma double up in the third bedroom. No one had a problem with that. After Emma came back and everyone unpacked, we met in the kitchen to discuss (again at my suggestion) meals, responsibilities, and other domestic arrangements. That was when we had our first fight.

Not really a fight—I shouldn't say that. Our first emotional moment. I was explaining why it made more sense to eat in tonight and go out tomorrow (we were tired of driving, we had steaks in the cooler ready to grill), and also suggesting certain tasks that seemed more appropriate for some people than others (Emma, for example, is a good cook but horribly messy, whereas Rudy is slightly less creative but just excellent at tidying up as she goes along)—when Emma, who had already opened a beer and drunk half of it, drew herself up straight and saluted. "Sir!" she shouted like a marine.

Well, I'm used to her not-so-veiled sarcasm, so I let that go. But a few minutes later, as I was trying to organize cleanup shifts for the common areas, the living and dining rooms, the kitchen, the outdoor decks—and I don't apologize for this, it was *not* officious of me, *someone* needs to say these things once in the beginning, to prevent misunderstandings later on—Emma made a crack. Under her breath, and supposedly to herself, but we all heard it. It was a reference to my sex life. And who was probably "in charge" of it, me or Henry.

I turned away. Everything went quiet until Isabel said, "Oh,

Emma," very softly. I don't know if it was Emma's crack or the gentle disapproval in Isabel's voice, but for some reason I started to cry.

And then I couldn't stop. I kept trying to turn my back on everybody and Isabel kept trying to turn me around. I sat down at the kitchen table and covered my face.

Emma knelt beside me. "Oh, Lee, I'm sorry," she said, "I'm so sorry," with real fear in her voice, and Isabel hovered behind me, stroking my hair. Rudy brought me a glass of water.

I was mortified. "It's the fertility drugs," I told them, "I'm on Clomid and it causes mood swings. I can't help it."

"No, it's my fault," Emma said. "What an unbelievably stupid thing to say. Lee, come on, don't pay any attention to me."

"No, it's me. It's not working, I can't get pregnant, and I feel like such a fool. I waited too long—I'm forty-one years old! It's my fault, and I can't stand it."

"It's not your fault," Rudy said, "it's Henry's sperm."

"It might not be. The doctor said there might be something else wrong, because it should've happened by now. I think he thinks it's me. And I honestly think Henry is *glad*! Because it's not just him anymore!" I tried to stop crying because I could see I was scaring them, but I couldn't. And I couldn't stop talking.

"What did I do? Is it something I did? Is this happening because I was too promiscuous when I was young? I had a one-night stand!" I said hotly when Emma and Rudy laughed—even Isabel smiled. "I could have gotten an infection and never known it. And I just *had* to have an IUD when I was thirty, to make it *easier* to have sex, and now we know what *they* can do!"

"Lee, this is not—"

"If I just hadn't waited so long, but no, I had to have everything perfect, my career, my house, my husband—why couldn't I have gotten married in my twenties? Oh God, it's just that I've always known what I wanted, I've always planned for it and worked for it, and I've always gotten it. And now everything's failing. It's like I'm paralyzed. I can't do anything, I can't fix it." More tears. This was too embarrassing for words.

Rudy had pulled a chair up close to mine. "And it must be so hard for you at work," she said, "being with all those children. I mean, of all the jobs for you to have."

"*Yes,*" I said, sobbing, and so glad somebody had finally acknowledged this out loud. Maybe it was too obvious, but for some reason nobody had ever said it before—that me being in charge of a child care center was a terrible cruelty, a trick life was playing on me for no reason but meanness. "It's *awful.* I don't know if I can keep doing it. It really, really hurts."

"Poor Lee." Emma wrapped her arms around my knees.

"It's too much, it's like constant torture, but what else can I do? I could do consulting, I could write articles, maybe a textbook—but it's still—"

"It's still children," Rudy said. "Constantly."

"Yes, and anyway, what's the difference, even if I was a bank teller I'd still see babies in strollers, babies in car seats, babies being breast-fed in the ladies' room at Nordstrom's. I'd still see mothers buying Pampers at the grocery store, and I'd still read stories about teenagers throwing their newborn babies in the garbage."

Isabel hugged me from behind, laying her cheek on my wet one. "Go on, it's good to cry. Do you tell Henry? I bet he's dying to talk to you."

I pulled away. I felt ashamed, not worthy of her sympathy, but I still had to say—"I'm so *angry* with him. I try not to be, I know it's irrational, but I can't help it. I'm on these awful drugs, I've taken a million tests, peed in a million cups, I've been probed and poked and injected and penetrated, and all he has to do is masturbate." I had to smile when Emma pressed her face to my thigh and snorted. "It's true. Deep down, I'm furious with him, and it doesn't matter that it's not his fault, and I *know* this whole thing is almost as bad for him as it is for me. For Henry, sex is private, and he can't stand this openness, all the questions he has to answer to a lot of nurses and doctors about our personal business. He even said something snotty about the group."

"No. He did?"

"Not about anybody in it, just that he guesses you all know everything about him, every little secret, and he *hates* that. And he hates having to go to the clinic and give his sperm, everybody knowing exactly what he's doing. It makes him feel ridiculous. Plus it's his sperm that are making all this have to be, so—"

"He feels guilty," Rudy said. "He wants to give you everything, and he feels like he's failing at the thing you want the very most."

I nodded. "He won't talk about it, but part of the reason he wants to be a father is to make up for not having one himself. I think a lot of pain from his childhood is coming back. Which makes everything worse."

"God," said Emma. "A double whammy."

"Exactly." It felt wonderful to get all this out and to be understood and sympathized with. But there was even more I *couldn't* say. Like my secret wish that I'd married somebody else, anybody else, just so long as he could give me children. And of course I couldn't tell them how bad sex between Henry and me had gotten. We didn't even do it anymore unless we had to. What was the point? For "passion"? We didn't have any. I felt unattractive and asexual, and Henry felt like a failure. Making love was so mechanical, so self-conscious; the last time we tried, I couldn't climax, and he barely could. I should have pretended, but I didn't care enough. The whole episode embarrassed us so much, we haven't done it since.

"What about counseling?" Rudy said. "What if you both went to somebody and talked about it?"

"Henry won't. And I'm not going by myself."

"It'll work out," Emma said. "Everything could change overnight, you know, Lee. One phone call from the clinic. One blue stick."

"But that's what I've been telling myself for months! Wait and hope, wait and hope—that's what my life has shrunk down to."

"Lee," Isabel said quietly, "you never mention the possibility of adoption."

"No, because Henry doesn't want to, he wants his own. So do I—so do my parents."

"Your parents?"

"Wait, now," Emma said, "Henry doesn't want to adopt? He says that?"

"Jenny says his father was killed in Vietnam, but the truth is—this is a *secret*, now—Henry thinks she doesn't even know who his father was. So he—he really wants his own child. We talked about it a long time ago, and we agreed."

"Well, but maybe now—"

"No. I'm in this, and I'm not giving up. I am going to be pregnant."

"But if it's making you crazy—"

"It's not making me *crazy*, Rudy. I'm determined, that's all. I won't be defeated. There's a difference between being crazy and being determined."

"Of course, I didn't mean really crazy. Not like me, Lee. You're the sanest one here."

"I resent that," Emma said, and we laughed, all of us glad for the levity.

"Oh, enough," I said. I was uncomfortable being the center of attention for so long, plus I didn't want to talk about my parents. I was sorry I'd let that slip—that they want a natural grandchild from me, another little Pavlik to carry on the genius genes. Their attitude embarrasses me; I could already hear what Emma would say about it.

"You're right, it'll work out somehow." I stood up. Everybody fell back, away from me. "It just takes time, and it makes me tired. You guys are great. There, that's my fifteen minutes," I said, laughing, "and I feel a lot better."

They didn't believe me, but they stopped hovering around me and started making drinks to carry out to the front deck. It was as if we'd all realized at once that our anniversary weekend was getting off to a dangerous start, and we'd better shift gears before we spoiled it. They would talk about me as soon as I wasn't around, I knew. "Oh, poor Lee, I had no idea, I've never seen her like that, it was so unlike her." I've never seen me like this, either. I hardly know myself anymore. I want my old life back.

The sunset was blinding; we had to turn our chairs away until it dropped under the haze on the horizon. "This is the life," we took turns saying, lolling on our backbones, bare feet up on the railing. "This is what it's all about." Rudy couldn't remember if this was the third or the fourth time we'd come to Hatteras to celebrate, and everybody started reminiscing. "Why don't we go for a walk on the beach?" I interrupted to suggest. I had a surprise in store for them, but not until tomorrow night; too much nostalgia this early could spoil it.

The tide was running out. We went along the shore two by two, Rudy and Emma in the shallow surf with their pants legs rolled up, Isabel and me higher up on the wet sand. Isabel wore a pretty red and green scarf around her head, and she looked wonderful, you would never suspect anything was wrong with her. She claimed the drugs were making her gain weight, but I couldn't see it.

"How do you feel?" I asked.

"Great."

"It was a long drive—I'm tired myself. Sure you're okay?"

"I'm fine."

"How's Kirby?"

"Great. Sends you his regards."

"I really like him." She smiled. "I wasn't sure about him at first," I admitted. "But after that night. That first chemo night."

She nodded. "What a night, huh?"

Her second treatment was last week, and it had gone a lot better than the first. She wasn't as sick, and the nausea hadn't lasted as long. I didn't stay with her, Emma did, and not all night this time.

"So," I said. "Is he still in love with you?"

She shook her head slightly, not to say no but to shake off the question.

She would never talk about Kirby except to say that his romantic interest came at the wrong time, and that she was grateful she still had his friendship. I can't tell if she's sad about that or not. Isabel's serenity isn't always a blessing. Sometimes it's a wall.

I kept slowing my steps to match hers, until finally she stopped. "You go on, Lee, I think I'll sit for a while and look at the water."

"You *are* tired. I'll sit with you."

"No, go on, catch up with Emma and Rudy. Pick me up on the way back."

These are the little incidents I can't bear. She lulls me into thinking not much is wrong with her, and sometimes I even *forget*—and then she'll tire out much too soon, or I'll catch her sitting down in a chair too carefully, like an old woman with arthritis. Reality closes in, and it's a new shock every time. I suppose it's the same for her, but worse. Oh, much worse.

We ate dinner in the dining room, with candles and soft music and a bowl of the wildflowers Emma stole from the next-door-neighbor's yard. Everything tasted delicious, even the microwave-baked potatoes. We made a lot of toasts, and by the end of the meal we were quite a merry group. I won't say my outburst in the kitchen was forgotten; in fact, I think it overshadowed the whole evening and made us more careful of one another. Emma in particular was on good behavior, speaking gently to me and never being sarcastic; she kept touching me, too, her hand on my hand, a soft nudge on my arm to share a joke. I must've really scared her.

We took our coffee outside and sat in the deck chairs to listen to the surf and watch the clouds slip past the moon. It was a fine night, soft and starry, with a steady breeze blowing in from the ocean. Neap Tide isn't a waterfront cottage, but from the front deck you can easily see the Atlantic on the left and the Pamlico Sound on the right, and at night, after the traffic on Route 12 dies down, you can hear the waves almost as clearly as if you were sitting on the beach.

"Well, I'm not pregnant, either," Rudy said out of the blue, during a lull in our lazy conversation. "In case anybody was wondering." She had her long legs stretched out on the wooden ottoman, long arms bent gracefully behind her head. The rest of us looked vague and shadowy, but the moonlight glinted on Rudy's black hair and glittered in her gray eyes. Even in the dark, she stands out. I started to say something, but she sat up and leaned toward me. "I just didn't want you to think I was hiding it, keeping it a secret not to hurt you. Because I wouldn't do that, it would be . . . "

"Condescending," Emma supplied. "And not necessary." She smiled at me.

"Yes," Rudy said. "So, I just wanted you to know."

To tell the truth, I'd forgotten she and Curtis were trying. I guess I'd put it out of my mind. "Are you worried?" I asked her. "How long has it been?"

"Since January. Yes, I am, a little. Because I was reading somewhere that if nothing's happened in six months, there might be a problem."

"Well, that's what they say." Something I wish I'd known myself two years ago.

Emma peered at Rudy in the dark. "You really think something's wrong? Are you doing it right, taking your temperature and all that?"

"Well, not at first, but for the last two months, yes."

"Oh, two months is nothing," Isabel said.

"I know." Rudy heaved one of her long, heavy, dissatisfied sighs.

"How's Curtis?" I asked. "How is he liking his new job?"

"Curtis . . ." She hesitated for so long, all three of us stopped staring into space and looked at her. "Oh . . ." More silence. Finally she said, "He's okay," in an airy voice, and stood up. "I'm going for a beer, anybody want one?"

How odd. While she was gone, we stared at one another and made soft noises, "Hmm," and "Ha . . ." but we didn't speak. This was too new; we didn't know what to think yet. If there was anything to think. Emma in particular looked bewildered.

"What a beautiful night," Isabel said. "Feel that breeze. Anyone mind if I take off my scarf?"

We scoffed, we disclaimed, Emma even swore—"Jesus, Isabel, how could you even *ask*"—but the truth is, it's always a shock to see Isabel's bare head for the first time. But you get used to it quickly, and then I honestly think she looks cute. I do. She doesn't agree, of course, and even for me it's hard to separate her appearance from the reason for it—hard to appreciate how she looks but not suffer over why she looks that way.

"So how's it going?" Emma said softly. She reached her hand out to the back of Isabel's chair and held on to it. "How's every little thing?"

Isabel looked over and smiled at her. "It's okay. I get tired easily. That's the worst of it."

"What about your hip?" Isabel had been having some pain there lately. She minimized it, but when it was bad it made her limp.

"When it gets worse, the doctor says I can have radiation. That'll take care of it."

"You mean *if* it gets worse," I said.

"Yes."

"Because the chemo should cure you. That's what it's for, I mean, that's it's *job*."

She nodded, smiled. Sometimes I think I have a better attitude than she does.

"Okay, that's the body," Emma said. "How's the spirit?"

"It's fine, too. I'm hopeful."

We listened to the sound of that word. Isabel usually says the simple truth. If she was saying it now, I guess we couldn't ask for more.

Rudy got up and went to stand behind Isabel's chair. "Let's try something. I've been reading about healing touch."

"Think you've got it?" Emma smiled on one side of her mouth.

"I could. So could you, smarty. You don't know till you try."

"I imagine it helps if you believe in it," I said a little coolly. Sometimes Emma's cynicism annoys me. Isabel closed her eyes and smiled.

"Shh," Rudy said. "Think healing thoughts, everybody. I put my hands like this, not touching you but almost, and I feel your aura, Isabel." She moved her long-fingered hands slowly, cupping the air an inch from Isabel's head. She slid them down lower, along her neck and then her shoulders, her arms. "I'm doing your whole body," Rudy murmured, and Isabel nodded slowly. "Do you feel anything?"

"I feel heat where your hands are."

I turned my head to send Emma a victorious glare, but she had her eyes closed. She was concentrating.

"I know I can feel your energy," Rudy said positively. "Which hip hurts?"

"This one," Isabel said, and Rudy did healing touch there.

I shut my eyes and did my favorite healing meditation. I imagine a sort of Mexican firing squad. Isabel's cancer cells are outlaws dressed in black, with gun belts across their chests—not that they have chests; actually they look more like kidney beans, but with sombreros—and they stand in a long line while a knot of good soldiers takes aim with long black rifles and shoots them. They fall over dead, and another line of cancer cells steps up. *Pow*, they're dead, and another line steps up. It's very efficient and it can go on indefinitely.

Rudy finished her healing touch and sat back down. "Want to try?" she said to Emma.

"Hell, no. Isabel's a friend, I might send her into relapse."

They laughed, but I thought the joke was in poor taste.

I got up to go to the bathroom. Even with the door closed, I could plainly hear Emma's voice gradually rising, getting shrill with anger. When I hurried back, she was on her feet, her back to the rail. Ranting.

"I really hate the mind-body connection, if you want to know the truth, and I can't stand that guy Shorter. I think he's done more harm to sick people than anything since leeches."

"Who's Shorter?" I asked Rudy.

"That doctor who wrote the book about—"

"He's a jerk, and he pisses me off. If you believe his spiel, then you believe Isabel gave herself cancer by being an emotional cripple. Well, fuck you, Shorter, Isabel is not guilty of cancer."

"Em, that's not exactly—"

"What gets me is how a *doctor* could be so stupid about *medicine*. And so destructive. Now whenever Isabel gets depressed—which seems like a pretty logical way to feel once in a while, wouldn't you agree? Given the circumstances?—Shorter's telling her she's making her tumors grow! What an idiot!"

Isabel tried again. "I don't think he's really saying—"

"I mean, what a gigantic *crock*. Whatever happened to science? Isabel, he's as good as telling you you made yourself sick. What about germs? Hm? What about heredity? What about smoking and asbestos? Nitrites! Smog!" The sea air made her hair stick out like a witch's broom. She prowled back and forth in front of the railing, and a couple of times she banged her fist on it for emphasis. She wasn't the least bit drunk, she was just mad.

"What's the difference between Shorter blaming your neuroses for your cancer and Jerry Falwell blaming your sins for your HIV? Cancer *happens*. You aren't responsible. Life's not fair—Jesus, do I have to *say* this? What happened, Is, is that you got a raw deal. That's it. God's little joke. Sorry, better luck next time."

"I understand what you're saying—Sit, Emma, would you stop pacing?—and sometimes I feel the same way. But whether we like it or not, there is a connection between our physical and spiritual selves. People with no religious faith die sooner—just for an example. That's been proven."

"Not to me."

Isabel clicked her tongue. "Well, I can't explain it to you, but it has to do with neuropeptides and T cells and endorphins or something. Your brain *communicates* with your body. It does. Take my word for it."

"Okay." Emma flopped down in the chair, sullen.

"I know what you're saying," Rudy said sympathetically. "I don't like it either, the idea that anyone would make herself sick—"

"That *Isabel* would make herself sick," Emma started up again. "It's bullshit. You're going along, living your life the best way you can, trying not to hurt anybody, and *wham*, one day you get cancer. And then this—*twerp* comes along and writes a best-seller about how it's all your fault. Insult to injury!"

"You know you're exaggerating," Isabel chided. "Nowhere do any of these writers, Shorter or anyone else, say it's our *fault*."

"But that's the implication."

Rudy said, "Emma, do you think our healing circles are a crock? Do you think when Isabel meditates, it's pointless?"

"No. No. I don't."

Isabel said, "Well, then, if you believe I can help to heal myself with positive mental energy, why can't you accept the converse—that my own negative energy might've contributed to my disease?"

Emma turned to her fiercely. "Do you believe that?"

"I don't know. I think it's possible."

"Well, I don't. Somebody else, maybe, but not you, Isabel. *Not you*."

There was a long, charged silence, during which I wasn't sure what might happen, maybe we'd all burst into tears at once.

I'm the one who broke it to say, "I agree with Emma." My voice came out thin and strange; they looked at me curiously. I cleared my throat and said with force, "I think sometimes we can make ourselves sick, and sometimes it just happens. But Isabel isn't toxic to herself. There's nobody"—I searched for the word, and finally came up with—"purer. I mean it. No one gentler." I had to whisper, "And nobody who deserves this less."

Isabel held out her hand. I took it and she pulled me close. Instead of weeping, we four looked at one another with sharp, intense stares. I felt a thrill of fear and excitement. I don't know how much I believe in the mind-body connection, but if everything they say about it is true, I know there was so much psychic energy crackling and snapping among us just in that moment, we four could have cured a hospice full of dying people.

We spent Saturday morning on the beach, listening to Emma warn us about sun exposure. "Don't be fooled because it's overcast," she kept saying, huddled in a beach chair, swathed in terry cloth and smeared with sunscreen and zinc. I don't blame her—she's fair; she freckles first, then burns, then peels. But she sounded like a broken record. "Okay, fine, but when we're old and people come up and ask why a nice-looking young thing like me took a job as nurse-companion to three wrinkled old crones, you'll be—"

"We'll be really sorry," Rudy mumbled into the crook of her arm, facedown on a striped towel. Rudy would never be a wrinkled old crone. Looking at her, lean and long and tan in her bikini bathing suit, I was jealous of her body—well, we all were, who wouldn't be?—and until last night I was jealous of her love life. No, I mean her sex life: definitely not her love life, her marriage, or anything to do with Curtis Lloyd. But I always imagined she and Curtis had an incredibly passionate and satisfying time in bed, although I had no better reason for thinking it than that they're both beautiful. Now to learn that, so far at least, they couldn't conceive—it made me feel shallow and silly, for thoughtlessly mixing up physical attractiveness and fertility. You'd think I'd know better, being married to Henry.

And—something else that's hard to confess. There was a dark, ugly place in me that was secretly glad when she'd told us about their problem. I'm ashamed. But it's true. I want Rudy to have a child, of course I do, *but I want Henry and me to have one first.*

"Going for a walk," Isabel said, shaking sand off her towel and draping it around her shoulders.

"Want company?" I asked.

"No, thanks. I won't be long." She strolled away. We watched her, and when she was out of earshot, we talked about her.

It's what we do when we're together now, we three. At first it felt disloyal, but we've gotten over that. We tell one another everything we know, what we've heard or read lately about cancer, what Isabel said the last time we saw her, how she looked, how she sounded on the telephone.

"She looks good."

"She walks so slowly, though."

"She hasn't been in swimming yet."

"Think she will? She loves to swim."

"She's not very strong. If she goes in, one of us has to go with her."

"I don't think she's eating enough."

"She says the chemo makes her mouth taste bad."

"Her attitude still seems really good, though."

"You don't think she's pretending? Acting more positive for our benefit?"

"Even if she is, it's good for her. Remember that study that showed that smiling makes you feel happier?"

"She's going to get well. She's doing everything right, and the chemo's working."

"If it doesn't kill her first."

"Thank God for Kirby."

"Do you think they'll get together?"

"I do. After she gets her strength back."

"Did you see her collage?"

"No."

"Her collage?

"On the wall in her bedroom. She made a poster of her life. Her past and her future, milestones, major events. She cut out photos of herself when she was little, and her parents, her wedding, pictures of Terry. Us."

"Us?"

"And drawings of herself with cancer, and what she's doing to defeat it."

"Isabel can't draw."

"It's just cartoons, stick figures representing her."

"What did she put for the future?"

"Pictures from travel brochures—places like India and Nepal. A drawing of a diploma. A photograph of her with Terry. Another photo of us. Oh, and the banner from the top of an AARP newsletter. And at the very end, a picture of a baby."

"A baby?"

"She said it's herself. Reincarnated."

"Ah," Rudy said, nodding.

"Whatever," Emma said, smiling. Hopefully.

We went out for dinner, as planned, to a new, almost trendy seafood restaurant in Hatteras. It had been cloudy all day; while we were driving home, it began to rain. "There goes our moonlight walk on the beach," Rudy mourned. "Let's stop at the video store and rent a movie." Nobody but me had any objections. "No, let's not, let's do something else," I kept arguing, and when they said, "Like what?" I had no answer. The conversation got more and more ridiculous. Finally I had to tell them. "Oh, all right, then, ruin the surprise. I've already *got* a video for tonight."

"You do?"

"What is it?"

"I'm not watching any musical cartoons," Emma warned, obviously tired of being nice to me. She was making an ungracious reference to the last time I rented our beach movies. I got *The Hunchback of Notre Dame*, *Pocahontas*, and *Aladdin*. I should've realized she's just the kind of person who would hate Disney.

"It's not cartoons, it's us," I said. "Ten years of the Saving Graces. I had all our old film bits spliced together on one tape for our anniversary. It's twenty-six minutes long."

"Oh, that's wonderful," Isabel exclaimed, and Rudy took her hands off the steering wheel to clap. Even Emma looked pleased, although of course she had to slide down in her seat and say, "Oh, Jeez, home movies," for a joke. But she was glad, they all were, and that was gratifying. Occasionally, not often enough, the thoughtful, competent, organized member of a group gets the appreciation she deserves.

"Lose the bangs, DeWitt." Emma made a face at her image on the screen. "Talk about a bad hair year. How come nobody told me?"

"Shh, I can't hear it."

"I want to know who let me out of the house in that dress," Rudy said. "I'm a summer, I should never wear beige."

"God, remember when we got our colors done?"

"I think you both look beautiful," Isabel said. "We all do."

"Wow, look how skinny I was," Emma marveled, pointing. "What year is this?"

"You're skinny now, you just can't see it," Rudy said.

"Yeah, right."

"I read that women who have positive body images have twice as many orgasms as women who don't."

"Yeah, well, don't worry about me, I'm just fine in that—"

"*Shh*," I repeated. If you kept quiet and listened, sometimes you could actually hear what we were saying on the tape. But usually it was only a crackling din, because we were all overlapping or talking at once. This always surprises me when I look at our old movies, the fact that we never shut up, and what we say rarely sounds important or even particularly coherent. Yet at the time, I always think we're being quite lucid and succinct.

"Fitness camp! Remember that?" Emma pointed at herself on the screen. "I lost seven pounds in six days."

"I lost three."

"Four, and I gained it all back."

"In the first week."

"We ought to go there again," Rudy said. "That was so much fun."

We laughed at the pictures of Emma and Rudy cutting up in the rustic cottage where we stayed for a week, back in 1990. "Fitness camp"—the poor woman's health spa—was just a YWCA camp in the Poconos. We'd gone there instead of someplace nicer because, at the time, Emma didn't have any money.

"You are such a jerk," Rudy said affectionately, ruffling Emma's hair. "Why can't you ever look normal?"

It's true—whenever I point the camera at Emma, she either turns her back or makes a face, or else she makes some subtly obscene gesture, like resting her chin in her hand and extending her middle finger alongside her cheek. All with a sly smile that's funny, I suppose, but childish: I can't tell you how many perfectly nice still photos of the group she's spoiled by putting "horns" behind someone's head at the last second.

I'm rarely in these videos; I'm the cameraperson, a thankless job the others barely tolerate—until it's time to look at the finished product. Then you can't get them away from the TV set.

"Oh, here it comes. I hope," Emma said, rubbing her hands together. "Lee, did you put it in? Did you? I bet you took it out."

I should have. But I didn't, and I hope that squelches for all time anybody's claim that I am not a good sport. And this is why I like being the photographer—because look what happens when someone else (Emma) gets her hands on my camera.

We were having a regular dinner meeting at the house on Capitol Hill Rudy and Curtis had just bought, and I'd brought the video camera to film it, intending to give Rudy the tape afterward so she could send it to her mother or sister or whoever she wanted—her family never visits, and I thought it might be the only way they'd ever see her new home. The other thing was, I had just come from ballet class; I was hot and sweaty and I didn't feel fresh. I asked Rudy if I could take a shower before dinner.

"Oh, here it comes, here it comes," Emma said gleefully. Rudy and Isabel were giggling already. The shaky, inexpertly held camera showed a closed door, and a hand reaching out to turn the knob. Emma's innocent voice on the tape, saying, "Hm, wonder what's in here. What could be behind this door? Shall we see?" Steam poured out when she opened the door. My voice over the sound of running water: "Yes?"

That always cracks them up; I sound too dignified or something.

The camera keeps coming. Through the steam, you can see the blue and white stripes of the shower curtain. "Hello?" I say from behind it. Emma says, "Just getting a—" something inaudible, and I say, still gracious, "Oh, okay."

A hand pulls the curtain back, and there I am. Full frontal nudity. But I'm washing my hair with my eyes closed, and so I am unaware of this indignity for fifteen seconds. (I know, because Henry once timed it.) Fifteen seconds is a long time to be naked on film and not know it. It might have gone on even longer if Emma hadn't finally said, in a breathy, sexy voice, "Hi, there."

I open my eyes, open my mouth, and scream.

Blackout.

Oh, hilarious. My friends fell against one another on the sofa, convulsed with mirth. Even Isabel. I laughed with them, although not quite as heartily. This incident happened over seven years ago, and I am still trying to think of a way to pay Emma back. Nothing nearly good enough has occurred to me yet, but it will. Oh, it will.

The tape skipped ahead to Rudy's wedding.

"Oh God, look at Henry! Look at his *hair*!"

"What a hunk."

This is my favorite part of the video—our first date. Rudy had a formal wedding, and yet Henry had worn a corduroy sportcoat, brown slacks and no tie—and *it didn't matter*. I didn't care! When I realized that, I knew I must be in love. And his hair, oh, it was long and flowing, streaky and gorgeous, prettier than Emma's hair and about the same color.

"Wow, you guys look *hot*," she said, and it was absolutely true. Someone, Isabel, I think, had filmed us dancing at Rudy's reception. The band was playing "Sea of Love," and Henry and I certainly looked lost in it. If I'd had any idea we were moving that way, that that was how we looked, I'd have gone through the floor. Because it's embarrassing. But nice, too. I like looking at it, and frequently run the brief clip back again, because for me it doesn't last long enough. I get caught up in the way Henry's arms are pulling me in around my waist, the way my hands look on the back of his neck, my fingers stiff and flexing, twining in and out of his hair. Our faces are touching; we look as if we're going to kiss, although we never do. It was public foreplay, that dance. A few hours later, we were at home in my bed, making love for the very first time.

Next came a backyard party at Isabel's. Summer 1995. Emma hissed when Gary appeared, but Isabel only looked a little wistful. I think she's really forgiven him. He looked chubby and self-important—the camera never lies, they say—in checked trousers and a sweater with the sleeves rolled up to show off his furry, bulging forearms. He saw the camera and grinned, held his arms out wide—*Look at me, I'm such a teddy bear.* I remember when I used to like him; I thought his flirting was cute, even a little bit flattering. Now, just the sight of him makes my lip curl.

"Lisa Ommert," Rudy exclaimed. "I wonder how she's doing. Anybody ever hear from her? How long did she last, Lee, a year?"

"Nine months," I said, watching Lisa, who was a Saving Grace until she and her husband moved to Switzerland, engaged in a very animated-looking conversation with Gary, Emma, and Emma's boyfriend at the time, Peter Dickenson.

"You have to wonder," Emma said in a strangely grim undertone, "what we could possibly have been talking about."

"It's the tail end of the party," Rudy pointed out. "We were probably all loaded."

"Oh, no question."

I glanced at Emma out of the corner of my eye. She and Peter broke up suddenly—in love one day, bitterly split the next—and we're still not allowed to ask why. Rudy knows, but Isabel and I don't. Well, Isabel might, but only from intuition. My intuition says there was another woman, and that Emma found out in some awful, humiliating way. I don't know what else could have been so hurtful that, this many years later, it's still unmentionable.

"How is it going with Clay?" I asked casually. Clay is the man Sally Draco fixed Emma up with. I couldn't believe it when she agreed, and I was even more surprised when they went out together a second time. The first was supposed to be a double date, but at the last second Sally and Mick canceled; he wasn't feeling well or something.

"Okay," Emma mumbled.

"Just okay?"

She shrugged and kept her eyes on the screen. Her face took on a stubborn set, as it seems to do a lot these days whenever the subject of men comes up. It means, Keep out.

So I wonder why I said, "You haven't mentioned that married fellow in a long time. Is that over now?"

"Well, since it was never *on*, I guess it must be over." She said that through her teeth. "Lee, could we just watch this?"

"Well, excuse me. I didn't realize you were so sensitive."

"Ladies?" Rudy said.

Emma sat hunched forward, forearms on her knees, tense-looking. "Sorry," she said, sitting back abruptly and smiling.

"Sure," I said, meaning *Me, too*. I didn't even know what we were sorry for, but it was nice to make up.

The last few minutes of the video were from exactly a year ago, here at Neap Tide when we'd come to celebrate our ninth anniversary. Watching it, I realized that in some ways it was the perfect ending to a Graces retrospective, because the camera had captured us all being so . . . idiosyncratic, I guess is the word. Ourselves. There was Emma, sitting in a beach chair in the sand, swaddled in towels and a hooded sweatshirt, her nose in a book; Rudy tan and gorgeous beside her, swigging from a thermos of Bloody Marys; Isabel trotting back from a swim, her hair dripping, lips turning blue, laughing at nothing—just gladness. Even the shot Rudy took of me is characteristic, I suppose: I'm in the kitchen, taping to the refrigerator a chart I'd just drafted, "Suggested Chores/Division of Labor, 6/14–6/17." (Emma, I recall, added a new chore category later, "Sleeping," and penciled her name in every block, all the way across.) It was a gay weekend, yes, and yet, watching the images of the four of us in all our silliness and crankiness and sweetness—it made me sad tonight. We looked so innocent. So much was in store for us, but we were too busy being "ourselves," and taking it for granted that we always would be, to give a thought to the future.

The last shot was very artistic, if I say so myself. I took it from behind the dark heads of Isabel, Rudy, and Emma as they stood on the deck and gazed out at a deep red sunset. It's only their heads in silhouette, black against crimson, with the murmur of their voices low and awed-sounding in the background. At the last second,

Isabel heard me and turned. There's just enough light left to see her smile.

Fade-out.

"Do you remember what we talked about that night?" Isabel said after a quiet, appreciative pause.

"I do." Emma reached for the remote and flicked off the staticky screen.

"I do," said Rudy.

"Life goals," I said.

"Yes." Isabel smiled. "I said I wanted to finish my degree, get a job helping old people, and travel."

"I said I wanted a baby."

"I said I couldn't think of anything." Rudy turned to Emma. "*You* said you wanted to live on a dairy farm and see James Brown in concert."

"And spend the night with Harrison Ford," Emma recalled. "By the way, I've changed that to David Duchovny."

I remembered the exercise better now. It had started out as a discussion of life goals but shifted to things we wanted to do before we got too old—things we would regret, on our deathbeds, not having done. I'd wanted to win a PBS auction and dance in *The Nutcracker*. Such a safe topic, it had seemed to us then, only a year ago. Fun. A game.

I couldn't look at Isabel.

She broke the quiet to say, "My goals haven't changed much since that night. That's strange, isn't it? I have more regrets, but exactly the same ambitions."

"What regrets?" Rudy asked shyly.

"Oh . . ." She had on her scarf tonight. She fingered one of the tasseled ends that lay across her shoulder, smiling into space, so sweet-faced and melancholy. "Well, the biggest is still there—that I didn't try harder to make my marriage work. For Terry's sake," she clarified when we all started to interrupt. "Maybe it's a delusion, but if Gary and I had found a way to stay together, Terry might not have gone so far away. Maybe. I don't know."

"No, you don't." Emma pressed her lips together.

"But now I have new regrets, too," she went on. "Ones that never occurred to me before."

"Like?"

"Like . . . I never learned to play the piano. Never watercolored. I never met Carlos Castaneda and asked him if it was all true," she said, laughing. "I never learned the stars, never learned birdsongs—I can't tell a finch from a wren. And wildflowers." Rudy slipped her arm through Isabel's and rested her head on her shoulder. "I never got to be the weather girl on Channel Five," Isabel mused softly. "I never acted or sang or danced, I've never even written a poem. I have no grandchildren."

"Why don't you do them?" Emma said after a forlorn pause. I could have kissed her. "You can do them all. Maybe not weather girl, but that's their loss."

"I think I heard that Carlos Castaneda's dead," Rudy mentioned.

"Okay, but the rest—why can't you, Isabel? I'm serious! You could write a poem right now, nothing to it. I'll help you. Next week, you get some watercolors and an astronomy book and—what was it?" Isabel started laughing. "Birds, you get one of those CDs that plays all the songs while some deep-voiced Audubon guy tells you who's who. Wildflowers, big deal, you get another book and go for a walk in Rock Creek Park. What else? Grandchildren? Well, there you have me, you'll have to take that up with Terry."

"I see." Isabel put her head back against the sofa. Her sadness had disappeared; she looked relaxed and amused and tolerant. Truly, I'm not an envious person, but if I could turn people's moods around the way Emma can (sometimes; when she feels like it), I would be blessed.

"You want to know what I regret?" Emma held up her index

finger. "I've never driven a car at a hundred miles an hour." She added her thumb. "I've never had a long, attitude-adjusting chat with the pope. I've never seen Graceland— "

"Wait," Rudy broke in, "wait a second. I want to say something. To you, Isabel, and—*for* all of us. I know I'm speaking for all of us, I don't even have to ask. I just want to say out loud that we—well, first of all, we know you're going to get well, so that's the bottom line." Emma and I nodded vehemently. "And the second thing is, I think it would be good if we made a commitment right now. I know it's understood, but sometimes it's important to say things in words. So I want to say, for everybody, that no matter what happens, we're here. I mean—we're here for the long haul. You won't be alone. Ever. I'm not saying this right— "

"Yes, you are," Emma said. "It's a good thing to say—that you won't have to face anything by yourself, Isabel. Anything. In fact, you won't be able to get rid of us."

I couldn't chime in and agree, although I knew it was expected of me. I was so afraid of crying, I couldn't say anything. If I did cry, it would be out of anger as much as grief. How dare they speak to her like this, as if she were dying? *She's not.* She is recovering. But they lied, they *don't* believe it, and that felt like a betrayal, not only of Isabel but of me.

She was moved, of course. She hugged them both, blinking so *she* wouldn't weep. I wanted to protect her from their pessimism, but what could I do? When she smiled at me, moist-eyed, and held out her hand, I stood up. "Let's have some ice cream," I said, and walked out. I had my cry in the kitchen.

18

Rudy

"Do you think Lee's going nuts?"

Emma spoke in a low voice, almost a whisper; Lee's room was next door, Isabel's across the hall, and we'd left our door ajar to get a draft of sea breeze from the window.

"You mean about having a child? Well, no," I said, "I think it's good she told us all that. She keeps too much inside, she's—"

"No, I don't mean for letting go a little with us. I agree, that was good for her, that was healthy. I mean the whole baby thing."

"Oh."

"It's like she's gone blind except for that, it's all she can see. And I believe her when she says she'll never give up. Why don't they adopt a child, Rudy? Why? No, she's driven, she's on a course, she's so caught up in the world of baby-making she can't see anything else."

"I know. What was she saying about her parents?"

"I have no idea. Just something else to keep her mind on one track. I wish we could *do* something."

"But what?"

"Nothing. There's nothing to do."

"Just be supportive," I said.

"Yeah." She looked over at me. "Hey, Rude. That was a nice thing you said to Isabel."

"Oh, well. I don't know. I just tried to put myself in her place and figure out what would be the scariest thing. If I thought I might be dying. And it was being alone. So I wanted her to know she never would be."

"Is that the scariest thing?"

"To me. I think."

A candle in a glass hurricane shade burned on the table between our two bunk beds. Between it and the moonlight, I could see Emma clearly, stretched out in her old blue UNC nightshirt, pressing a finger into the top of her white thigh—checking to see if she'd gotten too much sun this afternoon. "To me," she said, "the scariest thing is oblivion. Being, and then not being. Even if everyone you ever knew was with you at the end, everybody holding your hand and telling you it was okay and they loved you and all that, you're still alone at that last second. Wherever you're going, nobody's going with you."

"Wow. That seems so morbid."

"No, it isn't. Why? You can't tell me you don't think about that stuff."

"No, I think about it." But I'd been much better lately. "Could you believe Lee thought we were drinking in the car yesterday?" I guess that sounded like a non sequitur, but after I said it, the connection came to me.

"Well, you know Lee. If you're having that much fun, you must be drunk."

"I haven't been drinking much at all lately," I told her. "Last night was the most I've had in weeks."

"I noticed. Any reason?"

"Well . . . I guess I just feel a little stronger. More comfortable in my real life."

"How come?"

"I don't know. Well, one thing, Eric and I have been doing really good work. Hard work, but it's felt like we're really getting somewhere for a change. He says it's not unusual to go along for a long time without any progress, and then all of a sudden—breakthroughs."

"Like diet plateaus."

"Exactly."

"Oh, like you'd know," Emma scoffed. "Eric—he's very gentle, isn't he? Patient. He doesn't mind going slowly."

I thought I heard a second meaning. "You mean I'm not getting anywhere. He's not doing anything. Really, you think therapy's a waste of time."

Emma rolled her head on the pillow to look at me. "I used to think that," she said—surprising me; I thought she'd deny it. "But now I'm thinking Greenburg may actually be smarter than I am."

"Oh, Emma, the ultimate compliment. He'll be thrilled when I tell him."

We smiled in the dark.

"Hey, Em."

"What."

"You know that landscaping course? Remember the—"

"Sure I remember."

"Well, I've decided I'm going to go ahead and take it."

She sat up. "Oh, *Rudy*."

"It starts in September."

"That's fantastic. What did Curtis say?"

"Um. Well."

She sank back down, but still facing me. "You didn't tell him yet."

"Not yet. I've sort of been waiting for the right time."

"Okay. So, Rudy, what do you think about the fact that you haven't told him because you know he won't like it? I mean, what kind of—"

"I know what you mean. You sounded so much like Eric when you said that, Emma, it's spooky."

"Well, what's the answer?"

"The answer is—I don't like it. I don't like what it says about me *or* Curtis."

"*Or* Curtis. I like that."

"We have to confront some things, I know that. I need to tell him what I'm thinking. It's one thing to tell Eric, or you. I need to tell *him*."

She leaned toward me. "This is new, Rudy, this is good. This is something really different with you."

"I know. About time, don't you think?"

She didn't say anything. Once in a while, Emma's tactful.

"It's not just drugs, either."

"Excuse me?"

I stuck my feet up on the mattress overhead, pushing on it, flexing my knees. "I'm taking this—antidepressant." *New* antidepressant, I might have said. "And it's true I haven't felt depressed, but I don't think that's the only reason. As Eric says, just because the crazy pills are working doesn't mean you're crazy."

That line had never struck me as particularly funny before, but Emma laughed so hard I had to shush her.

Eric also says laughter is cathartic and cleansing, that it's good for the body and the soul, and when it's real it's better than sex. How many hours, I wonder, over the last thirteen years have I shared helpless, snorting, side-aching laughter with Emma? If I'm crazy *now*, what if I'd never met her?

Another thing about shared laughter is that it comes from trust. Which must've been why this popped out of my mouth next: "We didn't have sex for the whole month of December."

"December—last year?"

"Yes."

"You and Curtis?"

"Well, who else?"

"Um . . ." Emma stared at me, feeling her way. "Any particular reason?"

"Well, that's the thing. If there was a reason, I don't know what it was. I hadn't done anything he could've been punishing me for. He never—he just wouldn't—we never did it, that's all. I didn't say anything. I know I should have, but I didn't. I didn't even tell Eric."

"You never said anything at all? To Curtis?"

"No." I winced. How embarrassing. How cowardly of me. "And then on New Year's Day—we did. As if nothing had happened. So afterward I said, 'Well, happy *New* Year,' or something, you know, sort of suggestive, so Curtis could say something if he wanted to. But he—he just looked at me very coldly, so . . . So that was the end of that, and since then we've been fine, normal. Sexually."

"Sexually."

"Yes."

"But not otherwise."

It's funny how it's easier sometimes to talk about your sex life, as intimate a subject as that is, than it is to talk about how the rest of your life is going. "Oh," I said, "it's just a combination of things. Different things adding up over a long time. No one specific thing. Just some thoughts I'm having, and thinking of talking to Curtis about. Soon."

Emma sighed. "Like *what*? Give me an example. So we can say we're having a conversation here."

"Well, for example. Tonight on the videotape. That part when we were all standing around outside my house, getting ready to leave for fitness camp. That shot of Curtis kissing me good-bye."

"Yeah, that was a little weird."

They'd picked me up last, and we were giddy and excited, anxious to get on the road. Each of us had weight-loss goals, but part of the plan was to stop en route for one last glorious, fattening meal at a country inn we'd found listed in a guidebook; that way, we theorized, we'd be at our heaviest for the camp's first-night weigh-in. So we were silly and giggly, already looking ahead, already gone, you might say. I should have known, and in the back of my mind I probably did know, that that kind of inattention or obliviousness on my part hurts Curtis's feelings. Well, more than that, it actually scares him. He needs me to be *aware* of him all the time. He needs to be the center. Otherwise, it's as if he doesn't quite believe he exists.

And so—anyway—when he kissed me, it wasn't that sweet, private peck husbands and wives exchange when they're in front of people who they know are watching. You know the kind I mean—"Bye, honey," "Take care," "Love you," with lips touching briefly, maybe a quick, hard hug. Playful and tender, but pretty impersonal as kisses go. No, this wasn't like that. At all. Without even drawing me away a little from the group, and knowing Lee was filming everything, Curtis put his arms around me and gave me a long, slow, *movie* kiss, very passionate and erotic and forceful—when I tried to stop, he wouldn't let me go. He made every thought in my head revert back to him. He did it on purpose. Kissing me, taking control of me like that, was his way of saying, "Think about *me*," to me, and "She's *mine*," to the Graces. In a way, it was worse watching it on film tonight, years later, than it had been when it happened. Because now it matches up with a lot of other memories. Similar ones, and some of them are even more disturbing.

"I think," I said slowly, "I don't want to be possessed anymore. And I used to."

"Possessed? No, I know what you mean," Emma said, "it's just . . . an odd word."

"I suppose. But I'm afraid, too, of anything changing. I hate change."

"Sure about that? Sure it's not Curtis who hates change, and what you hate is challenging him? Upsetting him?"

"Hm." Food for thought.

"Well, you're going slowly, but that's okay, that's probably good. Like losing weight on a diet—again, not that you would get that analogy. Just as long as there's movement. We have to assume your shrink knows what he's doing."

"I've been smoking in front of him," I said.

"Who? Eric?"

"Curtis."

"Get out."

"Not in the house when he's there, because I think that's rude, but when he's gone. But I don't gargle or spray room freshener on the curtains afterward so he won't know—none of that. And I smoke right in front of him when we're outside or in a restaurant or a bar. Eric says it's great. Well, he says it's *terrible*, he *hates* it that I smoke, but he likes it that I'm not hiding it from Curtis. Much healthier, he says."

"Well, I guess so. Yeah. It's actually very brave of you, Rude, in a perverted sort of way. Rotting your lungs while you stand up for yourself. Personal growth through emphysema."

"Care for a fag?"

"Sure."

We lit up.

"I never did this when I was young," I told her.

"Did what?"

"You know." Propped on our elbows, facing each other in our narrow bunk beds, stretching over occasionally to share the ashtray on the floor, we looked like teenagers on a sleepover. "Had a best girlfriend. Told secrets in the dark. Snuck cigs. I just never had this."

"Because you were too fucked up," Emma said matter-of-factly. "Your family screwed you over, but now you're getting over it. Now you're getting well. Slowly."

"You think?"

"Yes, I do."

She said it so adamantly, I pulled back, out of the candlelight so she couldn't see my face. The fledgling hope on it. I didn't want to look pathetic. "Hope so," I said.

"Oh yeah, I see it happening. Smoking in front of Curtis, my God. Whoa, Rudy, you are a wild woman." She wasn't being sarcastic. "That is fucking fantastic."

And to think that Curtis once asked me to stop being friends with Emma. "For your own good," he'd said. How *despicable*, when you stop to think about it. I couldn't tell Emma about that, it was too embarrassing, I felt ashamed for Curtis. It was proof, I had realized afterward—Eric helped me to see this—that Curtis had been pretending all along about Emma, making me believe he liked her in spite of her antagonism. Not in a good way, either. Not the way Emma bites her tongue and doesn't say what she truly thinks of him. She does that for my sake. She does it out of respect, and tact, and love. Curtis pretends because he's dishonest. It's another way he *possesses* me.

Emma yawned. We put out our cigarettes, blew out the candle.

"We always talk about me," I said sleepily.

"I know." She already had her eyes closed. "It's because you're such an egomaniac."

I snorted. "It's because you make me *ask* everything. You never volunteer, I have to drag it out of you. Oh, I forgot to tell you—Lee asked me what I thought about inviting Sally to join the group."

"Did she? She told me she was going to. What'd you say?"

"I said I was all for it."

"*What*?"

I laughed.

"You jerk," Emma grumbled, settling back down; she'd almost hit her head on the top bunk when she sat up. "Tell me what you really said."

"I said the same thing you did, that I didn't think it was a good time because of Isabel."

Emma got comfortable again. "Think Lee was disappointed?"

"No, not at all. I don't even know why she asked me. Just to be evenhanded, I guess. But that friendship's cooling off, you know." Which reminded me. "How come you told Lee you'd stay down here two more days?" Emma opened one eye. "That doesn't sound safe and sensible to me, Em. In fact, that seems positively out of character."

"You think I'm safe and sensible?"

"Well, compared to me."

"Oh. Compared to you." Even in the dark I could see her smile.

Tonight Lee had begged us—one of us, two, all three, she

didn't care—to stay over until Tuesday and then drive back with her and Henry. Nobody volunteered. We kept asking why, and finally she admitted it: she'd fallen out of her infatuation with Sally Draco. She had invited the Dracos down to the cottage months ago, but now she didn't want to spend two whole days in the exclusive company of Sally, with no one but the husbands to break up the intimacy.

"Why don't you like her anymore?" Emma had asked—trying to sound nonchalant.

"Oh, I don't know, no real reason," Lee had said. "There's nothing wrong with her, I just don't feel quite as comfortable around her as I used to. That's all."

Well, I don't either, but then, I never did. Maybe it takes one to know one, but I think Sally has big problems. And Emma's probably the least of them.

Isabel and I couldn't help Lee out, we both had to be home on Sunday. I could see Emma was thinking it over, but I couldn't have been more surprised when she said, "Okay, I'll stay if you want. I brought some work, I can do it down here as easily as at home."

I'd stared at her; she wouldn't look at me the whole time Lee was thanking her, telling her again it was no big deal, Sally was fine, nothing wrong with her, this would just make things easier. Isabel never said a word.

"So, Em," I said again, "why did you say you'd stay? Don't you think that's dangerous? Don't you think, seeing Mick with Sally for all that time and everything, don't you think it might . . . hurt? Hey, Em," I whispered. "Are you asleep?"

Maybe, maybe not. She didn't answer.

19

Emma

Rudy and Isabel got a late start back on Sunday afternoon. As soon as they left, I went for a walk on the beach. I should've stayed and helped Lee tidy up the cottage—Mick, Sally, and Henry were due within the hour. But I didn't. Why not? It wasn't laziness—I didn't want to be there when they drove up. I couldn't face standing beside Lee at the deck rail, looking down, waving and grinning, "Hey, how are you, you made it!" Also, I wanted Mick to have some warning. He wasn't expecting me, and his face can be so transparent; it would be bad enough if he looked too glad to see me, but worse if he looked . . . what's the word? Speculative.

I guess it was a gorgeous day. Lots of blue sky and white clouds, lacy surf, gulls and sanderlings, shells. Sand. The tide was moving in, not out, I know because I saw people dragging their blankets back and pulling up their umbrellas. But on the whole I was oblivious; I could've been walking along the streets of downtown Poughkeepsie. "Don't you think it might hurt?" Yes, Rudy, I think it might. Why didn't I consider that sooner? I guess because love is not only blind, it's a masochist.

Since Lee's party I'd seen him one time, at his studio. And talked to him once on the telephone. Both were intense, unsatisfying affairs, everything between us unspoken, everything unshown. Believe it or not, I do not thrive on trouble with men, and I'm not one of those women who choose the same dysfunction, whatever it might be, in man after man and obliviously revel in it. No, my pattern is to pick a different dysfunction every time, discover it, and run away as fast as I can. So why am I tormenting myself with Mick, who isn't dysfunctional at all? Why does he keep calling me? We're not reckless people—why are we doing this?

If you cut through the backyards of the three cottages between Lee's and the shore, you can avoid the road entirely, which is convenient if you're barefooted. Lee has forbidden this shortcut because it's "illegal," but when she's not with us we take it anyway. I was one cottage away from Neap Tide II (what is a neap tide, anyway?) when I heard a peal of Sally Draco's loud, high, enthusiastic laughter. That's when I knew I'd made one of the biggest mistakes of my life.

I couldn't see them yet, just hear them, Henry's slow baritone drawl, Lee's voice clear and clipped, Sally's higher, shriller, wound up tighter. I paused, listening for Mick's, and finally heard the low, noncommittal sound of his laughter.

What had I done? I didn't belong here. They did: they belonged to each other. Too late—no escape. A pall of loneliness settled on me, and I shivered under it, wretched and bleak from the knowledge that I deserved everything I was going to get.

Nobody noticed me, even though I stomped up the outside wooden steps to the deck. Too busy talking and laughing. No—somebody noticed me. I started back in surprise, as if a small animal had suddenly darted across my path. A child—Jay, Mick's little boy—I'd forgotten all about him. Had Lee been expecting him? He sat cross-legged on the porch floor, pointy-kneed, yellow-haired. He looked up, not startled at all, from the absorbing task of tying knots in a kite's tail. Blue eyes studied me with serious, shy curiosity for a few seconds. As soon as I smiled, he looked over his shoulder at his parents. *Social help!* you could almost hear him calling.

"There you are," Henry boomed, finally seeing me. Everybody turned around. I went forward, smiling, smiling, "Hi, how are you, how was your trip," kissing Henry, hugging Sally when she made me. Mick, Mick I waved to, a playful little hand salute from six feet away. I barely looked at him, kept him in my peripheral vision only, as if he were the sun. But I saw he'd gotten his hair cut, and it made him look younger, practically callow. It was a bad cut; his white scalp showed through on the sides. And he looked too pale, his face strained, the stubble of his beard blue-black against his white skin. Had he been ill?

"I'm so glad you decided to stay," Sally bubbled. She actually took both of my hands and looked me in the eyes. "How *are* you, how have you *been*?"

The panicky thought occurred that she knew everything and she was torturing me. How *are* you, how have you *been*—I don't give my mother straight answers to those questions. "Fine, *fine*," I said, trying to match her intensity. "Is this your little boy?"

That worked: she dropped my hands and called him. "Jay, come say hi to Emma."

Oh, poor kid. Why do people do that? Just what Jay wanted to do, come over and meet some old lady friend of his parents. He scrambled up and dragged himself over, dutifully mumbling, "Hi," and sticking out his hand to shake while staring at my knees. Mick put his hands on his son's skinny shoulders, and the kid leaned back against him, relaxing. He looked just like his picture, which is to say, angelic. And superficially like his mother because of the fair hair and light eyes, but there was also something dignified and noble about the shape of his head, and that could only have come from Dad. Not that I'm prejudiced.

"Suit up, everybody, we're off to the beach," Henry announced, to Jay's delight.

"Not me," I demurred. "I've had enough sun for one day."

This brought on the usual incredulous laughter and jokes at my expense. Henry was especially inventive, calling me "fish white" and comparing my complexion to that of Casper the friendly ghost.

"That's okay," I told him, "I'm used to the scorn of the ignorant and deluded, who won't be laughing so hard when they drop dead from melanoma."

But the real reason, of course, was because I didn't care to witness all that wholesome family fun, the laughing and splashing and cavorting, just one Kodak moment after another. When everybody finally went away and left me alone, I mixed a gigantic gin and tonic and drank it in the shower. I wouldn't mind drowning, I thought lugubriously. I could slither down the drain with the water and the soap scum and disappear, and nobody would even miss me.

I sobered up in time for dinner. Six of us piled into the Pattersons' station wagon and drove to Brother's, where we pigged out on barbecue and fried fish and potatoes and mountains of mayonnaise-drenched cole slaw. I sat across from Sally, who never stopped talking. Her hair was a new, expensive-looking shade of pewter blond, striking with her high-arched black brows and huge blue eyes. She would be a fascinating woman if she'd just close her mouth. She had an obsessive habit of looking at everyone after she said anything, no matter how commonplace, compulsively checking our facial expressions, monitoring our reactions. A false laugh punctuated almost every utterance, as if she had to announce in advance, *this is going to be funny*. I wondered if she could possibly be high. Probably not, but she was wound up like a spring, trying too hard, shrill.

Maybe they were fighting. Beside her, Mick sat in virtual silence, smiling with strained politeness. But solicitous of her, somehow. I still couldn't look at him directly, but I could see fatigue in the way he held himself, even the tilt of his head. No, they weren't fighting, I didn't think. This was how they lived.

"Mick might get a job," Sally announced. I jerked my head up at that. She gave the nervous laugh and leaned playfully against his stiff arm. I caught his eye for a second and saw dismay. "You know, a real job, one that pays actual money."

Lee shifted with embarrassment. Sally's discontent was uncomfortably transparent. Then, too, public talk about personal finances broke a cardinal rule in Lee's etiquette book. But she stared at Mick expectantly—we all did.

He said lightly, "Yes, I've been thinking of taking a part-time job."

"You wouldn't stop painting," I said.

"No." He flashed me another lightning-quick glance before we both looked away. "No."

"Too bad you don't plumb, you could come and work with me," Henry said in a hearty voice that dissipated the tension. "What kind of a job are you looking for?"

"Night watchman," Jay piped up.

Mick laughed, and Jay grinned up at him in surprise. "That was a joke," father explained to son. "Like working at McDonald's."

"Oh. But you could carry a gun if you was a night watchman."

"Were," Sally said automatically. She laughed the fake laugh again. "Jay wants Mick to work for either the zoo, McDonald's, or the rodeo."

"Or the air force," Jay put in.

"While I," she went on, "would be thrilled if he hired on as a Kelly Girl. Anything for a steady income. Ha!"

I stirred cold french fries around and kept my head down. The stiff-sounding silence stretched to infinity. What galled me was knowing he probably didn't even blame her. She'd convinced him that he'd failed her, but she couldn't come out and say it, she could only snipe.

"They're raising the rent on my studio," Mick explained presently, as if no awkward moment had occurred. "It's still all outgo and no income for me, so I'll probably hook up with my old law firm, do some part-time research for them on patents, claims, that sort of thing." He looked straight at me. "It won't be so bad."

Oh, but his paintings, his beautiful paintings. I felt sick. And scared, and furious at the injustice. And if I hadn't known before that this was love, I knew it now, because the truth is, his paintings still don't make a lick of sense to me.

By the time dinner ended and we drove home, the thought of spending several more hours in Mick and Sally's company was intolerable. Tough luck, Lee, you're on your own. "Are you okay?" she asked when I said I was going to bed early. "Sure, fine. I think I got too much sun." A good distraction; that's always worth several minutes of good-natured ribbing. Good-natured on my part. I said good night and disappeared.

Then I lay in bed and listened to them talking and laughing on the porch above me. Sometimes I could hear the words, usually just the cadences. Rising and falling, opinionated and tentative. I felt like a child, sent to bed at the height of her parents' cocktail party. Jay, speaking of children, was sleeping on a cot at the foot of Mick and Sally's bed. I could have offered to let him sleep with me in Rudy's empty bunk. But I hadn't. Guess why.

Around eleven o'clock, I heard footsteps descending the outside stairs and crunching off down the sandy driveway. I got to the window too late to see which couple it was, but a few minutes later I heard Henry's voice upstairs. So I knew. Mick and Sally. They'd gone for a walk. Full, romantic moon tonight. And they had a child in their bedroom, so . . .

You deserve it is not a solace when you're suffering the scalding agonies of sexual jealousy. Every sixty-second click of my travel clock felt like a bullet in the brain. I struggled against picturing them twined together on the cold sand under the blue moon, but once the image gelled it was indelible. She's lovely, she is, especially when she shuts up, and he's a passionate man, I know that for certain, no matter that he's never touched me.

Eleven-thirty-four, the clock read when Lee and Henry tiptoed down the hall and closed the door to their room. At eleven-forty, I got up and went into the bathroom I was sharing with the Dracos. Ostensibly to swallow a Sominex but really—I amazed myself, what a surprise—to look in Mick's shaving kit. Just look in it. See what he took on trips. A pathetic, embarrassing way to be close to him, but I had lost all shame.

Shaving stuff; he used Mennen soap and a Gillette razor, no aftershave. An ace bandage. Comb, but no brush. Nail clippers. A bottle of generic aspirin, a tube of Chap Stick, a roll of Tums. Sun shades, the kind you clip onto your regular glasses. No condoms. Dental floss. Some Neosporin. Brut stick deodorant. Crest toothpaste and an Oral-B brush. No condoms. Matches and safety pins and a lot of old Band-Aids at the bottom of the bag.

Why no condoms? Three possibilities. One, she took care of the contraception in the family. Two, they were trying to make a baby. Three, they didn't have sex anymore.

Far and away, I liked number three best.

Sally's flowered makeup case sat on top of the toilet, but I didn't touch it. In spite of the condom discovery, I'm telling you it wasn't *information* I was looking for. I just wanted to see his things. Really. Pitiful, I know, but I wanted to run my thumbnail along the teeth of his comb, check out how many aspirins he had left, sniff his shaving soap. See if there was an underarm hair on his deodorant. I don't care—laugh. I tell you, I was *gone*.

At eleven-fifty-six, they returned. They took turns in the bathroom, and by ten after twelve they were in bed with the door closed, the light out. No, I wasn't peeping through the keyhole, I could see it go out in the reflection on the pine tree outside our side-by-side windows.

Silence.

Now I could *really* obsess.

It's not easy to admit that imagining your beloved in the arms of another is not only unmitigated torture, it's also titillating. Sorry, but it is, it's sexy. Why not? Emotional anguish and physical arousal don't always cancel each other out. No, indeed. The anguish only makes the arousal sharper. Darker. And relieving it yourself, if you're reduced to that, only makes you feel worse, even more alone and—superfluous. Expendable. In the gray, nauseating hour before dawn, I thought about packing my things and leaving, but the logistics defeated me. I'd have to steal a car.

When I finally went to sleep, I fell into a coma and slept half the day away. This is a pattern with me, I see; the night after I threw Peter Dickenson out of my apartment—years ago; don't even ask—I went to bed and slept around the clock, a dead woman. Nothing wrong with that; safer than drugs or booze, much cheaper. Call it nature's Nembutal.

I woke up and stumbled upstairs—the common areas in the cottage are on the second floor, bedrooms on the first—to find the house empty. Good, I thought, until the third cup of coffee and the second cheese and tomato sandwich; then my company began to seriously bore me. I put on my bathing suit and headed for the beach.

How quaint—the men were playing Frisbee while the women watched. I endured the inquiries about my health and, after I assured everybody I was fine, the jokes about my shiftlessness. To catch the shade from Lee's umbrella, I spread my towel sideways behind hers. Sally lay next to her. I got all my stuff arranged—book, lotion, sunglasses, hat, rolled-up towel for a pillow—and stretched out on my stomach. And joined the women watching the men.

It was a three-sided game, Henry and Mick at the ends and Jay in the middle. The men flung the disk at each other with muscular, grunting, Olympian hurls, lobbed it softly and gently to the child with scrupulous accuracy. There's something reassuring about watching men play games with children. When they're patient and delicate, when they make allowances, when they compromise and camouflage their own superiority—in other words, when they behave like women—it reinforces our illusion that they're civilized.

Underneath the mindless pleasure of watching this game, though, I was worried about Lee and Henry. I studied their faces, but neither of them was showing anything except bland enjoyment. But how could they not be suffering? Like Rudy, I was glad when Lee had lost it a little, as much as she ever loses it, and opened up to us about her fears and her anger over their childlessness. Because she's the most self-sufficient, Lee uses the group for therapy less than the rest of us. So even though I'd known on some level that she was feeling all the ugly emotions of resentment and jealousy and fury and guilt, it was still a shock to hear her admit it. And now to watch Henry play so prettily, so sweetly with Jay, who's like this golden cherub, this epitome of Perfect Kid, this everyman's dream son—how could it not cut her to the heart?

But they're doing okay, I think. I hope. Deep down. Because these two really were made for each other. From the beginning, Lee's been amazingly frank with the group about her passion for Henry, and when you're with them you can actually *feel* it. Nothing blatant or overt—heavens—but I'm telling you, heat practically vibrates in the air between them. It's partly the way he looks at her, like she's the goddess of sex and he hasn't had any in a hundred years, and partly Lee's prim, buttoned-up manner. Watching them together always starts my imagination moving down a sexy path. Gets me a little hot, if you want to know the truth.

Before I made my early escape last night, I wandered out on the deck for some air, only to find that Lee and Henry were already there, relaxing against the rail in a dark corner. "Oops." I almost mumbled an excuse and backed out. And they weren't even doing anything—he had his arms around her from behind and she was leaning back against him, her hands wrapped around his wrists. They smiled at me, then went back to staring up at the moon. My presence didn't bother them in the least, but *I* felt as if I'd walked in on a love scene. That's how intimate it was, that wall, that blur of tenderness they'd put around each other. When he leaned over and casually rubbed her cheek with his, slow and soft, a purely loving gesture, I had a lump in my throat. I said good night and got out.

Oh, I want what they have. I yearn for it. It's what everybody longs for, isn't it? Sweet, deep intimacy with another? And I know it's a chimera, a dream, it comes in flashes at best, it's hardly ever what it seems—I don't care. The way they blended into each other, the way they turned into one there in the shadows . . . what a well of loneliness that opened in me. Real or not, there are times when I would gladly settle for the dream.

"I'll really miss ballet," Sally said, sitting up to rub sunscreen on her legs. I looked at her blankly. "I was telling Lee," she said in a solicitous tone, anxious to include me. "I've got to drop out of our class. We just can't afford it anymore, too many other things are more important. It's the only activity I do just for myself, so it's hard. But what are you going to do?" Brave, plucky smile.

"Yeah, that's a shame," I said. Lee, I noticed, didn't say anything, barely looked at her. Hm. More of a strain here than I'd expected. And I'd been evading the one task Lee gave me, which was to be the buffer between her and Sally this weekend. I felt bad about that, but God, had she ever tapped the wrong person for the job.

I didn't see the Frisbee until it smacked me in the shoulder—caught the bone and hurt like hell. Henry came trotting over, sweaty and grinning, panting like a dog. "Sorry, Em. You okay?"

"Sure." I handed it up to him with a good-sport smile. His red-white-and-blue-striped suit hung to his knees, baggy and uncharacteristically hip. He heaved the disk in the air, high over Jay's blond head. Mick flexed his knees and executed a stunning vertical leap that made his son shout with approval. Shielding my face from Sally with the side of my hand, I stared at her husband.

He'd definitely lost weight. He was too thin. I shouldn't have blamed her, but I did. Except for his forearms, he was nearly as pale as me. I wanted to touch that tender demarcation line on his biceps, white to golden tan, run my lips along it, my teeth. Everything about him stirred me, everything was exactly right. It felt illicit, practically taboo to look at him like this, stare openly at his thighs and his calves, the ribs in his sides, his chest hair, his collarbone. To see him run and bound, when before I'd only seen him walk or sit.

It was the fact that Mick and his legs and his long back and his hard stomach were *forbidden* to me that made them so unbearably attractive—I knew that—and yet he was beautiful, truly he was, no matter that he was too thin, too pale, his hair too short. "He looks a little bit like Daniel Day-Lewis," Isabel once said, a long time ago. I, of course, said nothing to that, but I remember thinking, *Daniel should be so lucky*.

But why do I keep obsessing about him? What is this doomed, lunatic, self-destructive need to keep him in my mind? Why can't I forget about him—why can't he forget about me?

In my case, it's because I just can't resist. Over and over, I find that my need (not my desire; I'm beyond that) is stronger than my discretion (not my conscience; we still haven't done anything wrong). I rationalize that our infrequent meetings are indiscreet, not immoral. They don't hurt anyone but me. And him.

Oh God, that's the dangerous, seductive part, the chance that he feels what I do. I think it's true. He's not very good at disguise—I'm much better—so he doesn't hide his gladness when we're together, and he isn't cool or suave on the phone. Our conversations get more and more personal. In the last one, I started to tell him about the last time I saw my mother, and ended up describing my childhood. How it felt when my father walked out, how it felt when he died. Now he knows things about me that, before, only Rudy knew.

I know things about him, too. I can picture the earnest overachiever he used to be, winning track medals and getting straight A's for Mom and Dad, dedicating his young life to making his adoptive parents proud of him. Proud and not sorry. He told me it wasn't only Sally he let down when he gave up the law, it was his parents, too. In a way, it was even harder to disappoint them, because their expectations had been even higher. Now they laugh about him to their friends, he thinks—but gently, fondly; philosophically. *What are you going to do?* he imagines them saying. That hurts him so much.

So—we know things about each other. We're intimate in the strangest way, like jail mates who communicate through the plumbing, or bang out a code with our tin cups against the wall. We share secrets, but never touch.

Jay got tired and came slogging through the sand to our umbrella encampment. He collapsed between my towel and his mother's, and asked for a soft drink from the cooler. He drank it noisily, his eyes still on Mick and Henry, whose game had ratcheted up several notches on the macho scale now that it was just the two of them. "Hi," he said to me with a shy, sideways grin.

"Hi, yourself."

"So you slept late," he observed.

"Yep. Guess I was tired."

"How come?"

"Mmm." I thought. "Bad dreams?"

He nodded. "I have them. Nightmares, I have. I wake up, and my dad comes. Or my mother sometimes. Then I go back to sleep."

"Me, too." Except for the mother and father part. "What do you dream about?"

"Monsters. What do you dream about?"

"Well, usually I dream I'm late for something, and I can't find it." Lost and late; I have these dreams incessantly. "I don't know where the train station is, or sometimes it's the bus station, and everybody's giving me different directions. Then the bus comes, or the train, but I don't know where it goes, I can't read the number, and I'm late, I'm so late, and everything keeps repeating and repeating, until finally I wake up out of boredom."

Jay stared at me for a long second, then belched.

"'Scuse me," he muttered, with a glance at Sally. She only smiled and raised her eyebrows at him.

I wish I could say she's a bad mother—No, I don't, no, I don't, that was a figure of speech, even I am not so far gone that I'd wish a lousy parent on a helpless child. In any case, she's *not* a bad mother, she seems like a very good one from what I've seen with my jaundiced eye, very attentive and low-key, very affectionate. And yet—you knew there was an *and yet*—Jay behaves differently with Sally than he does with Mick. He's giggly and loose with Dad, silly and relaxed and happy, a normal, well-adjusted kid. But with Mom, he sobers up fast. His youthful brow furrows and he watches her closely, worriedly. At five and a half, he's already a little caretaker.

Not that I'm an expert on children. Hell no, they scare the daylights out of me. They're so autonomous or something. So unforgivingly straightforward. Irony's not in their vocabulary, so they never get my jokes. As a rule I stay out of their way—but you'll understand that this one fascinated me, so I was paying special attention to him. What I saw was a polite, anxious boy, bashful and very sweet, but wary and much too observant for his age. As if he were compelled to check the temperature, over and over, of whatever emotional atmosphere he found himself in.

Incredibly, Jay has decided he likes me. It happened last night at Brother's, and I could see the change so clearly, see the decision as he was making it in his naked, guileless, child's face. Don't ask me why, I've forgotten the context, but I had launched into a minirant on the perversities of anthropomorphism and the amazing arrogance of us humans toward the so-called lesser creatures—all right, I'd had a couple of beers—and for examples, I was mentioning names like "panfish," "box turtle," "pocket mouse," "fur seal," humble creatures whose very existence we've limited and defined by naming them according to how they relate exclusively to *us*. For some reason the word "panfish" struck Jay as the funniest thing he'd ever heard, and he went off.

He couldn't stop laughing, and he's got this lovely, low, gurgling giggle, just the essence of delight. It's irresistible, and pretty soon we were all snickering along with him. Then Henry and I started naming the silliest-sounding fish we could think of, to try to get him going again—scrod, kipper, fluke, smelt, croaker, you get the idea. I said "crappie," and Jay lost it—he almost slid off his chair. What fun; I think I've found my best audience ever. And when he finally recovered, he kept beaming at me with the goofiest, the most charming, sweet-faced appreciation.

Question: Am I that vain, or is this really the nicest, brightest kid I've ever met?

The day drew to a lazy close that seemed early to me—I'd gotten up so late. We had dinner at home, burgers and hot dogs on the grill. Afterward, Lee got me alone and demanded to know what was wrong.

"Wrong? Nothing. Wrong? What do you mean?" I tried to look astonished, but panic flickered in my chest. Did she know?

"It's Mick, isn't it?"

"No," I denied, horrified.

"What I can't understand is *why* you don't like him."

"But I *do*—"

"I shouldn't have asked you to stay. I'm sorry, Em." She'd been cleaning the stove within an inch of its life. She sat down at the kitchen table, damp dish towel in one hand, a glass of ice water in the other. She looked hot and irritable. She pressed the glass to her forehead, and for the first time I noticed she also looked tired.

"No," I insisted, "I was happy to stay. Really, I'm having a great time."

She dismissed that with a wave. "I don't blame you for hiding out. I would if I could, too. To tell you the truth, it's Sally's company I don't enjoy that much anymore," she all but whispered. A needless precaution, since no one was in the house but us: Henry, Mick, Sally, and Jay had gone for a moonlight walk on the beach. Lee ran her fingers through her short brown hair, sighing. "I just wish she'd stop telling me things I don't want to know."

"Personal things?"

She nodded. "When we were first getting to be friends, I told her a few things about me—us, Henry and me. Nothing really intimate," she said quickly, "not like I would tell the group—"

"No, no."

"But somewhat personal, you know—"

"Sure."

"But I've quit, but she *keeps* telling me things."

"Like . . ." I waited hopefully. Shamelessly.

"Like—they've been in couples counseling for five of the six years of their marriage."

"Wow." Mick had never even hinted at such a thing. How discreet. In the same situation, most men would have, don't you think? What a rationale: *My marriage is a wreck, let's go to bed.*

"And I hate the way she talks about her husband," Lee went on, leaning close. "Henry's crazy about Mick, and I like him, too. We feel more loyal to him now than her."

"What does she say about him?"

"Oh, you know, how she resents his job change and what it's done to their lifestyle, how it's changed everything. She's from Delaware—apparently her family has money. She actually said to me, 'I didn't buy into this.' She laughed afterward, pretending it was a joke, but it wasn't."

"No."

"It's so—it just makes me angry. I married a plumber, but I've never been ashamed of Henry, never. It's part of who he is, which makes it part of what I love about him." She sat back, blowing her bangs out of her eyes. "Then again, what if he decided all of a sudden to give up plumbing and take up—I don't know. Winemaking. How would I like that?"

"Well, how would you?"

She shook her head. "I wouldn't care."

"No, you wouldn't. Because he'd still be Henry."

"And that's who I love."

I thought about Sally and who she loved. Presumably she used to love Mick the lawyer. Michael Draco, Esquire, was worth loving, especially in his three-piece suit and suspenders. But Mick the penniless painter wasn't. She hadn't bought into that.

Oh, she was a piece of work, all right. Her insecurities made you pity her, and her insincerity made you dislike her. But she was a good mother; somehow with Jay she transcended all her neuroses.

Poor Mick. Even I could see that he was trapped.

Around ten o'clock that night, Jay woke up screaming. I didn't even hear him at first; we five were upstairs with the TV on, although only Henry was watching it—some basketball game. Mick jumped up first, but Sally said, "I'll go," and hurried out of the room.

Lee had been reading. She laid her magazine aside and asked, "Does he have nightmares a lot, Mick?"

"Just lately, yes. They're coming almost every night." The crying stopped all at once. He relaxed slightly; some of the tension went out of his face.

"It's not that unusual at his age," Lee assured him. "In fact it's probably more common than otherwise. You shouldn't worry too much. Really."

He thanked her with a smile. "I know it's normal, but still—"

"It's upsetting."

He stood up again. "I just want to go see. Check. You know, make sure," he muttered apologetically, and disappeared.

He came back a few minutes later, looking relieved. "He's asleep and everything's fine," he reported, and we all said, "Good, good." "Sally's going to bed, by the way. She said to say good night."

So then it was just the four of us, spending a quiet last night reading and watching television. Henry had the whole couch to himself; he had a warm beer on his chest, and occasionally he would mutter things like, "*What* loose ball foul?" and "Shoot, *shoot*, what the hell are you waiting for?" Lee sat at the dining room table, absorbed in the July *Vogue*. Mick divided his attention between the game and his book, a library hardcover called *Murder at the Hard Rock*. Me? I was doing an impression of someone reading the latest Louise Erdrich, which I'd brought along on purpose to impress people, but in fact I was watching Mick. And sometimes, he was watching me.

Lee yawned, stretched. "Well, I'm going to bed. Henry?"

"Yep. In a minute."

"Night, you guys," Lee said to Mick and me. We said it back.

Henry's minute stretched to fifteen as his team kept calling time-outs. *I should leave before he does*, I kept advising myself. It was going to be just Mick and me, and it was going to be awkward. But I reread the same paragraph over and over and didn't move.

Henry vaulted off the couch, energized by his side's win at the buzzer. "Great game. Lee go to bed?"

We chuckled and said she had.

"So, early or late start back tomorrow?"

"Early for us, I'm afraid," Mick said. "Sally's folks are driving down for dinner." From Delaware, I assumed. The folks with the money.

"What about you, Em? Any rush?"

"No, not really. Whenever you and Lee want to go."

"Great. Morning on the beach, then." I've never known anybody who likes the ocean as much as Henry, not even Isabel. He's like a kid. "Course," he had to add, "you might've maxed out by now. How many minutes have you spent in the full, undiluted sun this weekend? Ten? Fifteen? Ha ha!"

"Ha ha."

Still laughing, he tossed his beer can in the trash—"Three points!"—and went downstairs.

He'd left the TV on. Mick and I glanced at each other, then turned as one to stare at two sports announcers, a black guy and a white guy, recapping the game. We did that for a while. A new announcer's voice came on to tell us that if we stayed tuned, we could hear all the sports news and scores from around the country. I stood up.

I don't know why the tension was so tight. We'd been alone together before. We were *friends*. But when I looked at Mick, my muscles gave out. I stood there with rubber knees, taking shallow breaths and feeling as if my skin didn't fit me anymore, it had gotten too thin and sensitive, too tight.

He stood up, too. One look at his face, and it was all over. I honestly don't know who moved, who put out a hand first. Even up to the last second, it could've been innocent—just a touch, a good-night brush of fingers. But we gripped hands hard, and in the next second we were holding each other.

We broke away quickly. Fatalistic, I clutched at the phantom memory of his hard shoulders, the cottony smell of his T-shirt, thinking that was all I could have. He said something. I couldn't understand him, my senses were dazed. "What?" He snatched at my hand and pulled me outside, out onto the deck.

Too bright—too open. We went down the outer stairs as quietly as we could, me barefooted, Mick in his unlaced sneakers. Under the house, in the shadowy space between his car and a padlocked storage shed, we stopped. One last second of sanity while we faced each other, hands off. We could go back up, we could just talk—

We kissed. It was painful, not joyful, but I couldn't stop—like drinking seawater if I were dying of thirst, it would kill me in the end but I had to have it. I clutched at his arms, covered his whole mouth with mine, grinding my body against him. He turned us, pressed me back against the side of the shed. My head struck something—the metal fuse box. "Ow." Mick started to take his hands off me, but I grabbed him back, urgent.

"Kiss me," I said, even though he already was. I kept saying it, like some exciting obscenity, because it felt good to say the *truth* for a change, tell him for once what I really wanted. He wasn't as articulate—he murmured curse words in between kisses, but to me they sounded like love poetry. He put his hands in my hair. "So pretty," he said, and my heart just sang. He'd never given me a compliment before. It meant so much. I kissed him tenderly, not like a madwoman, and we both started shaking. He slid his hands up from behind, inside my blouse. Skin on skin.

Shuddering, hissing in my breath, I gasped out the fatal question. "Mick, Mick, where can we go?"

Glare from the outside spotlight glittered in his eyes when he turned his head, looking around. I saw the same outlaw indifference to consequence that I was feeling. He took my hand. We picked our way past the pilings and stepped off the concrete pad onto the grass, along a narrow, half-beaten path to a row of scrub pines separating Neap Tide from the beach house behind it. From there the path turned toward the sea. Where was he taking me? Would we drop between the pines and kiss some more in the dark? Would we keep going till we reached the water and make love in the cold sand in the moonlight? I followed him blind, thoughtless, loving the feeling of being tugged along, and so glad the choice was his and not mine.

I stepped on a burr.

Mick caught my elbow when I started hopping on one foot and swearing. I stuck my foot out behind me and tore at the stinging thistle, but I only got part of it; as soon as I took one step, I was hobbling again. "Sit," he said, and we sank down together in the sand.

Wasn't this just like my life? A living analogy? Accidental performance art? He made me straighten my leg out and put my foot in his lap. He tried to be gentle, but by the time he plucked out the last of the spiky, prickly nettles in the soft part of my arch, we were different people. We had turned back into our old selves. Our thinking selves. I mourned the loss so sharply, I wanted to weep.

The wind blew the feathery fronds of sea oats and stirred the beach grass, carrying the heavy smell of the sea. So many stars, more stars than black sky, and a moon one night past full. We stayed where we were, enclosed in the steady roar of the surf, watching each other. Mick studied the look of his hand around my ankle, pale on paler, and I measured the weight of my calf on his thigh. He had on gray sweatpants and a black T-shirt. Moonlight picked out the silver in his too-short hair, and I leaned closer to touch him, overcome by a stabbing, irresistible tenderness. We started to speak at the same time. I gestured—*you first.*

"When we got here and I heard you were staying," he said, and stopped. I scooted closer. "I thought I'd just see—remnants of you. I was looking forward to finding an old book you'd read and discarded, a—" He laughed with no sound. "A wet towel."

"I looked in your shaving kit," I blurted. "Just to see. I touched your things." He put his hand on the side of my face, and I closed my eyes. "I shouldn't have stayed. Oh, Mick. I knew it as soon as I saw you."

"But I'm glad you stayed."

"I'm glad, too, but it's crazy."

"I know."

"What are we going to do?"

"I don't know."

So much for having my will taken away from me. That had been my secret hope, that Mick would take charge, make all the decisions, tell me what to do, *make* me do it if I put up any resistance. Kind of like a father and his little girl.

I embarrassed myself.

"Emma—I don't think I can leave my family. I can't leave Jay."

"I know, I know that, I'm not asking you to," I said quickly, stumbling over the words in my haste. That he should think for a second that I wanted to wreck his marriage—and yet he broke my heart with his finality, his lack of equivocation. I didn't want games, but I needed something, some slender thread of made-up hope to hold on to.

I covered his hand on my cheek with my hand. "I have so many things to tell you." He bent his head, leaning closer. "But also, I have nothing to tell you. If you can't leave her."

He swallowed, his face bleak with pain.

I was in pain, too. "Do you still make love to her? Have you had other women besides me? I don't know anything about you. How can I be in love with you, we've never even gone to the movies. I *hate* this. I want—I just want—I want to hold hands with you, Mick, call you up on the telephone—"

This was torture. He didn't say anything, didn't answer. Even now, he couldn't talk to me about his marriage, couldn't bring himself to betray Sally to me. And now would have been the perfect time to say, "Emma, I'm miserable, she doesn't understand me, let's be lovers." But Mick had no rap, no married-guy patter, he couldn't excuse himself by enumerating his wife's failings. Most especially, he couldn't walk out on his little boy, who already worried about Mommy, and woke up screaming in the night from bad dreams.

"This is it, isn't it? This is all we're going to get." I touched Mick's mouth, his raspy cheek. I put my fingers in his hair. "Darling, who gave you this godawful haircut?" I said, choked on tenderness, feeling tears sting behind my eyes.

He said, "I didn't want this to happen. The last thing I wanted to do was hurt you."

"I know that. Anyway, it's too late."

"Emma . . . "

Then we were kissing again, eyes shut tight as if we could stay blind to the truth that this was hopeless, this was just putting off the inevitable. But, God, it felt right to hold him, it felt like the most honest thing I'd done since we met.

It had to stop. We backed off shakily, breathing hard, like teenagers in the backseat at the drive-in. "God," I said, and he said, "Emma, Christ," and we sat back on our haunches and stared at each other.

"Okay. Okay," I said, "it's over. No more. Because this is killing me."

He helped me to stand. That sounds silly, but I needed help. He glanced over my head, back at the cottage, and I looked back, too—a reflex. There was nothing to see, no lights on upstairs, no suspicious wife on the side porch, hands on her hips, surveying the dunes. But his anxiety infected me. It made me feel sick.

"Do you want me to go back first?"

He looked at me sharply. "No."

"You see how we would be at this?" I said a little wildly. "We wouldn't even have any fun. We can't see each other anymore, Mick, not at all. Don't call me, don't do anything."

He nodded once. He put the palms of his hands on his forehead and pressed. "Lee and Henry are bound to have something."

"I know. If I hear you've been invited, I won't go."

"No, you go, I'll stay away."

"No, you're friends with Henry, and I can see Lee anytime. You go."

I turned and started back toward the cottage, keeping my eyes on the path, wary of rogue nettles. Another metaphor for my life. Mick and I had never even made it to the beach, never made glorious, swept-away love beside the crashing waves. Because of a burr, we'd hunkered down in the chilly sand and made do with a few furtive kisses.

I never cry in front of people. It's a matter of pride, or maybe it's a phobia. Anyway, I don't do it. Imagine my chagrin when we got to the bottom of the wooden steps at the side of the house and I realized I couldn't stop. I could have waved good-bye and run up alone—he'd never have known then. But I didn't want to leave him yet.

"Shit," I whispered when he put his arms around me. Were we safe here? What if someone came out—Henry, to smoke a cigar? Jay, sleepwalking? Lee overcome by a sudden compulsion to sweep the porch? "I hate this, I hate it."

"I hate it, too, and it's my fault. I swear I never wanted this."

"Stop saying that, it's nobody's fault. Anyway, we haven't done anything."

"I've made you miserable."

"That's true. I forgive you."

We kissed, smiling. But then I spoiled it by starting up again. "I'm not like this," I assured him, using his T-shirt to dry my face. "I'm really not, this is a first."

He pretended to believe me. He stroked the tears from my cheeks with his fingers, and then he leaned in and pressed his face to mine. "Sorry to hurt you. Not sorry this happened. I've been lying since the beginning."

"I've been lying, too."

"At least . . . "

"Yeah." At least we weren't lying anymore. There was some chilly comfort in that.

"I'll miss you," he whispered.

"Oh, don't." But I didn't break away, I wanted every futile, agonizing second.

A last kiss, very soft. No passion, just—good-bye. I don't like the feel of my heart breaking. It's very romantic, but it stings like acid.

"Bye. I'm sleeping in tomorrow, Mick—I don't want to see you."

Those were the last words. Car lights swung off the highway onto our cul-de-sac, a stranger's car, but it scared us. We backed away from each other. I turned and ran up the steps, tiptoed inside, slunk down the hall past the closed door to Sally's room, and ducked into mine.

Closed the door. Sat on the bed in the dark and waited until I heard Mick in the hall. His door opened and closed softly. I listened like an animal, like a wolf, but there was no sound, no murmur of voices. Nothing.

I had a long time, all night, to suffer for my disappointment. I'd wanted her to catch him. I'd wanted the jig to be up.

He's wrong—he should leave her for me. I could make him happy, and I could fall in love with Jay. In fact, I already have.

But.

But what I love about my lover is that he's true. Damn him. He's killed me.

20

Isabel

I've discovered purgatory. Not hell—it's too boring. Purgatory is low-lit and industrial-carpeted, mauve-walled, library-quiet except for a wall-mounted television permanently tuned to CNN. It's called the Diagnostic Imaging Department.

My heart rate invariably drops in the waiting room. I sit on one of the thinly upholstered, pine-and-tweed chairs and feel my facial muscles go limp. I don't see well; the air is blurred, grainy. My nerves, my energy, everything drains into the pastel walls and the soft-tiled ceiling, the flaccid Renoir reproductions. *Someone take care of me, please*, I'm reduced to pleading. *Be tender. Don't hurt me*. It's a giving over, a relinquishment, the medical version of "Into Thy hands." Utter passivity. Nothing I can do. It's a relief to let go, stop trying to be in charge of my life, if only for this little bit of time.

Today I'm here for a chest X ray. Before, it was days and days of radiation therapy for my hip. Whatever they did, it fixed me up—I have very little pain now, and I walk without a limp. Given that, you might think I'd like this place better. But no. I remind myself of Grace: they've never really hurt her at the vet's, but she begins to shake in terror as soon as she sniffs the parking lot.

But no one looks frightened here, not even the children. I make a covert study of my radiology comrades, hunting for signs of despair, panic, devastation. I'm never successful. No one weeps silently, huddled into herself; no one ever breaks down. Do I look like these people? They could be waiting for their insurance agent, the dentist. Is my face that flat and accepting? That empty of drama?

"Mrs. Kurtz?"

A thin young woman with freckles and wispy hair smiles at me from the double doors. I follow her down two short corridors to the changing area. "Hi, how are you today?" she asks as we walk. She zips a curtain back from one of the tiny booths. "Everything off from the waist up, and put on one of these robes. I'll be back to get you in a minute. Okay?"

I strip out of my sweater, blouse, prosthetic bra, and put on the blue cotton robe. It makes me look hippy, cinched in at the waist over my slacks. My face is ghastly in the fluorescent glare, and yet I feel a rush of love for myself, a painful tenderness. Oh, poor Isabel.

The technician comes back. The tag on her uniform says she's Ms. Willett. Inside the spacious X-ray room, I start to undo my robe, but she says, "That's okay," and stands me up in front of a white square of wood or plastic, like a basketball backboard, my arms at my sides. She disappears. I hear her voice from across the room; she's gone behind the protective shield. "Okay, very still. Deep breath. Hold it, hold it. And relax."

Another picture from the side, and then one more from the back. "Okay, that should do it. Wait here for a minute, okay? I'll be right back."

It's never a minute, it's always longer, five, frequently ten. She's finding the radiologist, who will check to see if she got the pictures right. Sometimes they have to take them over again. This is the worst part, waiting for the technician to return. When she does, she never tells you anything, so the tension is pointless, but I feel it anyway. My fear and fatalism and self-pity reach their peak at this stage. I always go to the magazine stand and pull out *People* or *Woman's Day*, anything. I stand with my face to the wall and flip the pages of slimming chicken recipes, articles on the miracle of antioxidants, fashion ads, "pants that slink and shimmer are the sexiest option for after dark."

"All right," Ms. Willett says brightly, coming back into the room empty-handed. "You can get dressed." I search her face. Was that sympathy in her voice? She knows what the X-rays showed. Did the doctor point to a spot on the film and shake his head with her? No, it couldn't be. Her smile is too chipper. I couldn't have a lung metastasis—she wouldn't look like that.

Right or wrong, I feel better by the minute. Getting dressed in the booth is the precise reverse, emotionally, mentally, of getting undressed. Riding up in the elevator to the first floor, striding through the automatic doors to the sidewalk, breathing in the clean, nonmedicinal air—I'm a new woman. Out here, I'm one of the normal ones, not defined by my illness anymore, indistinguishable from the rushing, bustling, oblivious, healthy people. Just like them, I could be immortal.

I walked across Pennsylvania Avenue and started up K Street, taking my time. On my way to the hospital, I hadn't much noticed what kind of day it was. If I had, I might have resented it. Because it was perfect, one of those golden days when summer is ending but autumn hasn't begun. The air smelled sweet and the sun slanted in the tired, aging, still-green leaves of the trees as if through a sympathetic photographer's gauze filter. Rush hour had just begun, but passersby looked relaxed, not harried, as seduced by the softness of the afternoon as I was.

But I was tired by the time I reached Farragut Square, too tired to stand on Connecticut and wait for the bus. I bought a cup of coffee from a street vendor—the only vice I have left is caffeine; otherwise my diet is strictly macrobiotic—and sat down on a bench in the park.

And fell into a morbid game I catch myself playing at odd times. Wrinkled old ladies, children, young men, pretty girls, mothers with toddlers, surly teenagers, old men—to each of them as they strode or hobbled or ambled past me, I thought, *You're dying. You're dying, and you're dying, and you're dying, and you're dying, and you're dying, and you're dying, and you're dying.* I didn't do this for comfort, certainly. Perhaps it was a way to persuade myself of the unthinkable, the outlandish—that no one gets out alive. The truth is, I still have trouble believing in death. Yes, even now.

Perhaps it's not important anyway. Maybe it's enough to be alive and know it. In this never-to-be-repeated instant in the vastness of time, I, Isabel, have the miraculous privilege to exist. Sipping hot coffee softened with a delicious nondairy powdered creamer. It's really tasty. Starlings are tuning up in the oak trees. The air smells like perfume, then auto exhaust, then perfume again. I love the worn feel of this bench under my fingers, smoothed to velvet softness by a million behinds. Here I am in the world, right now, this minute. I never was before, never will be again. I simply exist, and it's glorious. An honor and a privilege. A marvel beyond belief.

"Mind?"

I looked up to see a man bending toward me at the side of the bench, smiling widely. I was perplexed until he made a stiff-armed gesture toward the empty space beside me. "Yes—no, I don't, go ahead." I moved over a few inches, pulling my purse closer to my hip.

He came around with a series of short, dragging steps and slowly, creakily, lowered his backside to the seat. His breath came out in a long *ahhh* of relief, and he sat back by degrees, settling himself on the bench the way an old dog settles itself on a front porch floor. From the corner of my eye I saw him take a handkerchief out of one pocket of a heavy maroon cardigan, much too warm for the mild September afternoon, and dab under his nose daintily with a horny, discolored hand. He turned to me, full-faced, and pulled his thin lips into the widest smile I've ever seen, practically ear to ear, and said, "Pretty day, isn't it?"

"Beautiful," I nodded.

"I don't like that humidity."

"No, I don't either. None today, though."

"*Pretty* day today."

"It's lovely."

He pushed his mottled cheeks out, froglike, and turned his affable, pale-eyed gaze from me to the branches overhead. He shoved his hands under one knee and hauled it up, crossing it over the other with a huff of breath. His feet bulged out of beige socks and worn brown sandals, as if he had bunions and corns and who knew what else. "Where'd you get that coffee?" he asked.

"Across the street." I pointed.

He smiled and said, "Huh," nodding his head. "Smells good."

"Do you want some? I could get you a cup."

"No, no! Thank you very much!" He grinned, showing bright white false teeth. "I've given it up, it was getting on my nerves. Still like the smell, though. Not like cigarettes. Gave them up, and they smell horrible now, smell like hell. You smoke?"

"No, I never did."

"Very wise. My wife didn't smoke, either." He broke off to cough into his handkerchief, a rough, wet, old man's cough. He turned away to spit discreetly into the handkerchief, then stuffed it back into his pocket. He reached inside his sweater and brought out, presumably from his shirt pocket, a photograph. No, two photographs. "Here's Anna, my wife. We met over in Italy during the war. She was Italian."

He wanted me to take the pictures, not just look at them in his hand. I did, and saw two versions of Anna, slim and pretty in the first, plump and pretty in the second, smiling the same mysterious smile in both. Mysterious to me—it's hard to know what a stranger's smile means.

"I lost her in 1979." He pushed his cheeks in and out, in and out.

"How did she die?" A too-personal question I couldn't stop myself from asking.

"She had cancer of the cervix."

"I'm sorry. Do you have children?"

He shook his head. "A baby," he said, "but we lost her very quickly, very quickly. After that, we couldn't have any more."

"I'm so very sorry." I barely stopped myself from touching him. And I'd said that too fervently; it was so long ago, my sympathy must sound extreme.

He spread his fingers wide over the knees of his shiny brown trousers, a kind of digital shrug. "Thank you," he said with much dignity. "Are you married, if I can ask?"

"No." For some reason I added, "I have a son."

"Is he married?"

"No. But he lives with someone." A woman I've only heard about, never met. Susan; she's an elementary school teacher. When did I lose Terry? He went away to school in Montreal and never came back. I tried for a long time not to call it an escape, but after so many years, that's no longer possible. Terry ran away from his father and me. I don't blame him, and I don't believe in lifelong regrets, but that failure is the singular tragedy of my life.

"They do that nowadays, don't they," the old man said. "Nobody thinks a thing of it."

I nodded. "Shacking up, we used to call it."

"That's right. Shacking up." He laughed merrily. "My name's Sheldon Herman. I won't shake because I've got a cold."

"I'm Isabel."

"Pleased to meet you. Look here." He took out another picture. "That's Moxie." A floppy-eared mongrel, mostly German shepherd, red-eyed from the flashbulb. "Man's best friend," Sheldon Herman said, rough-voiced. "She was quite a girl. Lotta heart. Kept me good company after I lost my wife. She passed on in '88, age of thirteen."

I made a sympathetic sound.

"I buried her in the backyard. Gave her a little funeral, you know, flowers on top, and her tennis ball down there with her. Near her paws."

"Yes."

"After that I had to move. You know how it is when you get old, they make you move. So now I live in a home for old fellers. It's okay. Could be worse." He turned his slack, shapeless body toward me. Crevasses that probably used to be dimples scored his white-whiskered cheeks. It was hard to say what his coloring might have been, fair or dark or in between. He was washed out now. He was almost gone.

"What I missed most," he said, "was having something to take care of. Where I live we're all on our own, pretty much. They got me in a private room. It's all men." He looked me over, smiling the nice, wide-faced smile. "You a squeamish kind of girl, Isabel?"

"Pardon?"

"You the kind of a lady who's scared of spiders and whatnot?"

"No," I said slowly, "I wouldn't say I'm squeamish in that way. Why, Mr. Herman?"

"Now, don't go swooning on me," he said, looking down, reaching into the far pocket of his bulky sweater. I stiffened a bit, not really alarmed but definitely on guard. He brought out—something, I couldn't see what until he opened his spotty, veiny hand. A mouse.

"Found 'er in a trap they set in the kitchen. Her paw's smashed, see? She limps. I could show you, but you might faint dead away. I call her Brownie. She's my little pal now."

"Cute." She was. Bright-eyed and pink-toed, with a smooth, russet coat. Perched on his hand, she looked around nervously, twitching her whiskers.

"I feed her cheese and bread and whatnot. Salad. I don't know if they know I've got her, but nobody bothers me about her. Pet her?" His faded eyes twinkled, daring me.

I stroked my finger along the mouse's satiny back. "She's company for you," I said.

"That's it. You got to have something. Anything, as long as it's alive. Can't be a thing, it has to breathe, but that's the only requirement. I've always thought that. More than ever these days. Part of getting old, I guess."

"I guess."

"You know, I cared for my wife more than anything, more than my own life, but when I look back it doesn't feel like even that was enough. I wish I had her again, so I could do it better. I would, too."

He lifted the mouse and kissed the top of its head with his thin lips. Then he put it back in the pocket of his sweater with great care, like a mother laying her baby down. "Pretty day," he said with a sigh, leaning back to stare up at the tree branches over our heads. "Summer's about up, hm? Not too many more days like this, I'll bet."

"No," I agreed. "Not too many more."

A few minutes later, I saw my bus coming down K Street. I said good-bye to Mr. Herman and left him on the bench, smiling after me while the waning sun threw shadows over his slope-shouldered figure.

When I got home, I didn't go inside immediately. I wandered around to the back of the building to look at my garden. Kirby's garden, really; he did the heavy work of digging and tilling for me last spring, when I was reeling from my first chemo sessions. He did plenty of weeding and watering in the summer, too, when I'd drag home from a late class, too exhausted for anything but bed. Without Kirby, I wouldn't have bothered with a garden this year, although it's by far the nicest perk that comes with my lease. Mrs. Skazafava, my landlady, used to cultivate all the grounds behind the building herself, an area of two thousand square feet or so. Now she's too old, and a few years ago she divided it into four plots for the use of the tenants. Surprisingly, not all the plots get taken every year, even though the building has twelve units. I've taken one every summer since I moved—this is my third year. I love to garden. It's a passion.

Kirby found a wooden spool in the alley last spring and rolled it in to use for a garden seat. My legs had begun to ache; I sat down on the spool. Most of the tenants grow vegetables, but I prefer flowers. This late in the year I had more foliage than flora, but the pink and white cleome were still blooming, and the asters and nicotiana, my transplanted boltonia, the hardy *Chelone obliqua* with their pink turtle heads. Twilight closed in. A bee buzzed in the coleus, then flew up and headed home. The birds were tuning up for one last fling before dark. Across the alley, my neighbor Helen put her head out the back door and sang the hopeful, two-note croon mothers use to call in their children.

I heard a step, and turned to see Kirby coming down the concrete walk that bisects the garden plots, two on a side. He had on his summer uniform—cut-off army fatigue pants, dun-colored T-shirt, and old Birkenstock sandals, no socks. The sandals made me think of Mr. Herman and his bulging, pained-looking feet. A soft drift of melancholy settled over me.

Kirby stopped beside me, hands in his flap pockets. "Hi," we said in unison, smiling and nodding. But his hooded eyes looked sharp. "It's almost time to plant chrysanthemums," I said. "Look how well the anemone's doing, and the cimicifuga. You put them in the perfect spot."

He squatted down beside me, resting his forearms on his bony knees, clasping his hands. "How did it go?"

I didn't know what he meant for a second. "Oh, the X ray? Fine, it went fine."

"Did they say anything?"

"No. But they never do—the doctor calls you if there's anything."

"I see." He frowned, but said no more. He's lovely that way. I know he cares, but he confines his sympathy for me to deeds, not words. And he's one of those rare men who don't feel bound to have an opinion on everything. Or worse, a solution.

He bent his head to gaze at the ground. His slender neck

looked naked and tender, like a young boy's. I had an urge to touch the tight tendons, the soft hair that came to a point in the center. I put out my hand. He turned, and my fingers just grazed his cheek. Instead of withdrawing, I let my hand fall open and press lightly against the side of his face. I caressed him.

"Isabel," he said, quietly astounded.

"I might die," I said. "I might get out of it, there's a chance, but I might not. Probably not. You know that, don't you?"

"Yes."

"No, but do you really? Do you know it, do you really understand?"

"Yes. I know all about it." He moved the palm of my hand to his mouth. I started to pull away, but he held on. We hadn't touched, not like this, since the night he'd kissed me under the streetlight.

I brushed my fingers across his gaunt cheekbone. His lashes swept down, hiding his eyes. "I'm sick, Kirby, and I'm bald, I'm not the real Isabel in my body. I don't know how you could want that, but if . . . "

"But if . . . "

"If you do . . ." I was struck dumb by the most idiotic shyness. And a superstitious dread of putting into words the thing I'd just realized I wanted most.

He stood up, still holding my hand, and carefully raised me. "I haven't changed. Not at all. I've just been waiting." He looked so thankful. He put his arms around my shoulders and held me.

It felt too good, I could hardly trust it. "Only if you want me," I mumbled against his shirt, "not for sympathy. Please, please don't lie."

He pulled back, gripping me hard. "What's happened?"

"Nothing— "

"You're not worse?"

"No!"

"You swear?"

"I'm fine, nothing's happened. Truly." Nothing I could explain to him yet, anyway. A change of my heart. It had to do with regrets, and trying to eliminate as many as I could, while I could. And realizing it doesn't matter where love comes from, or when, or what it looks like. I don't want to end wishing I could do everything over again, better, differently, fuller. This is it. My life. Here, now.

"All right, then," Kirby said. "Stop saying stupid things, Isabel, and let's go inside."

I dreamed I was locked in a tall black closet. I kept flailing with my hands, my fingertips, at the thin, faint strip of light at the bottom of the locked door, crying out, "Help, someone help me, let me out," until the light dimmed and disappeared, and I was alone in absolute darkness. I screamed and screamed, but I had no voice, and when I woke up my face was streaming with tears.

Kirby slept on his side, facing away. He never stirred when I eased the fingers of my right hand under him, between the mattress and his warm-skinned waist. I waited while the soft throbbing of a pulse, his or mine, calmed me down.

Anyway, it was an old dream. I knew what it meant, and I'd dreamt it so often it had lost the power to squeeze me in an icy vise until dawn. I concentrated on the rhythm of Kirby's breathing, soothing as a heartbeat, and drifted back to sleep.

When I awoke, it wasn't to that moment of vague anxiety that suddenly bursts into cold, bright panic. It stops my heart, makes me flush with heat. *Cancer is in my body again, and this time it's going to kill me.* I waited, but for a change the act of waking was safe, not treacherous.

Turning my head, I saw Kirby's sharp-nosed profile in the chalky dawn light. He was either meditating or sleeping. Sleeping, I supposed, although the lines of his austere face weren't lax, and the breath coming and going through his fine white nostrils was inaudible. I thought of Gary, and tried not to make comparisons.

Making love with someone for the first time is always awkward—I assume; until last night, I'd only had the experience once before. Making love with a one-breasted bald woman for the first time—that ought to outdo awkwardness. For me, after Gary, the novelty of lying with a man *shaped* like Kirby was enough to smother passion and fill me with skittishness and misgiving. And sometimes the anticipation of disaster is a self-fulfilling prophesy.

Kirby saved us—I take no credit. I almost ruined it. When we took our clothes off and got in my bed, I lay there and marveled at the toughness of his body, and thought about Gary, and wondered if Kirby were thinking of his wife, and worried that he might feel only pity now that he had me, pity and regret—and all he did was touch me. He had such caring in his hands. Another first, for me.

In the end, I was so easily seduced. "Don't think," he said, pressing hard inside, giving me his fierce, romantic kisses. Easier said than done, I thought, and yet I did forget. He made me forget the strangeness, my clumsiness, the freakishness—some would say—of our joining. For a second I even forgot the worst thing, the deep fear that never leaves. Light burst in and dazzled me. But immediately I thought, *This letting go is a rehearsal*—spoiling it. A morbid fancy; I rather shocked myself.

But the long night was only beginning. Before we fell asleep in each other's arms, Kirby had managed to cure me of morbidity, at least for a while. He's a man of many varied and surprising talents.

I do not believe sex, the act of love, transforms people. Emma would argue, but the fact is, I am not a romantic. Having said that, I have to admit I felt different this morning. I lay very still, and presently it came to me what was missing.

Dread.

The colorless sunrise seeped in around the edges of the curtain, and by its grainy light I studied the lines on my palm. According to this one, which all but winds around the base of my thumb, I will live to be about a hundred and ten. I don't take that lightly, and yet it occurs to me that it doesn't really matter. Yesterday's revelations continue. Ultimately, in the very grand scheme of things, it's irrelevant whether my life lasts fifty more years, or five. Or two. The point is to live it, not wait through it. And I'm alive now—I can pick flowers, pet the dog, eat cinnamon toast. How foolish I would be to let my mortality, which has been there all along, since the second of my birth, spoil my love of these things. So I won't. I'll have to remind myself constantly, but starting now, I intend to live until I die.

I woke Kirby up to tell him so. He went from sleep to full wakefulness in two blinks of his eyes. His smile was blinding. "Thank you," I said, instead of telling him about my epiphany.

"For?"

"The gift you gave me."

"Gift." I could tell he was thinking I meant the sex. It's actually rather refreshing when Kirby acts like a typical man. "You're under a delusion," he said gruffly, running his tongue over his teeth. His hairy forearm lay dark and startling across the virginal pink of the blanket. "I didn't give you anything, Isabel, I took. For me."

"You ruthless cad."

His lips curved. "Just don't turn it around. Don't make it me being selfless and giving," he advised, growing serious. He reached for me, cupping my face in his hands and stroking his thumb along the skimpy hair at my temple. He's very romantic. To me, everything he does is just right.

"How lucky I am," I realized all at once, kissing him all over his surprised face. Starting now, I remembered. No more waiting, nothing but living from here on. "Take advantage of me again," I suggested. A fine beginning.

21

Lee

I was dozing when Henry answered the phone in the hall on the third ring. I heard him say, "Hey, Em," in a glad voice, and start clumping up the stairs. "Yeah, she's still in bed. Well, she's still sore. Yeah. A day or two, they say. Yesterday. No, everything went just fine."

He stopped in the bedroom doorway. "Hold on, I'll see." He put his hand over the receiver. "You awake? Want to talk to Emma?"

I stared at him coldly. "Everything went fine?"

His face closed up; he didn't look so damned happy anymore. "Here she is," he said into the phone. "She'll tell you all about it."

I took the telephone from him and covered up the mouthpiece. "Why did you tell her everything went fine?"

"I meant," he said, "there weren't any complications." He had the nerve to sound exasperated.

"You're glad, aren't you? Why don't you admit it?"

"*What*?"

"It's not your fault anymore."

"Lee, you're—" He took a deep breath, made a big deal of reining in his temper. "You're nuts," he said quietly, and went out of the room.

I blotted my eyes with a new tissue and said hello into the phone.

"Hi! How was it, how are you feeling?"

Oh, knock it off, I thought. What was she trying to sound like, a nurse? "I feel okay. Tired."

"Yeah? Not in any pain?"

"Not anymore."

"What did they do to you?"

"They did an HSG, a hysterosalpingogram, and later they did a laparoscopy."

"Wow. Were you asleep?"

"For the laparoscopy. Not the HSG."

"Did it hurt?"

"Yes."

"Oh, Lee. Was Henry with you?"

"He had to work. He picked me up afterward and brought me home."

Pause. My flat voice finally got through to her. She said hesitantly, "Is it bad news? What did they find?"

"I've got SIN. That's pretty funny, isn't it? I thought you'd appreciate it. Salpingitis isthmica nodosa."

"What does it mean?"

"It means a tubal blockage. It means that little things like eggs and sperm and embryos can't get through."

"Oh, no. Oh, Lee. Can they fix it?"

"Sometimes. Not in my case, though. Because I've got bipolar disease—damage to the tube at both ends, not just one."

"Shit."

"Yes."

"But there must be something they can do. Nowadays—"

"All that's left is in vitro."

"That's like a test tube—"

"They take an egg from the ovary, fertilize it with sperm in a lab environment, an embryo forms, and they put it in the uterus."

"I see. So—that'll work?"

"Possibly. The chances increase if they use donor sperm."

"Donor sperm. You mean—not Henry's?"

"Correct."

"Do you—would that be—"

"At this point, I really couldn't care less."

"Aha. And Henry's okay with that, too?"

I was tired of answering questions. "This is getting a little personal," I said.

She took a quick breath. "Hey, sorry, excuse me, I just—I shouldn't have asked, it's just that we've usually—Well, anyway, sorry."

"Okay."

"So. In vitro next. Well, I'm sure that'll work. In fact, they probably should've started with it, but hindsight's twenty-twenty and all that."

I waited.

"Well, um, you sound tired, so I guess I'll let you go. I'll tell Rudy how you're doing. She'll probably call you."

"Fine."

"Can you believe she's started that landscaping course? I can't believe it. I was sure Curtis would stop her, or else she'd chicken out. I just think it's great. Our Rudy, flexing her muscles."

"Yes, it's great."

"Have you talked to Isabel?"

"Last night. Briefly."

"How did she sound?"

"Fine. She was sorry about what they found. The tubal blockage."

"But how was she? Did she sound okay?"

"She sounded fine, she sounded peachy. I have to get off the phone."

"Lee? Honey, I'm sorry, I know this is rough, but—"

"No, you don't, you don't know anything about it. And I just hope it never happens to you, Emma, because then you won't think it's so damned trivial."

"I don't think it's trivial! What do you mean? Where did that come from?"

"I have to get off the phone."

"Well, get off, then."

"All right."

"Oh, Lee—"

I hung up. I'd told her I had to get off, so I wasn't hanging up on her. Technically.

I got up and got dressed.

Henry was stirring a big pot on the stove. He turned around when he heard me. "You're up." He looked surprised, although not particularly pleased. "You sure you should be out of bed? They said—"

"A day or two, and it's been a day. I feel fine. I'm going over to Isabel's."

"Isabel's? But I'm making dinner—it's seven o'clock."

"I know what time it is. I'm not hungry. Especially for chili." It's all he knows how to make, but still, how thoughtless. Wouldn't you think *anyone* would know that chili isn't the dish you offer someone who's convalescing from surgery?

But everything about him annoyed me, his flannel shirt, the wooden spoon he was dripping sauce on the floor with, his new haircut that made him look like a girl. That's what we'd fought about last week. "You're too old for long hair," I'd told him—so he'd gone out and gotten it cut without consulting me. He didn't like it when I said, "Now you look like Prince Valiant. If you're going to get your hair cut, do it right, try to look like a normal man for a change." We didn't speak again for two days.

"All right," I said to him now, "I'm going."

"When will you be back?"

I put on my jacket gingerly; if I stretched too quickly, something pulled in my abdomen. "I don't know."

"Well, call before you leave," he said, going back to stirring.

"Why?"

"So I'll know."

"Know what?"

He looked around in irritation. "That you're leaving."

"What difference does it make?"

He turned away, angry. Good.

"If I get carjacked, what are you going to do about it? If somebody mugs me in Adams-Morgan, how does my calling you before I leave—"

"Don't, then." He banged the spoon on the stove. "Don't call, who cares?" He walked out of the kitchen into the TV room.

My stomach hurt. I followed him, seething.

"You're glad, aren't you?"

"Shit." He slammed the remote control on the coffee table.

"It's not your precious sperm anymore, it's me."

"You're losing your mind."

"No, I'm not. Tell me you're not secretly relieved—you can't!"

"Lee, it's *both* of us."

"Yes, and you're glad. Somebody to share the blame with."

"The blame?" He swore, which he knows I hate. "Why does anybody have to be to blame? It just happened, it's nobody's fault—"

"Oh, you'd like that."

He stuck his fingers in his hair, messing up his pageboy cut. "What the hell does that mean!"

I had no idea. "It doesn't mean anything." I started to cry.

He didn't move, didn't come over to comfort me. We stood on opposite sides of the room and stared at each other.

"I'm going to Isabel's," I told him, and left.

Kirby answered the door. He carried a napkin in his hand, and he had to swallow before he said, "Come in."

"Oh, no. You're eating—I'm sorry, I thought you'd be—"

"Lee?" Isabel called. Kirby widened the door, and I saw her in the little nook off the kitchen she calls the dining room. "Come on in, we were just finishing."

"Come," Kirby seconded, gesturing. Even Grace plodded over to greet me.

I went in.

The apartment looked like a bower—a church. Every table, every shelf on the bookcase held a vase or a bowl of flowers, dahlias, petunias, cosmos, asters. Classical music played softly on the stereo, and the air smelled exotic, a combination of incense and something gingery. Chinese food? The last rays of the sun were streaming through a stained glass plaque of an angel in the living room window, and the only other light came from candles—they were everywhere, like the flowers.

"What is it?" I asked stupidly. Kirby was trying to get me to take off my jacket. "What's happening?"

"What do you mean? Just dinner, and we're done." Gripping the edge of the table for support, Isabel pushed back her chair and stood up. She reached behind for something, standing at an awkward, half-bent angle, opening and closing her hand until she found it. A cane.

"I've interrupted something. Don't get up, you're having a special evening, I can—"

"No, no." She kept coming, taking slow but normal steps. She reached the natural light in the living room, and I saw how pale she was. Her unlined face was beautifully gaunt, her dark-circled eyes too big, her cheekbones too sharp. The new drug—it had to be that. Making her sick again. The doctor took her off the old drugs and put her on Taxol. She smiled at me, trying to put me at ease. Kirby was still hovering. I burst into tears.

I felt two pairs of hands on me, patting, soothing. I looked up to see Isabel send Kirby a message with her eyes. He said, "Well, I think I'll just," and then he headed for the bedroom, mumbling the rest.

"Oh, no," I wailed, "now look, I've banished him, he's—"

"Shh, shush. He lives here, he's just going to his room, you didn't banish him. Have you eaten?"

"He lives here?"

"Well, virtually." She was leading me back to the dining area, one hand through my arm, the other on her cane. A wooden cane with a brass handle. "Sit. Look at all this food we have left."

"I'm not hungry. Good Lord, Isabel, what is that?"

"This? Miso soup. And tofu and brown rice. Would you like some plum juice?"

"No, thank you."

"We were trying out a new cookbook. I'll bet you didn't know that macrobiotic food likes to be stirred counterclockwise in the northern hemisphere, but clockwise in the southern."

"It likes to be?"

"I can't wait to tell Emma. Are we sitting down, or would you rather talk in the living room?"

"Living room." And by the time we were settled on the sofa, Isabel with a glass of plum juice and me with Grace grinning at my feet, I had pulled myself together, no more snuffling and weeping. "Sorry," I said, blowing my nose for the last time. "This is all you need. I should've called first, but I just—"

"It's all right."

"I sort of escaped. From myself as much as the house. Emma called tonight and I hung up on her."

"You what?"

"I know, it's crazy. I'll call her tomorrow, try to apologize. She didn't do anything, it's me, I'm not myself anymore. And Henry—oh God, we're fighting about the stupidest things. Isabel," I interrupted myself, "is this how you live all the time?" I gestured to the flowers, the candles. "It's *beautiful*." The sudden question came to me—How could Isabel die? She had that pretty rug she loved, she had these pillows, those wildflower lithographs on the wall. The poignancy of all her things, her belongings, somehow struck me as proof that she couldn't leave, she had to stay. Otherwise, it would be too cruel.

She smiled. "Yes, it's deliberate. Kirby's idea. A place for healing, he says. Now, tell me about the surgery."

"It was awful. You have to lie under this huge X-ray machine with your feet in stirrups. They thread a catheter through your cervix into your uterus. They gave me Advil and told me it wouldn't hurt, but it was absolutely excruciating. My muscles went into spasm."

"Oh, my Lord." She squeezed my hand, wincing.

"They send a dye in through the catheter. If there's no obstruction, it goes to the end of the fallopian tubes, but if there's a block it stops. Mine stopped, so they knew I had to have the laparoscopy. To see how bad it was."

"And?"

"Bad. It can't be fixed, surgery's not possible. I can't have a child except by in vitro fertilization, and the chances of that working at my age are about twelve percent, even with donor sperm. Plus, every time you do it, it costs a fortune."

"How much?"

"About eleven thousand dollars." Isabel's mouth dropped open. "Henry's—he can't even talk about it. So we're barely speaking."

She shook her head in sympathy. "What do you think you'll do?"

"In vitro."

Isabel sat back. She started to say something, then didn't.

"Well, it's *my* money, not his."

"Yes, but it seems like so *much* money."

"What difference does it make? If I had a terrible disease—"

"If you had a terrible disease, what?" she said when I stopped. I wasn't saying *anything* right tonight.

"I just mean, if I needed an operation or something to save my life, he wouldn't mind spending the money for that."

"No."

"Well, it's the same thing."

"Is it?"

"It is for me."

Isabel made a loose fist and pressed it to her lips thoughtfully. Her soft eyes regarded me for so long, I leaned over to pet the dog. "What about adoption, Lee?"

"No, I've told you."

"I know, but—"

"We're not considering it."

"I see."

I sat up and faced her. "The in vitro can work, Isabel," I said, letting my excitement show. "Twelve percent—that's not very good, but each time you do it it's twelve percent, so it adds up. That's how I'm looking at it. I feel hopeful, I really do. I just wish we'd *started* with this, I wish we hadn't wasted so much time."

"Lee . . ."

"What?"

She smiled, and I realized I had snapped at her. "I don't have any advice," she assured me, "don't worry."

"I don't mind advice," I said contritely.

"It's just that I'd hate to see you hurt again. That's all."

"I know. I do know, and you're right—I can feel it happening again, the hope revving up. Every time—every month—" I pressed my hands over my eyes. "I'm so afraid it won't work, and then I think it will—a miracle. Then it doesn't, and I'm scared again. I'm so tired, if I could just have some rest—"

"Why don't you—"

"There's no *time*, I've already let too many years slip away. That's what kills me, or one thing. I've always, always been in control of my life, every part of it, and now the most important part is out of my control, and I'm stuck, I can't move, and I can't stand this uncertainty anymore."

Isabel sighed. She sat back slowly, pulling a pillow against the small of her back. Her fragility disturbed me, but it was the Taxol, I was sure. So much of chemotherapy is worse than the disease it's supposed to cure.

"Lee," she said wearily. "No advice, just a question. Something for you to think about. Okay?"

"Of course. Go ahead." I leaned over again to pet Grace.

"Is having a child the most important thing in your life? More important than Henry?"

My throat closed; I couldn't answer.

"Ask yourself if the need to have your own genetic, biological child outweighs every other need in your life, including your marriage. I know you love Henry, there's no question of that. But if your answer is yes, you may lose him. Why did you marry him?" she asked kindly. "There's no right or wrong—if it was to have a child of your very own, no one else's, well, that's the answer. But you may not be able to keep your husband. Are you crying?"

"I can't help it."

I felt her move closer. She put her arm around me. "I know. All that pain—most of it comes from trying to avoid it. The tyranny of wanting things. Poor Lee, you want this so badly."

"What is that, Buddhism?"

She hugged me. "Yes, as a matter of fact. Sorry."

"I don't mind it. Don't mix me up with Emma." She laughed. I blew my nose. "I know I'm . . . what's the word? Not *obsessed*."

Isabel raised her eyebrows.

"I'm *not*. I'm . . . *consumed*, that's it. I know I'm consumed by our infertility, and that's not fair to Henry. We must've had problems before now, but I can't even remember what they were. He says I blame everything that's wrong between us, everything that's wrong with my whole *life*, on the fact that we can't have children. It's true. I know—I know I'm driving him away, but—"

Isabel leaned against me while I cried some more. What finally made me stop, once and for all, was realizing how badly I wanted to lay my head down in her lap and let her hold me. In fact, I almost did it. My only excuse is that it was the lowest point on one of the most miserable nights of my life, and that Isabel had always been there for me, as caring and tenderhearted as a mother.

But now it was different. She was going to recover eventually, I was sure of that, but for the time being her problems made mine look embarrassingly small. I sat up straight. "I feel much better. Thanks for listening to all that. Let's go in the kitchen, I'll do the dishes while you tell me how *you're* doing." She protested, but I won by ignoring her. "That's new," I said casually as we stood up.

"This? Kirby got it for me." She smiled, running her fingers over the curved brass head of the cane, which was shaped like—something; a horse? "The dragon," she said. "It's a symbol of hope."

"Oh." Did that mean she didn't need it? Or she needed it for luck, but not to walk? I was afraid to ask.

She never did tell me how she was doing, not really. She said the new drug didn't have as many side effects as the old ones, which surprised me. Because she didn't look well. Beautiful, but not well. "I'm just tired," she said, sponging crumbs off the counter into the sink. "I feel like I could sleep for a week."

"How's school going?"

"All right," she answered after a pause. She sounded vague.

"Really? Still taking a full course load?"

She found a spot on the counter that needed scouring and didn't answer.

"Isabel?"

She can't lie. She can evade, but she can't lie. "I've had to drop a few credits. It was a little too much. I'll make them up next summer."

"But you're still enrolled, you haven't—"

"Oh, yes," she said positively. "I'm working hard and really enjoying this semester. Some great courses. I've got a paper due tomorrow, in fact, in Society and Aging."

"Oh, *no*. Is it finished?"

"Just about. I've still—"

"Why didn't you tell me? Oh, Isabel!"

"What? Oh, don't be silly." She followed me into the living room, laughing. "What are you doing, running away?"

"First I drive Kirby out before he's finished eating his dinner—where's my coat, did he hang it up?"

"Lee, you don't have to go."

"Then I go on for half an hour about my problems and you don't get a word in, and then—"

"I got a few words in."

"The only good thing I did was the dishes."

"Don't go, you don't have to. All I have left to do is the footnotes."

I kissed her. She felt different, brittle or something, I was afraid to hug her very hard. "Tell Kirby I'm sorry." She made a face. "I'll call you tomorrow. Thanks for everything. I mean it."

"Be careful driving."

"Bye."

"Good night, Lee."

I was all the way to the elevator, in fact I'd already pressed the button, when I remembered. I hurried back to Isabel's apartment.

She opened the door. "Hi, long time no see," I joked. "Can I do one more thing?"

"Sure." She stood back to let me in. "What?"

"Call Henry. Tell him I'm coming home."

22

Rudy

Eric's office is on Carolina Avenue in Capitol Hill, catty-corner to Eastern Market. I can walk there from my house, and usually I do, but today I was driving. And late. I know—as usual. I found a parking place that might or might not have been legal, and raced through the cold rain, not even stopping to open my umbrella. The building is an old red brick town house converted to offices, and Eric's is on the top floor. I dashed right in, didn't stop in the waiting room to take off my coat, which was dripping wet.

"Sorry, sorry, the traffic, you wouldn't believe, plus no place to park, plus I was late anyway. Can I put this here?" Eric said yes, and I slung my coat over the radiator. "So, I'm here. At last."

I flopped down in the big black lounge chair across from his identical big black lounge chair. Our vantages were the same, except that my chair sat next to the little table holding the always-full box of Kleenex. "How are you?"

"I'm great. And you?"

He always says that. With a searching smile that makes you think he means it, he's really great, but he'd rather talk about you than himself. An excellent quality in a psychotherapist. I know amazingly little about Eric, considering I've been seeing him once a week, more during emergencies, for the last seven years. He's forty-six, and he lives with a slightly older woman, that much I know. Lately it's been tense around his house. He let that slip a couple of weeks ago, and it fascinated me. Out of all proportion. It was as if I'd finally located the whereabouts of my birth parent or something—it felt like I'd found out an important fact I'd never expected to, or I'd given up on.

"Well, I'm great, too," I said, "and how often do you hear me say *that*? I've just come from Emma's, and that was pretty grim, but I *still* feel great."

Eric shook his head wonderingly. "Something in the water?"

"Must be."

"So what's wrong with Emma?"

"Well, that's the other reason I'm late. She sort of let her hair down, something she hasn't done in a long time. With me, anyway."

Eric made his *Go on* face.

"Remember I told you she was in love with a married man?" That was all I'd said, though; I don't tell Emma's secrets. Well—once, to Curtis, just the bare fact that she liked Mick, but no details. And even that was an accident. Alcohol-related. "Well," I said to Eric, "nothing came of it, and I thought she was over him. Which was really deaf and blind of me, I see in retrospect."

"She's not?"

"No, she's just miserable. She isn't seeing anybody, and that's unusual in itself—there's always a man around somewhere with Emma. She's not writing. All she does is stay home. I told her she was in mourning, and she said of course, she knew that. She was so open about it, not hiding anything, which is also unusual. I think her only strategy is waiting, you know, lying low until she gets better. She's gone to ground, and that's definitely not her usual coping mechanism with men, not at all. She says men are like dogs, as soon as one dies, you should go out and buy a puppy."

"Ha."

"So while I was driving over here I was thinking how much safer Emma's way is—staying home and grieving by herself—than, well, say, some of the ways I've used to get out of depressions."

"Maybe her depressions aren't like yours."

"I know, but . . ." Well, that was obvious—mine are chronic, Emma's are acute. Mine are clinical, hers are—whatever. But that cheered me up, what Eric had said. I told him so.

"How come?" he asked.

"Well, because . . . I beat myself up a lot about making the wrong choices, doing crazy things. But everybody starts in a different place, and if you consider where I started . . ."

"What? Go ahead and say it."

"Okay." I took a breath. "I'm doing pretty well."

He beamed. "Very good, Rudy. Very, very good."

He looked so pleased, I thought of something else good to tell him. "Guess who got an A-minus on her planning midterm."

"Hey!"

"We had to design an urban backyard, only fifteen hundred square feet, with all the plantings and pavings, privacy screens, seating, terracing. I even designed a little fountain for mine. Anyway, I aced it."

"That's terrific."

"It was hard, too, I'm finding all the courses hard. But I love it, and I'm so happy I'm doing it. Thank you, Eric."

"For what?"

"Helping me get up the nerve." He opened his mouth to deny it—he always does—so I kept talking. "You did help me, and so did Emma, by nagging. Isabel, too, but in a different way. She never said anything, but I knew she thought I could do it. Not should do it, but could. She had faith. I didn't want to disappoint her—not that I would, not that she'd ever be disappointed in me, exactly, but—I just wanted to make her glad for me. I wanted to make her happy."

Eric nodded in understanding. "How is she?"

"Oh . . ." I sighed. "It's hard to say. She's evasive. She always says she's feeling better, but she doesn't look well. I've heard that you can gain weight on chemotherapy, but she's losing. I think she might even be on some steroid, but she keeps getting thinner. It's alarming. She says it's her new diet, but I don't know, no one knows. Kirby might, but we don't. We Graces."

"Does that bother you?"

"What?"

"That she tells Kirby more than she tells you?"

"No, not me. It probably bothers Emma a little. Lee, definitely, but she's closer to Isabel than Emma and I are."

Eric raised his eyebrows.

"In a way. Not in all ways. It's kind of complicated. Anyway—" There's a clock on the wall over Eric's head; he keeps it there so clients can see it and pace themselves. It said I was over halfway through my session and I hadn't even told him the main thing.

"Anyway—here's what I really wanted to tell you. I think, I'm pretty sure, I'm going to confront Curtis and make him talk about our relationship." I laughed, I even clapped my hands at his expression. "I know, it's amazing, I'm amazed, too! Where's all this gumption coming from? Is it the drugs?"

"What drugs?"

"I mean the new antidepressant. That's the only drug I'm taking."

"I should hope so. But you said drugs."

"Force of habit."

We laughed.

"Well, Rudy," he said, "this is very interesting. What do you think you'll say? Do you want to do some role-playing?"

"Umm . . . No, I don't think so." I could never tell him, but whenever we role-play and Eric tries to be Curtis, it's all I can do not to laugh. "I'm going to start by telling him I love him, which I do. You know, basically. But that I think some things haven't always been so healthy between us. And that there are some patterns I'd like to see us start working to break out of."

Eric waited.

"Such as my needing his approval so much. His controlling me with his approval. Or disapproval. His possessiveness. My allowing him to be possessive—liking it, even."

Eric stroked his chin; he looked mesmerized.

"I'm going to tell him there are some things we do together that I don't think are good for us. Mutual arrangements. A symbiotic relationship, you could say." Emma says that's not as clichéd as codependent. "And . . ."

"And?"

"I'm going to tell him I want joint counseling. With anyone he wants, which probably means not you."

He nodded readily.

"I wish it could be you. But Curtis won't, I can tell you right now—in fact, he won't want anybody, but I'm going to insist."

I stopped, so we could both listen to the sound of that. *Insist.*

"Well?" I said. "What do you think?"

"I'm very pleased," he said, and I squeezed my hands together between my knees, so glad. "This is an excellent, excellent step."

"I know. I'm very hopeful. He's been so good about the landscaping. Well, in the sense that he didn't forbid it or anything. He's not happy about it, of course. I think—" I sat back, deflated. "I think he thinks I'll bomb out, so why bother making a big deal of it. Oh, God, Eric, am I making a mistake?"

"Rudy."

"I know, but what if it makes things worse? What if I tell him all this and he . . ."

"What? What's the worst that can happen? That he'll get angry with you?"

"No. I'm used to that."

"What, then?"

"That he won't love me?" I said fearfully. "Is that the worst?"

"You tell me."

"I don't know! Oh, God." I scrubbed my face, sat up straight.

"But I'm doing it, I'm doing it anyway. Tonight. Maybe." A little thrill of fear made my scalp prickle, but it wasn't debilitating; if anything, it was invigorating. "I'm doing it," I repeated. Talking myself into it.

"Good," Eric said. "It's the right decision. Call me tomorrow, if you like. I'll be thinking about you."

I wanted to make Curtis his favorite dinner, but we were out of veal. Instead I made lamb chops with a peppercorn crust, which he likes almost as well. I felt like the mother on *Father Knows Best*, buttering up the patriarch before she asks him if they can buy a new living room suite or something. I suppose I demean myself with these tricks, but we all do what we have to do. If fixing Curtis lamb chops made me look foolish, I could live with the embarrassment.

I don't know if it was the dinner, but by the time we ate he was in a fairly good mood. A little quiet, but that's not unusual. We ate in the kitchen—he likes to keep half an eye on C-SPAN (with the sound off) while he eats, and I don't mind much anymore. I've gotten used to it.

I was bursting to tell him about the grade I got on my midterm, but I kept it to myself. The method I'm using to make the landscaping course palatable to him involves keeping it out of his sight and hearing as much as possible. I'm always here when he gets home, I never study in front of him, never talk about the course or my teachers, my grades, the people I'm meeting in class. I especially never talk about where it all might be leading, what sort of job I might get when I've earned my certificate.

It's not easy living in two completely separate worlds. But so far it's working, and you can't argue with success.

After dinner, Curtis got his briefcase and carried it into the living room. A good sign. He'd work there while I did the dishes. Some evenings he works upstairs in his office, and then he's off limits, not to be disturbed. Working in the living room meant he was available; he was still in my world.

I came close to pouring myself another glass of wine. It was so tempting—but, no. It was normal to be nervous at a time like this. I would be much better off with a clear head than a glib tongue.

I brought him coffee in a special cup, one I made a few years ago as part of a tea service. I'd used a pale celadon glaze, trying to match with color the airiness and delicacy of the pieces. Really, I was getting pretty good at potting before I gave it up. I still keep my best pieces in the living room, in a little display that both cheers me up and makes me sad when I look at it. It reminds me that I had talent, and that I can't seem to stick to anything.

Maybe, I thought, handing Curtis his pretty cup, I'd take up potting again one of these days. Maybe, if he knew what it meant to me because I *told* him, he wouldn't mind the night classes, or complain about my wheel crowding out his exercise equipment in the basement. Maybe this conversation we were about to have would mark the beginning of a lot of new things.

Curtis said, "Is this decaf?" without even looking at his cup.

I sat down beside him. "Of course."

He took a sip and smiled at me. "How was your day?"

"Fine. Curtis?"

"Hm?"

Deep breath. "We have to talk."

"Oh, no. The four most dreaded words in English," he teased. "What about?"

"Us."

He turned away to set the cup down, and when he turned back, his face was set and cold. "As you can see, I'm a little busy right now."

"I know, but this is important."

"So is this."

"Curtis." I got up and moved to the chair on the other side of the fireplace. Distance and objectivity. I'd forgotten my speech, though. Already this was going badly.

"First of all, you know I love you. That's the main thing—that we love each other. But we have some habits, don't you think, some ways of behaving toward each other that aren't always so—helpful. I just feel we've let ourselves fall into some patterns that don't always work well."

He stood up. He'd taken off his jacket; he looked so tall and handsome in his vest and shirtsleeves, his polka-dotted tie loose. But he rubbed his forehead with both hands in an odd way, as if he were confused or in pain. "Rudy. Please."

"What?"

"I'm not feeling very well."

"You aren't? You were fine about two seconds ago."

I was afraid that would make him mad. He didn't say anything, though. He went a few steps to the mantel and leaned his folded arms against it, keeping his face turned away from me.

I started again. "I just feel we need to discuss some things about our relationship. Any marriage can get—any couple can—just because it's easier, pretty soon you don't even think about what you're doing, and years go by and you realize—" I closed my eyes and did a breathing exercise. "I feel—I want—I'd like us to make some changes. Maybe. Or talk about it, at least. Curtis, are you listening?"

"Rudy, not now." Even his voice sounded strange.

"What's wrong?"

"Nothing."

"Are you really sick?"

"No, I just can't . . ."

I got up and went closer to him. Now or never. "I was thinking about couples counseling," I said in a rush. "It might be just the thing for us. Get us talking, you know? I really think it might be good for us."

I touched his back. He felt hot, damp. "Curtis?" I tried to see his face, but he kept turning. Finally I caught sight of him in the mirror over the mantel. "What's wrong?" To my horror, his knees buckled before he caught himself. I threw my arms around his waist.

"I'm all right." He stood up straight, pulling away. "I'm fine." He made his way to the couch and sat down carefully, turning off the lamp on the side table.

I sank down beside him, tried to take his hand. What was this? He still wouldn't let me look at him.

I saw a tear on his cheek before he could dash it away—it stopped my heart.

"What is it?" I whispered, terrified. "What's happening?"

"I don't want to tell you." His voice was choked, as if his throat hurt. "Don't want you to know."

"Is it something terrible?" He nodded. "Don't tell me." I put my hands over my ears. My skin felt like it was shriveling and puckering, pulling in like a leaf in a freeze.

He didn't move, he sat with his shoulders hunched, his profile pale and frightened.

"All right," I said. "Tell me."

"I might be dying."

I laughed.

"I've known it since Tuesday."

"Stop it. What? Stop it, I don't like that. What are you saying?" He looked me full in the face. "Curtis!" I screamed it, and he folded me up in his arms.

He shook and trembled, holding me tight. "My last checkup. I told Dr. Slater I was tired, that's all. A little dizziness sometimes, some pain in my stomach."

"No, no—you didn't say anything—this didn't happen." My teeth began to chatter.

"I didn't think it was anything. Flu—I thought it was flu. I almost didn't even tell him. But—he ordered tests, and the blood test came back with too many leukocytes. Rudy—I've got CLL. Leukemia."

"No, it's a mistake. Who told you? This is not true."

"It's not a mistake." His eyes were swimming. "They're good doctors, Rudy, they're the best."

"Where?"

"Georgetown."

"Oh, God."

"Don't cry. I'm sorry. This is why I didn't tell you. You've already got Isabel to worry about, I didn't want to add this."

Through a glaze of tears, I saw his strained, anxious face—worried for *me*, solicitous of *me*. I was crushing handfuls of his shirt, kneading his shoulders, unable to reconcile the thing he was telling me with the tough, alive feel of him.

"I don't have any other symptoms yet," he said steadily, keeping my gaze, not letting go of me. "That's a good thing—it means it might be progressing slowly. I could live for years and years and not even need treatment. Or—not. They can't say yet. It's too early to tell how it'll go in my case."

"No, no, no, no, no—"

He pulled me close and rubbed my back, told me it was all right. It wasn't all right, it was an avalanche, the ceiling falling on me, rubble and dust and chunks of plaster cutting off the air, covering me, heavy blows to my head, my back. I could hardly understand what he was saying, he sounded so muffled and far away.

"We can't tell anyone yet, Rudy. If they found out at work, I could lose my job. We can't afford that, not until it's unavoidable."

"Not tell anyone?" I tried to concentrate on that. Not tell anyone? "That's crazy. Isn't it?"

"I know, but that's how it works. And anyway, I couldn't function if anyone knew. Anyone but you—not my family, not yours, not your friends. Greenburg."

"Oh, but—"

"Promise me you won't tell them."

"What?"

"Please, Rudy. I just—I couldn't take it yet. Can't you understand? I couldn't possibly talk about this with anyone but you. Promise. It's important to me."

"All right." Oh my God, oh my God.

He held me again. "We'll fight together, darling. We'll be strong together."

"Yes."

"Us against the world, Rudy. The way it used to be."

I didn't know what he meant. When? When we first fell in love? Those days in Durham when we didn't care about anything but each other, no one else existed. It's true that was the best, the safest time. We've been trying to get back to it ever since. And now we have.

He wanted to make love. I wanted to die. I let him do everything he wanted, and he wanted it right there, in front of the cold hearth with our clothes half on, half off—he likes it that way sometimes, he thinks it's wanton. I couldn't feel anything except fear and cold, as if a ghost was penetrating me. Nothing was real. Curtis could not be dying. What is leukemia, how does it kill you? *Not real, not real*, I thought all the while he moved over me, not minding my passivity, accepting it without a question.

We lay on the prickly rug afterward, and I pretended it was a dream, I'd wake up soon and say, "Curtis, I dreamed you were dying—oh, it was awful, what a nightmare!" I turned to look at his peaceful face, his eyes closed, mouth relaxed. He looked different to me—less defined, insubstantial. Where was his solidity? His skin, his fingernails, the hair on his forearm, everything looked vulnerable and impermanent and tender. But he was smiling slightly, eyelashes fluttering. I had helped to put that smile there, I thought. That would be my job from now on. I wouldn't think about anything but that.

We went upstairs together. While he showered, I thought of calling Emma. I almost did—I had the phone in my hand. Did my promise count? How could I not tell her? How could I not tell Eric!

But I hung up and didn't call anyone. It's hard to explain why. In a way, I've betrayed Curtis for the whole of our marriage. He's a private man, intensely private, and at one time or another I've told secrets of his to everybody I love.

I won't now. This is happening to him, not me. If keeping it a secret makes it easier for him to bear, then how could I not be his accomplice?

"We'll get through this," he told me in bed, holding my hand under the covers. "You can't know how much better I feel now that I've told you. The last few days have been the hardest of my life."

"Darling," was all I could say.

"Maybe I shouldn't have told you. Maybe it was selfish."

"Oh, no."

"But I couldn't help it. I started to feel dizzy, I was even afraid I might faint. So then there was nothing else I could do but tell you. It's nothing to worry about, the faintness, by the way. They told me there might be episodes like that from time to time. Night sweats, too. Fever."

I pressed my face against his shoulder.

"And, Rudy?"

"Yes."

He switched off the bedside lamp. "I just want you to know. I asked them about secondhand smoke, and they said no, probably not."

"What do you mean?"

"I couldn't understand why this had happened to me. I tried to think of anyone in my family—but there's no one. So—no genetic predisposition."

"Secondhand smoke?"

"It's all I could think of. But they said the chances that that had caused it were very slim. Almost nothing, in fact. So that's one thing you don't have to worry about."

He settled the covers over us, making me turn away from him.

He put his heavy arm across my waist, his hand on my breast. "I'll sleep well tonight," he said against my hair. "Thank you, Rudy. I love you, darling."

"I love you, Curtis."

He fell asleep in no time.

I lay still, waiting until he began to snore before I crept out of bed and tiptoed into the bathroom. I had a nearly full bottle of Noludar, because I hadn't taken any in months. I shook out four and swallowed them with tap water. Four was safe, since I wasn't drinking. Yet. All sorts of bad habits were smiling at me, though, waving, dying to get reacquainted. It was hard to know where to begin.

23

Isabel

In late November, Terry came to see me. It was a short visit, only Friday to Sunday, and I had to share him a bit with his father. Gary picked him up at the airport and brought him straight to my apartment on Friday afternoon. My nerves were in knots. I'd been cleaning my three rooms and bath for days, planning meals, vacillating over what to wear. I hadn't seen Terry in nearly two years.

Father and son hid identical expressions of dismay when I opened the door. Terry embraced me stiffly, as if afraid I would break. Gary couldn't stay, had to go, good to see you, you're looking fine, Isabel, he lied. I barely glanced at him; he'd put on weight and lost some hair—that's all I noticed. It was Terry, twenty-seven years old and a man now, not a boy, that I couldn't stop touching, looking at, marveling over.

"You've gotten better-looking," I said, mixing tuna salad for a sandwich while he prowled around the kitchen, making the room seem even smaller in a way Kirby never did. He was nervous, too, I realized; he had the same apprehensions about this visit that I did. "No, it's true," I insisted when he made a face. "Your hair's darker. You've gotten taller."

"Mom, I couldn't have."

"You did. Your eyes look more like Gary's, too. Your father has beautiful eyes." But I could see my father's sternness in Terry's straight, narrow-lipped mouth, and that worried me. I wanted to tell him to bend more, flex more, life doesn't have to be such a struggle.

I sat across from him and watched him eat. "Didn't they feed you on the airplane?"

"Sure. What time's dinner?"

We laughed as we settled into the agreeable fiction that we were still mother and son, that we knew each other intimately enough to joke and mock and hector one another at the kitchen table. But in truth, a scrupulous kind of courtesy had sprung up between Terry and me years ago. Time and distance have only nurtured it, and now we behave like cordial, respectful strangers—like the mother in the host family and the polite foreign exchange student.

But maybe we could foil it this time, break out of our pattern. If ever there were a time, certainly this would be it.

"How's school, Mom?"

"Oh, it's wonderful, I love it. I've been taking a little time off just lately, but I plan to start back in January."

"Time off?"

I hadn't wanted to get into this so soon. "The chemo blindsided me a little bit," I said, shrugging. "I had to miss some assignments. So I decided it was better to back off for a while than risk bad grades."

I couldn't tell him what a blow it had been when I'd realized I couldn't take my finals. School meant everything to me, and not just because it held the key to my working future. It represented normalcy, wellness. The routine of classes, the hard hours of studying, the process of going and coming, adhering to a schedule—all that had given my days shape and structure when cancer was working so hard to turn them into chaos.

"What kind of drugs have they got you on now?"

Oh hell. But maybe it was better to get it all out of the way now and not have to talk about it again. My illness is like a noxious, uninvited guest, too unpleasant to ignore. But Terry always wanted to discuss strategies, protocols, percentages, and I had so many other things to say to him.

"I'm not taking anything at the moment."

"What do you mean? Nothing at all?"

"We're on a break."

"But, Mom—"

"It's all right, the doctor doesn't disapprove. I've been taking chemotherapy for the last eleven months, Terry. We thought my body could use a rest."

"Yes, but . . ." He stopped protesting, suddenly diffident. Becoming my medical advisor at this late date probably struck him as out of line.

"I know it doesn't sit well with you. You're a scientist, why should it?" His specialty is enzyme molecules and substrates, but he understands the significance of a breast cancer metastasis to bone. "You'll be even sorrier to hear that I'm about ready to renounce the medical model altogether."

"In favor of what, crystals?" He laughed—I laughed with him. It was better if he thought I was joking.

"I think I'll try to heal myself. You know, *heal* and *cure* aren't quite the same thing," I said, and he smiled, thinking he was humoring me.

Kirby arrived in time for dinner, according to plan. One of my many worries was what Terry would think of him. Well—and what he would think of the fact that his very ill mother had a lover. I watched them all night like a spy. Kirby has an odd way of behaving in company as if he's alone. At first it's off-putting, then appealing. To most people. But I fretted that Terry would find him aloof instead of self-contained, might take his reticent silences for coldness, even arrogance. I shouldn't have worried. Kirby worked his low-key spell slowly but surely, and by the end of the evening Terry even got his jokes, which are dryer than chalk dust, dryer than hot desert sand.

Sleeping arrangements were something else I'd stewed over at length. My couch is comfortable but short, and it doesn't fold out. Terry's over six feet tall. How sensible to offer him Kirby's room upstairs, a whole apartment to himself, while Kirby slept where he always does: with me.

How sensible—but I couldn't manage it. It would have violated a principle that's as old-fashioned as it is deep-rooted, a code I won't defend and don't even particularly approve of, yet I'm stuck with it. Call it a product of my upbringing. And don't think I'm blind to the charge of hypocrisy in this. In self-defense, I could say that that was part of my upbringing, too. In any event, Terry slept on the couch and Kirby slept upstairs in his own bed.

On Saturday Terry and I went for a ride in Kirby's car. He wanted to see the old neighborhood, the high school, his favorite hangouts. "The Hot Shoppe is *gone*?" He couldn't believe it. "Where's People's? Where's the Bank of Bethesda? When did everything get so swanky?" A long time ago, I could have told him. He'd been away for almost ten years, but his clearest memories were much older. "No wonder you moved out, Mom. You'd have to be stinking rich to live here now."

He pointed out landmarks to me. "That's where you taught me to drive"—the parking lot of the Catholic church on East-West Highway. "Dad tried it one time. One time only. Remember?"

"Vividly. He came home looking like a zombie. I thought he was having a coronary."

"How come you were so calm?"

"Drugs. Rudy used to give me Quaaludes."

"Really?"

"No." I laughed. "Anyway, you were a good driver."

"Dad didn't think so. There's the Domsetts' house. Do they still live there?"

"I don't know, I guess so."

"I used to mow their lawn. I'd always try to collect from her, not him, because she tipped better. Remember when I used to run away from home? You'd pack Fig Newtons for me."

"You wanted them in a bandanna tied to a stick—you'd seen that in a comic book."

"You said it was okay to run away as long as I didn't cross any streets. You'd kiss me good-bye, and I'd walk around and around the block till I got tired, and then I'd come home."

He told me a new, horrifying story about getting drunk on prom night and drag racing with his friend Kevin on Old Georgetown Road. "I could have lived the rest of my life without knowing that," I said. He told me about Sharon Waxman, a girl in his high school home room who committed suicide last year. He asked me if I'd liked being a stay-at-home mom.

I looked at him curiously. He looked like a man, not a boy, maneuvering Kirby's old sedan through the Saturday traffic with care and competence. "Yes, I liked it," I said. "Usually. Did you think it was old-fashioned of me not to have a job?"

"No," he said, sounding surprised. "Anyway, you were always doing something. It's not like you were eating bonbons and watching the soaps. You made the home," he said seriously. "You were the home maker."

I felt ridiculously flattered.

"I guess you weren't that fulfilled, though. Going back to school for your master's now. I guess you wish you'd done that sooner."

This was a new kind of conversation we were having. It happens to most of us eventually, the moment when our parents become real people, with motives and hopes as authentic as our own—but I couldn't help ruing the fact that it was the nature of my situation that had accelerated this adult revelation in Terry. "Yes, in some ways," I answered him truthfully. "It would've been nice to feel more independent. Less reliant on your father. As I'm sure he would agree."

The unspoken subject of Gary hung between us. If Terry had asked me about the divorce then, I would have told him anything he wanted to know. But it had to start with him. When it didn't, the moment passed, and I wasn't sorry.

In the afternoon, Terry visited with his father, then played basketball with old friends from high school. They went to a bar afterward, and he came home late for dinner in high spirits.

"You haven't said a word about Susan," I mentioned over coffee in the living room.

"Nothing to talk about." He lifted his arms over his head, stretching sore muscles. "We've broken up."

"Oh, Terry, no."

"It's okay, Mom. It was mutual."

Mutual, maybe, but obviously it wasn't okay. I still knew all my son's diversionary tactics, the body stretches, the fake yawn, the casual-looking avoidance of my eyes.

"What happened? If I may ask."

"Nothing happened, it just wasn't working out. We had different expectations."

"What were hers?" I asked.

"Oh, the usual. You know, marriage, children."

"Aha. Do you still love her?"

"I don't know, Mom. I guess." He looked surprised by my audacious question. How forthright I am these days. It saves a lot of time, and time doesn't tick past for me in the same rhythm it used to. "It's complicated," he said. "We're still friends."

I waited, but that was all he wanted to say. And somewhere along the way in the last ten years, I've lost the right to pry. But I didn't care for that cynical note in his voice when he said, "Oh, the usual." Most parents feel guilty for every inch their children fall short of perfection, and I'm no exception. Terry's disinterest in the conventional family ("marriage, children") was a failing I feared he could lay directly at my door, mine and Gary's. The subject I'd ducked in the car this afternoon hovered again. But Terry yawned, lay down on the floor, and promptly fell asleep.

I woke him at ten o'clock and helped him make his bed on the sofa. I kissed him good night in a muted panic, and lay awake while the clock marked off the hours of our dwindling time together. I can't bear to acknowledge the most likely result of my situation to the people I love. It's too hurtful; I don't have the courage or the will to inflict such pain. But on Terry's last day, with so much left unsaid between us, I couldn't avoid it any longer.

Kirby and I were to drive him to the airport. I sat on the edge of the couch while Terry crammed dirty clothes into his canvas duffle. He knelt on the floor in his faded jeans, the sleeves of his yellow sweater pushed up to the elbows. Unthinkingly, I reached out and brushed the hair back from his forehead. He grinned at me and went back to his work, but in that second, with his head cocked, eyes merry, he looked so much like himself as a baby and then a boy—the Terry I remember best—my heart twisted.

"I wish you had a brother or a sister, Terry. Sometimes," I added dryly, "I wish I did, too."

"What do you mean? You've got Aunt Patty."

"As I say."

"Oh," he said, grinning. "Yeah, I guess you two aren't that close."

"No, we're not. There's the age difference, of course, but that's not all. I wasn't close to my parents, either. Our house was so cold. Strict. Because of my father, mostly, but my mother was a very closed-up person, too. I never wanted that for my own family. One reason I married your father was because of his passion." Terry looked up, interested. "He's an emotional man. Especially when we were younger. Lots of fire and warmth."

"I guess," he said uncertainly, thinking it over.

"But things didn't work out the way they were supposed to. I blamed everything on Gary when we separated, but it wasn't all his fault. Not by any means." I leaned toward him, intent on getting this right. "If we drove you away, Terry, it was the last thing I wanted. Nothing was ever your fault—do you know that? You were the best thing in my life. I'm sorry if I didn't show you how much I loved you. I did love you. I do. As much as I've ever loved anyone, as much as I can. It feels like a lot—it takes up my whole heart. But if it doesn't feel that way to you, I'm so sorry."

I hadn't seen my son cry since he was twelve. He put his head in my lap to hide his face. His shoulders shook; I could feel his tears through the knees of my jeans. "Oh, it's all right," I told him, stroking his hair, stealing a kiss. I hoped he wasn't ashamed. "It's good to cry, I've found out. Definitely not something to be avoided at all costs. It shows you feel something, that's all."

I brushed Terry's tears away and smiled at him. It was easier to talk now, as easy as talking to my little boy.

"I've never told you what broke up your father and me. You haven't really told me what separated you and Susan. The details don't matter. But, Terry, be sure you have good reasons. Not having perfect happiness—that might not be good enough. Do you love her? Life is so short. It looks endless when you're twenty-seven, I know, but . . ."

I hated to preach, but I'd waited too long and now I had things to tell him.

"Never throw love away, never neglect it. Never assume you'll find better love somewhere else. Take it wherever you're lucky enough to find it, and always try to return it in kind." I pressed my lips to his forehead. "Don't take so much for granted," I whispered. "That's my final bit of wisdom, and it's the most important."

Kirby, as I've said before, has wonderful timing. He chose that moment to give one knock at the front door and walk in. Terry didn't start guiltily or turn away in embarrassment; he dug a handkerchief out of his pocket and blotted his face, blew his nose manfully.

"Ready?" Kirby asked with suitable blandness. "It's just about time to go."

We stood up. Terry shrugged into his jacket, hefted his duffel onto his strong shoulder. "You know," I said, "I've decided not to go with you two after all. I think I'll just say good-bye here."

Terry looked stricken, but he didn't argue. "I'll call you when I get home tonight," he promised, holding me tight. "And I'll come back, Mom, as soon as I can. Or you could come see me—how would that be? Maybe for Christmas."

"That's an idea," I said, entering into the conspiracy gladly. "Take care of yourself in the meantime."

"You, too. You take good care of her, Kirby."

"I will."

"I love you," I whispered, kissing his damp cheek.

"I love you. I love you, Mom." He couldn't break the thread.

I swallowed hard and gave a little sniff that pulled my tears back inside. "Better hurry, you don't want to miss your plane."

"I'll call you," he said again, following Kirby to the elevator. It came almost immediately. "And I'll write more often! I will, Mom."

I smiled and blew kisses until the doors closed.

And then I was so tired, I couldn't make it to the bedroom. I collapsed on the sofa and covered myself with the afghan. Old, smelly-fragrant, holey afghan I knitted myself, years and years ago when I was unashamedly a housewife. Homemaker, as Terry said. There had been many, many happy times in those days that, for no good reason, I had fallen into the habit of dismissing. Nostalgia drifted over me like a pleasant fog, numbing a little the exquisite pain of Terry's leaving. Gary used to take a nap on Sunday afternoons under this blanket. I'd sit with him, reading or knitting with the radio on low, looking up to see his paunchy stomach rise and fall under the then-bright squares of wool. I used to wrap it around my nightgown and run outside for the newspaper. Terry liked to drape it over two dining room chairs and pretend he was a soldier in a fort.

Was Gary home now? I could call him. Just to talk. "Hi, how are you? What do you think of our son? After all, we didn't do so badly, did we?" But the phone was too far away, I was too tired to get up. I closed my eyes and drifted into a dream. A sweet, bright dream about a family. I gave it the happiest ending.

24

Emma

My birthday is three days after Christmas, which makes me a Capricorn. The goat. How unamusingly apt, but never more so than this year.

I often go away for Christmas, drive down to Danville to see my mother, and sometimes I keep going, drive on to Durham and Chapel Hill to visit old friends from grad school, spend New Year's with them. This year, even the thought of packing made me nauseated, never mind leaving, arriving, greeting, smiling, and talking. Especially smiling and talking; those were by far the most retch-inducing. So I stayed home.

It wasn't a pity party, though. No, no. I got fully dressed, called all my loved ones, I even roused myself to go out and take Isabel her present. No, I was saving myself, bathos-wise, for the twenty-eighth, when I could turn forty all by myself. Now we're talking heroic, orgiastic self-pity on the grand scale.

My solitude was by choice—my friends didn't desert me. In good conscience I couldn't inflict myself on them, and so I asked them to stay away. (Rudy was out of town anyway.) The day started out normally, i.e., full of frustration and self-loathing. That novel I started last spring? I threw it out in August. A mercy killing, believe me. It was what they call a coming-of-age novel. Preternaturally articulate adolescent learns about love, life, sex, and redemption among colorful characters in the New South/urban ghetto/Jewish upper-class/soul-stifling Midwest. I set mine in a nasty little town in southern Virginia named Tomstown. As I say, a mercy killing. So much for writing what you know.

Now I'm working on something entirely different (although "working on" may be a tiny euphemism). It's a mystery, a thriller, lots of intrigue and suspense, a woman-in-jeopardy deal, bodies piling up. I think it's got excellent best-seller and movie potential. Too bad it bites. One thing writing this story has taught me, though, is that I really enjoy killing people. I mean I really get off on it. So I keep doing it. The danger here is that all my characters could be dead before the book ends. It might turn out that God was the narrator.

The other thing this book is teaching me, it and its precious, hackneyed predecessor, is that I might be a fraud. All my life I wanted to write fiction, or at least so I've been saying for most of it. Nonfiction didn't satisfy; I wanted the story to go another way, the truth never got to what was really true, et cetera, blah blah. Well, guess what. Turns out I was a much better journalist than I am a novelist. So now I have to wonder if I was only drawn to the image of what it means to write fiction. I wanted to *look* like a novelist. I wanted to answer the "What do you do?" question at cocktail parties with "I write books."

If that's true, I don't know what I'll do. It feels like smashing into a glass door. I thought there was a vista, a future, but maybe there's just shock and embarrassment and bloody lacerations.

Happy birthday, Emma.

What I needed was a cake. An ice cream cake, one of those Viennetta or Violetta things they advertise on TV around the holidays. They always make my mouth water. I almost bought one once, then I read the fat/calorie blurb on the back. Well, fuck it, I'm forty years old, I can have any damn thing I want. Like wine. Wine and ice cream cake. A really good wine, too, not that eight-dollar Mondavi in the refrigerator.

Going outside and getting in my car felt like setting foot on a new planet. How long since I'd been out of the house? Almost four days. God. There's something to be said for a real job. Not much, but something. The low, late-afternoon December sky was that old-diaper shade of gray, heavy with either rain or snow, it couldn't decide. Until I parked on Columbia Road and started to walk the block and a half to the liquor store—then it decided. Sleet.

On Christmas Eve morning I put on some old black sweatpants, a black blouse, and my most comfortable sweater, a snarly, dung-colored cardigan with big pockets and one remaining leather button. I liked this outfit so well, I put it on the next day, too. And the next. And today. I hadn't washed my hair in a week—why bother?—and it goes without saying I hadn't put on any makeup. I'd left the house in a trenchcoat and my beaded bedroom moccasins, no socks. Got the picture?

Mick got it when he opened the door to the liquor store and we almost smacked into each other. He said, "Excuse me," and stood back—for two seconds he actually didn't recognize me. Later I couldn't decide if that was an insult or deeply flattering. Then he did a double take, probably humorous to an impartial observer, and stopped dead.

Me, too. "Mick, hi," I think I said, very casual. Inside, it felt like cardiac arrest. I think I went white, but his cheeks turned red, two streaks of bright color like slap marks. "How are you," I said, "how've you been." I was pressed back against the door frame, clutching a bagful of clanking wine bottles, and he was squeezed back on the other side, holding the glass door wide open with his outstretched arm.

"Emma." He couldn't even smile, he just looked at me with his burning eyes. His shock helped me get over mine. I was ready to say something bright, maybe even true—"I've missed you," something like that—when he jerked his head toward the street. "I've got my family."

Ah, yes, so he did. In the car; I recognized the small white Celica at the curb half a block away. Couldn't see the occupants, though, just their hazy outlines through the sleet and the streaky windshield.

"Well. Tell them I said hi. Really good to see you."

Neither of us moved.

"How are you, Emma?"

"Fine, I've been all right. You?"

I'm not that great a liar, but at least I try. Mick doesn't even try. "I'm terrible," he said.

I felt my face get hot. "Not fair," I whispered. "Damn you, that is no fair."

One customer and then another one, both wanting to use the door, put an end to the torture. We had to separate; I walked out and Mick walked in. We never said good-bye, but we waved to each other through the door. How inane. I thanked God my car was in the opposite direction from his, and I didn't wave to Sally. I slogged through the freezing rain with my wine bottles and went home.

That night when the phone rang, I knew it was Mick. You know how sometimes you can just tell who it is by the sound of the ring? I'd been sitting in front of the fire for so long, it had burned out. To my credit, I wasn't drunk; I'd had a glass or two of a very expensive Cabernet, and given up. Lack of interest.

I picked up the phone in the kitchen on the third ring and said, "Hello?" in a firm, deceptively healthy, clearheaded tone.

"Happy birthday."

"Thanks." It was Lee. I collapsed on a stool and waited for my heart rate to subside. "How are you?"

"Okay." Not that long ago she used to answer that question with, "I'm not pregnant," but she's stopped. Nobody's amused anymore, especially Lee. So far, in vitro isn't working. "How's your birthday going?" she asked.

"Lousy."

"Oh, no. Would you like to come over?"

"No, thanks."

"We're not doing anything. We're not even fighting. Come on, we'll cheer you up."

"No, but thank you, that's nice. Really. How're you doing?"

"Okay," she repeated. "Rudy's back from the Bahamas."

"Oh, yeah? Since when?"

"Today."

"Did she call you?"

"Yes."

Well, shit. Rudy won't say boo to me on my birthday, but she can call Lee to say she's back from her "second honeymoon"—honest to God, that's what she called it. "How did she sound?" I asked.

"The same as before."

"Which is to say . . ."

"Not very good. I think the only reason she called was to say she's not coming to dinner tomorrow. So it'll just be you, Isabel, and me."

Christ, we were falling apart, all four of us. "Did she say why?"

"Something about something she has to go to with Curtis."

I said some really vulgar swear words that made Lee hiss in her breath like a mongoose. I had to ask, "Does she talk to you? Lately? Is she telling you anything about what's going on with her?"

"No. So . . . she's not telling you, either?"

"No, and I know she's not talking to Isabel because I asked her."

We heaved simultaneous sighs.

"Well," Lee said dispiritedly. "See you tomorrow night, I guess. Don't forget to bring salad."

"When did I ever forget?"

"And you'll pick Isabel up?"

"Of course."

"Happy birthday, Em."

"Night, Lee."

We hung up.

Before I could get off my stool, the phone rang again.

"Hello?"

"Emma? It's Mick."

Everything receded, nothing left but my hand on the receiver and his voice in my ear. And I felt sick with wanting, with knowing it was him and this was real. I had come so close to convincing myself that this wasn't true—that he's the only one and I'll never be over him.

"May I see you?"

"Are you all right?"

"I'm fine." He laughed, a huff of breath. "Except that . . ."

I imagined I could hear, in his silences and his deep, frustrated breathing, everything he couldn't say. I pictured him in his house, probably in the kitchen, with Sally upstairs putting Jay to bed. "Are you at home?"

"No, I'm in my car. Sally's cell phone."

"Oh." So much for my intuition. "It's very clear."

Another exhalation of humorless laughter. "That's probably because I'm around the corner from your house."

"Oh, God."

He was quiet for a few awful seconds, then he said thickly, "It's okay, don't worry, I was driving and I just ended up here. I won't—"

"Give me five minutes."

"What's that?"

"I need five minutes. I have to—I'm not quite dressed. But then come."

"Are you sure?"

"Yes. Okay, I'm hanging up now."

He laughed, and it was a real laugh, not sad or forced. I waited until it was completely over, just reveled in it, and then I hung up.

Five minutes. I should've said ten. I raced upstairs to the bathroom and looked at myself in the mirror. I should've said an hour and a half.

Too late to shower or change clothes. Clean my house, buy a

new wardrobe. I took off my ratty sweater and brushed my wine-stained teeth. I tried to comb my hair, but that was impossible, so I piled it up in a bun. I put on mascara, a little lipstick. God, God. I'd keep the lights low.

Downstairs, there wasn't even time to rebuild the fire. I scooped up the newspapers strewn all over, straightened the sofa cushions, blew crumbs off the end tables. I put on music, then turned it off. Would he like my house? It wasn't very artistic. I had some pictures, some prints I liked a lot, but they were probably gauche. Oh God, now he'd find out, he'd see that I was cheap and fraudulent and shallow. What a stupid idea this was. I liked it better when we were a neat, clean tragedy. No potential, no messy reality. Then we were perfect.

The doorbell rang. My heart gave a dangerous leap—if this kept up I'd be dead by morning. Deep, cleansing breath. I put on a normal face and opened the door.

"Hi," we said. He brought in the cold and damp on his wool overcoat. His face was pinched, his ears livid. "Take off your coat," I said. When he gave it to me, I felt his icy hands. "You're freezing. Were you walking?"

"For a while." He moved into the living room, drawn to the hearth, but he stopped when he saw the fire was out.

"It burned down," I said idiotically. "Shall we sit here?"

He took the chair, I sat on the edge of the sofa. A mistake. How could we talk like this? Too weird—Mick and me in the living room, facing each other across my tony sisal carpet. We weren't ourselves, we were actors in a play.

"Would you like a drink? I happen to have a lot of wine."

"No, thank you."

"Coffee?"

"That would be great."

I jumped up. "Come with me."

Much better in the kitchen. He leaned against the counter,

watching me while I filled the kettle, measured the coffee, poured hot water over the grounds a little at a time. Very labor-intensive, the Chemex coffee system, very good for keeping the hands busy. "It's Jay's birthday today," he mentioned, to fill the industrious silence.

I looked up. "Is it really?" What a coincidence.

"He's six. I took the afternoon off for a little party he had at the zoo this afternoon. Only eight friends—that didn't seem like so many when we were planning it." He rubbed his forehead as if his head hurt. "Jesus."

"Oh, you're just trying to make excuses for being in the liquor store."

We laughed. It loosened the tension a little.

He began to pace in front of the black squares of the windows. I watched him out of the corner of my eye. He looked different—again. He had on gray slacks and a good sport coat, a loosened blue tie. He must dress like this, like a businessman, for his part-time job at his old law firm. If he still had it. The fact that I didn't even know, that there could be a hundred new things about his life I had no idea of, struck me as the saddest thing in the world.

"How is Isabel?" he asked, picking up and setting down the red rooster salt shaker. "And Rudy. Sally tells me about Lee sometimes, but I don't hear about the others anymore."

It's no wonder I love him. He wasn't filling silence, he really cared how my friends were doing, and not just because of me.

I poured coffee into mugs, added a lot of milk to his. "Isabel's very sick. I don't know what's going to happen."

"I'm sorry, Emma."

"Yeah." His sympathy almost did me in. I was really on some kind of an edge. I gave him his mug and reached for the cookie jar. "Want a tea biscuit? Rudy's no good, either. She's dropped out of school. Did you know she was studying landscape design?" He shook his head. "Well, she quit. God knows what she's doing now, I sure don't." I sounded so cold and careless.

He just said, "I'm sorry," again.

"Yeah, life sucks." I was on the verge of making an ass of myself by crying or something. "Why did you come here, Mick? Just to chat? Do you want to have an affair with me? But we already know exactly how that will turn out." I hated the tone of my voice. This was crazy—why was I being hateful to him?

"I can go—"

"No, don't, I'm sorry, don't go. I'm—you should know, it's only fair to tell you—I can be an awful bitch, Mick, when I'm—miserable."

"I don't want you to be miserable."

"Too late. Nothing you can do about it." Was there? Why *had* he come?

He set his cup down carefully. "I kept thinking I'd see you. I couldn't believe it when we never ran into each other. Months."

"I know. I *did* see you. On the street, or in a car passing by, on line at the movies. But it was never you." Just some fraud, a Mick look-alike. Sometimes they didn't even look like him; I'd only conjured him up out of some good-looking schlub's generic eyes, hair, mouth. A mirage.

"Then, today," he said.

"Yeah. A vision of loveliness." Oh, shut up, Emma.

"A vision of loveliness." He smiled, but he wasn't kidding, and my fatuous phrase didn't sound stupid when he said it. "It was like taking one drink," he said. "Smoking one cigarette. Readdicted."

Oh, God help me. I'm falling.

"I had to see you. Don't laugh at this. I thought—I had some idea that if we were together, just once, we could leave each other in peace afterward."

"Really." I nodded seriously, not disagreeing. It sounded specious in the extreme to me, if he was talking about what I thought he was talking about. But I wanted it too badly to point out the flaws.

"Just never seeing you again—" He touched the side of my

hand, which was gripping the edge of the counter. "It's worse than being together. It seems that way to me. Unnatural, Emma. More of a—sin."

"A sin." As an ex-Catholic, the word arrested me. "Is that what it would be to you? Sleeping with me would be a sin?"

He shook his head, smiling, helpless.

"Well, I don't care anymore. I don't care about your guilty conscience or your immortal soul, what do you think of that? And I don't care about your wife or your happy home or your—" I choked up, couldn't get it out. It snuck up on me from behind and pounced, all the reasons why this was the same bad idea it's always been. "Your son," I finished, trying to sound bold while I was losing my nerve.

He did the best thing—he put his arms around me and held me.

I closed my eyes to block out the pain and doubt in his face. Words had never gotten us anywhere—they never do when the situation is untenable to begin with. I kissed him for a distraction, and it worked: everything melted in a slow dissolve, all but Mick's hot mouth and the whisker stubble on his cheeks and the feel of his hand on the back of my neck. We kissed until we were out of breath and groping, until it was stark sex, not for comfort, not to show we cared. I made a choice to let go, stop thinking, just do it. Maybe something would change if we let it happen, something we couldn't foresee. And it felt so natural, opening my legs so Mick could move between them and press me back, back, the sharp edge of the counter hard and bruising against my spine. I didn't care that it hurt, I wanted sensation, I wanted his hands all over me. "Upstairs," I muttered—I could have more of him if we were horizontal.

We took hands and went blindly down the hall, up the stairs, into the bedroom. I almost didn't turn on the light—afraid of his face again—but the blue, bitter moonlight chilled me. Craving warmth, I closed the curtain and turned on the bedside lamp.

We stood on opposite sides of my handsome, unmade sleigh

bed, watching each other. I was right to be wary of his face—he looked tragic. "What?" I said, and started to unbutton my blouse. Not terribly romantic, but one of us had to go first. Mick turned around and sat on the edge of the bed. But then—he didn't move, he didn't undo his belt or start to take off his shoes. I knew exactly what was going to happen.

I thought of screaming at him, making a scene, letting hot, humiliated fury take over from here—see how that went. I discarded the idea, but I was angry and hurt enough to want to hurt him. I didn't fasten my blouse when I came around the bed and stood in front of him. I have great breasts, twenty men have told me so, they're my best feature. So it was consoling to show them to Mick, gratifying to watch his eyes drop and darken. *See what you missed,* I thought spitefully, sticking them out a little.

He smiled. He looked at me with such tenderness and understanding, I started to cry.

"I'm such an ass," he said, taking my hand and tugging me down next to him. "I know it. You couldn't feel any more contempt for me right now than I do."

"I don't. I don't." But I had to whisper, "What happened?" Between the kitchen and the bedroom, what went wrong? Should we have done it on the counter?

"You know what happened. I've been telling lies."

"What did you tell me that was a lie?" I asked fearfully.

"That we could do this once."

"Oh. That lie. Did you think I believed you?"

He smiled, and we started at the same moment to kiss each other's hand. A little tug-of-war. I rested my head on his shoulder.

"So basically," I said dully, "nothing's changed. You just came here to torture me. Again. I was almost over you. No, I wasn't."

"I came because I . . ." His shoulder lifted and fell when he sighed. "Everything sounds stupid. I can say I couldn't resist. I can say I was sick of needing you, that I had to see you. I don't know if nothing's changed, Emma—something must have. I've been suffering enough for something to have changed."

"Me, too."

He faced me. "There haven't been any other women. You asked me that on the beach. There's only you."

"I asked you something else."

By the downward flick of his lashes, I could tell he remembered. He was quiet for a long time. "I sleep with my wife. Yes. Not often. She needs—the illusion, and I try to provide it when there's nothing else I can do."

"The illusion?"

"That we have a marriage."

"Ah. And you think that's a gift?"

He shifted, almost flinched. "I have no hope of making you understand this."

"Try."

"Emma—I'm all she has. Even though I think she hates me most of the time. I'm afraid to give Jay to her and I'm afraid to take him away." It was as if he had glass in his throat, it was so hard for him to talk. He still hated betraying Sally to me, even this much. And that hurt, too.

"Mick, why did you marry her?"

"Because she was pregnant."

"Oh."

Bleak silence.

He resumed wearily. "She's the opposite of you. She's not strong. She's always defined herself by what other people think, her family, friends."

"You."

"Especially me."

"Did you ever love her?"

"I love you."

"Oh, God." I dropped my head in my hands. "Why did you

come here?" I asked him again. Some strange exhaustion was making me almost ill.

"I think—I must've come to ask you to wait."

"Wait. Because you still can't leave her? You still think staying with her is better for Jay than splitting up?"

He pulled at his hair. "I don't know."

I was pretty sure that meant yes. "Go away, Mick," I said, standing up.

"Emma—"

"I'm not your therapist. Don't come to my house and spill your troubles to me. This is—this is the first selfish thing you've done, and I don't appreciate it. I had a scab over you, and you ripped it off. And you won't even sleep with me. Go away, please, disappear for six more months. I'm no masochist, I'll be over you by then, and that's a promise."

He stood up. He never gets angry—I didn't like that about him now. "I'm sorry," he said, "I'm sorry," and then something that sounded like, "I was freezing." And he walked out.

I caught him in the hall, snaked my arms around him from behind, pressing my cheek against his tweedy coat. A symbolic position—no face-to-face contact; me holding on to the man who keeps leaving me.

He tried to turn around, but I held still and wouldn't let him. Better to say it like this. "Listen to me. I want to marry you, Mick. Have babies. Be a starving artist with you. What I don't want is to be a forty-year-old spinster who's having an affair. Or *not* having an affair, that's even worse." I could feel his heart pounding under the smooth cotton of his shirt. "I can't wait for you," I said, and my stupid voice quavered. "You shouldn't have asked. I have to get on with my life. Don't call me or come over anymore, it just makes it worse."

"I know. I won't." He bowed his head. "I love you. That's not so you'll change your mind. It's just so you'll know." He squeezed my arms around him once, just for a second, and then he left me.

* * *

Late that night, much later, I called Rudy.

"Oh, Christ, you were sleeping."

"Emma?"

"I'm sorry."

"What's wrong? Wait a sec—" She put her hand over the phone. Muffled silence for about half a minute. Her bedroom phone is cordless; I imagined her telling Curtis to go back to sleep, then slipping out of bed and going out in the hall or the bathroom.

"Emma?"

"I didn't even think about the time, Rudy. I'm really sorry."

"It's okay."

"I guess Curtis is pissed."

"No, of course not."

I shouldn't have said that, I could tell by her tone. She was always prickly about him, which was why I kept my rapier Curtis wit sheathed around her, but lately she'd gone beyond touchy. Something really bad was happening, but for the life of me I couldn't figure out what.

"So, Rudy, how was your vacation?"

"Great."

"Was it?"

"Yeah."

"You don't sound like it was great. Are you okay?"

"I just woke up."

"Oh, right."

Silence while she waited for me to come to the point. This was such an unnatural conversation for us, I started to get lost in the weirdness. I could hardly remember why I'd called her.

It came back to me. "I saw Mick today."

"Oh."

Oh? "Yeah, at the liquor store on Columbia Road. You should've seen me, I looked like the wrath of God. As my mother would say.

We didn't—we just looked at each other, couldn't really talk much. It was such a shock, you know? Plus he had his family waiting for him, so . . ."

"Yikes."

"Yeah. Then tonight, he called me. He was in his car. I told him he could come over."

"Oh, Em."

"I know, but there was no way, I mean, I couldn't not see him, you know? Wait, how many negatives is that?"

"Did you sleep with him?"

"No. Almost."

She sighed. It sounded sympathetic.

"It was pretty much a repeat of the beach scene, except this time we really . . . we finally talked about his situation, which is hopeless. So, that's that. It's over, and I'm . . ." I'm bleeding. Help me.

"I'm sorry, Em. Really sorry. Maybe it's for the best."

"Possibly." I waited, but that was it. No more comfort and sympathy coming from Rudy tonight. I should've called Dial-a-Shoulder.

"Well," I said, "it's pretty late."

"It is. I should go. I'll call you."

"Will you? That'll be a novelty."

Oh, I shouldn't have said that, either. That mild reproof should not have passed my lips. I'd hurt her, I could hear it in the hush between us.

"Night, Rudy," I said gently. "Sorry I woke you."

"Night, Em. I really love you."

"Well, hey, that's—"

Click.

I replaced the receiver slowly, frowning and smiling, feeling a little breathless. "I love you, too," I said.

But I was worried sick. I couldn't get angry with her for not being the rock of support and understanding she'd always been. My broken heart hurt like hell, but it would heal. Someday.

Whatever was wrong with Rudy might not. If she would just *talk* to me. What is it, what could be happening to her? It's something to do with Curtis, that's a given, but what?

While we were talking on the phone, I kept thinking about a time, years ago, when she helped get me through another crisis involving a man. This one was Peter Dickenson. Peter the Prick. I was mad for this guy, totally nuts, I was ready to marry him. You think I'm cynical about men? You should've known me six years ago, P.P. Pre-Peter. I was like Gidget, I was like a goddamn puppy. This guy—he looked like Alec Baldwin's brother, the skinny one with the slicked-back hair, the one you can never trust. I was living alone in a great apartment in Foggy Bottom and really enjoying my solitude. But—this is the Gidget Goes to Washington part—I was so gone on Peter the Prick, I invited him to move in with me. We lived together in common-law bliss for almost four months.

Then one night—don't get ahead of me, now—I came home early from a Graces meeting, and guess what. Oh, shoot, you guessed. But you know, it doesn't matter how clichéd this story is, how many times you've heard it bleated about in a country-western song or overacted on some soap opera. When it happens to you, it's not funny. I walked in on it in classic in flagrante style, and it was going on in my own bed.

I exited swiftly, but the image was cauterized on my retinas. The lovers had seen me, too, so I went in the living room and sat on the sofa to wait. It didn't take long. Peter came out first, in his underwear. He knelt at my feet. Talk, talk. He was at the "She means *nothing* to me" stage when the girl came out. At least I didn't know her. She looked like an undergraduate, very leggy, lots of flowy blonde hair. She blanched when she heard she meant nothing to him—I actually felt a little sympathy for her. Then she left, and Peter kept talking. This I remember with crystal clarity: putting my foot in the center of his naked chest and kicking him over backward on his butt. *Get out*, I told him, but he wouldn't, so

I called the police. The first and only time I've ever dialed 911. Peter saw the light and left before the cops came.

So then—here's the point I'm making—I called Rudy. At this time we weren't really speaking. Long story; it was right after she married Curtis, and we'd had a fight about that, the worst in our history, and even though we were pretending all was well for the sake of the Graces, it wasn't. But I called her, and just about all I had to say was, "Oh God, Rudy," and she said, "I'll be right over."

She stayed with me all night. I cried a lot. We drank gin and smoked a thousand cigarettes, and at about 6 A.M. we went to the Howard Johnson's on Virginia Avenue and ate bacon and pancakes. I was a mess, but Rudy got me through it—this is the thing. Who knows how long I'd have pined for Peter without her? And who knows what kind of shit Curtis gave her when she went home at nine o'clock in the morning? That's the point. That's why the fact that she couldn't replicate that daring rescue mission tonight means nothing whatsoever to me as far as our friendship is concerned. Rudy and I are true-blue.

Not long ago I'd have said the problem is men. "Men ruin everything" is a saying of my mother's; I grew up with it, and after a while it's hard to argue with.

But now I'm in love with a man, and as the song says, he's a credit to his gender. I'm miserable, but I can't lay the blame at the usual place. I can't lay blame anywhere, and that ticks me off. Is this called growing up? If so, I'm against it. Middle age—I hit it today and already I despise it. I don't see anything in the future but loneliness and being mature and not having fun and taking hormone replacement therapy.

Happy birthday, Emma. Welcome to the rest of your life.

25

Lee

Dr. Jergens's office always calls late in the day. Good news or bad, 4 to 5 P.M. is the nurses' time to give patients their latest blood tests and lab results. So I knew who was probably calling me at home at four-forty-five on a cold, darkening Monday in the second week of January. I'd had a lifeless feeling all day. A premonition? I let the phone ring three and a half times, almost let the answering machine pick up.

"Mrs. Patterson?"

It was Patti. One of the nice ones. She always sympathizes when the news isn't good. Some of them don't; they could be reading off stock market quotations for all the warmth in their flat, rushed, telephone voices.

"Yes?"

"Hi, how are you?"

"Fine. And you?"

"Fine, thanks, and I'm calling with the results from your last IVF."

"Yes."

"Oh, I'm really sorry. No luck this time."

No luck this time. And Henry spelled *cheese* wrong on the grocery list. *Cheeze* he wrote. I have so many refrigerator magnets. Too many. They look messy. One says, "My karma ran over my dogma"—a present from Emma. It's stuck over a photograph of the Graces, all of us on Rudy's front porch steps last summer. We look leggy and tan in our shorts and sleeveless tops.

"Mrs. Patterson?"

Henry put another magnet, this one shaped like a turkey drumstick, over his Wizards' basketball schedule. Tonight they're playing against the Charlotte Hornets. An away game.

"Mrs. Patterson? You there?"

"Yes. Thank you for calling."

"Okay. Well, I was saying you'll want to make your next appointment before the end of the week, don't forget. You can do that now if you want to. Or, um, you can wait."

I have a magnet that tells how many fluid ounces are in three-quarters of a cup, how many milliliters in a tablespoon, how many tablespoons in a third of a cup. I thought it would come in so handy, but I rarely use it.

"Hello?"

I put the phone back in its cradle very quietly.

I didn't want to take my hand off the receiver. And then I didn't want to go outside. But I made myself open the back door and follow the sound of Henry's ax, sharp thunks of noise, *crack, crack,* that split the cold twilight like ice breaking. He uses an old elm stump behind the garage for a chopping block. I like to watch him heave the heavy, impenetrable-looking chunks of oak or hickory onto the block, haul back, and smash them in half with one clean blow.

He didn't hear me. He turned, reaching down for a slab of wood that had flown sideways. He saw me and straightened, started to smile. Then he stood motionless, the long-handled ax hanging limp from his fist.

"They called."

He came toward me, dropping the ax, crunching over wood scraps and bark in his ashy work boots. "Where's your coat? You'll freeze out here."

Everything got very clear again. Muddy dust on the black windowpanes of the garage, dark places between the bricks where the mortar's gone, a tear-shaped coffee stain on the breast of Henry's plaid jacket. "I'm not pregnant. It didn't work."

"Lee. Honey." He reached out to touch me, just my elbow with his fingertips. I flinched. He drew back.

"It's over."

"What?"

"Four times. That's enough. I'm not doing it anymore."

I waited for him to nod in sad understanding and then hold me, tell me it was the right decision. "It's over," he echoed, but more to himself. Perspiration was drying on the smooth skin of his forehead. He looked into my eyes—making sure I was all right. I felt very little; almost nothing. Fatigue, mostly. "Okay." Henry swallowed. "You're sure?"

"Yes."

He turned and went back to his chopping block, began to throw chunks of wood into the wheelbarrow. I waited while he bent and twisted, snagging pieces in both hands, lobbing them underhand, never missing. I caught a glimpse of his face. By accident—he was trying to keep it turned from me. He was crying.

Shock kept me from moving. I started to feel something. Heat, like a burn widening in the center of my chest. "Henry?" I grabbed for his arm—got the sleeve of his coat. I kept pulling and pulling until he had to face me. Tears streaked down his cold, ruddy cheeks. "Is it wrong? I'll keep doing it. Darling, I'll go back, we can try again."

"*No*. I don't want you to do it anymore, Lee, I want you to stop. I'm—it's—"

"Sad."

He undid the leather buttons of his jacket and pulled me inside, wrapped me up in it, and in a minute his body heat began to ease the burning in my chest. I put my hands on the wet sides of his face and held him. I had never seen Henry cry, never, never. It melted me. It thawed me from the inside.

"I'm so sorry."

"Don't say that—"

"So sorry. Oh, Henry, I'm so sorry."

"It's all right." He held me harder. "Lee, I love you."

"I know. Oh, I'm so sorry." I gave in and wept.

And it didn't hurt. It didn't sting like acid in the backs of my eyes, didn't make me feel afraid and desperate. Henry cried, too, and I thought maybe the mixing of our tears was helping to take the pain away. I know it was a beginning. Hopelessness is a blessing sometimes, Isabel told me once, and now I see it's true.

"Come inside with me. We can warm each other," I said, and that's how it started. Henry and I began to heal.

In early February, Isabel finally had the Graces' meeting at her house. She'd canceled at the last minute for the last two weeks in a row—once she was too tired, once she had a late doctor's appointment—but when I called to confirm on the Thursday afternoon, she said, "Yes, come, come, I can't wait to see you."

On the way to her apartment, I drove down Connecticut Avenue behind a Subaru station wagon. At every red light between Van Ness and the zoo, two little girls in the back waved to me. I waved back the first few times, even blew a kiss; but they grew wilder and sillier at each stop, and soon I put on a calm, adult face to settle them down. They were about six or seven, not sisters but best friends, I decided, one dark, one fair. They pressed their noses flat to the glass, stuck out their tongues, ducked below the window and then jumped up, "scaring" me with grotesque faces. The laughing and shrieking must have gotten too loud: they faced forward abruptly, mirth fading, while the woman in the driver's seat apparently laid down the law. After that the little girls only gave me a couple of backward glances and a grin or two—conspiratorial, I imagined. But I was quickly forgotten, and at Woodley Street the Subaru turned off.

I drove for a few more blocks before it hit me: I hadn't cried. In the past, and not so long ago, I would have. I believe I may be growing a shell around my heart. Henry and I are childless. Childless. I say it out loud sometimes, because I believe in calling a spade a spade.

This is a secret: I've thought of calling Dr. Greenburg, Rudy's therapist, and making an appointment. Wouldn't that amaze the Graces? Lee, the normal one, needing a shrink? I probably won't, though. These days it's old-fashioned, but I also believe in the ideal of self-sufficiency, the individual's responsibility for her own happiness. It's not that I disapprove of psychological counseling for others—I wouldn't last long in my profession with that attitude—but I don't think it's for me. It's not part of my heritage, if you will. Pavliks don't go to psychiatrists. Besides, how would I explain it to my mother?

At Isabel's, Emma answered the door. "Where is she?" I asked in a low voice. "Is she okay?"

"Sure, she's in the kitchen. Come on in."

Isabel was sitting at the table. She didn't get up, but she held her arms out to me. I gave her a long, soft hug. "How are you? How do you feel? You look beautiful." Yes, but also frail and tired. Her sweater and slacks dwarfed her body, just as her wig had gotten too big for her bony face. I wished she wouldn't wear it anymore; I liked her own short, patchy, brittle hair better.

She said what she always says—"I'm just *fine*," patting my back and beaming at me with so much gladness, I got a lump in my throat. "What have you got in your bag?" she asked.

"Dinner. Did you make the rice?" Even though she'd insisted on having the meeting at her house, we wouldn't let her do anything except make brown rice. That's the new staple in her diet nowadays.

"Kirby did," she said. "He's not here, he's acting in a play tonight. Said to give everyone his love."

"What a guy." Emma looked up from chopping vegetables for the salad. "Not many men send their love. They think it's not manly or something."

"That's true," I said. "Henry just sent his 'best.' Emma, what is that? Is that spinach?"

"Yeah?"

"Isabel can't eat that."

"Oh, shit. Isabel?"

She shrugged, smiled. "That's the theory."

"Well, I've also got chicory," Emma said defensively. "You can eat that, it's very yang. Rhubarb, though, is almost completely yin, did you know that? So don't eat it."

"Show-off," Isabel said. We've all bought macrobiotic cookbooks, and now we take turns bringing meals over to Isabel's a few nights a week. It gives Kirby a break.

"Rudy's late," Emma noted. "What else is new. Maybe she won't show up at all."

"Has anybody talked to her?"

"Not really," Isabel said. "She comes by to see me once in a while, but she never stays. She's in and out, and she won't talk about herself."

"A troubling anomaly in itself," Emma muttered.

I caught Isabel's eye. Whatever was wrong with Rudy, it was hurting Emma the most. Until now, as far as I knew, they had never kept a secret from each other. For myself, I couldn't help feeling Rudy had let the whole group down, not only Emma. Yes, she had problems—so what? Who didn't? Whatever was bothering her, and I had no idea what it was, it couldn't possibly be worse than Isabel's situation. If ever there was one, this was a time for rallying round, not wallowing in one's own private neuroses.

I didn't say that out loud, of course. It would have broken a rule—one I didn't make up, by the way; in fact, we've never even put this rule into words, never discussed it. If one person says something negative about another person in the group (Emma's "troubling anomaly" remark, for example), nobody else is allowed to chime in with another negative comment. Because that would throw off the balance; it would be ganging up. It's never happened, but I can imagine the rule relaxing slightly during those times when we have five members instead of four. But as I say, it's never happened. If anything, now that I think of it, we become even more homogeneous when we're five. We core four do, I mean. As if we're closing ranks, sending a message to the poor fifth person, the transient, that she'd better *not* criticize one of us to the others.

"At least she's not drinking," Emma said, as if she wanted to make up for being snotty before. "As far as we know. Then again, how the hell *would* we know?"

"She's unhappy, Emma," Isabel said.

"I know that." She was rhythmically pulverizing a broccoli floret. "But who isn't? You know?"

"How's your writing going these days?" When she glared at me, I realized I might not have timed that question perfectly.

"I threw it out," she snarled.

"Oh, no! Your mystery?"

"Is that what it was? Thanks for telling me, I never knew for sure."

"What will you try next?" Isabel asked.

"Well . . . I was thinking maybe a romance."

I laughed. "You?" But she wasn't kidding. "Sorry," I said when I realized it. "I just thought, you know, it's possible you're too . . ."

"What? I'm too what?"

"Cynical. Maybe. For romance. But what do I know."

"Yeah, what do you know."

"I don't think you're too cynical," Isabel said thoughtfully. "In fact, I don't think you're cynical at all."

Emma blushed.

After a moment, she surprised me by bumping my hip with

hers as we stood at our side-by-side cutting boards. "Your turn, Lee-Lee. How are you doing?"

That's a term of endearment Emma uses only on very rare occasions, mostly when she's had too much wine. Or when she's afraid she's hurt my feelings. "Oh," I said, "I'm all right."

"Really?"

"Really." I told them about the two little girls in the car, and how I hadn't cried. "Mostly, I think I feel relief."

"And still sure you did the right thing? *I* think you did the right thing," Emma said quickly, "I mean, for what that's worth, but I'd hate it if you had regrets."

"Well." There are regrets, and there are regrets. "We did everything, there was nothing left to try."

"Right. You did it all, so you can't look back and—"

"Although we could've gotten on an egg donor list."

"But enough's enough."

"We thought so. We both felt it was the right time to stop."

"How is Henry?"

"He's better, too. We're better together." I laughed. "We're starting to remember why we used to like each other."

"Oh, I'm glad." Emma gave me a shove with her shoulder—another uncommon gesture of affection. "Tell the big lug I send him my *best*."

"Should we wait for Rudy or should I start cooking?" I was making a stir-fry with winter squash, turnips, lotus root, and chickpeas. I'd made it before—it's not as bad as it sounds.

Isabel said, "Wait," at the same moment Emma said, "Cook."

"I'll wait a few more minutes," I decided. I joined Emma and Isabel at the table, bringing a glass of wine for me and a fresh cup of bancha tea for Isabel. Kirby makes about a gallon of it for her every morning. She swears it's doing her good.

"How's your love life?" I asked Emma. I felt a little self-conscious, introducing such a frivolous topic. Shouldn't we have been discussing important things, like the meaning of life? We never did, though. We talked about the same old things we'd always talked about. Isabel didn't seem to mind; these days she didn't say much herself, but she would smile her soft smile, letting her eyes rest calmly, peacefully on whoever was speaking. Sometimes I wasn't sure she was even paying attention to the words; she looked so dreamy, she might've just been listening to our voices.

"My love life?" Emma slid down in the chair on her spine. "It's an oxymoron." She had on all black tonight, black jeans, black sweater, black boots. Let's hope it's a phase, because it's not her color.

"I thought you were dating that real estate guy."

"Stuart. Not anymore."

"Well, what about the lawyer from EPA, Bill, Will—"

"Phil. That didn't work out."

I sighed. "Well, I don't know what to do. I ran out of people to fix you up with about a year ago."

"The lone firm spot in the quagmire of my life."

"Ingrate."

"Pimp."

"So there's no one?" Isabel's voice has changed, I can't imagine why. It's higher, lighter, a little breathy. She ran her index finger back and forth across the top of Emma's hand, a way of saying, *Let's be serious for a second.* I didn't like to look at her wrist bone poking out of the sleeve of her sweatshirt; it was too white and sharp, the skin stretched too tight. "Are you sure, Em? Nobody at all?"

Emma looked at her in alarm—as if she was afraid Isabel might know something she didn't want her to know. Then she ducked her head and stared down at the wineglass balanced on her stomach. When she didn't answer, I thought of something.

"Whatever happened to that man who was married?"

"The one I'd rather not talk about?" she snapped.

"Well, *excuse*—"

"Oh, Lee, I'm sorry." She smiled, trying to make me smile. "I'm sorry, I keep doing that. It's just that this guy . . ." She shook her head.

"But that was months ago, that was last *spring*. You're still not over him yet? Em, I'm sorry, I just didn't know. You should've said something." She'd never even told us his name.

She glanced at Isabel. "Maybe I should have. But the thing is, the man is married. So I haven't felt that comfortable talking about him."

"But you didn't *do* anything," I pointed out. "Or—" Hm.

"We *didn't*. As it happens." But she didn't look very happy about it.

"So—do you really love him?"

She scowled. "Yeah, but let's not talk about it. Nothing's going to change, so what's the point. What?" she demanded of Isabel, who was only watching her. "No words of wisdom from you?" She said it snidely, but I was sure I saw hope in her eyes.

Isabel gave Emma's hand a squeeze. "What a mess," she said softly. "The real thing at last."

"Yeah." She tried to smile. "My luck."

"It still might work out."

"I don't think so, Is. I think it's safe to say I lost this one."

We sat in a sad circle, not speaking until I couldn't help asking, "Why is everything bad happening to all of us at once?" I turned toward Isabel, and so did Emma—as if she might know the answer. "Is it karma? Some group sin we committed a long time ago and can't remember?"

"I know—it's because of that time we lied to what's-her-name, that awful recruit of yours, Lee, about the Graces breaking up, just so we could get rid of her."

Isabel laughed. "I don't think we've committed a sin. Karma—if there is such a thing," she said for Emma's benefit, "—isn't a punishment, it's a lesson. We have to learn them all sometime. If not in this life . . ." She smiled and let that hang.

"The karmic curriculum." Emma grinned.

"Exactly."

"Well, I don't like it," I said. "These are *horrible* lessons, I *never* want to learn them."

Isabel just smiled, but Emma said grimly, "I'm with you," and in that moment I felt closer to her. Closer, in fact, than I felt to Isabel.

We decided to start dinner without Rudy. I was sautéing the bok choy when the doorbell rang. "About damn time," Emma grumbled, but she was relieved, I could tell. "I'll get it."

Over the sound of popping oil, I heard her say, "Jesus! What's wrong?" I turned. Isabel crouched, half in and half out of her chair, staring into the living room with shock on her face. Rudy appeared in the kitchen doorway, ahead of Emma. I turned off the stove and ran to her.

"Rudy, what happened? Did you have an accident?"

"What?" She looked at me through a blur of tears. Her streaming face went bright red, and she made a strangled sound, like a sob. "Did I what?" Emma clutched at her coat sleeve, which was dotted with melted snow. When Isabel struggled to her feet and started toward her, Rudy finally said, "I'm okay, nobody died, nobody's hurt," and Isabel wobbled with relief—we all did.

"Sit," Emma ordered, taking her arms out of her coat and pushing her down in a chair. "Tell us what happened. You didn't have an accident, that's one—"

"No, I did. Just now, in front of your house."

"My house?" Emma stared.

"I forgot we were meeting. I've been driving and driving, and then I went to your house, and I hit a fireplug trying to park. But it doesn't matter, it was Curtis's BMW." She reached out for Emma's wineglass and drank two large swallows, gasping afterward.

We darted glances over her head. Was she drunk? I brought a box of tissues from the windowsill and set it in front of her. She plucked out three at once and buried her face in the pile. She looked awful, her hair sticking out in wet spikes, her eyes bloodshot and frantic. She balled the tissues in her fist and swallowed. "Okay. This is what happened. Curtis said he has cancer and he might be dying."

"No!" I cried. Emma hissed in her breath. Isabel said, "Oh, my God, my God," and collapsed in her chair.

"No!" Rudy grabbed her hand. "No, it's okay," she said, gray eyes swimming again, her hand squeezing Isabel's much too hard. "He doesn't, he's fine, it's all right!"

"What? Oh, thank God," Isabel breathed, staring, bewildered.

Rudy laughed and let go of her hand. Such a strange laugh; it made me shiver. "I've left him. Can I stay with you?"

Emma nodded stupidly. "You've what?"

"Rudy, for the Lord's sake," Isabel said, "tell us what happened."

Emma and I dropped down on either side of Rudy, and the three of us leaned in toward her, riveted. She gave a little hiccup of laughter, this one much more natural. "You guys—thank God—" She blew her nose again, and then she told us the story.

"Okay. Last November, Curtis told me he'd just been diagnosed with chronic lymphocytic leukemia—CLL. There's no cure, but it isn't always fatal. He said his kind was slow, he might not die for five or ten years, and they might even have a cure by then. He was very hopeful."

"Wait—but you're saying he doesn't have leukemia," I said to clarify. "He does not have it."

"He does not have it."

"Jesus fucking Christ." Emma stared, pressing her forehead up with her fingertips, making her eyes go even wider.

"I thought it was strange that he had so few doctor appointments, and when he did he'd never let me go with him. He didn't want me to be upset, he said. He took pills every morning, but that was all." Rudy looked around at us helplessly. "I think they were vitamins."

"Holy God."

"He seemed fine most of the time, and he was in really good spirits. I thought they'd put him on Prozac or even speed or something, to keep him from being depressed. Once in a while he'd say he was weak or dizzy because his white count was off, and I remember one time at the movies when he had double vision."

"Double vision? Caused by *leukemia*?" Emma's disbelief made us laugh, but the story wasn't funny yet. I didn't see how it ever could be.

"He said the doctors had told him his symptoms were normal, that he'd have episodes from time to time, I shouldn't worry. Now I can see that the *episodes* only happened when we were fighting. Not even really fighting, just arguing, or when he wasn't getting his way. Or when I begged him to at least let me tell Eric. And you guys," she said, but she was looking at Emma. "He wouldn't let me tell you. He made me pro—prom—" She broke down in fresh tears.

"Oh, Rudy." Emma put her arms around her. "It's all right, it's okay. Rudy," she said, rocking her, "it's okay, I forgive you."

Isabel and I both got misty-eyed. It sounded funny when Emma said, "I forgive you," and yet it was so clear to me that that's what Rudy wanted. Forgiveness.

"So I went to see Dr. Slater—he's our family doctor. I had a feeling Curtis wasn't telling me everything, and I wanted to know the worst. I thought it must be even worse than he was saying, and that's why he was being so secretive about it—to *protect* me. My God." She pressed her shaking hands to her cheeks. "Can you believe this?"

"No. Here," said Emma, pouring more wine and pushing the glass toward her.

But she ignored it and kept talking. "So I went to see Dr. Slater. Today, this afternoon—God, it feels like *weeks* ago. It might be funny when I think back someday and remember the look on his face when I asked him how much longer Curtis had to live."

Emma gasped, then laughed. Even Rudy laughed, horrified.

"He said he didn't know what I was talking about. I *argued* with him." She covered her face. "I was so *slow*."

"No—" Isabel started to say, but Rudy grabbed her hand.

"Wait," she said, "it's worse." Her eyes glittered. She pulled her lips back in a terrible smile. "Are you ready? I told Dr. Slater I'd stopped trying to get pregnant after Curtis told me about the leukemia, and he said—he said—"

"*What?*"

"He said Curtis had a vasectomy."

"No!"

"Last year. Remember I told you we didn't have sex for the whole month of December?" Emma nodded. "That's why! He was healing! And right after that, he told me he wanted us to have a child!"

She sat back, dazed. She wasn't crying anymore. She looked like she'd been knocked unconscious and she was just starting to come around.

Isabel and I were too shocked to speak, but Emma did enough cursing for everybody. "What the hell was the motherfucker thinking he'd do when his five years were up? That's what I want to know. And how the hell did he think he could keep a vasectomy secret from his own wife? Who went to the same family doctor? Didn't it ever occur to him that someday you might ask Slater why you weren't getting pregnant? I mean, what kind of arrogance is that?"

"What did he say when you told him you knew?" Isabel interrupted. "How did he defend himself?"

Rudy focused on her gradually. "Oh, well, I didn't talk to him yet. I just wrote a note and left. I should've packed a bag, but I wasn't thinking. I took his BMW," she added with a broken-off laugh.

"That'll get him," Emma gloated.

But we were disappointed. But nobody said so. We went over it again, all the gory, unbelievable details of Curtis's lie and Rudy's credulity, the misery she'd been in for the last three months. After a while she stopped shaking. I made her eat some bread, not just drink wine, and soon her color looked more natural, too, not as ghostly. But her eyes were still too dark and glittery.

Isabel, who hadn't said anything for a long time, announced, "Rudy, I think you should go home."

Stunned silence, then we all talked at once. "Never! Leaving Curtis is the healthiest thing she's done in years—Are you crazy?—She *can't*, how *could* she—"

"What are you going to do?" Isabel cut in to ask. "Stay with Emma for a while, I know, but then what?"

"I'll find a place."

"With what?"

She said, "Curtis . . ." and trailed off.

"I've got money," Emma said belligerently.

"I do, too," I said. But I started to think.

We were quiet.

"It's not just the money," Isabel began again in a patient tone.

"Which he'll keep," Emma figured out. "He could get the house, the credit cards, all your assets. Your health insurance."

Everything, we realized.

"At the very least he'll get first crack at it," I said, furious. "He's a fucking *lawyer*."

Their mouths dropped; I thought their jaws would hit the table. It's not that I'm incapable of profanity, for heaven's sake. Unlike most, I save it up for when it's warranted.

"Well, shit," Rudy said, waking up.

"And *you* abandoned *him*," Emma reminded her.

"It's not just the money," Isabel repeated into the dismal silence.

"What do you mean, Is?"

She ran two fingers around the lip of her empty teacup in a slow circle. "I've always regretted walking out on Gary. Not divorcing him," she said over our protests, "*leaving* him. I was the wounded party, and it gave me some small satisfaction to march out and leave him on his own. But he betrayed me, and he's never faced that, never even admitted it. Not to this day. It's beside the point that I've forgiven him."

"He cut a class in the karmic lesson plan."

"It's true," I said when Isabel only sent Emma a bland look. "He wronged you, Isabel, and he never paid for it."

"Yeah," Emma said. "Motherfucking bastard lied and cheated and screwed other women, and he never suffered."

"Like Curtis," I said.

"Oh," Rudy said, "but there's no comparison."

"Yes, there is."

"What Curtis did was *worse*," Emma declared, glancing at Isabel. "I mean, in a way. Don't you think? Sure, he's sick, but no amount of psychosis can forgive what he's done to Rudy. Gary thought with his dick and then lied about it. I hope he rots in hell for that, but it's not really *evil*."

"But Curtis—" Rudy closed her mouth. "No, I'm not saying anything, I'm not defending him."

"Better not," Emma warned darkly.

"Well," said Isabel, and we all looked at her. "The point I was trying to make is, Gary broke faith with me. I don't want to say he 'sinned'—"

"He didn't live up to his human potential? He wasn't sufficiently self-actualized?"

"Thank you," Isabel said. "Whatever you want to call it, he

never had to confront it, and he should have had to pay something. A recompense. And so should Curtis."

"You're damn right."

"Not for revenge," Isabel cautioned, catching the gleam in Emma's eyes. "For balance."

"Whatever."

"She's right, Rudy," I said. "For whatever reason, you owe it to yourself to get him out of there. Is he home now?"

"No, he's on a trip. He'll be back tonight."

"When?"

"Late."

We thought.

"I'm a little afraid of him," Rudy said in a small voice.

The temperature in the room dropped; Isabel and I exchanged a sick glance. "Why?" I asked casually.

"He's never really hit me or anything. Well, one time, but that was so long ago. It's more—it's probably just me, but—" We shifted in our chairs, made impatient noises. Rudy closed her eyes. "God, listen to me. I don't know what he does, how he gets me to do what he wants. It's not by violence. But I'm afraid of him anyway. He scares me, and I'm so ashamed to say that to you."

I put my hand on her arm. "Tell the truth, Rudy. Do you still love him?"

"I don't know, Lee. How could I?" Her nose turned pink. "I think it's dying. Right now. I can feel it. It's like a miscarriage."

Emma broke the bleak silence to say, "I'll go home with you if you want. Because the sonofabitch doesn't scare me."

"Me, either," I said. But I'd call Henry first.

"We'll all go." Isabel leaned on her cane and struggled up. "We'd better take two cars." We looked at her quizzically. "Since Rudy won't be going back to Emma's afterward. She'll be staying home."

26

Rudy

I went wild in graduate school. Not college—for some reason all the poison I ingested in childhood didn't hit my bloodstream until I was twenty-six or twenty-seven. It's a wonder I'm alive. No one who knows me now (except Curtis) knows what I was like then—I hadn't met Emma yet, and I've never told her, not all of it. I had to laugh that night Lee blurted out, "I had a one-night stand!" She looked so cute to me, all defiant and ashamed of herself. If I had a nickel for every one-night stand, every one-*hour* stand . . .

It's funny nobody thought of me as a tramp in those days—at least I don't think they did. For some reason I never got a reputation, as we used to call it. It might be because of the way I look (respectable), but I think it's also a knack I inherited from my mother, a way of projecting a sort of New England propriety in the midst of complete emotional chaos and breakdown. My mother—try to imagine if they'd cast Katharine Hepburn instead of Olivia de Havilland in *The Snake Pit*. You can't, I know, that's the point.

It wasn't just sex I O.D.'d on either, although that excess was the showiest one. I had sex with abusive men, wild men, married men, crazy men. I used it as an analgesic—and I even knew it, knew that word, understood the therapeutic context, got it all. Did it anyway. It helped that men really wanted me and I could have anyone I liked. It never occurred to me to stay to myself, not give it away. And as I said, it wasn't only sex; don't forget drugs and alcohol. I was in therapy—I've been in therapy since I was thirteen—

but the shrink I had in those days in Durham was especially incompetent. He was always good for psycho drugs, though, so I took a lot of legal stuff along with the illegal.

What I was doing was running as fast as I could, using prescriptions for white noise, sex for distraction, alcohol for oblivion, all to escape a growing terror that I either was or soon would be schizophrenic or full-blown manic-depressive. That was no paranoid delusion—both illnesses run in my family. But what a crazy way I chose to avoid craziness, you're thinking. I think so, too, but do you know, I haven't really changed that much. Eric says I have, but I don't believe him. My biggest fear—no, I don't even want to say it. But it's the same, it's always the same. Nothing's really changed.

Here's how I met Curtis. I was going out with a man named Jean-Etienne Leutze, a Swiss national supposedly studying drama at Duke, but what he was really doing was drinking himself to death. Naturally I was drawn to him. We made quite a couple. "Fiery," our smattering of friends in common called us, but they didn't know the half. One night we had a row in Jean-Etienne's cramped, filthy, one-bedroom apartment in a colorfully run-down student neighborhood nowhere near campus. Until that night we'd thrived on our fights, been really creative, I thought, with the insults we traded and the heavy objects we threw at each other. I had an exhilarating sense of breaking out, of opening windows and breathing in fresh, dangerous air. Jean-Etienne was the perfect man for me, I thought, at least in that place, that time.

It couldn't last. Violence always escalates. One night he beat me up and threw me out of his apartment—literally, out the door in a rush, *smash*, up against the wall in the stair landing. I wasn't hurt, no broken bones or anything, but I was very drunk and—this is embarrassing—naked except for my underpants.

Curtis lived next door. I'd seen him once or twice, briefly and only in passing, but long enough to think, *You don't look like you belong here*. Too clean-cut and wholesome. Blond, blue-eyed, and serious, always carrying a stack of books or a briefcase. He'd noticed me, too, but I assumed it was because he'd heard the racket through the wall, always either sex or yelling, and was curious about Jean-Etienne's partner in decadence.

He came out of his apartment and found me huddled on the staircase, half nude, hurting, very confused. It was late, well after midnight, but Curtis was fully dressed in chinos, polo shirt, and loafers—he'd been studying. All the time he looked at me, touched me, helped me to stand and stagger into his apartment, he never seemed to regard me in any sexual way whatsoever. This was novel in my experience. And seductive. It's a power he possesses that he's fully aware of and has put to good use any number of times since then. But it was new to me that night, and I fell under its spell without a thought.

He gave me his bathrobe to put on and coffee to sober me up. He wanted to call the police, I remember, and that moved me, made me feel so grateful, as if I had a knight looking after me. We talked for hours—I talked, rather, and he listened with complete absorption: again, very seductive. He was thinner in those days, and more callow, less all-knowing, but already he had a fine quality of self-restraint that attracted me powerfully. I had so little of it myself.

When it was time to go to bed, I assumed we would sleep together. But he surprised me by bringing sheets, blanket, and a pillow, and tucking me up all nice and neat on his sofa. He didn't even kiss me.

In the morning, I woke up first. I took a shower in his pristine bathroom—quite a contrast to Jean-Etienne's sty—and then I went into Curtis's room and slipped into bed beside him. This was my idea of a thank-you gift. A small favor for a small favor.

He rejected me. He wanted me—he slept naked, so that was obvious—but he wouldn't take me, and the way he put me away from him—no words, just a small, scrupulous smile, his hands kind but firm and somehow practical—made me feel ashamed of myself. And in his power.

A pattern began—I see it so clearly now—of me offending and Curtis forgiving. Me being outré, he disapproving, then relenting. We didn't become lovers for weeks. He made me wild with wanting him first, and even while it was happening I knew he was doing it on purpose. I liked it. I entered the game willingly, denying and disciplining myself because it pleased him, and getting addicted fast to his control over me. He wasn't like any man I'd ever known; he had single-mindedness and focus, and unlike me, he knew exactly what he wanted: a political career. The law he was studying was only to be a stepping-stone.

Our relationship never went smoothly, not even at the start. It looked one-sided to outsiders, Curtis in charge, me in thrall. But things aren't always what they seem, and they're never simple.

Just before we left Durham, I told him I didn't want to live with him anymore, that when we moved to D.C. I wanted to find a place of my own. I wasn't breaking up, I just needed some space, as we used to say. I wanted to slow things down. In a rare moment of self-knowledge, I understood that his possessiveness was hurtful, and that my complicity was borderline pathological.

Then, too, I simply wasn't prepared for total commitment. I still needed a lot of room to act out, a lot of freedom to self-destruct, and I didn't want all that stability Curtis's good side represented—well, I wanted it, but I was afraid of reverting to type and blowing it in some huge, spectacular way.

I couldn't believe what happened next. He tried to talk me out of it, of course, being very reasonable and methodical as only Curtis can be, but for once I stood firm. Then he mocked me and ridiculed me, and that was harder to take, but somehow I did. I wouldn't give in.

So he started drinking.

It's the Lloyd family vice. It's a bad one, no question, but what a luxury, I've always thought, to come from a family with only one serious flaw. But Curtis *didn't* drink, or hardly at all, maybe a beer on Saturday afternoon or one glass of wine in a restaurant, and I'd end up finishing it for him. He was supposed to take the D.C. bar exam in three weeks, and he'd been studying for it like a monk for months. The day after our big blowup over living together, I came home from school (I was still doing an art history master's then) and found him passed out on the couch. I thought he was sick—it just didn't register, not even when I saw the whiskey bottle sticking up between the cushions. When I figured it out, I thought, Oh, this is just an aberration, and I scoffed at him, gave him a stern, disapproving lecture while I poured coffee down his throat and pushed him into the shower. He never said anything, not one word: blind drunk, he could still control himself.

When he sobered up enough to function, he put on clean clothes and went out, still not speaking. (What a potent weapon silence is.) He came back with four fifths of vodka, and for the next six days proceeded to drink them behind the locked bedroom door.

I was frantic. As I've said, we had very few mutual friends, and no one I felt comfortable calling. I called his parents in Savannah. It was futile, the conversation surreal, like trying to interest a fish in the fact that its offspring is drowning. Once when Curtis was in the bathroom, I ran in the bedroom and tried to steal his booze stash. I thought he might die—I thought he was poisoning himself. He *was*—he looked like death, smelly and foul and unkempt, doubly shocking in a man who's usually so fastidious. He caught me before I could escape with the bottles, and for the first and only time in our lives, he struck me. Not a hard blow, he was too drunk, but I lost my balance and cut my forehead on the doorpost.

Curtis saw the blood and started to weep. He went back in the bathroom and vomited. I thought it was over, that that would end it, but he staggered back to his room and started drinking again.

I gave up.

"I won't leave you," I told him, both of us crying like children. "We'll find a place in Washington, a wonderful apartment on the Hill, and we'll be rich and happy and you'll be famous, you'll be president and I'll be first lady, and we'll always be together." He had the shakes, he couldn't stop sobbing, dry, racking barks of pain that I'll never forget, although nothing like that, nothing close to that, ever happened again. His life, once he recovered, went back to normal, and he was completely his old serious, sober, focused self.

That terrified me and thrilled me, the unimaginable notion that *I* might have power over *him*—that I could ruin his life by simply taking myself out of it. An awesome responsibility, I thought. I would have to be so careful and loving, so delicate with him.

It took years to see—and then I only saw it in blurred flashes, never clearly, never for long—that it was just another game, that he was still the one with the power, not me. Like a child holding his breath to get his way.

Well, that analogy is even truer now, isn't it—Curtis threatening his own *death* to get his way. But this time he's gone too far. His true colors are visible at last even to me, the blind woman. It's over. I think it's over. How could I stay with a man that much crazier than I am?

"I think you should throw all his clothes out in the street."

I glanced at Lee as she floored the BMW and merged into two lanes of speeding traffic on Rock Creek Parkway. Maybe letting her drive hadn't been such a good idea. She'd suggested it, Isabel had seconded it, and at the time it had seemed sensible—I was so upset, I had the hiccups. But I'd never seen Lee this angry before, and she was taking chances that had me holding on to the door handle and wishing Curtis's car had a passenger-side airbag. I should've gone with Emma, who was right behind us, trying to keep up in her little red Mazda.

"And definitely call a locksmith," Lee added. "You ought to

call one right now, in fact. You need to get every lock in your house changed, Rudy. I've got my phone, can you get it out of my bag?"

I got the phone out, but calling a locksmith was beyond me. I turned around to see what Isabel thought.

"It might not be a bad idea," she said from the backseat. "But you can probably wait till you get there."

"Okay," said Lee, in a don't-say-I-didn't-warn-you voice, "but they might not be able to come until tomorrow. Time is of the essence. Another thing—as soon as you get home, you have to start calling your credit card companies. If he gets vindictive, he'll try to cut you off, so you have to make a preemptive strike. You've got the edge right now because you know something he doesn't know, but as soon as he catches up, things could get very dicey. Do you know any good lawyers? I'll call my mother, she knows everybody. Isabel, would you recommend the one you used for Gary? To be frank, I think Rudy needs someone tougher. A piranha, that's what we want." She bared her teeth. *Fucking lawyer* still echoed in my head. Before tonight I'd never heard Lee say anything stronger than *damn*. She scared me. I was glad she was on my side.

"Give me the phone," she said, "I have to call Henry."

"I'll dial." She was taking corners at fifty miles an hour; I wanted both her hands on the wheel.

"Don't call the house, he's not home, he's at his mother's." She gave me the number. My fingers were shaking, I had to dial twice. I couldn't tell what I felt more of, fear or excitement, dread or anticipation. And underneath it all lay a streak of sickness, nausea almost, over the thing my husband had done to me. My best friend. The person in the world I had trusted most.

"It's busy," I told Lee. "Let me call Eric." I dialed, and listened in dismay to his answering machine message. "Eric? This is Rudy." I hiccuped, then laughed. "I've got the hiccups. I'm in a speeding car with Lee and Isabel, Emma's behind us, we're going to my house so we can lock Curtis out. *Hic*." Lee and Isabel snickered—

we all sounded hysterical. "This you won't believe. Curtis told me he has leukemia—this is what I haven't been able to tell you—and today I found out it's a lie!"

"Tell him about the vasectomy," Lee said, swerving onto Independence Avenue.

"And he had a vasectomy over a year ago. I'm not drunk, I'm not on anything, this really happened! So I'm leaving him. Or I was leaving him, but now I'm throwing him out. I've got all the Saving Graces with me. I wish you were there. If you get home soon, call me at my house. If you get home ever. Anytime tonight. Call me, please, I really, really want to talk to you."

"Hang up," Lee said, "I have to call Henry."

"Okay," I said into the phone, "signing off. Wish me luck." I dropped the phone on the floor. "Oh God, I'm a mess! How can I do this? Can I do this?"

"Yes." Isabel leaned over the seat and took the phone out of my hand. "Lee, what's your mother-in-law's number, again?"

It turned out Henry wasn't there anyway, he'd gotten an emergency call at Jenny's house and taken it himself instead of her. Lee told Jenny the problem in a few simple sentences, and Jenny said she'd try to get the message to Henry. "Yes, do," Lee said, "because it's really important. Where was his emergency? Oh, shit." Isabel and I stared goggle-eyed at each other. Lee was setting all kinds of records tonight. "He's all the way out in Burke," she relayed to us. "Well, tell him, as soon as he possibly can, to go over to Rudy's. Yes, he knows where it is. Yes. Capitol Hill. He knows. Okay, Jenny, thanks. Yeah. Well, we don't know, anything's possible. We will be. Bye." She clicked off. "She says to be careful. Hah. I hope he *does* try something. No, I don't," she said hastily, getting hold of herself. She turned onto my street. "Should I hide the car?"

"Should you hide the car?"

"If he sees it, he'll take it. Which do you want him to have, the car or the Jeep?"

"Yikes." I couldn't think. "This *is* his car. I think they're *both* his."

"Both of your cars are in Curtis's name?"

"I think so. I don't know. Maybe the Jeep is in both."

Lee mumbled more curse words. "Well, then, the hell with it." She found a place in front of the house and parallel parked. "I hope you like riding Metro."

We got out of the car, and that's when I noticed the porch light.

"Oh, no, oh, no, oh, no."

Isabel took my arm. "He's here?"

I nodded. He was home, so he'd read my note. *I saw Dr. Slater,* it said. *I know everything. I'm leaving you.*

Emma hurried over; she'd parked on the other side of the street. "Rudy, did you leave the lights on?"

"No."

"Uh-oh."

"He's here," Lee confirmed, and by the gleam from the streetlight, I saw anticipation in her eyes.

Emma took me by both hands. "You're freezing cold and your hands are clammy." She started chafing them, trying to warm me up. "Now, listen to me, Rudy. If you want, we'll stay outside." Lee said, "What?" but Emma ignored her. "It's up to you. If you want to talk to him alone, that's your business. Either way, we're with you."

"No, I want you to come in with me."

They all looked relieved.

"You can do this, you're strong," Emma declared, looking into my eyes. "And think, in a few minutes the hardest part will be over."

"And we're with you," Isabel said. "It won't be so bad if it's all of us."

"That's right," Lee said, "it'll only be one-fourth as hard, because we're together."

"Okay?" Emma said, and for a minute I thought she'd make us

do a secret handshake or something, a four-way high five. "Let's go, then. Okay? Let's *do* it."

We marched up the sidewalk arm in arm, a phalanx of slow-moving soldiers. Slow-moving because of Isabel's cane, plus we had to separate at the steps, which were too narrow for four abreast. But we didn't lose our militant spirit, and it *was* like marching into battle, four of us facing one clever, dangerous enemy, whose reactions were unpredictable and with whom, even now, part of me might still be in love.

I got out my key and unlocked the front door. The light in the foyer was on—Curtis was coming down the staircase. He stopped in the middle when he saw me. His face, pale and set before, broke into a glad, astonished smile.

I softened, started to melt like snow in the sun. Then I widened the door, and he saw who was behind me. Raw hostility replaced the relief on his face, and I got my resolve back. But that was a close one.

"What's this, a slumber party?"

That's right, I thought, be obnoxious, help me out. Lee, the last one in, closed the door. Somewhere between the car and the house, I'd stopped having hiccups.

"Curtis?" I said, my voice high and flutey. "Curtis, I want you to leave this house." I actually sounded composed. An act, of course; inside I was veering back and forth between panic and a kind of weird, out-of-body detachment. Seeing him looking exactly like himself but also knowing what I knew about him was disorienting, like trying to match the man with his dark shadow, line the two up perfectly to get the true picture.

"Rudy," Curtis said, as if I hadn't said anything at all, "we have to talk."

"Oh, no, I'm not talking to you. I want you to go. Stay in a hotel or something, stay with your friend Teeter."

"Rudy," he said through his clenched teeth. "Please tell your friends to go. I have a lot to say to you, but I'm not doing it in front of an audience." He put his hand out to me—a subtle capitulation. And he'd said "please."

The others looked at me. They'd hate it, but they would go if I asked them to. Well, Lee and Isabel; I wasn't so sure of Emma. But I said, "No," very firmly, "they're not leaving"—and I could tell in the clearing of their faces, the straightening of their postures, that my friends were proud of me. I felt bold. "Nobody's leaving but you."

A muscle bulged under his left eye. "You're mistaken. We'll talk later," he said, turned, and marched back up the stairs.

Emma, Lee, and Isabel were all looking at me. "Curtis!" I called. "I want you to go!"

No answer. He disappeared around the landing.

Whatever made me think this would be easy? "Now what?" I looked around in despair.

"You were great," Emma said, shaking my shoulder.

"You were," Isabel agreed.

"I was," I said weakly. "I didn't cave."

"But," said Lee, "you still have to get him out of the house."

"*How?*"

"You'll have to talk to him." *Oh, Isabel,* I thought, *I didn't expect naïveté from you.* "And," she added, "we'll go with you."

"You will? You mean—all of us?"

They nodded.

How bizarre. But I didn't want to think about it for long. "Okay, let's go."

Curtis's face when he saw us was—indescribable. He was bending over in front of his open closet; he'd taken off his tie and was starting on his shoes. "What the hell is this?" He tried a laugh, but his face was stiff with outrage.

I pointed a shaky finger to his overnighter, which he'd thrown on the bed. "It's good you haven't unpacked yet, you can take that with you when you go."

He looked at me as if he couldn't recognize me. Then he heaved a heavy, patient sigh; he got that forgiving air that's worked so well for so long. "Rudy, this isn't the time to discuss this."

"I agree. I'm not discussing it. I want you out of this house. I know what you did, and you won't even deny it. I shouldn't have to go, *you* should."

Isabel stood on my right, Lee on my left. Emma had taken a seat on the bed—an escalation of the offense, usurping more enemy territory. Possession is nine-tenths of the law.

Curtis tried a humorous look, a sensible man up against irrational females. "Isabel, can't you talk some sense into your friends?"

She took two steps toward him, away from us. She had her cane in one hand, purse in the other; she still had her coat on—we all did. "Rudy's only asking for fairness. A little generosity from you now. Do you think you might owe her that? To begin righting the balance a little?"

I loved her so much then. She was the best champion, the kindest friend. Surely her simple decency would get through to Curtis, help him to see his deviousness for what it was.

He smiled. Sniffed his breath out through his nose. Didn't even bother to answer her.

Lee cleared her throat. "You don't really think you can get out of this, do you? After what you did, you don't think Rudy's going to forgive you and you can just go back to normal. Do you?"

Curtis snarled, "Butt out."

She only got more dignified. "No one is butting out. You've brought this on yourself. Rudy wouldn't need us here if you weren't such a bully."

"A bully?"

"Yes. An emotional bully."

"Curtis," I said. He looked at me hopefully—he'd given up on my friends. "There's nothing to be said, no possible explanation you can give. I know what you did, I even know why you did it, so there's nothing to talk about. I'm just asking you to go. That's all I'm asking."

He brushed past Isabel and loomed in front of me, so close I had to will myself not to back up. "Then we'll talk later," he said softly but firmly, just to me. "I'll go if that's what you want, but I'll come back after your bodyguards leave and we'll discuss this. Rudy, you *know* we have to talk."

Was he asking so much? After five years of living together and six years of marriage? We *did* have to talk, didn't we? The tight, indecisive silence stretched out. In the mirror on the closet door, I saw Emma look down, her shoulders slump. She knew I was going to give in. And if he got me alone, she knew he'd win.

"No." All around me, I heard a soft gasp. "I'm sorry, Curtis. The next time we talk, it'll be in a lawyer's office."

He kept shaking his head. "You don't mean that. You'll see reason once you've thought about it. On your own. I know you, Rudy—"

"I'm seeing reason now. It's very"—I inhaled—"refreshing. Curtis, will you please, please *go*?"

"Listen to me," he said very fast, "I was going to tell you tonight. I couldn't live with myself anymore. I only did it to keep you—I knew it wasn't fair, wasn't right. Tonight I was going to tell you the truth, I honestly was, and suggest we get counseling. With Greenburg if you wanted."

"Oh, Curtis." I couldn't help it: I laughed. It started Emma and Lee off, and even Isabel smiled sadly. If he had just left Eric out, I might've believed him.

"*Fuck* you, then, just *fuck* you," he said, the malice finally revealed in his bared teeth and his hate-filled eyes. "Get out of my way." He blundered out of the room, smacking into Lee as he went, and pounded downstairs.

But we listened, and the front door didn't open or close.

Lee said, "Well?"

"It's up to you," Emma said. "I can keep this up all night."

Isabel nodded. "Room to room to room."

I couldn't figure out what I was feeling. "Is this funny?" I asked Emma, squeezing my hands together.

"Not yet, but it will be."

"Are you sure?"

"Yes."

"Okay, then." We trooped out. Emma snatched up Curtis's overnight case on the way.

We found him in the kitchen trying to make coffee. We squeezed in, three around the sides with their backs to the counters, me in the middle. The yellow light sallowed our tense faces. Four hunters and one hunted. Curtis had his self-control back, though, and that's a much deadlier weapon than his anger.

"It's hopeless. Curtis"—I felt the need to remind both of us—"*you told me you had leukemia*."

He finished measuring decaffeinated coffee into the maker and flicked the switch. He turned around. He cupped his hands around the sides of his face, like blinders, trying to cut out of his sight everybody but me. "Don't shame me," he said, and for the very first time, he sounded sincere. "If you would just give me a chance to explain why I did it."

Deep down, I felt another treacherous softening.

Thank God for Isabel. She said, "But that's not the only lie you told."

How could I have forgotten? It was good to feel the disbelief and the indignation come roaring back, so loud they made my ears ring. And Curtis had the decency, finally, to drop his eyes.

"That alone sounds like grounds for divorce to me," Lee said. "Telling your wife you want a baby right after you have a secret vasectomy." Her face got a baffled, incredulous look. "Did you *want* to get caught? For God's sake—you and Rudy go to the same *doctor*."

He opened his mouth, closed it. He was changing slowly, before my eyes, into a man I not only didn't love, I didn't even like. At last he thought of something to say to Lee. "This is none of your business."

How pathetic. He made me feel like such a fool. "What in the world have I done?" I said. "Why did I love you for so long?"

"Because he's good at what he does," Lee answered. "Which is to control and manipulate people. I think," she said to Curtis politely, "you're despicable."

"Why don't you go fuck yourself," he repeated. Pitiful! He had two dots of saliva in the corners of his mouth. "Rudy, would you get them *out of here*?"

"No. *You* leave."

He lunged, pushing me back by my shoulders. Not a hard blow, but Emma yelled, "Hey!" and she, Lee, and Isabel crowded up, surrounding us.

The doorbell rang.

It kept ringing, *ding-dong, ding-dong, ding-dong, ding-dong, ding-dong,* whoever it was was leaning on the button. The knot in the middle of the kitchen began to loosen. Curtis started for the door, but Lee made a quick move and beat him to it. I remembered—she'd called Henry.

Emma gave me a searching look as we moved into the living room—*You okay?* I was shaking all over, my whole body, uncontrollable. But the longer this went on, the better I felt. Curtis shoving me—it was like a jolt of amphetamine. I felt almost giddy from it. An unnatural high, but who cared, the danger excited me.

It wasn't Henry at the door, it was his mother.

I'd never seen Jenny in her work clothes. Lee's descriptions didn't do her justice. She had on denim overalls and a red flannel shirt. A leather tool belt around her hips, and muddy black rubber boots to the knees. A billed cap over her pompadour that said PATTERSON & SON and across the breast of her coveralls, *Jenny* in bright yellow script.

She broke off a low-voiced conversation with Lee when she saw us. "Hear y'all havin' some trouble out chere tonight," she said in her slow-as-syrup Carolina drawl.

"Ha ha ha ha," Curtis tried to laugh, but the sound was so phony I felt sorry for him. "This is great! Now the circus begins! Now we get dykes to the rescue."

"Watch your mouth, pretty boy," Jenny warned with a flash of good, clean temper. She was like fresh air in a sickroom.

Curtis felt it, too. Under a thinning, cracking veneer of contempt, he looked hounded. I knew what he was going to do the second before he did it.

"Don't!" I had time to say, and then he grabbed two sides of the tall, heavy, bronze-and-glass étagère beside the window. "Curtis, don't!"

He couldn't lift it, so he shoved it. *Smash*—six feet of glass shelves and ceramics shattered on the parquet. All my pots, my pretty vases and jugs, my bowls, all broken, nothing but clay rubble and shards in a sparkling snow of slivered glass. Gone.

Nobody moved. Curtis breathed hard through his mouth, winded, watching us, daring somebody to react. Emma made a strangled, furious sound. Isabel, I saw from the corner of my eye, had her by the arm and was trying to hold her back.

That sound and Emma's rage—they energized me. I left the protective circle of the Graces and moved toward Curtis, into his space, closer and closer until we were nose to nose. I wasn't afraid at all, and I was glad he'd broken my pots. Like the shove, it had cleared my head.

Still, my voice didn't sound like me in the least; it came out breathy and high, each word standing alone. "Get. Out. Or I'll call the police."

He laughed.

"And. I'll tell Teeter. Tell him what you did."

He froze. Paled. At last, at last I'd found it—the stake through his heart.

"If you ever try to hurt me. You won't get elected. To anything. Dogcatcher."

He shook his head, couldn't believe his ears.

To make it clearer, I enunciated. "Ratcatcher."

Somebody laughed. Jenny, I think.

Curtis whirled. We five closed ranks. I think he still might have done something, committed some violence on us, or me, the house, but we cowed him with our numbers. Also, one of us had a cane and one of us had a twenty-inch Stillson wrench.

"Go," I said.

He went.

Jenny built a fire in the fireplace. Lee poured the coffee Curtis had started. Emma kept saying, "Could I please get some credit for not saying anything?" I had stopped shaking enough to call Eric, but he still wasn't home. I left an incoherent message that ended, "I'm glad you're gone, I am, because this way you couldn't help me, I had to do it myself."

Which wasn't true—I couldn't have done it without the women.

"Here's one that's not broken." Isabel held up a small, purple-glazed vase, eggplant-shaped. An early effort and not very good, but I'd always liked it; it must've survived because it was so heavy. "And I think one or two can be glued, Rudy, I really do."

"You watch out for that glass," Lee warned her from the sofa. "Come over here by the fire, Isabel."

"I knew if I said one word, I'd set him off, so I just kept my mouth shut."

"Emma," Lee said dutifully, "you were wonderful."

"No, but, it wasn't like when you guys rescued Grace and I didn't do anything. This time I didn't do anything on *purpose*. Honestly, it was a real act of will."

I hugged her, and she finally grinned and looked mollified. "You were great. You were. And I knew what you were doing."

"No, *you* were the one," she said. "Oh, Rudy, what a moment. You were awesome."

"Ratcatcher," Lee recalled. "I *loved* that."

"How'd you get mixed up with a crazy ol' boy like that anyway?" Jenny wondered, leaning back on the ottoman. She'd taken off her boots and her tool belt, pushed her cap around backward. She looked like that woman in the old Ma and Pa Kettle movies—Marjorie Main?

"I keep thinking of his face when we all went in the bedroom," Lee said, rubbing her hands together. "Was that priceless?"

"You were great, too," Emma told her. "'I think you're despicable,'" she said in Lee's voice.

"I do. And he couldn't say *anything*, he had absolutely no excuse. Rudy, don't you feel good? You shouldn't have any guilt at all, you should just be proud of yourself."

"I do, I am." But once in a while my teeth chattered and I had a fit of shuddering. The fire, the coffee, the blanket Emma had tucked around me, nothing seemed to be able to touch the cold, shaky center of me. Maybe a drink?

"He won't do anything now," Emma said. "I mean, he'll never stalk you or anything. You really got him where he lives with the dogcatcher thing."

"Yeah," Lee agreed, "threatening to tell his partners, that was brilliant. You can call the shots now, get anything you want out of him."

"I don't want anything."

"You say that now."

"No, I really don't. Enough to get by till I figure out what I'm doing." I hugged myself under the blanket, shivering again.

"Rudy, if you don't take that son of a bitch to the cleaners, I'm never speaking to you again," Emma said, and she was only half joking.

They started to talk about changing the locks and calling the banks, the insurance companies, getting names of good lawyers. Lee was full of advice; you'd have thought she'd been divorced six times. But that's Lee, she always knows everything. Slowly, slowly, I began to unwind, untangle inside. Could this really work? It was looking as if it might. But even that scared me, just the prospect of success. Early days yet, I consoled myself; still a million chances for everything to blow up in my face. And I had the strangest, strongest urge to call my mother. Where did *that* come from? I got up to call Eric again.

"I have to go," Lee said, forestalling me. "Who's driving us back—Emma? Jenny, it's too far out of your way." Henry had called from his car an hour ago, heard we didn't need him, and gone home. "Isabel, are you ready?"

No answer.

"She's asleep," Emma said. "She fell asleep on the floor."

Lee moved quietly to where Isabel lay on her side, half on the rug, half on the hardwood floor. "Is, are you awake? We're getting ready to leave." She knelt down. "Isabel?"

Emma and I froze. We went closer, drawn by something in Lee's tone. Then Isabel opened her eyes and smiled—and I let go of a dark fear that had gripped me so fast, I didn't have time to name it.

"Get up, sleepyhead," Lee murmured.

Isabel put her thin white hand on Lee's knee. "Don't think I can."

"Why? Are you sick? What's wrong?" She craned her neck around. "Rudy, call an ambulance!"

"No, no." Isabel wet her lips. "Call Kirby," she said slowly and carefully. "Lee? Just call Kirby."

27

Isabel

February—

Going through some old letters and papers, I found my last address book, the one I used for about fifteen years before the current update. I read the names I'd written in so carefully, some with reminders to myself of the spouse's first name, the children's birth dates. I don't know what to make of the fact that a fair number of these people, closer to a third than a quarter, didn't even make it into the new book. Natural attrition? Cold words for one of life's little tragedies. People move away, drift away, drop by the way. When Gary and I separated, a lot of acquaintances simply disappeared into the blue. But the loss of others is more mysterious.

This woman—Fay Kemper—lived on Thornapple Street; we met at the dog park, the same place where I met Lee. We both loved gardening; we went on a house tour together; she had a daughter Terry's age, we talked on the telephone for hours about our children. And yet, she slipped away. Didn't make the cut. Our husbands never quite got along, that was one obstacle, but it doesn't explain everything. I was fond of Fay, but I didn't fight to keep her. She didn't fight for me. We simply let each other go. There are a dozen more like her, and I know these near-friends come and go in everyone's life, it's a ruthless necessity occasioned by circumstance, taste, chance, apathy—and yet it makes me sad.

All my life I've wanted to tell people I loved them. Fear usually held me back, that they wouldn't care, or they wouldn't hear, or they would take too much from me once they knew.

It's different now. The years pile up like snow against the windowsill. I don't have a moment to lose.

This time of the day frightens me. I don't want to die in winter. Don't want my last glimpse to be of that blighted sunset through the bedroom window, the sway of bare branches against the twilight sky. The wind is so cold and heartless; I imagine it calling me under its harsh breath.

I want to go when it's warm and the air is blue. I'd like to hear a fly buzzing against the screen, an airplane droning in the cloudless sky. A conversation in another room. Laughter. Smell of grass.

I can't forgive my body for betraying me. I am my best friend, and I've let me down. Who's left to trust? That's silly, I know. But the myth of my immortality is still with me, although necessarily fraying at the edges. It gives way to attacks of panic. *I'm dying*, I'll suddenly recall after a period of inexplicable forgetfulness, and my veins light up like Christmas tree lights in terror. My stomach contracts. I cry quick, hurtful tears. Then the deep breaths, the squaring of the shoulders. The weighty, unshareable sadness. For myself, for everyone in the world. What a burden we carry under the shadow of dying. The dark bird's wing.

Why is death such a mystery? It's taboo, like sex to a virgin, a secret locked carefully away. I lived my whole life believing everyone would die but me.

It's the only way we can live, I suppose. It comes from believing we are our bodies. It's not natural to regard flesh, blood, and bone as temporary housing from which we'll soon be evicted. But lately I'm moving closer to learning the secret, I think, the lesson: that death isn't a bizarre, detestable, unspeakable catastrophe. Life's a circle, not a straight line, the longer the better. The circle never ends, it only widens.

* * *

March—

Emma comes to see me nearly every day. She always makes me laugh. "Oh, God," are a Christian's last words, she tells me; an atheist's: "Oh, shit!"

She has never mentioned Mick Draco's name. So the last time she visited, I brought him up myself. (Waiting for "the right time" is a luxury I don't indulge anymore.) She looked impressed and relieved, but not particularly surprised that I knew who he was. "I thought you might've guessed," she said. "So many times I've wanted to tell you."

"But you thought I'd disapprove. Because he has a wife."

"No, I don't think you would *disapprove* of anything, Isabel. That I did, I mean. Or anyone else you love."

"Not be pleased, then."

"Okay. Not be pleased."

"It's true," I said, "that adultery in the abstract is something I dislike. Abhor, even."

"Well, that makes two of us."

"But in the particular, it's a bit more complex, isn't it?"

"But we still didn't do anything, Mick and I."

"And now it's over?"

"Yeah. I broke it off. He asked me to wait for him. He's trying to get out of his marriage without hurting his wife." She made her dry, sardonic face. "Which doesn't seem too likely to me. Especially since Lee says they've been in couples therapy for the last five years. Put it this way—I'm not sitting around waiting for a breakthrough."

"And are you happy now?"

"No. I'm miserable."

"Maybe you should've told him you'd wait." I have no trouble at all offering advice these days. I'm a fountain of it.

"But waiting is suffering, Isabel. I don't have room for any more."

She meant me—she's suffering because of me. I find myself

comforting the people I love more than I grieve for myself. I'm constantly consoling. It's exhausting. But a good thing, too. Because in the process of convincing them what's happening to me is not a tragedy, I almost convince myself.

Lee is not easy to console, and impossible to convince. She's so very unhappy. The solution to one of her problems seems simple to me, but even I, in extremis, don't quite have the presumption to solve it for her.

She took me out for a ride in her car. I hadn't been out of the apartment in weeks except to see the doctor, the acupuncturist, or the massage therapist. To them I take taxis; Kirby goes with me. But I was feeling unusually strong, and this was a pleasure trip for Lee and me. Pure pleasure. We took Grace with us. Winter is finally over—I thanked all my gods for that: one nuisance worry about dying out of the way. It felt wonderful to speed along with the windows down, the wind in our faces. We drove out to Virginia, those pretty little roads around Purcellville and Philomont. Grace put her gray muzzle out and let her ears blow back—she looked like a flying dog.

"Will you take her for me?"

Lee pretended not to hear me.

"Kirby would take her if I asked him. But I'd rather it was you."

I thought she would let it go, just not answer. But a little time passed, and she said, "Yes, I'll take her." Then we both pretended it was the wind making our eyes water.

Sweet old Grace. These days *grace* means something else to me, too. I've been given a grace to see—well, our connectedness. It's almost primitive, it's so easy. Literally, we're all in this together, and my anger has almost completely dissipated into a feeling of oneness with everything. Everyone.

A gift.

Still. How much easier it would be if we could go with somebody. A partner, a companion. Oh, if only we could take a friend with us. How much less lonely it would be.

* * *

I have help two days a week now. A lady from social services came and interviewed me, and then a nurse began to visit on Tuesday and Thursday afternoons. Roxanne Kilmer is her name; she's young, only twenty-seven, and I worry she's gotten into the wrong line of work, or gotten into it too early. A woman should have more experience, more of life before she has to see the things Roxanne sees.

I like her, though, and I'm selfish enough to want to keep her. She helps me bathe, changes the bed, plans my meals, manages my medications. I like her competence and briskness, the way she's kind to me but not sorry for me. I'm so lucky—I have Roxanne, I have Mrs. Skazafava who happily walks the dog every day at four o'clock, I have the Saving Graces. One of the hardest things to bear by people in my situation—the worry that when the bad time comes there won't be enough caregivers—has been mooted. It's simply not on my list of anxieties anymore.

Then there's Kirby. The social services woman wrote down that he's my "primary caregiver," an obvious, self-evident fact that for some reason I hadn't quite realized or accepted. Because of his capacity for self-effacement, I suppose. And because he slipped into my life so quietly. Like a fast-growing sapling you plant one spring, and seemingly the next it's a strapping maple tree, perfect in its setting, you can't remember that spot in the yard without it. I only worry that he's taking too much time from his job to be with me, but he won't discuss that or let me nag him about it. It's off limits.

These days it tires me to talk for too long anyway, so the balance between us has had to shift: for once, Kirby talks more than I do. He was rusty at it at first, and even now he's not exactly voluble. But he perseveres, because he knows I love to listen. He tells me about his father, one of the highest ranking army officers to die in the Vietnam War, and about his mother, who once danced in musical comedies on the New York stage. I can see both of these contradictory influences on the son, who camouflages his creative, unconventional side with a deceptively quiet, gray-looking conformity.

I've asked him why he stays with me. "Because I love you," he said gravely. "It's simple." But is it? Does it matter? Should I, should anyone, be concerned if he stays with me because it's a way to say good-bye? A proper, humane, dignified way he couldn't have with his wife and his babies because it was stolen from him? Either way, the motive is love. So what does it matter?

He's helping me write a letter to the Graces. I dictate and he types on his laptop computer. In the evenings he reads to me. I lie on the sofa under the afghan with Grace on the floor at my side, and Kirby sits under the lamp in the easy chair, long legs crossed, head tilted back so he can peer down through his half-glasses. His theatrical voice is wonderfully expressive; I can listen to it for hours. He reads classic plays to me, Shakespeare's comedies and Ibsen, Molière, Oscar Wilde. And novels I loved as a child that he finds for me in the library—*Girl of the Limberlost, The Secret Garden, Little Women*. And the Bible, the Koran. Poetry. They're a great comfort to me, these other voices, these other people's worlds. I'm thankful for how completely they take me out of mine.

He helps me with my mail, too. So many get-well cards, so many kind, nervous, graceful, inept, tactless, elegant notes, some from people I haven't communicated with or even thought of in years. Just as interesting to me is the number of people who *don't* write, don't call, don't acknowledge my illness in any way. I forgive them absolutely, and lately I've been scrawling little messages to them to say so—not in those words. I understand that, for some, what's happening to me is unspeakable, literally. They can't help it. I don't take it personally. I did once, but no more. No time.

Gary is one of those who can't speak. I called him on the telephone, hoping for something, closure, acknowledgment, maybe my own forgiveness. It was awkward. No, it was impossible. So: Gary and I are going to die separately and far from each other. I know that for certain now, and it makes me sad. To think that, after all, our vows came to nothing.

April—

Kirby and I don't have sex anymore; it's simply not possible. But we make love. There's an Indian healing ceremony that involves foot-washing and the application to the body of scented oils. He does that for me, chanting the low, slow meditation that goes with it. He makes me feel as if my weakening, withering body is a shrine.

At night we lie together and talk about what our lives have been. We used to plan trips, but not anymore—just lately we've given up that fantasy. That conceit. I'm not greedy the way I once was, I don't ask God to let me live for five more years, or three, or two. My ambitions have dwindled. I don't want to die in winter, and not in a hospital—that's all. How diffident. God, do you see how modest I am?

I think about writing down a word, an allusion to something we've shared—I don't know what it is yet—and Kirby opening it after I'm gone, and remembering. It would be a little way of staying alive.

A surprise—there is something left when there's no more hope. Something you make up. Acceptance—believe me—has a kind of joy in it. Yes, and from there, it's not that far to celebration. I'm longing to be with my dearest friends. I'm having a very good day today—maybe tomorrow will be the same. I want to call Lee and Emma and Rudy and tell them to have the women's group meeting here tomorrow night. It's been so long. And I have a lot to say. Ha. The hardest word is good-bye, and yet I almost think I could say it. I believe I could.

What is the best I can say for myself? That I loved, and I was loved. All the rest drops away at the end. I'm content.

28

Emma

Isabel died in her sleep sometime after midnight on the tenth of April. She had an embolus—a blood clot; it blocked an artery to her lung and killed her instantly. I hope. Kirby wasn't with her, he was sleeping on the sofa in the living room because she'd been restless earlier and he thought she might fall asleep more easily alone.

He found her in the morning, lying on her side with her eyes closed. I like that—I think it proves she was sleeping when she passed away. He said the covers were neat and tidy, not thrown off. She looked peaceful, he said. I believe she was dreaming. A sweet dream, with all of her friends in it, all of us who loved her. And then—I believe she just drifted away.

She didn't want a funeral, she didn't want to be buried. She specified in her will that after her body was cremated she wanted her son, Terry, to have the ashes, to dispose of as he saw fit.

Nobody liked this plan, especially Terry, who had no idea what was best to do with his mother's remains. We particularly hated it that there was no wake, no ceremony, no nothing. And so about three weeks after she died, I invited as many of Isabel's friends, family, and acquaintances as I could track down, and we had a memorial service for her at my house.

The place was packed. Standing room only. People spilled out into the dining room and the hall, the foyer, they sat behind the banister rails halfway up the stairs. We didn't have a minister—Isabel had belonged to most of the major religions and all the minor ones; how could we have chosen?—but we did have Kirby, and that was even better. There's something so gloomy and clerical about him, a priest-like quality that served him well as the master of ceremonies, so to speak, at Isabel's last service. I always thought there was something mysterious about Kirby, too, especially in the beginning, before I knew him. But the mystery turned out to be nothing more than that he loved Isabel with his whole heart, and that's no mystery at all.

I wish now I'd tried harder to know him while she was alive. I wish I'd been nicer to him. Not that I was ever mean, but—oh, I guess I was jealous of him. He was a stranger, an interloper. A man. We Graces don't always cotton to newcomers. But Isabel loved him very much, and I know, I really do know that that took nothing away from the love she had for the rest of us. For me. Isabel had enough love for everybody.

She had so many friends, a lot of them had to sit on the living room floor because there weren't enough chairs. I'd made coffee and put out sweet things, cookies and brownies, a bakery cake. When the crowd thinned, I planned to break out the booze and get into more of a wake mode for the closest mourners. I thought Isabel would appreciate that.

Kirby had brought some of her favorite CDs, and when people weren't eulogizing her we listened to New Age pinging and ponging, Mozart, and Emmylou Harris. New people kept arriving and departing, as if it were an open house, which I guess it was—people from her old neighborhood, classmates and professors from school, women from her old bridge club, cancer support group people, healing circle people, meditation group friends, miscellaneous Adams-Morgan neighbors. It astonished me how many of them stood up, cleared their throats, and spoke movingly and unselfconsciously about what Isabel had meant to them.

I had a small heart stoppage when Mick walked in. Without Sally. He maneuvered through the crowd to where I was standing, in the archway between the living and dining rooms, and he hesitated for what seemed like an hour but was really a split second before he leaned down and kissed me on the cheek. He was approximately the fiftieth person to murmur to me, "I'm so sorry," but *his* words I heard, his sympathy I took to my heart. I parroted, "Thank you so much for coming," and then he left me and found a place to sit on the floor across the room.

By chance, I caught Rudy's eye. She lifted one eyebrow a millimeter. It said everything.

Then she went back to listening to Mrs. Skazafava tell about Isabel's amazing green thumb, and how her little garden plot behind the building put everybody else's to shame. Grace, Isabel's dog, lay at Rudy's feet, her white muzzle draped over her instep. She's Rudy's dog now. She was supposed to be Lee's, but her arrival sent the overly refined Lettice into a decline. Meanwhile Rudy moved out of her house (I know, after all that) and into an apartment that allowed pets, so the solution was obvious. It's a good fit, too, Rudy and Grace. For now, each gives the other exactly what she needs.

Lee cried through the whole service, beginning to end. Henry held her hand, gave her his big red handkerchief, put his arms around her, and let her sob on his shoulder.

Someone read a poem. A woman from the healing circle stood up and sang a song she'd written especially for Isabel. A cappella. And she made everybody join in and sing it with her after teaching us the treacly chorus. I accidentally made eye contact with Rudy again. Big mistake. I had to turn my back to the room and bury my face in my hands, as if overcome with emotion. My good laugh dissolved into a good cry, and then I blew my nose and pulled myself together.

Terry had flown down from Montreal the day after Isabel died, and he hadn't gone back yet. His girlfriend, a beautiful black woman named Susan, had joined him a few days ago, and he'd brought her with him to the memorial service. I thought he might stand up and say something about his mother, but he didn't. I think he was afraid he would cry. (That's why *I* wasn't talking.) He'd brought an oblong mother-of-pearl box with Isabel's ashes in it, and set it on my mantel. Which sounds like it might be weird, but it wasn't. Not in the least. I'd put some lilies around the pretty box, made a little arrangement. Everybody's eyes went to it, over and over, and it looked dignified and peaceful and sweet. Like Isabel.

Gary didn't come. He sent flowers, though, and wrote a short and very nice note, which Kirby read out loud. I had no desire to see or speak to Gary ever again, but I did wonder how he was feeling about losing Isabel. I hoped he hurt. A lot. I hoped he hurt one-tenth as much as I did.

The impromptu speeches began to wind down. Kirby stood up. I'd never seen him in a suit before; he had on a dark gray one with a vest, a white shirt, no tie, and he looked good. Wasted, but good. Isabel's beauty, her facial purity, if you will, had grown more pronounced the sicker she got—and in a strange way, the same thing had happened to Kirby. Isabel's illness seared away everything in their faces except the character.

"I don't have much more to say," he said, hands behind his back in an at-ease military posture. "Isabel never despaired, even though I think she knew everything that was going to happen, right from the beginning. There was a Walt Whitman poem she liked, especially the part that went—'All goes onward and outward,/Nothing collapses/And to die is different from/What anyone supposes/And luckier.' She tried to believe that, and it gave her some comfort, I know. She was very brave. Always. She hid her anguish and sadness, although I know she felt them. Because she wasn't losing only one person she loved—as we have. She was losing all of them."

Kirby got his handkerchief out of his pocket and unashamedly blew his nose.

"Isabel believed death is a process, not an end. She said it was her job to hold on to life for as long and as well as she could—her karmic duty, she called it. But she also had faith that something comes after, something better. Not that she was anxious to get there," he said with a grim attempt at a smile. "She talked very openly about her fears, her grief. But her absolute faith that death isn't the end always kept her from despair. She just wished—she just wished she didn't have to go alone."

He looked helpless, gazing around the room at us with watery eyes, as if he wished he hadn't ended on that note.

"Well, I want to thank you all for coming. Isabel would've been moved by all your kind wishes and your—your eloquent words. Thank you. Thank you all very much."

Nobody from the Saving Graces had talked. Kirby was calling an end to the formal part of the service, and none of us had said anything about Isabel.

Lee had her mouth covered with Henry's kerchief, her head slumped on his chest. She was a hopeless mess. I sent Rudy an urgent look—*Get up! Get up and say something*. But she only smiled tragically and shook her head. I wanted to kill her.

"I would like to say something." My voice came out embarrassingly nasal, as if I had the world's worst cold. People who had started to get up sat back down. All the austere, expectant faces staring at me started my heart pounding.

"I just want to say—thank you, also, for coming, and thanks to Kirby for everything. And I also want to say . . ." How much I'll miss my friend, how much I love her, what she meant to me. How to start? My mind kept skipping back, back, looking for the beginning of what I should tell them about her.

"I should thank Lee, too—Lee Patterson—because about eleven years ago she had the idea for our women's group. The Saving Graces." On the floor at Rudy's feet, Grace heard her name and lifted her head to look at me. "That's how I first met Isabel. In fact, we had our first meeting at her house. I met you that night, too, Terry. Do you remember?" He smiled and shook his head. "You were sixteen and very surly."

Laughter.

"There were five of us in the group then, but over the years we've boiled down to four. Basically. Isabel and Lee, Rudy Lloyd—Rudy Surratt now, sorry—and me. I—if I could—for me—" I stumbled again. "If I tried to tell you what the Saving Graces have meant to me, we'd be here all day and I still wouldn't get it right. Isabel was older than the rest of us, and she was different. I don't mean *because* she was older, but just because she was—unique. I always felt we didn't deserve her. Me, anyway. She was the gentlest person I ever knew. Very quiet. She was a wonderful listener. She watched people, but not to judge them. She never judged anyone. I always knew she loved me. Very much."

Oh, shit. I was going to screw this up by bawling.

"I think," I soldiered on, "our friendships teach us a lot, make us grow and change. The Graces taught each other so many things, like how to tolerate our differences. How a good marriage works. How to understand another person's spiritual . . . longings. A sillier sense of humor, maybe a—sharper sense of irony. Hugging. A hundred other things. And Isabel, she wasn't our leader exactly, but I think she was our spirit. She was behind everything good or unselfish we did. I don't know how to explain this very well, but in the very best way, Isabel was our mother. And—I'm lost without her. I feel like an orphan."

I kept talking, not looking at Lee or Rudy. I knew if I did, we'd all break down.

"I just can't believe she's gone. A thousand times since she died, I've wanted to call her up and tell her something, something only she would get, or care about, or react to just right. I've even picked up the phone and started to dial. Then I remember. Lee does it, too—she's told me. We've lost the dearest friend, the most loving, unselfish friend. I try to think of something good, anything to make this bearable, but I can't. She died before she was in excruciating pain—that's all I can think of. Well, okay. Thank God for that.

"Toward the end it was hard to come and visit her. I never knew what to say. Good-bye was impossible. Because—then there's no more hope. Before you say good-bye, you can always say more, you can still fix things. Get it right. One more try. I think we live our lives like that—putting off getting it right, saying to ourselves, Maybe next time. And then, when there isn't going to be a next time, we can't bear it.

"So I couldn't tell Isabel good-bye. I don't know if she wanted me to or not. She was so kind—she took her cues from us. I think she was dying the way she thought would be easiest for the people who loved her. That was so typical of her.

"And—she was so easy to please. At the last, after I finally accepted the fact that there was nothing I could do to change things, nothing I could do to heal her or make it go away or get better or disappear—after I really knew I was going to lose her—everything got much, much simpler. Since there was no future, everything had to be in the moment. So I could make her face light up when she first saw me. I could make her laugh at a joke. I could say, 'I love you, Isabel,' and she would smile. That's all I could do, but it seemed like enough. And really, it's all we can *ever* do for each other, but we live with the illusion that time is infinite, that we're all immortal and there's no need to get anything exactly right, not now, not yet. Isabel taught me a lot of lessons, but I think that one was the most important.

"Well—I'm sorry, I didn't mean this to be so therapeutic. I wanted to talk about her, not myself. But I think she's smiling right now. She's thinking, *Jeez, she's not even drinking*. She used to say I talked a lot when I had more than one glass of wine. Which is true. So I'll stop. And just say—I love you, Isabel, and I'll miss you so much. Rudy's taking good care of your dog, and we're all going to watch out for Terry. And Kirby—we'll take care of him, too, because he'll be lonely. And we hope you're in some wonderful place now, someplace that deserves you. And that you're at peace. And—we'll never forget you." I hung my head and whispered, "Bye, Isabel." And because that was unbearable, I added to myself, "Talk to you later."

Rudy and Lee got up and hugged me. We made a sniffling, swaying tripod in the middle of the living room, and I guess that was the signal people were waiting for that the service was over.

Many of them left, but a lot stayed to eat and drink and party. That always gets me, how we can do that at wakes and such. I do it, too—I'm not saying it's wrong, just amazing. I've gone to funeral homes where the dead person is lying there in his or her coffin, and except for the immediate family—but sometimes them, too—everybody's carrying on like it's a class reunion. Well, it's just what we do, I suppose. Our primitive, cowardly way of dealing with too much grief or too close a call with death. If anybody would understand that and forgive it, it would be Isabel.

So I turned into a hostess, making drinks and passing food, thanking and thanking and thanking all the people who said it was brave of me to speak, it was good of me to host this service, it was just what Isabel would have liked. Meanwhile, I was constantly aware of Mick. He talked to Lee and Rudy, then to Henry for a long time. Whenever I let myself look at him, he was already looking at me. It was four months since the night we broke up in my bedroom, and I hadn't seen him since, not once. Lee didn't hang out with Sally much anymore, so that source of intelligence had dried up. He looked the same. Which is to say, beautiful. Healthier than he had last winter, not so white. The godawful haircut had grown out, and it had more silver in it than before. Very attractive. I could look at him and feel weak in the knees. So—had *nothing* changed? Maybe it was habit. Pavlovian mouth-watering based on nothing but conditioning. What a stupid affair we'd had anyway, pathetic, hopeless from the beginning. *Quit looking at me with your brown eyes, damn you.*

He must've heard. He turned his back.

Terry took me outside in the backyard for a private word. He's all grown up, very tall and handsome; he's got Gary's blue eyes, but something of Isabel's softness in them. We don't really flirt, but he likes it when I joke about wishing he were fifteen years older.

"Thanks again for having this," he said. "It's really meant a lot to me."

"I'm glad, but I didn't do anything."

"I wish she'd had a regular funeral."

"Well." I did, too, sort of. "But that's not what she wanted."

"I know. Listen, Emma." He squeezed his nose between his fingers, a manly gesture of indecision. I just can't get over how he's grown up.

"What?"

He looked away to say, "I don't know what the hell to do with the ashes."

"Oh."

"I just have no idea. Should I bury them? They have places where you can do that, memorial gardens. But would Mom have liked that?"

We shook our heads in agreement: no.

"Do you know if she had a favorite place? I asked my father, but he didn't know. What do you think I should do? I thought of giving them to Kirby, but . . . I just don't know."

"Hm." It was a problem. Terry would go back to Montreal, probably marry Susan, probably fly home once in a blue moon to see his father. What business did Isabel's ashes have in Canada?

"I was wondering," he said, looking at me hopefully. "I was thinking maybe the Saving Graces would, you know, like to have the responsibility."

I was thinking the same thing. But I said, "I don't know, Terry. She gave them to you. She must've had a reason."

"Well, she said I was supposed to do with them *as I saw fit*."

"Hm." He'd given this some thought. "Did you say anything about this to Lee?" I was more used to her making the big group decisions.

He shook his head. "She's kind of wrecked. I thought I'd ask you."

"Oh." I actually felt a little flattered. Imagine me being the grown-up. "Well, um. Okay, I think I can say for all of us, Rudy and Lee and me, that we'd be honored. So I'm saying yes, but I'll call you or write you and let you know what we're going to do before we do anything."

"That would be great." He grinned with relief, and I got a hint of what a burden this had been to him. How funny. I guess it's understandable. But the thought struck that it was possible we Graces knew Isabel better than her own son did, and that he was mature enough to realize it. And he was handing over her remains to the ones she'd trusted most to do right by them. Was that sad? Or was it a comfort? Something to think about later.

Terry and I hugged, and cried a little, and I told him again how much Isabel had adored him, how proud she was of him. He said he regretted more than anything that she'd never met Susan. I said she'd have loved her, too, and we cried some more.

Back inside, the crowd was thinning out, mostly the hard core of friends left now. People thanked me some more, I thanked them for coming. Out of habit, I looked around for Mick—and found him right behind me. "Emma," he said, "I have to go."

I walked out with him on the front porch. The sun was dying, sinking down orange and gold behind the houses on Nineteenth Street. It was late April, high spring, but still the cruelest month; the spent azaleas along my walk shivered in a frigid breeze, and my front lawn was still more mud than grass. I hugged my arms and thanked Mick for coming.

"I wanted to," he said. The absence of Sally curled around us like smoke. *Where's your wife?* I wanted to ask. *Does she know you're here?* Mick had liked Isabel, of course, but he hadn't known her very well. He'd come because of me.

"I liked what you said," he said.

"I talked too much."

"No."

"Yes. I embarrassed myself. I'm a writer, not a talker."

That reminded him. "How is your—"

"Don't ask."

He smiled, and oh, my idiotic heart turned inside out.

A man and his wife, Stan or Sam and Hilda something, came outside. The husband had been in Isabel's cancer support group. He looked healthy enough now, I noticed with some resentment. "Do you have to go? Well, thanks so much for coming," "Yes, it's late, thank you for inviting us," "Good luck to you," "God bless you"—and so on while Mick stood aside, awkward, waiting until we could be by ourselves again. It seemed to me we did a lot of that.

Stan and Hilda finally went away. Mick and I stood side by side at the porch rail and looked out at nothing, the car-lined street, the row house opposite mine. "You'll miss her," he said.

"I thought I was prepared, but I'm not. I miss her so much."

"At least you have your friends."

"Yeah." I sighed.

"I've always envied you for that."

"What? The Graces?"

"There's a fellow I go trout fishing with every spring, up in the Catoctins. The rest of the year I see him maybe three, four times. I call him my best friend."

"Oh, well, that's because you're a guy. Guys don't have friends the way we do. You have your—wives or your girlfriends for your best friends. We have each other." Oh, just keep talking, Emma, cram your foot all the way in. But it was mortifying to think he might think I was hinting around at the Sally question, when really I'd just been blithering, saying the first thing that came into my head.

"Emma," he said presently. I'd really missed hearing him say my name. "Can I call you?"

"What for?"

He laughed, looking down at his hands gripping the white wood railing. He had on a brown corduroy jacket and a blue shirt. While he kept his head turned, I looked at the line of his profile, the curve of dark stubble his beard made on his hard cheek. I didn't feel elated by his question. All I felt was weary.

"Has anything changed?" I hated having to ask. Anyway, I could see the answer in his face. "No, please don't call me, I don't want to see you. Oh, Mick. I hurt so much. If I added you—"

"Okay. It's okay, Emma."

I have never wanted anyone to hold me so much. But we didn't touch, not even our hands, and after a while it felt right, having absolutely nothing. Isabel was gone, and there was a hole in the world, and I had no hope of filling it.

Mick's bowed head moved me, though. His hair was disturbingly beautiful. I drew away from him abruptly—he looked up. Now his eyelashes, the curl of his nostrils, the shape of his mouth, everything about him was like a heavy weight pulling me under. I had to snap the line before he drowned me.

Luckily some more people came out on the porch, people I had to deal with. "Good-bye," I told him, and I meant it. He knew it—we both knew this was it. I turned away and said all the obligatory things to the departing couple, nice people, one of Isabel's instructors and her husband. When I looked again, Mick was gone.

So then I went inside and said everything that was expected of me, including good-bye, to about twenty more people. You'd think I'd have gotten better at it, smoother, more facile, you'd think the word would be tripping off my tongue. Good-bye, good-bye. Good-bye. By the end, though, it stuck in my throat.

Rudy noticed. Oh God, Rudy, help me, I thought, but she knew already. She got rid of the last of them, and she stayed with me that night. "Maybe I should get a cat," I said, watching her with Grace, their easy, admirable, human-dog relationship.

"That's it," she said gently. She lit a cigarette and handed it over to me. "That's what we'll do next, Emma. We'll get you a cat."

29

Rudy

Nobody thought about the logistics of ash strewing until the time came to do it. "We'll sprinkle them out at sea," we said, not considering past those six words, which sound perfectly feasible, even romantic. Isabel would like it, we agreed; she loved the ocean, particularly the Outer Banks and Cape Hatteras, which was our place, the Saving Graces' special spot. Also she was a water sign (Aquarius), and she believed in things like that, astrology and such. Strewing her ashes at sea would be just right.

But you can't do it, there's no such thing, at least not from the land. The wind blows the ashes straight back, *inland,* not at all what you intended. Luckily we—I should say Lee—discerned this before we opened the mother-of-pearl box, thereby saving Isabel's ashes from being blown back onto the Carolina dunes. Which wouldn't have been so terrible, I didn't think, but we really wanted them *at sea.*

Lee suggested we charter a boat and sail out a ways before strewing the ashes—she'd seen that in a movie, she recalled, and it had worked out quite well. Emma said maybe we could walk out to the end of the fishing pier in Frisco and strew them from there. But eventually both of these suggestions were rejected for the same reason: they involved the presence of other people. We wanted privacy when we said good-bye to Isabel for the last time.

The solution we hit on was another one that's a lot better in theory than practice. We put on our bathing suits and simply swam out as far as we could. The tacit plan was, we'd each say a few words, Lee would open the box, and the wind would take the ashes and blow them gently out to sea. Which it did, finally, but we didn't have time to say much of anything because Emma almost drowned. We'd swum out too far, and we'd forgotten what a poor swimmer she is. Those were our two mistakes.

"Have to go back!" she sputtered, dog-paddling, swallowing saltwater. "I can't go any farther. Do it now, Lee, do it now!"

Lee swims like a dolphin—she'd gotten all that way out with her arms over her head, careful to keep the box out of the water. "Okay," she said, "well, wait, we'll do it here, then, this is far—"

"Now, hurry! I have to go back!"

"Okay. Okay—we commit these ashes of our dear friend to the ocean she loved so much when she was with us. Isabel, we—"

"Help!"

I caught Emma by the hair just before she went under. "Hurry it up, Lee, just do it," I yelled, trying to pull Emma on top of me. "Hold still, I've got you, I've got you. *Say something.*"

"What?" Emma coughed up water and spat.

"Say something about Isabel."

"Bye, Isabel!"

Lee glared at her, treading water strongly. "We commit these ashes to the sea. Okay, I'm opening it. Rudy?"

"I'll miss you, Isabel. I love you. Rest in peace." I had something better planned, but Emma was going to swamp both of us. Lee opened the box—the wind caught the chunky ashes in a blinding, smoky billow, *whoosh*. They lay on the water for an instant, then melted like snowflakes. When the next wave came, they vanished.

"I'm throwing the box, too."

"Oh, no," I said. "Well, okay. But I don't know. Emma, should she—"

"Jesus Christ!"

Lee threw the box, and I started back toward the beach with

my arm around Emma's chest, towing her along like a lifeguard. I didn't even know I could do that. Lee stayed for a minute or two longer, then struck out for shore behind us.

You can laugh later at farces like that, and we did try to even then, but the truth is, we were upset. Maybe if we'd waited longer, a year instead of only two months after Isabel's passing, the perspective of time might have lessened our sense of failure. But we sat in the sand while the sun went down behind us, silent and miserable and, in Lee's case, mad. It wasn't our finest hour. What was supposed to have been moving and important and even cathartic had turned into an undignified fiasco that didn't do Isabel credit. We felt we'd let her down.

It was the first of our two nights at Neap Tide. We hadn't had time to shop for groceries, so we went out to dinner that night at Brother's, our old standby. But not even good, greasy, North Carolina barbecue could cheer us up. Too many memories. And I hadn't been drinking for the last three months, so I couldn't even synthesize a good time.

We moped back to the cottage, where things didn't look up. Nobody said it, but I knew we were all thinking, *Why was this ever fun?* What's special about sitting around playing gin rummy or watching silly television shows you wouldn't be caught dead watching at home, eating too much, reading books you can't concentrate on because somebody's always interrupting? With trivia and nonsense, not anything you'd really want to talk about, because you've already said everything you had to say on the interminable ride down and nothing's left but mindless chatter?

It didn't used to seem like mindless chatter. Maybe it hadn't been profound, but it wasn't mindless when Isabel was here. Maybe we were no good without her. Maybe the group was finished.

Maybe we'd keep meeting for a while, then gradually, imperceptibly, taper off, everyone pretending all was well, until one day we stopped meeting at all.

I always thought it was bossy, officious Lee who kept the Graces in line, kept us going. Had it been Isabel? But she'd been so quiet. Emma said she was our "spirit." What if we were lost without her?

"I think I'll go to bed," I said at ten o'clock. Emma and Lee looked up at me, hollow-eyed as owls, and then quickly away. Neither of them said, "So early?" "Night," we told one another dispiritedly, and I wandered downstairs.

I had a room to myself this time, the one with the bunk beds Emma and I had shared last summer. It was lonely by myself. I missed Grace. I'd wanted to bring her, but I'd asked Kirby to keep her over the weekend. Her back legs are too crippled with arthritis, she couldn't have made it up and down the wooden steps.

Lying in bed, I took it as a good sign that I felt homesick, considering I don't even have a home. I gave it to Curtis—yes, I know, after all that—and now I live in a big, sunny, one-bedroom apartment on the western edge of Georgetown. Curtis isn't fighting the divorce at all. But then, I'm not asking him for much. A cash settlement, that's all I want, enough to keep me on my feet until I start earning a living wage. (At what?) After that, we're done. Dissolved.

This doesn't sit well with Lee and Emma, all this magnanimity from me. Even Eric thinks I'm being hasty. It's worth it, though; anything to make this go smoothly. I'm terrified it's going to backfire. It's working too well, I don't trust my good fortune. I'm walking through a minefield carefully, carefully, panicky at the thought of a bomb exploding under my feet. I used up so much psychic energy leaving Curtis, I'm depleted. But slowly restocking. These things take time.

For instance, I haven't gone back to landscaping class yet. But I will, fall term for sure. So what do I do with myself? I've been throwing pots again, and that's such a pleasure, I can't believe I ever gave it up. I've been keeping a journal. Seeing Eric. Not drinking. Taking long, slow walks with Grace. Doing some volunteer work.

Almost every day I uncover some new way in which Curtis . . . "exploited me" isn't right. Tricked me? Whatever—here's a miniature example. We liked different TV programs. All Curtis ever wanted to watch were CNN, CNBC, and C-SPAN. Period, nothing else. Me, I liked stories—plays, movies, hospital dramas, sitcoms, *Masterpiece Theater*—anything with a story in it. He knew this about me but he ignored it, never acknowledged it. Intelligent people watched the interior secretary address the Senate or the Ways and Means Committee chair give a press conference. And when those were over, intelligent people turned the television off.

The way Curtis got my passive complicity was to make fun of the kinds of shows I liked: they were trite, sentimental, melodramatic, banal, badly acted, phony, meretricious, sleazy—and he always pretended I agreed with him, that we were both above that kind of trash. I know I was a coward, but his scorn was so cutting and dismissive, I *did* agree with him. I lied. I don't know how to explain how he did this to me, all I can say is I was helpless. He made up look down. When I was under his spell, I'd have sworn black was blue if he'd wanted me to.

Now he's gone, and I watch *E.R.* and old movies and *Seinfeld* reruns. I'm a couch potato! It's not so much the programs that perk me up, it's the guiltlessness I feel when I watch them. I feel like a delinquent let out of reform school. I'm on probation, so I still have to watch it, no acting out, no having *too* much fun. But I have something now I can't remember having for ages, maybe ever. Hope.

"Night, Em."

"Night, Lee."

They were whispering; they closed their doors softly, trying not to disturb me. Would they lie awake now like me, fretting and frustrated, mulling over their troubles and wondering why we three couldn't seem to connect? We don't trust ourselves as a group anymore. It's like—if you had four legs and one was amputated, you'd be in a lot of distress while you learned to walk on three, if you ever did. And you probably wouldn't like yourself very much, because you'd be so awkward, so . . . graceless.

I remember the last time I lay in this bunk bed, and Emma lay on that one, and we stayed up late and talked about our lives. Things were just beginning to change for me, I was just starting to feel stronger. Emma said, "Whoa, Rudy, you are a wild woman," when I told her about smoking in front of Curtis. That's when he must have begun to feel the change in me, right around then. So that means he had six months to be afraid of losing me—the old me, the dependent one whose whole life revolved around his—before he took the fatal step of telling me he was dying.

My God, what a desperate act. I still can't get over it. Pathological, Eric calls it. He says Curtis needs therapy a lot more than I do.

Yes, well, I think I've always known that. We were coconspirators in neediness, and it was only an illusion that he was in charge. We held each other up. You can call our relationship sick, but people do all sorts of things to survive, and at least we never hurt anyone but each other. I don't hate him. Eric and I are still working on what I feel, but it's not hate, it's not even anger anymore. I understand Curtis too well, I'm too much like him, I can't honestly keep vilifying what he did to me.

But I can't go back to him, and that proves there really is such a thing as change. For so long I thought there wasn't—well, all my life. I think it's the heart of despair, not being able to believe in change.

Now I've not only seen it, I've *provoked* it. I *am* a wild woman. I alternate between euphoria and stark terror, but it's not like manic depression, you know, it's more like—*normal* insanity. Garden variety neurosis, you could call it. How refreshing and delightful, theoretically.

But I'm frightened, and I need a lot of help, and it scares me to think the Graces might not be able to give it to me. Could that really happen? We're all in mourning, locked away in our private griefs. Isabel is our shared grief, but we have personal ones, too. Mine is Curtis, Emma's is Mick. Lee's is a baby.

Maybe we just need time to adjust to our three-leggedness. But I'm afraid. Not all change is good change. Oh, I wish you were here, Isabel! You wouldn't tell us what to do. But somehow, if you were here, we'd know.

30

Lee

The Graces always make clam chowder at the beach. Well, we did for two out of our four years here. This was the fifth year, and if ever we needed a tradition, now was the time. So I insisted.

"You two start peeling the potatoes," I told Rudy and Emma—I'd brought five pounds down with us; why buy new ones when I had so many at home?—"and I'll go buy fresh clams. Back in twenty minutes."

It turned out to be forty minutes, but they were still peeling when I returned. They sat at the kitchen table, their heads nearly touching, dropping potato peelings into a paper sack on the floor between them. How many dinners have we made in one another's kitchens in the last eleven years? How many glasses of wine have we drunk, how many secrets have we told? They glanced up and smiled at me, then went back to work. The stillness between them was easy and comfortable, they were like an old married couple. I envied them—each still had her best friend. Rudy's thinner these days, though. And Emma's quieter. What am I? Sadder.

Rudy looked up at me curiously. "Did you get the clams?" I hadn't moved from the doorway.

"Yes." I put the bag on the counter. "I went to the post office, too. Sometimes there's a bill in the mailbox, or a tax form or something. I forward it to my mother."

"And?" Emma frowned at me. "What's that?"

I turned the envelope over in my hand. "A letter. It's from Isabel."

They stared. They shoved their chairs back and stood up.

"What do you mean?"

"That's not her handwriting."

"It's her address, though."

"Let me see it. What's the postmark?"

I kept the letter and sat down at the table. "It's Kirby's handwriting. The postmark says May eighth."

"May eighth. But she . . . "

"Kirby mailed it," I said. "Afterward. It's to all of us, and it's to Neap Tide. She must've known we'd come here. She must've wanted us to read it here."

I laid the envelope on the table and we stared at it, our names on separate lines in Kirby's neat script. Isabel's return address in the corner.

"Should we open it?" Rudy stood stiff and straight, gripping her hands under her chin.

"Nah, let's pitch it in the trash. We've got potatoes to peel here."

She stuck her tongue out at Emma. "I mean should we open it *now*? Maybe we should wait until after dinner."

"Why?"

"I don't know. It's more . . . "

"More like a ceremony," I said. "Everything else out of the way. Then we could take it out on the deck and read it."

"It's raining, and it'll be dark," Emma pointed out.

"It could stop by then. We could light candles."

Emma lifted her hands and let them fall, slapping her thighs. *"You want to eat dinner before you read Isabel's letter?"*

So we read it before dinner. But first, Rudy went downstairs and got a fresh pack of cigarettes. Emma opened the best bottle of wine, the Chardonnay we were saving to drink with the chowder, and poured glasses for her and for me. Rudy made herself some iced tea. I went in the bathroom and filled my pockets with Kleenex.

"Who's reading it?"

"I am," I said.

Emma raised her eyebrows, but didn't say anything.

It was still drizzling out, so we sat on the floor in the living room, ashtrays and drinks and tissues placed in strategic spots around us. I slid my thumb under the flap of the envelope, and Rudy said, "Wait," and jumped up. "I have to go to the bathroom."

Emma scowled and sipped her wine while we waited, not looking at me. Steeling herself. She doesn't like to show her emotions in public. Oh, and God forbid she should cry, that would be the end of the world.

Rudy plopped back down and lit up. "Okay," she said, shaking out the match, exhaling a strong stream of smoke. "I'm ready."

Inside the envelope were three typewritten pages, and a fourth page in handwriting on top. "This one's from Kirby."

"Read it."

"'Dear Emma, Lee, and Rudy.'"

"Alphabetical order," Emma noted.

"'In the last few weeks of her life, Isabel began to feel detached from the things she had known and even the people she had loved. She said it was a gift dying bestowed on the still-living, one that, on the whole, she could have done without. She said it was hard to remember who she had been, the "old Isabel," and she found it especially difficult to care or even talk about many of the things that had once been such vital concerns to her.

"'But she wanted to write a letter to the Saving Graces, and so she had to come back. It was a trip she didn't always want to make. A trip back for love, she said, settling on her left side against the sofa cushions, the only position she could be comfortable in at the last, and slowly dictating the words in this letter that I typed on my computer. It took several sessions; as you know, her strength had diminished significantly by then. I know she wanted nothing more than to slip away, and in fact part of her had already gone. She would lie for long periods without speaking, not sleeping but perhaps dreaming, detaching from this life, moving to whatever comes next.

"'I think the speed of her physical deterioration at the end took her by surprise—she thought she had more time. When she realized the truth, she had no choice but to use me to say the things she still wanted to say. I hope you don't mind my part in this. It was unavoidable. That Isabel trusted me to be the intermediary is a point of pride for me, and a deep satisfaction. You had the privilege of knowing her longer, but I don't think it's possible you could have loved her more.

"'With kindest regards, Goodloe Kirby.'"

"Who?"

"Goodloe Kirby."

"Goodloe?"

We smiled. A fitting name.

"Okay," Rudy said softly, and I started to read Isabel's letter.

> My dears. I hope I'm right, and you are all three at Neap Tide. I want to think you're together and hearing this—Lee, you read it—at the same time. Is it a beautiful day? I'm picturing you on the deck in late afternoon, with the sun going down over the sound. Emma's safe from too much exposure now, so she's in her cutoff jeans and her faded red sweatshirt; she's had her nose in a book all day, and she's ready for a drink and some conversation. Rudy, sleek as a long black cat, what have you been doing? Sketching on the beach, I think. And taking walks by yourself. But now you're sipping a Coke or something, ready to be sociable. And Lee, I think you've prepared some clever hors d'oeuvre, or maybe you've mixed up a fancy drink in the blender. You look smashing in something simple and tasteful you just got at Saks; it's the latest color, and it makes you look very beautiful.

"If you're going to cry," Emma warned, "you can't read it."

I thought of writing three separate letters, private letters, but decided against it. We've all kept a secret or two over the years, or shared it with only one other, but most of the time we were a group. So I'm writing to you all at once. Besides, secrets take too much energy.

Rudy—You're my hero. I was never so proud of anyone as I was of you the night you made Curtis move out of the house. So brave! I wish you knew how strong you are. You said you couldn't have done it without us, but I don't believe it. Anyway, even if it were true, isn't that what friends are for? But look at your life—look how gracefully you live it. You don't believe me, I know. Emma, Lee—try to convince her. Rudy, you're so kind, so empty of malice toward anyone. I admire your strength and valor, all your courage in the face of a childhood, a heritage that would've leveled by now anyone less brave than you. I'm sorry to say I don't think you will ever have an easy time of it, not in this life, but I know you'll live well. Never forget your true friends, who will always be there and will always love you.

Now, men. I hope you can learn to trust one again. I know you will, but I hope it's sooner rather than later, because you have so much to give. Share yourself with someone who deserves you the next time. And be careful. Borrow some of Emma's skepticism—just a little. Pray for some of Lee's good luck.

I have one more bit of advice. (I'm allowed that, don't you think, from my exalted position.) If you can, make peace with your mother. Heal that wound. I don't know for certain—Eric would know, ask him—but I don't think you can move on until you try. I can say this to you myself as a daughter and a mother. It may not work, but the trying is everything. You'll never be able to control your family's instabilities, but you won't catch them—they're not contagious anymore, because you've grown immune. You have, Rudy. You're not that little girl anymore, the one who stayed with her mother in the bathroom, lay with her on the bloody tiles until the grown-ups came. You're Rudy Surratt, all grown up, clever and creative, and so lovely with your huge, forgiving heart.

I love you, Rudy. I have so much faith in you. I'll be watching you, because your new life is going to be so interesting. Take good care. Only treat yourself with a little of the gentleness you show others, and you'll thrive.

I paused. "That's all," I said. "The next part is to Emma."

Rudy lay down on her back and folded her hands over her eyes. "Keep going," she said thickly. "What's she say to Emma?"

First I had to blow my nose.

Emma—You know what I'm going to miss most about you? The way you keep it to yourself that you think all my New Age beliefs are bullshit. Such forbearance! I love it when you turn your head and roll your eyes, but never say a word. Tolerance, you know, is the essence of friendship. Your tolerance, thank goodness, came from love, not indifference. Oh, you are so dear to me.

I have advice for you, too, of course. Oh, lots of it. It comes in smug-sounding little epigrams, for some reason:

Fear kills. Protecting yourself backfires eventually. Failure isn't failure, it's a step, and life is nothing but steps. Or failures, with occasional, widely spaced successes. If you don't screw up pretty regularly, you're only running in place. Also, pain isn't all it's cracked up to be. Speaking from experience. And living in fear of pain isn't really living at all.

Got that?

Specifically—How can you not know what to write about? "I haven't found my subject yet," you claim. (And when you tell me about some of your experiments, I must say I can only agree.) I see the problem very clearly: you've been hiding behind stories. They might be good stories, but they're not true, so you hate them. Then you hate yourself. Stop doing this.

Telling the truth is scary, I know, but you have enough courage. You do. Emma, don't you really know what to write about? Us, my darling. Don't you think? Write a book about us.

As for the man you're in love with. This advice may surprise you—you probably think I have no sympathy for the other woman, considering my marital history. I do believe that good behavior is important, and so is honor, and honesty. But if everyone perpetuates a wrong out of the very best of intentions, it's still a wrong. The child you're both protecting can't be protected, not like this, and neither can the woman. It's time to move, Emma, let life go on. It's so short, oh, it's so short. You can take what you want now. I think you really can.

Try not to be so afraid. You told me you didn't have room for any more suffering. Well, I'm gone now; I've freed up a little room for you. Ha. I can't deny that love sometimes requires suffering, but if this man is the one for you, he'll be worth it.

Oh, must I keep calling him 'this man'? For heaven's sake, tell Lee who he is. I promise you, she won't be shocked.

Thank you for the gifts you've given me—so much laughter, your lovable insecurities, your loyalty. There's no one else like you. It's been my privilege to love you. Now, be brave—follow Rudy's example! And all will be well.

I looked up. "That's the end. Okay, who's the guy?" Emma looked close to tears. That was so upsetting to me, I made a joke. "It's Henry, isn't it?"

She gaped—she believed me! It was wonderful—this *never* happens, it's always the other way around. Then she got it, and burst out laughing. "Oh, God," she said, and flopped over on her back next to Rudy. I watched their stomachs bump up and down in time to their teary-faced giggling. Oh, so Rudy knew, too.

"Am I the only one who doesn't know who this man is?"

Emma popped up. "I'm sorry—it was sticky, Lee, I just couldn't tell you."

"Well? So? Tell me now."

She shrugged, trying to look careless, but I could see she was nervous. "Okay. It's Mick."

"Mick! Mick Draco?" I couldn't have been more surprised. "But I thought you didn't even like him!" I wanted details—but first I wanted to read Isabel's letter to me. "Why didn't you tell me? I hardly even see Sally anymore, if that's what you were worried about."

"Well, you know. Yeah. Partly."

"Henry talks to Mick, though," I said. "You know Sally's moved back to Delaware."

Emma's slack-jawed expression said no, she didn't know.

"What's this, now?" Rudy said, sitting up, too.

"They've separated. You didn't know? Mick's probably going to move to Baltimore so he can study art at the Maryland Institute."

"But—Jay—but what about Jay—" Emma couldn't even make her tongue work. First she went white, now she was pink-faced.

"They're working it out. Sally's got him for now, but they're talking about sharing custody. This just happened, according to Henry. Like about a week ago."

"Why didn't you *tell* me?" She went white again. Before I could answer that ridiculous question, she whispered, "Why didn't *he* tell me?" and covered her mouth with her hands. "I told him I wouldn't wait," she mumbled through her fingers. "What if he doesn't care anymore? Oh, but at the service, he was so— But why do you think he didn't tell me? Should I call him? Would that be pushy? What if he's not interested anymore, what if he's moved on? What if he found someone else?"

"In a *week*?"

"It's possible!"

"Well, then you'll suffer," Rudy said.

"Isabel says suffering's worth it," I said.

Emma took her hands away. "Right. Okay. I'll call him." She started to get up.

"Hey!"

"Oh." She dropped back down, laughing, blushing with embarrassment. "Sorry, I'm sorry, go ahead, finish the letter."

"Well, not if it's going to inconvenience you in any way, God knows I wouldn't want to—Stop it, cut it out, would you? That's enough—" But I couldn't help laughing when she put her arms around me and kissed me all over my face. Rudy cracked up. I *hate* when Emma does that, which of course is why she does it.

But it worked—the three of us finally, finally felt normal again, like our old selves with one another. It was the best time for us since Isabel died.

"Okay, I'm reading this now. Do you mind? Get hold of yourselves."

"Right," said Rudy.

"Right. We're serious. Read." Emma drew her knees up and hugged them. Even her face looked different—sharper, as if her skin had tightened or the bones were sticking out more than they had five minutes ago. She was like a stretched wire; if you plucked her she'd make a high, tight, pinging sound.

I turned back to Isabel's letter. I really wanted to read it by myself, but that wouldn't have been fair.

> Lee. Sweetest Lee. What should I say to you? We've talked so much in these last days, there's very little left to say. Except that I'll miss you so much. Have Rudy and Emma thanked you lately for starting our women's group? They should. Once a week at least, I should think.

Watery giggles from Emma and Rudy.

> You're the sane one, we always said. Sometimes, because of that, we forgot to be soft with you, believing you were strong

and didn't need us to be so gentle. You are strong—but also tender in the center. I can't imagine the last dozen years of my life without you. You've been my friend and my daughter. My delight.

Nobody said anything while I stopped for a minute.

A little time has passed since you and Henry gave up trying for your own baby. Mourning time. And I'm gone—you won't mix up those two losses so readily now. You can see more clearly. Lee—good news. Did you know there's a child looking for you? I tried to tell you this before, but I didn't say it right. I've been thinking about it a lot. Emma won't want to hear how I know this, so I won't say—but I do happen to know for certain that there's a child somewhere right now who's looking for you and Henry. You have to try to find him. (Or her; even I don't know this detail, Emma.) And when you do—and you will—you'll have to love him with your whole heart. And you will.

I'm so happy for you. This is a deep, deep comfort to me, knowing this about you. And your baby—ah, what a wonderful mother he'll have. Lucky, lucky baby.

There's so much more I could say. My beloved Graces. Lee, Rudy, Emma, the friends of my heart. Then again, there's really nothing else to say. I feel so close to you. I've thought of something you can do for me. In fact, I insist on it; I'll brook no argument. You have to find a transient member who'll stay. A nontransient; a permanent. Really, you have to try, no halfhearted measures, no false welcomes or disingenuous goodwill. Two new members would be even better. Our group can't be allowed to fade away—you know that. Do this for me. Please. Because it's not really for me, it's for you. I wish it for you.

Thank you for all you've given to me. Lee, Emma, Rudy, I love you. Thank you for staying with me to the end. Do you know what I regret? That I won't be there when what's happening to me happens to each of you. To give back a little of the love and solace and sweetness you've given me.

But then again—Emma, you knew this was coming—maybe I will be. Yes, I think I will. In fact, now that I've thought of it, I'm counting on it. Just not, please God, anytime soon.

All my love,
Isabel

31

Emma

I made Rudy and Lee go outside on the deck when I called Mick. Well, the only phone is in the kitchen, and they'd have been able to hear me. It wasn't raining anymore. Just a little damp. They were fine.

But guess what, the line was busy. Who was he talking to? Any number of loathsome possibilities crossed my mind.

"The line's busy, you can come back."

They returned, and together we set the table and finished making the chowder.

"Okay, go out now, I'm calling him again. Here," I said, sensing mutiny, shoving a bag of pretzels at Rudy. "Eat these if you get hungry."

They left, muttering snide things, and I dialed Mick's number again.

"Hello?"

From now on, I will associate the great emotions, fear, dread, heart-stopping relief, with the smell of cooking clams.

"Mick? This—"

"Emma?"

"Yes. Hi. Um . . . hi. I was just talking to Lee, and she—"

"Are you at home?"

"No, I'm at Hatteras."

"Did you go down today?"

"Yesterday. We got here yesterday."

He laughed, the oddest sound. "That explains it."

"What?"

"I called you all night last night. I was sure you had a date. One of your ubiquitous men."

My legs started to tremble. I slid to the floor slowly, carrying the phone down with me. "One of my ubiquitous men?" Euphoria. I was aware of my jaw, my throat; my lips felt swollen; I didn't sound like myself. "I called you just now," I said, "but the line was busy. I figured it was your new girlfriend."

He laughed again. Giddy. "No, that was Jay."

"Oh." That sobered me up. "Where is he?"

"With his mother. Sally's staying with her parents in Wilmington. While she looks for a place. For her and Jay."

"Oh. So you . . . "

"We've separated. As of about ten days ago. I have a lot to tell you." He paused, then blurted out, "Emma, why the hell are you so far away?"

"I know! Oh, Mick." And then I had to ask, "Why did you wait ten whole days to call me?"

"Well, for one thing, I wasn't sure it would make any difference."

"How could you think that?"

"Because the last time we spoke, you were very clear. About us. Don't you remember?"

"Of course I remember." That excruciating interval on the front porch. "But that's because you didn't give me any hope. You didn't see anything changing."

"I know. It happened all of a sudden. The other reason is because I wasn't sure she'd really go. Stay gone. Now I'm sure, but if she had come back, it would've been bad. For you."

"Why?" I asked fearfully.

"I wouldn't have stayed, that's not what I mean."

"Oh."

"If she'd come back, I'd have left, Emma. Because it's really over."

"Oh."

"But I didn't want you in the middle of that, if it happened. That's why I didn't call you."

"Oh." That was a good reason. It made me grin like a hyena and quietly bang my fist on the floor. "How did it happen? If you want to tell me. I know you've always—"

"I want to tell you. I want to *see* you. What if I drove down there tonight?"

Now I was really coming undone. "Well, you could, but I'll be home tomorrow."

"Tomorrow. I don't know. That's a long time."

"I know."

"I could meet you in Richmond," he said, and we laughed like teenagers. "Or Norfolk."

"I guess that wouldn't make much sense."

"Guess not."

"Fredericksburg, though . . ." More giggling. "Oh, Mick. This is . . ." Just what I've always wanted. To say stupid things to you long-distance.

"What?"

"Good. This is good."

"Yes."

Long, smiling pause.

"What are you doing?" he asked. "Where is everybody?"

"I'm sitting on the kitchen floor. Rudy and Lee are out on the deck—I banished them. They're fine, it stopped raining. Where are you?"

"I'm in the kitchen, too. You've never been in my house before."

"No. Is it nice?"

"Come and see."

"I will." I could not, simply could not, stop grinning. "So are you okay? With the separation? How's Jay?"

"He's much better than I thought he'd be. Unless I'm kidding myself. I miss him—that's the worst of it. Emma, I might move to Baltimore, try to go to the Maryland Institute. If I can get in—it's one of the best private art colleges in the country."

"You'll get in. What would you do, get a master's?"

"Yeah. And I'd like being closer to Jay. Sally surprised me. She's not fighting custody, she wants us both to have him."

"Thank God. That was the main thing."

"So when I see you, you can rub it in about how I should've done this years ago. Except that it couldn't have happened any sooner. I don't think."

"Not one word. I'll be a model of self-restraint."

I could hear him smiling, feel it in the pauses.

"So," he said. "What do you think about Baltimore?"

"I think it's great. It's only an hour's drive. We'll work everything out."

"That's what I was hoping. You know, it's . . . "

"What."

"Hard to switch over from the daydream to reality."

"How do you mean?" I knew, I just wanted to hear him say it.

"The things that seem to be happening now. About to happen. I've been imagining them for a long time, almost since I met you."

"Have you?"

"But I was afraid to hope."

"I know. Me, too."

"But now. Now it seems to be working out."

"It's terrifying. Because it's too good."

"Or else . . . "

He didn't finish, but I knew where that was heading, too. *Or else it won't work*. Always a possibility. Mick didn't have much of a track record for failed relationships—only one that I knew of—but I sure did. And we'd been pining for each other for a year and a half. If that's not a setup for disaster, I don't know what is.

"How come we're not even *more* afraid?" I wondered. "I should be paralyzed. But instead I've got this—ridiculous—*faith.* I feel silly even saying that. But I have it, I do. Because this isn't like anything that's ever happened before. To me. Oh, Mick, I can't say these things to you over the phone."

"I know. Tomorrow."

"Tomorrow. Okay. Oh, *man.* I feel very . . . lustful. All of a sudden."

"Lustful." The way he said it, surprised and glad and in agreement. Mmm.

"Lustful." It was beginning to sound onomatopoeic.

"Call me," he said, "as soon as you get home."

"Don't worry."

"Do you want to come here?"

"I don't know." Ah, the delicious logistics. "No, you come to my house. Is that okay?"

"Yes."

We talked a little longer. But it wasn't very satisfying. Too much to say, and definitely too much lust. And we couldn't even talk dirty because I wasn't really alone. He told me the bare outline of how the split with Sally had come about. She'd asked him point blank, over dinner at the Yenching Palace on Connecticut, if he loved her. He could have said yes and meant it in a charitable, faraway, technical sense; he'd done that often enough before, he said. Instead he told her the barer, harder truth. He said no.

She cried, but she didn't break down and she wasn't destroyed. He thought she might even have been relieved. "Or else I'm kidding myself," he said again. Either way, it was her idea to go back to Delaware. Jay would be with her more than with him at the beginning, and he was almost reconciled to it. "He loves his grandparents, and they're great with him. I think he'll be all right. I'll see him all the time. I'm rationalizing, I know—"

"No, but it's true, you *will* see him."

"But it won't be the same."

"No, it won't. But after a while, maybe it'll be better."

Had I really said that? I wanted to get up and look in a mirror, see if my appearance had changed, too.

"Okay," I said eventually. "I guess I should go. They probably want to eat. Lee and Rudy." I could see their outlines through the screen, lying in the deck chaises, Rudy's cigarette tip a waving red dot in the dark.

"Okay," Mick said. Halfhearted.

Such a juvenile pleasure. It took us ten more minutes to hang up. This is how it's going to be, I thought. Maybe it won't work (but I think it will), but in the meantime we get all this happiness.

"I love you," I whispered. Very brave. *Isabel, are you listening?*

He said it back, and added my name. I can't get enough of that, Mick saying "Emma." Oh, Jeez. Pretty soon I'll be scribbling his name in my geography book.

"See you tomorrow," I said.

"Good night, Emma."

"Night."

"See you tomorrow."

"Yeah. Or you could call me later."

"Okay."

Startled silence, then we laughed at the simplicity of the solution. It made saying good-bye so much easier.

"Well?"

"Well?"

"We talked." I drifted over to the railing and hunched over it, too scattered and dreamy and romantic to sit.

Rudy got up and came to stand beside me. "You talked?"

"We heard that." Lee got up and moved to my other side.

"Right there," I said, leaning over farther. "Well, you can't see from here; farther in."

"What?"

"We kissed for the first time."

Rudy sighed.

Lee gasped. "That *weekend?*"

"Yep."

"I want to hear all about this, every single detail."

"Okay." No problem. I had never felt more generous.

"But first, are you going after him?"

"Am I *going after* him?"

"Isn't that what Isabel said you should do?"

"I guess she did."

"So? Are you?"

I smiled. Wasn't it written all over my face? Lee can be so literal. "Are you going to adopt a child?" I countered.

"Oh, Em." She wrapped her arms around herself and squeezed. "It's looking for me," she whispered, staring up at the sky. The clouds had blown away; the stars were out and winking.

"I take it that's a yes?"

She nodded slowly, dreamy-eyed. "Why did I wait so long?"

Rudy and I exchanged a look. "Well," I said, "why *did* you?"

"It's—I don't know. Now it's obvious, but before—We ruled it out without even really thinking about it. Henry said he wanted his own, but—and I used that, I put it in my ball of reasons, I had this long list of reasons for why it had to be ours, and they didn't even make any sense. Isabel tried to tell me, but I couldn't hear her."

"You were so determined."

"And another thing is, they don't talk about it in fertility clinics. I've spent the last two years in doctors' offices, and not once in all that time was the word *adoption* mentioned. Not once. Isn't that amazing? Not even by a nurse. So I didn't think about it."

"And Henry won't mind?"

"Oh, no. He won't mind."

Now I wished *I'd* had the guts to say something to her sooner, or that Rudy had. But we were too tactful or something, or too intent on being accomplices to her obsession, trying too hard to be "supportive" to bring up an alternative.

"Rudy says we should try for a foreign child because that might be quicker," Lee was saying. "Maybe a Russian orphan, or Romanian. I was thinking a little Ukrainian Jew." She stopped looking at the sky and turned practical. "As soon as we eat, I have to call Henry."

"And if it's a girl, she'll name it Isabel," Rudy said.

"Well, of course," I said. "And if it's a boy, Isadore."

We smiled in the dark.

"Do you think we really have to get a new transient?"

"A permanent," Lee corrected. "She said we did."

We sighed.

"There's this woman at work," Lee said.

We groaned.

"I guess I'll call my mother tonight." Rudy flipped her cigarette over the rail. "Sheesh, I'm surprised she didn't say I had to give up smoking."

I don't know why—I just turned and gave her a strong, hard hug.

"Wow," she said, pleased. "You're getting so much better at that."

"Am I?"

"I've noticed it, too," Lee said.

"Hey, is anybody starving?" I said. But nobody moved. We didn't want to go in quite yet.

"You know what would be nice?" Rudy said. "If we all got old together."

"Why wouldn't we?"

"No, but I mean *together*."

"Yeah," I said, "in an old ladies' home." I'd had this fantasy for years. "We'd sit out in our rocking chairs on the front porch of some neat old house in the country."

"We'd still have all our faculties," Rudy decided, "we'd just be old."

"And you'll still look great. I'll be fat, but Lee'll push me around in my wheelchair, because she'll still be tough and wiry."

"Maybe I will, maybe I won't. If you want me to push you around, you'll have to be a lot nicer to me."

"And we'll still like each other," Rudy said.

"We'll play a lot of canasta."

"Bridge," Lee corrected.

"And whenever one of us dies," I said, "we'll be cremated. But we won't dispose of the remains until the last one goes."

"Okay, but then who'll do it?"

"Isadore. Right out there." I pointed in the direction of Isabel's spot, about fifty yards out in the invisible sea.

"Isadore?"

"Your son. He'll be about sixty by then. I hope he keeps himself in shape for the swim."

"Unlike some people."

The moon loomed over the water. The crickets got louder and louder until they drowned out the sound of the waves. Across the street, two little boys and their father came out to shoot hoops in the driveway.

"Write a book about us," Isabel said. Could that be my subject? I couldn't quite see it. Real life was too damn chaotic; it didn't translate well. Fiction, now, fiction's a lot simpler. I've been thinking a mystery with some romance, some danger, maybe a little amnesia. I always like an amnesia story. It could still be about four women. Who belong to a club, and one gets killed. No, that's too sad. One's *sister* gets killed, and they team up to solve the crime. If this caught on, I could make it a series. The Four Femmes. The Four Yuppie Femmes.

Title needs work.

But she said, "Write a book about us." Oh, Isabel, I don't know.

(I talk to her like this now, as if she's standing next to me, shooting the breeze. I think we all do.) That sounds so adult, so mature. Let me dick around a little while longer, okay? Yes, I know, the time factor; life is short, and you never know how short, I know, I know.

All right, I'll think about it. But if I get stuck, I'm putting in amnesia.

"Dinner?"

We went inside. The table looked pretty. We lit candles, used the cloth napkins. Didn't talk about how much less three is than four. Isabel was absolutely right, we had to get a new transient.

Afterward, everyone wanted to use the phone, Lee to call Henry, Rudy to call her mom, me—I just wanted the line free so Mick could get through.

All this business, all this outreach—we weren't prepared for it. We'd come here for a specific purpose, an *ending*, and here we were making all these new beginnings. Are you liking this, Isabel? Are you smiling and rubbing your hands together, feeling pretty complaisant up there? Over there? Wherever you are. Well, fine, good, I don't begrudge you a thing, not even smugness. I just wish you were here. You know? I just miss you.